A Dead Sister

Jessica Huntington Desert Cities Mystery #2

Anna Celeste Burke

A DEAD SISTER

Copyright © 2014 Anna Celeste Burke

www.desertcitiesmystery.com

Published by Create Space

Cover Design by Anna Celeste Burke
Photo by StockLite From Shutterstock.com

ISBN-13: 978-1497473973
ISBN-10: 1497473977

Books by USA Today Bestselling Author, Anna Celeste Burke

A Dead Husband Jessica Huntington Desert Cities Mystery #1
A Dead Sister Jessica Huntington Desert Cities Mystery #2
A Dead Daughter Jessica Huntington Desert Cities Mystery # 3
A Dead Mother Jessica Huntington Desert Cities Mystery #4
Love A Foot Above the Ground Prequel to the Jessica Huntington Series

Cowabunga Christmas! Corsario Cove Cozy Mystery #1
Gnarly New Year Corsario Cove Cozy Mystery #2
Heinous Habits, Corsario Cove Cozy Mystery #3
Radical Regatta, Corsario Cove Cozy Mystery #4 [2017]

Murder at Catmmando Mountain Georgie Shaw Cozy Mystery #1
Love Notes in the Key of Sea Georgie Shaw Cozy Mystery #2
All Hallows' Eve Heist Georgie Shaw Cozy Mystery #3
A Merry Christmas Wedding Mystery Georgie Shaw Cozy Mystery #4
Murder at Sea of Passenger X Georgie Shaw Cozy Mystery #5
Murder of the Maestro Georgie Shaw Cozy Mystery #6 [2017]

DEDICATION

To sisters everywhere, especially mine.

CONTENTS

ACKNOWLEDGMENTS

To my husband, Victor, for his continued love and support. He reads every word I write. There's nothing more encouraging than hearing him laugh where I hoped the reader would!

To *my sister*, Brenda, who painstakingly edited **A DEAD SISTER.** I am blessed, and would be so lost without her!

Special thanks to Peggy Hyndman for carefully reediting this book after I made significant changes to it. Her contribution has made this an even better edition than the first!

To readers of **A DEAD HUSBAND**, the first book in the Jessica Huntington Desert Cities Mystery series. Thanks for the kudos, comments, and suggestions. Feedback is a gift to me and every author.

PROLOGUE

Palm Springs, CA. January 10, 1999

Kelly Fontana ran for it as well as she could. She had fooled the thug who came to shoot her up again, pretending to be out cold from whatever it was he was giving her. Trying to escape was scary. The first time she fought the huge ugly man with the misshapen head and a scar on his cheek, he had hit her hard. Hard enough to make her ears ring and her teeth rattle. Then he had bound and gagged her.

What scared her more than that was the fact she almost didn't want to stop him. She was beginning to like the drug: the rush of something akin to euphoria, followed by oblivion. It was tempting just to lie there and let him shoot her up again. But, Tommy, what about Tommy? It would be his sixteenth birthday any day now, if she hadn't lost track of time altogether during her captivity. Her younger brother was going through a lot and he needed her.

It had been several days since she was confined to the luxurious hotel suite. Once they had her under control with the drugs, they had untied her hands and feet and removed the gag. That made it easier to get her back and forth to the bathroom, to give her water, and a bit of food. The food didn't always stay down so then it was back to the bathroom again to clean her up.

What the ugly man and an assortment of helpers hadn't realized, what any junkie knows, is that she was developing a tolerance for the stuff. After the third or fourth or fifth day, the drug had started to wear off a little sooner each time. She could get a window of near-lucidity before the next injection closed the curtains. Those brief interludes had been used to check out her surroundings. The doors were locked and the windows too. Not a way to escape, anyhow, with such a long drop to the ground from her second-floor accommodations. No phone. No response when she pounded as hard as she could on the door or the walls of the hotel room, calling out for help. On one occasion, someone had heard her, peering up at her from the parking lot. Kelly shrank back in horror. It was the ugly man. By the time he made his way up to her room, she was back in bed and seemingly out cold.

It was just a matter of time before they'd shoot her up not to knock her out, but to shut her up, permanently. She had overheard her captor arguing on the phone about what to do with her. They had not believed her when she promised not to tell what she knew. It wasn't clear why she was still alive at this point.

Stumbling from the hotel room after she stabbed the ugly man, Kelly headed down the nearest set of stairs under the exit sign. He had bent over her so close that she could smell the sour odor of his breath, tainted by more than a hint of alcohol. He was startled when she shoved the knife, secreted from the room service tray, into his throat. Pushing past him, she stopped long enough to put on her shoes and grab her purse. Then Kelly took another few seconds to retrieve the hypodermic needle he had just loaded. She might need a weapon if she ran into one of his assistants before she could get downstairs to the lobby and help.

Holding tight to the rail, Kelly made her way to the first floor and through the door from the stairwell into a long corridor. Not one, but two of the ugly man's assistants spotted her and headed in her direction. They had that same startled look she had seen on the ugly man's face, but quickly recovered. A grim determination carried them toward her as swiftly as they could without drawing attention to themselves. Kelly moved back through the door she had exited and out another leading from the stairwell and the hotel. The creosote-laden evening breeze hit her as she stepped into the hotel parking lot. She lurched forward as fast as she could, hoping to stay ahead of her pursuers long enough to get around to the front entrance. Maybe someone would help her.

The bright lights rushing toward Kelly made it impossible to see the make of the car or the driver. She tried to step out of the way. When it struck, she flew through the air and collided with the windshield before landing hard. Her last thoughts were of the gift she had bought and the little handwritten note: "You are sweet sixteen, Tommy. I love you just the way you are! Sis."

CHAPTER 1

Rancho Mirage, CA. June 29, 2013

Jessica hurled the book she was reading by Pierre Teilhard de Chardin across the room. She sighed and walked the short distance to pick it up. It wasn't hers to destroy. Father Martin had loaned it to her, hoping it would help her find answers to the questions that dogged her. She checked the book to be sure she hadn't dinged it when it collided with the wall in the exquisitely furnished bedroom of her childhood home in Mission Hills.

The desert modern wonder of glass and stone and steel wasn't hers, either. She glanced at the wall to make sure it wasn't damaged. The house was an architect's dream come to life, a cathedral to domestic bliss. It was a dream her father, Henry "Hank" Huntington, yes, as in the Huntington Beach Huntington's, brought to fruition before his marriage to her mother fell apart.

Her parents' divorce was the first terrible thing that had ever happened to Jessica Huntington-Harper, the pampered only child, born into the lap of luxury. She was just Jessica Huntington then. The hyphen came later, when she married her law-school sweetheart, now turned scumbag, Jim Harper. The hyphen was gone again now, along with the scumbag.

When Jessica was a "tween," her parents began to spend less time together and started bickering behind closed doors. Eventually, unable to contain themselves any longer, they squabbled in front of anyone who happened to be in the room. At that stage, Jessica became an integral part of the free-for-all, throwing herself into the fray. She didn't take sides, but hated them both. They were equally to blame for making shambles of the

1

idyllic life they led in the tony desert resort town of Rancho Mirage, California.

To get even, she became the most unbearable little beast, mouthy and defiant about anything and everything. Not just at home. Jessica managed to get herself kicked out of two private schools in the Coachella Valley before landing at St. Theresa's Catholic high school in Palm Springs. She was scared, angry, and out of control for much of her early adolescence because of her parents' divorce. Now she felt that way again. This time it was *her* marriage on the rocks.

"Why do bad things happen to good people? No, make that, why do bad things happen to ordinary people trying to get by the best they can?" She moaned. She put herself into that category of person. Maybe not always good, but not so bad either as to deserve the comeuppance she was being dealt. That was only one of the questions that pressed down upon her as she struggled to recover from a series of blows.

What did Chardin know, anyway? A learned man, sure, but he was still a man—and a priest to boot! Jessica glanced down at the open book in her hands. The hair on the back of her neck prickled as she read.

"In the final analysis, the question of why bad things happen to good people transmutes itself into some very different questions, no longer asking why something happened, but asking how we will respond, what we intend to do now that it happened."

She snapped the book shut, placing it gently on the writing desk, pondering what she had read. How could he grasp the heartbreak of being humiliated and dumped by an unfaithful husband whose girlfriend had "accidentally" become pregnant? Jessica had failed at that, too. Three years of trying to have a baby, to no avail, even with fertility treatments. There had been several false starts, and sad endings, accompanied by a few extra pounds of baby fat, but no baby.

"Accident! No way!" Jessica shouted as she stomped back to her enormous bed and threw herself down into its plush, silky embrace. An accident, for Jim, maybe, but no way that conniving skank made such a mistake.

Yesterday, Jim Harper, her soon-to-be ex-husband had brought an apt end to what had been the worst week of her life. When he had arrived at the gate to the Mission Hills Country Club, her beloved Bernadette had given security permission to let the rat into the community. Then, as if it were the most natural thing in the world, Bernadette announced his arrival, allowing him to join Jessica on the back patio.

Sprawled on a chaise, in a bathing suit and a coffee-stained robe, Jessica hadn't even combed her hair. She wore no makeup to hide the remnants of a black eye from one of several fights for her life in less than a week. Her knees were skinned, and there were bruises on both her legs and arms. Her wrist, sprained but not broken, was in a sling. Unable to swim with the wrist injury, she had retreated to the patio, hoping the triple digit summer heat would purge her of the loathsome things she had seen and endured.

"We need to talk," Jim Harper had said, seating himself on the chaise beside her. He did a quick little double take, taken aback by what he saw as he intently peered at her.

"Sounds like you've had quite a time. You look like hell."

"Apropos, since that's where I spent a good part of the last week," she said, glancing at him warily. "Make that the last few weeks, really, or months. No, how about the past three years?"

Jessica was growing angrier as she stared at the polished, well-dressed man. He wore an open-collared bespoke shirt, in a cool minty green shade of Egyptian cotton, with tan linen shorts. On his feet were custom-made moccasins worn without socks. The whole ensemble created a relaxed, easy feeling that didn't match the look on his face. Stress sat there. It had been there long enough to take a toll on his boyish features, etching lines that would cost a pretty penny to remove. A sprinkle of gray had begun to appear in the dark umber of his perfectly coiffed hair.

She flashed on the image of Jim as she had last seen him at their home in Cupertino—in their marital bed with a well-known Hollywood blond. The blond had a name, but she couldn't bring herself to use it. Jessica had developed a list of names she preferred for the vile woman. It was small consolation to see that they had obviously used a body double for her nude scenes in her recent banal hit. She was, nevertheless, a younger, thinner, more artfully enhanced creature than Jessica. Add to that her notoriety, and it all made a sad, sick kind of sense. Jim had acquired the platinum blond as the newest venture capital investment, in the love division, of his fully integrated corporate existence. His world of ruthless wheeling and dealing brought home in the most poignant way possible.

Jim's growing addiction to deal-making, ladder-climbing, and money-grubbing had become a near-constant source of antagonism in their marriage. He wanted her to understand, to share his enthusiasm for outwitting his opponent and amassing wealth. She didn't. They were both rich when they married. Surely, their marriage—their lives—could be about other things? It was a wish, an assumption that she had made without even knowing it when they said, "I do."

According to Jim, there was rich and then there was RICHER and RICHEST. Not content with the tens of millions they each possessed, Jim wanted more. He kept Jessica up-to-date about newly-minted billionaires each year, noting those who had reached that pinnacle with some tie to the Silicon Valley.

Jessica closed her eyes, hoping that image of Jim and the skank, along with the more recent carnage she had witnessed, would just go away. There had to be some mental equivalent to chlorine bleach that could remove the vivid stains from her weary mind and beleaguered soul.

"Trust me, Jim, I gave, as good as I got. It's my new motto. No more of that "lemons into lemonade" crap. If life kicks you in the ass, kick back. And, I might add, you appear a little worse for wear, too." Jim ignored her last comment.

"You want to tell me what happened?"

"It's not worth hearing all the gory details. I'm not even sure you know the key players, anyway, except for Laura. You know, Laura Stone? Her husband, Roger, was murdered a little over a week ago and we got caught up in the aftermath. Aftermath is an understatement." Jessica gazed out over the large, free-form pool sparkling in the late afternoon light. The palms were dancing in the afternoon breeze, picking up as it often did this time of day. Vivid blue skies provided the backdrop. Blue skies signaled fair weather and promising prospects. Sometimes blue skies lied.

Murderous hooligans, trying to retrieve something that had been taken from them, had stalked her and her best friend, Laura Stone. It had gotten Laura's husband killed. Convinced they had conspired with him, they pursued Laura and Jessica to get it back. That Jessica had held her own with scoundrels and hoods, a mob-boss wannabe and his psychopathic moll, was testament to her stubborn determination to survive.

Or perhaps it was sheer dumb luck. That bothered her, too. Another of those haunting questions: how had she escaped death when Laura's husband had not? Her shrink said it was normal to have some sort of survivor's guilt after going through such a calamity. Why not come in and talk about it?

A Dead Sister

"Why not? Because I no longer live in Cupertino, that's why not. And I can't stand the thought of ever setting foot in the place again. That's why not!" She was shouting at that point, and her perceptive, three hundred-dollar-a-visit shrink, sensing Jessica's distress, promised to get back to her with a reference for someone local in the Coachella Valley.

She tried to refocus on the slickly dressed slime-ball-du-jour sitting next to her, wondering once again how she could have gotten him so wrong. "Let's just say that all's well that ends. How about, all's well that ends and you're still alive?" Jessica registered the first anxious flutters of a body that sometimes betrayed her by subjecting her to a full-blown panic attack.

"Laura's husband murdered? Sounds like an ordeal. I'm glad you're okay," he said, shifting in his seat. Jim seemed relieved, but the comments were perfunctory. Given his "time is money" credo, he was more likely relieved that she had cut the story short than that she was okay. That was harsh. It was hard to believe that the guy who had betrayed her after promising to love, honor, and cherish her forever, was capable of any genuine concern.

"Yeah, well you can imagine how deeply moved I am by your expression of concern. So, what is it you really want to talk about?" Her time was valuable too, and she could tell that he was here on business. The tone in her voice gave him pause, but only for a moment.

"This may not be the best time to do this, but is there ever really a best time when a marriage ends?" He didn't wait for her to answer but rushed ahead with his pitch. Social amenities out of the way, he was ready to get down to the matter at hand. It occurred to her that she hadn't even inquired as to his well-being. She didn't care to know. How strange to feel so little for a man she had loved so much. How was that possible? *I'll just put it on the to-be-pondered list,* she thought, trying to pay attention to Jim's words.

"I'm convinced it's in both our interests to get this matter resolved. We had some good years together, but those years are behind us. We both need to get on with our lives." Jim added a couple of well-practiced gestures as he spoke. She was almost touched that he had gone to the trouble of rehearsing his spiel before making his presentation.

She also realized he was well within kicking range. Jessica squelched the thought before the more impulsive side of her nature could take command. Besides, he just wasn't worth the effort, and too many of her body parts were still aching from recent encounters with other bad guys.

Anna Celeste Burke

"By *this matter*, I presume you mean divorce. It's okay, you can use the word. I can take it. You're here because you want me to sign the divorce papers, right? Shall I go get my copy or did you bring another?" She hoped he had brought a copy. Jessica wasn't quite sure where her copy was, and besides, it had seen better days. The last time she *saw* her copy, it was wrinkled, marked by the circular imprint of a coffee cup, and streaked with an odd assortment of things. Ice cream, finger print dust, makeup, and a little blood, most likely her own, but she couldn't guarantee it.

Jim appeared stunned. Jessica wasn't sure if that was because she had cut him off mid-spiel or if her willingness to expedite matters caught him off guard. She was a little surprised, too, by how much she wanted closure in this part of her life.

"Why yes, I did bring a copy. I thought you might have, uh, uh, destroyed, or, uh, misplaced the copy sent to you, and that's why you hadn't responded. You'll sign it then?"

"Sure, hand it over."

It was like a balloon had been pricked and all the air had gone out of him. For a moment, the confidence he wore crumbled and something more unfamiliar took its place on his countenance. Was it an expression of doubt? No, not that. It was more like apprehension or maybe dread. He lied as he spoke again.

"I am so relieved. I was afraid you might need more time and I just don't have it. Cassie wants to get married as soon as possible. She, uh—we—uh, had an accident of some kind. And, and, anyway, she's pregnant." There was nothing resembling relief in the look on his face or the sound of his voice as those last few words tumbled out of his mouth. Jessica cocked her head. What she saw was the look you might expect to see on a bear with its foot caught in a trap. The analogy worked better if she visualized a different body part caught in the trap.

"Wow, you're going to be a dad. Congratulations, right?" She asked, with only the slightest tone of sarcasm in her voice. Three years ago, when Jessica had embarked on the baby-chase, Jim had been more than a little ambivalent. Each month she failed to get pregnant, each false alarm, and even the miscarriages fueled Jessica's determination to go on. Jim lobbied harder to call it quits. The effort became a wedge between them, rather than a rallying point to salvage their relationship and find a new way to be a family.

A Dead Sister

"Of course, thanks." He ran a hand along the back of his neck as he picked up the satchel at his feet. A sleek, exquisitely crafted piece, it was made from finely tooled leather and bore his monogram. It was exactly the sort of thing that Jim hated. Way too small to be useful in his work as a lawyer putting together mega-deals. Too pretty for a man who had lived in a hoodie and tennis shoes until he decided to become a master of the universe. Not to mention the fact that James Harper did not do monograms! Jessica quickly surmised it was a gift from the she-beast. She couldn't resist twisting the knife a little, as he pulled items from the bag.

"What a gorgeous bag," she said sweetly, "and your initials, so you can always spot it in a crowd at the club." It didn't matter what club. He would find it irritating to behold at any of the many clubs and other venues he frequented. Jim looked up, distracted, but that faded as their eyes met. The jig was up. He knew that she knew he had a tiger by the tail with his latest "joint venture," a savage creature with a rapacious appetite to get her way.

"There's something else. Cassie wants me to sell the house in Cupertino. I know we've talked about that and I do have an offer. What I want to know is if you'll agree to take it. Prices have come back a lot in the area already, but I'm sure we can do better if we hang on for another year or so."

There was almost a pleading tone in his voice. The sort of tone that, a few months ago, she imagined he might use to get her to take him back. She wasn't sure if he was pleading for her to sign the papers or to refuse to sign, giving him an excuse to hold out for a better deal.

Ouch, she thought, but didn't say aloud. This was the unkindest cut of all. The predacious tiger lady was already costing him money. Worse than that, he was being denied the bragging rights that would have gone along with making a killing off the little piece of paradise she and Jim had created. Of course, back then, they had cared more about making a comfortable home for themselves than making a good investment, as they painstakingly renovated the pricey fixer-upper. Or, at least, she had.

"Let me see," she said, getting anxious for this little tête-à-tête to be over. Reviewing the sales agreement, she had to suppress a gasp. The offer on the house was substantial. It was way more than they had paid for the house. More than she imagined they would ever realize from a sale after the real estate bubble burst. The market *was* making a comeback. Jim would have plenty to crow about. So, what was the problem?

"This seems fine to me. How do you want to handle the sale?" After another of those, "huh?" glances that lasted only a microsecond, Jim went to work in a very lawyerly fashion.

He must have expected the worst. Why not? The day she found Jim in her bed with another woman, she'd lost it. In addition to foul-mouthed epithets, she'd thrown every movable object in the room at them. Her aim, blinded by fury and disappointment, hadn't done them any physical harm. She'd scared them, though, as they scrambled, buck naked, for the bathroom to evade the bombs she was lobbing. The room was trashed by the time Jessica left. Drapes ripped from the windows, and the flat screen television, lamps, art, and mirrors all smashed.

She'd gone straight to her lawyer's office to file a petition for divorce. Jim was served immediately and vacated the premises. Jessica could have kept the house, but the idea made her nauseous. Like the thought of her friend Laura moving back into the house where her husband had been murdered. The Cupertino house was a crime scene too. She had taken a bullet to the heart, figuratively speaking, but just as vicious as the more tangible projectiles that had felled poor Roger Stone.

Jessica slept in one of the guest rooms in the Cupertino house while she had arranged to get out for good. With the help of a team of movers, she'd sorted through years of accumulated "stuff." She packed and moved out of there in a matter of weeks. That included helping herself to the contents of the wine cellar. The wines were now ensconced in the room her father had built at the Mission Hills estate. She also took her favorites from the art pieces she and Jim had collected over the years. Those were packed away. Still too painful to display or sell.

Since that awful day when she had discovered the inescapable truth about her marriage, Jessica had ridden a roller coaster of emotions. Those emotions ranged from shock, to rage, to unbelievable sorrow and regret. At times, she was overcome by the shame of being betrayed and of reacting so violently to that betrayal. What bothered her most was the disorientation she felt. The abrupt end to her marriage had smashed her compass, and she had lost true north.

That had been in March. Now, well into June, she was more in control, but still far out to sea in so many ways. Now, all she wanted was to get this traitorous sleazebag out of her life, once and for all. *Grrr!* She thought, as she gritted her teeth.

Within minutes, Jessica had signed the divorce papers and the sales agreement. She signed other documents, too. They allowed Jim to handle the sale of the house, at the agreed-upon price, without another face-to-face meeting with her. When the transaction was complete, she'd get a check for her half of the proceeds of the sale. At least his baby would never occupy the nursery Jessica had spent hours designing and decorating.

Jim lined up all the papers she'd signed before putting them back in the leather satchel. Jessica made a stab at being polite. "So, have you found a new house?"

"We have—in LA, though. Cassie figures she needs to be close to where the action is for her career, so we've bought something in Beverly Hills. We're planning to have the wedding there, nothing too big. She'll have to take some time off late in her pregnancy, but can manage her work *and* a baby better if we're living in town. I'll do the commute. I spend a lot of time on the road anyway, and some of that's in LA, so it's no big deal."

No big deal? What was he saying? One of his arguments against having a baby was the distraction it would be to their careers. He was adamant that someone would have to give up something to raise a child properly! The implication that she would have to choose between her law practice and a baby did not sit well, even though Jessica's career had tanked with the collapse of the real estate boom. She was having another of those "who the bleep did I marry" moments. The man was a mass of contradictions. She must have been shaking her head or something.

"What? What is it?" She was about to speak and would have said something that filled her with regret later. Terms like wimp, jellyfish, or wuss, and words that were even more vulgar sat upon her lips. Fortunately, Bernadette opened the sliders at that very moment and called out to her.

St. Bernadette, as Jessica called her on occasion, was a surrogate mother, friend, and confidant. She'd been hired as a housekeeper by Jessica's parents when they built the house decades ago. She soon became much more to all of them. She did little housekeeping herself, but managed the estate, overseeing the service providers required to keep it in tip-top shape. Things hummed smoothly even during all the chaos wrought by warring spouses and a daughter bent on wreaking havoc. Bernadette kept it that way, even after everyone left but her, making it easy for Jessica to take refuge at a moment's notice. The fact that her mother was absent, jet-setting around the Mediterranean with husband number four, also helped. Bernadette, more than the house itself, represented safety and comfort to Jessica as her life careened out of control.

"Jessica, somebody's here to see you. Are you and Jim about done?"

"Oh, we're done. Jim is just putting things back in his scrumptious bag so he can leave." Jim shot her an irritated look and then went back to shoving papers into the bag. It had been a lot easier to get them out than it was to put them back in again.

Bernadette moved out of the way and a mountain of a man stepped through the open sliding door and onto the patio. Peter March, with his square jaw, bulging muscles, six-foot four frame, and marine-style buzz cut, looked menacing, even while standing there holding an astonishing bouquet of flowers. Peter and Jim looked each other over. It was hard to determine who regarded the other with more suspicion.

"These are for you. I intercepted a delivery guy as he was bringing them to your door. Once I made certain he was who he said he was, he was more than happy to let me complete the delivery. They're from Paul, so I accepted them for you. I hope you don't mind."

"Oh, she doesn't mind. That was very thoughtful of you, wasn't it Jessica?" Standing beside him, Bernadette looked even more diminutive than usual. Her tiny, sixtyish, maybe seventy-year-old frame belied a will of iron and a heart of gold. If she stood up straight, she might be all of five feet tall; dripping wet, she weighed a hundred pounds. Bernadette exuded kindness from every pore, but could be tough as nails when she had to be. Jessica had learned that before the age of twelve, and had seen her in action again in the past week. Her smile was sheer comfort, and the sparkle in her dark eyes challenged you to believe anything was possible, but Bernadette did not suffer fools. Jessica and several of her friends were convinced she possessed special powers that made it unwise to get on her bad side.

"Stand up. I got you something for you to put on before everybody gets here." Bernadette helped her slip out of the sling, removed the stained robe. The plum Karla Colletto one-piece asymmetrical tank suit that lay beneath it had been the easiest thing to put on with only one arm to wriggle through. It fit perfectly.

Despite the extra pounds put on while desperately-seeking-baby, Jessica's 5'4", thirty-four-year-old figure was well-proportioned. The skinned knees and bruises here and there were not what caught the attention of the men in her presence. Bernadette dropped a slinky, diaphanous cover-up over Jessica's head and then put the sling back in place to cradle her wrist. Bernadette stood by while Jessica sat back down on the chaise. She whipped out a hairbrush and gave Jessica's hair a few swipes, then, placed a floppy hat on her head.

A Dead Sister

"Aren't those gorgeous flowers? That lawyer friend of yours is so thoughtful." With that, Bernadette took the enormous bouquet from Peter and placed it in Jessica's lap. Bracing the flowers with her free arm, Jessica looked like she had just been crowned Miss America.

"I brought something for you too. I made a batch of my organic super green smoothie. You've been through a lot. This will help, guaranteed." Peter set a liter bottle of bright green liquid on the table beside her. With that, he paused and glanced sideways at Jim.

"Sorry, I didn't get your name. I'm Peter March, Jessica's security consultant." He held out his hand.

"Geez, where are my manners? Peter March, meet my ex-husband, James Harper. We were just wrapping up some unfinished business."

Jim stood awkwardly, still fumbling with the latch on the bag in which he had finally managed to stash the papers. He winced as he shook hands with Peter, whose grip was firm, to say the least. As Jim stepped aside, Peter slid into the chaise next to Jessica.

"Like I said, you've been through a lot. This will give you a real boost."

"What will give you a boost?"

Heads snapped in the direction of the voice that had come, not from the house, but from the yard. Around the corner strode Brien, their half-clad, bleached-blond twenty-something pool boy. He was loaded down with brand new pool cleaning equipment. His old equipment had been ruined fighting off bad guys this past week, so Jessica had directed him to replace it all at her expense.

The sun shone off his ripped abs, glistening with sweat and suntan oil. How he managed to stay in shape was a mystery, given the amount of junk food and beer he put away on a regular basis. He grinned from ear-to-ear as he spotted Jessica. Setting down the equipment he was carrying, Brien rushed to her side, kneeling like a knight before his lady fair.

"Yo, you look more like you. Kinda awesome except for a few dings, you know?"

"Thanks. Your new equipment looks kinda awesome too." Jessica shifted the bouquet so she could reach out and give Brien a pat on the head, knocking a lock of hair down over his eyes. He flicked his head, tossing the hair back. He was beaming like a puppy as he perched himself, gingerly, on the end of Jessica's chaise.

"Yeah, it sure helps to have all the right equipment. Those flowers are righteous. Did you bring them, Peter?"

"Well, yes and no. Paul Worthington sent them as far as the driveway. I hauled them through the house and out here."

"Paul Worthington? The Paul Worthington we knew in law school at Stanford?" Heads whipped around again toward the house where Jim was still standing near the back door. In the commotion, they had lost track of him.

"Yes, that's the one. He was a Godsend this past week in so many ways," Jessica said, burying her nose in the fragrant plumeria blooms tucked in among huge creamy white, vibrant yellow and pale pink roses. Paul Worthington had, indeed, been a lifeline as Jessica dove off the cliff into unfamiliar legal waters. Fearful that she would be accused of murdering her husband, Laura begged Jessica to keep her out of trouble with the law.

With little experience in criminal defense work, Jessica had turned to the law school alum for advice even though they hadn't been in touch for years. The man had not only given her advice, but loaned her a P.I. to help investigate Roger Stone's murder, offered her a job, and invited her out to dinner. Jessica was drawn to this waspy middle-aged lawyer with striking blue eyes and the insouciance of a man used to privilege and success. She had never thought of him as her type. But then again, having been tied to Jim Harper for more than a decade, she couldn't recall if she had a type.

Paul was considerate and generous with his time as a colleague. Jessica was flattered that he not only remembered her, but also held her in high regard. She was grateful, but not ready to make more of his attentiveness than that. Of course, Jim didn't need to know that. Let him wonder.

"He's part of a big firm in LA with lots of high profile clients, right?" She wasn't sure why Jim was asking. Maybe he was doing some sort of calculation on his "success-o-meter" set off by the mention of Paul's name. Or maybe he was hoping to use the connection to make inroads among high rollers in the Los Angeles community. *Who knows? Who cares?* She thought.

"That is correct. As it happens, he's also opening a satellite office here in Palm Desert on El Paseo. I may join that office in some capacity. We'll talk about it more when we have dinner tomorrow night." She poked her nose back in among the flowers and inhaled their heady fragrances.

Jim's eyes narrowed. He was getting testy for some inexplicable reason. "Criminal defense work is hardly your area of practice."

In fact, she hadn't practiced law of any kind for several years, except for pro bono work at the legal clinics associated with Stanford or other community agencies. She had not been *paid* for work as a lawyer since the Great Recession tanked her burgeoning career as an environmental law specialist. Working with progressive developers in and around the San Francisco bay area, committed to innovative eco-sensitive community development, she had hit the floor running right out of law school.

Three years later, she was dejected as project after project, undertaken with such idealism and excitement, failed. Environmental issues were hardly relevant when development of any kind had come to a screeching halt. Fortunately, even though her law job vanished and her portfolio of stocks, bonds, and real estate took a major hit, Jessica was still quite well off. Thanks to substantial inheritances from both sets of grandparents, even in hard times, she and Jim didn't have to worry about money.

Jim and his cronies *had* worried, though. Their firm depended on Wall Street and the free flow of capital to fuel the deals that kept them afloat. When all hell broke loose, they were busily writing and reviewing contracts, setting up esoteric organizational entities, and arranging transactions that made it possible for Silicon Valley wunderkinds to bring the next big thing to market. Like a lot of firms, they were caught with their pants down, so to speak, when the bubble burst.

Not all firms were as nimble or as willing to reinvent themselves as the one where Jim worked at the time, bucking to be made a partner. Jim and his colleagues skillfully shifted their focus from venture to vulture capitalism. There was a ton of money to be made from sorting out the legal issues related to picking over the bones of defunct investment ventures, their carcasses swarming in fine print. Until their maneuvering proved successful, though, there was a lot of hand-wringing and some sleepless nights. Many of their acquaintances lost everything.

That was old news. Today, she had signed off on her marriage, making their divorce final. Well, final, as soon as the six-month mandatory waiting period required by California law was fulfilled. Jim now had nothing more to say about her career or any part of her life, for that matter. She clenched her teeth, trying to keep herself from growling out loud.

Anna Celeste Burke

"As it happens, his firm has a broader scope of practice than criminal law, but that's none of your business now, is it, Jim?" Jessica bristled. He was overstaying his welcome and Jessica was just about ready to throw him out. One word from her and Peter would be more than able to oblige her. Before anyone could say anything more, Bernadette hustled over to her.

"I should take those flowers from you and put them in a vase. They'll look great as a centerpiece for our dinner tonight."

"How about if I give you a hand with that and you pour Jessica a glass of the smoothie I brought for her. That's what I was talking about, Brien, when I said she was going to get a real boost. You want to try it too?"

"Sure, why not?" Brien replied, though he looked askance at the bottle of green liquid as Peter reached over and, in one fell swoop, scooped up the bottle from the table and the luxuriant bouquet from Jessica's lap. Jessica felt a sense of loss as she let Peter take the flowers from her. "You're going to drink it, right, Jessica?" Brien asked, seeking reassurance.

"Of course," she said with more certainty than she felt. Peter-the-giant was a devotee of health foods. So far, he had not taken her too far afield from her own preference for mostly healthy, but more mainstream cuisine.

Peter and Bernadette headed toward the house with Jim leading the way. Before Jim even touched it, the patio door slid open. Jim stopped and backed up abruptly. He was almost run down by a stunningly handsome man, as tall as Peter, but less bulky. That didn't mean he wasn't in great shape, as evident by the t-shirt and tight jeans he wore. Instead of the rugged soldier of fortune look that Peter sported, Jerry Reynolds had the classic good looks of a movie idol. He was the sort of man you could describe as beautiful without taking anything away from his masculinity.

Jerry's hair was a light shade of brown, his eyes a dazzling green. His face, a marvel of symmetry, was set off by a smile that revealed a perfect set of gleaming white teeth. He conjured up images of the glamorous stars that had made the Palm Springs area their playground for decades like Randolph Scott, Cary Grant, Rock Hudson or, more recently, George Clooney. Just because Jessica wasn't ready to put herself out there on the dating scene again, did not mean she no longer appreciated the male form. He was a joy to behold. Jerry, however, preferred men, and was madly in love with one of her dearest friends. But Jim didn't need to know that either. Let him wonder.

"Excuse me, I didn't see you. My eyes are still adjusting to the sun. I

14

A Dead Sister

should slow down," Jerry said, towering over Jim and flashing that dazzling smile. He slipped the sun glasses perched on top of his head back down over his eyes. Jerry stepped around Jim, gave a little "hey" to Peter, and then wrapped his arms around Bernadette. He brushed her cheek with a kiss and spun her around, making her giggle like a schoolgirl. She gave him a little push.

"Stop that. Go see how our girl is doing. Brien says she's looking a whole lot better."

"I don't doubt it. A day or two without tangling with desperados has got to be good for her. It's a whole lot better for the desperados, too." The smile that spread across his handsome face radiated warmth. His eyes danced with good humor as he gave Bernadette a last little squeeze. Then he hustled over to the chaise just vacated by Peter and sat down.

"Brien and Bernadette are both right. You are looking much better." With that, he took her hand and planted a gentle kiss on her palm before leaning back on the chaise. The trio waiting to get into the house made another move in that direction. The patio misting system came on, cooling the patio instantly. Tommy Fontana, Jerry's paramour, burst from inside the house.

"Hi, everybody, let's get this party going." He stopped as he caught sight of Jim. "Not you! What are you doing here? If you've done anything to her, I swear you'll have to deal with me. She's been through enough this week. Jessica, are you alright?" He rushed to join Jerry and Brien at Jessica's side.

"Tommy, sweetie, I'm fine. Jim was just leaving. Congratulate me, I signed those papers, and I'm single again." A spontaneous cheer rose up among the little group assembled on the patio. Jim Harper plunged through the mist and disappeared into the house and, hopefully, out of her life for good.

15

CHAPTER 2

It had been more than two weeks since that encounter with Jim Harper. Despite her bravado, Jessica was still struggling with the idea that her marriage was over. Her wrist had healed faster than her heart. There were fewer bad days when she felt like never getting out of bed again. Hours passed without wondering what went wrong or plotting some heinous act of revenge on that she-devil and her beastly ex-husband.

Then, out of the blue, she would be waylaid by another tidal wave of sadness, anger, or paranoia. Like Dorothy in the Wizard of Oz, she was swept up into a tornado of unanswered questions. Had Jim ever really loved her or had she been duped all along? Were there others before the Hollywood hellion? She ruminated, willing herself to think, think, *think*: when had he met her? What signs had she missed that he was two-timing her with that billowy-lipped bimbo? Eventually, she would either wear herself out, or the storm would pass, and something resembling blue skies would prevail.

Soon after Jim left that afternoon, Laura had arrived. The Cat Pack, as Jessica fondly referred to their little group, was assembled. Cat Pack was an homage to the sixties "rat pack," a name supposedly given by Lauren Bacall to friends who hung out with Humphrey Bogart. After Bogie's death, the title had lived on, ascribed to a reconfigured group of friends: Frank Sinatra, Dean Martin, Sammy Davis, Jr., Joey Bishop, and, for a time, Peter Lawford. On stage and off, they epitomized midcentury cool and the swinging sixties, in perfect sync with the Palm Springs vibe. Enjoying the convenient proximity to both Hollywood and Vegas, they had done their share of ring-a-ding-dinging in Coachella Valley resorts and in the homes they bought in and around Palm Springs.

A Dead Sister

Jessica's little band was a lot less flashy. They were given more to wandering aimlessly, like a herd of cats, than ring-a-ding-dinging. That evening, they toasted Jessica's recovery and the fact that they'd all survived harrowing experiences. Each had saved the day in some way during that awful week following Roger's murder.

Peter insisted that Jessica toast with a cup of his organic green smoothie. Jessica obliged. The concoction was dominated by the flavor of banana, which didn't account for the color. Jessica wasn't too interested in knowing what did.

"Not bad," was the best she could do in the way of an enthusiastic endorsement. That was enough for Peter, who flashed a big grin at her. That grin seemed out of place on his weathered, battle-scarred face. Jessica didn't relax completely until his usual, more implacable, expression settled back into place.

The food and drink that followed was more to her liking. Jessica had implored Bernadette to take the night off, and arranged for dinner to be catered. The caterers set up buffet-style indoors, to let guests serve themselves. Appetizers included a wonderful chilled avocado soup, roasted mixed peppers with capers, and a bruschetta with figs, honey, and feta cheese. For the main course, Jessica and her friends could choose from a vegan zucchini frittata with mushrooms and herbs, savory roast chicken, or red snapper on angel hair pasta with a citrus cream. As if that weren't enough, there was a delightful red potato and green bean salad with Dijon vinaigrette, and a pilaf with pistachios, as well as an assortment of flaky rolls—including some specially made for Peter-the-vegan. For dessert, the caterers brought out lime granita with candied mint leaves and crème fraîche, a mixed berry crisp with vanilla ice cream, and vegan carrot cake.

Jessica had raided the wine cellar and set out several good vintages to complement the summery fare. That included a refreshing 2000 Domaine Marcel Deiss Pinot Gris Beblenheim to get them started. The symphony of fresh ingredients, paired with well-chosen wines, nourished the body and delighted the palate, inspiring a festive mood.

Even Laura, who had endured the devastating loss of her husband to murder, was buoyed by the good food and camaraderie. The week had taken a toll. Laura's clothes hung more loosely than they should have. Her eyes seemed to have turned a deeper shade of brown. Dark circles sat beneath her eyes, and her skin was paler, with less color in her lips and on her cheeks. The overall effect was not unattractive. It cast a soulful aura that added, rather than detracted, from her natural beauty.

Jessica marveled at the grace in her manner and bearing. A characteristic that she'd attributed to Laura's athletic ability, she now regarded as more an expression of some interior quality. Jessica had been drawn to Laura by her openness and willingness to reach out. Everything in Jessica's world was so fractious when they first met all those years ago at St. Theresa's. Jessica had been wary and a little wild, kind of like she was again with her marriage on the rocks and her life in tatters. Laura had displayed a friendly, easygoing confidence, not offended by Jessica's petulance or impulsiveness. She had been a stabilizing influence in Jessica's life and they had become steadfast friends.

Jessica could recall conflicts with other girlfriends, but not with Laura. Although she had regarded Tommy Fontana's sister, Kelly, as her closest friend in high school, Laura anchored their little group. She brokered truces and mended fences when squabbles erupted among their circle of friends at St. Theresa's. Laura still did so much good, not just as a friend, but also in her chosen profession as a nurse. Those memories evoked the Catholic schoolgirl within. Jessica found herself saying a Hail Mary for her friend.

After dinner, the Cat Pack got down to business. Their Saturday night gathering was intended to allow Jessica to treat them all to an escape. Figuring out where they wanted to go was easy—Hawaii. The "boys," eager for Brien to take the surf safari he had long dreamed about, were headed to the North Shore of Oahu. Once their travel dates were sorted out, Jessica finalized the reservation she had made for them in a gorgeous, fully staffed beach house. A personal chef, housekeepers, and a driver would tend to them.

The "girls," Jessica, Laura, and Bernadette, had settled on a trip to Maui for a stay at the Grand Wailea. Coordinating their schedules, Jessica put her black AMEX card to work. In no time, she had their trips booked. Laura had also finagled some dates out of her sister, Sara, who was making a swift recovery from her own blood-curdling encounters with the dark side during hell week. The Cat Pack cheered Jessica on as she booked Sara, her husband Dave, and their two children on a Disney cruise.

The following week, Jessica, Bernadette, and Laura were borne aloft, in body and spirit, by the jet speeding them from one resort paradise to another. Their ten days in Maui at the Grand Wailea were splendid, restoring Jessica's faith in the miraculous nature of spa treatments. They were all polished, pampered, and massaged. Brazilian blow-outs, facials, "manis" and "pedis," along with more exotic fare, evoked "oohs" and "aahs" day after day. The shops nearby made it easy to indulge her shopping "jones." The tropical drinks flowed as they watched the sunset

A Dead Sister

cast vivid colors over the horizon, turning the Pacific waters from aqua to indigo. It was a welcome respite from the desert heat. Jessica's body was still struggling to readjust after a decade-long absence.

This morning, on her first day back home, the house was too quiet. Laura, who had moved in with Jessica and Bernadette during the investigation into her husband's murder, had left. She was living with her parents, for now, so they could all support each other while mourning Roger's death.

Peter March, already back from Oahu, had returned to work. His job as Jessica's "security consultant" no longer involved taking up a post in her front yard. He'd installed surveillance cameras and upgraded their home security system, but wasn't scheduled to check back, in person, until mid-July. Tommy, Brien, and Jerry weren't due home for a few more days, staying in Oahu for the Fourth of July. Bernadette was rushing around getting things done. She would leave after Sunday Mass tomorrow for a few days, celebrating the holiday with family members living just outside the Coachella Valley in Beaumont.

Jessica sat on the patio after a lengthy workout in the pool. Feeling alone and adrift, she sought solace in the beauty of her surroundings. Less lavish than the tropical splendor of Maui, the Coachella Valley, in the Sonoran Desert, captivates in its own way.

Some of what holds sway is the contrast between the austerity of the desert and the lushness of oases, natural and manmade, that populate the valley. The seven desert resort cities, strewn along Highway 111 south of Interstate 10 beckoned, each in its own way. Wilder, mostly unincorporated areas north of I-10 possess their own fascination. Especially to those who regard themselves as true "desert rats."

Encircling the valley, mountains cradle desert-dwellers in their embrace. They keep the rain at bay, and help create the desert climate. Jessica liked to imagine that the mountain ranges also staved off danger. She was not the first to regard the Coachella Valley as a sort of Shangri-La. Even now, after so much evil had found its way into her life, Jessica took comfort from the steadfastness of those ancient craggy peaks.

Two of them, Mt. San Jacinto and Mt. San Gorgonio, stood watch like gargantuan sentinels, posted on either side of I-10 at the Banning Pass. It was a marvel to behold them when they were covered with snow in winter, while inhabitants below cavorted among the swaying palms in shirtsleeves and shorts. When overtaken by the urge to play in the snow, that was possible, too. The Palm Springs Aerial Tramway moved revelers from palms to pines, depositing the chill-seekers near the top of Mt. San Jacinto, in a matter of minutes.

This morning, the green of the manicured golf course posed in startling contrast to blue skies, magenta bougainvillea, and mountains cast in varied hues of browns, gold, russets, pinks, and purples. The palette of colors shifted depending on the angle of the sun and the time of day. Golfers darted here and there in speedy little carts, determined to get in eighteen holes before the triple-digit heat stomped them into the ground. Cries of triumph and tragedy followed in their wake. Jessica had added another kind of color to her vocabulary, early in life, by overhearing encounters with errant balls and unyielding holes on the course. But their banter was generally cheery, the sound of happy humans at play. Jessica welcomed their presence today.

While she was brooding about what to do with the day ahead, her phone rang. She cast about for a moment, trying to find it. Pulling it out from under a nearby towel, she answered on the third or fourth ring.

"Hello, Jessica speaking."

"Hey, Jessica. It's Frank. Frank Fontana." She couldn't have been more surprised. Until he showed up for Roger's funeral, she hadn't seen him for years.

"What a nice surprise, how are you doing?"

"I'm fine. But, we need to talk."

Oh no, she thought, flashing on the words Jim-the-swine-hearted had uttered as he sat down beside her recently. Right before he delivered his let's-get-this-marriage-over-with speech. *Grrr! That was not Frank's fault. Down girl*, she said, silently, to her inner pit bull.

"Of course. What's up?"

"I need your advice—legal and otherwise. Any chance I could drop by tomorrow? I was planning to bring the kids out to the desert for a visit with Mom and Dad. Could you free up some time for coffee or a drink?"

Frank, a police officer with the Riverside County Sheriff's Department, lived in the city of Riverside about sixty miles west of the desert. His dad, Don Fontana, was a Sergeant with the Palm Springs police department and had to be nearing retirement by now. When Jessica was growing up, Don

A Dead Sister

Fontana had been "Uncle Don" to her and to her friends. He was, in fact, a real uncle to Tommy Fontana and his older sister, Kelly.

Jessica hadn't spoken to Uncle Don for some time before the recent events surrounding Roger Stone's murder. She'd called on him for his help, as a police officer and as a family friend. Uncle Don and his wife, Aunt Evelyn, had an ample backyard at their pool home in Palm Springs. Their house had served as the backdrop for countless barbeques and pool parties. For gatherings of all kinds during the years, their son, Frank Fontana, his cousins, Kelly and Tommy Fontana, and Jessica all went to school together at St. Theresa's.

"Sure, that would be nice. We didn't have much chance to catch up at Roger's funeral. I wasn't in a mood to socialize under the circumstances, but I was glad you were there. Especially since you and your dad showed up in uniform that day. Given all the trouble we were in, it was a real comfort to Laura and to me. You want to come over for lunch or dinner?"

"Nah, Mom will feel bad if she can't feed me. I thought that maybe I'd stop by after lunch, if that's okay. That way I can be back at the Fontana homestead again by dinnertime. It's a small thing, but it makes her so happy to believe she's still taking care of me. Now that I'm divorced and, I quote, 'a man on his own who needs a good home-cooked meal now and then.' I don't put up any resistance, even though she knows I'm a decent cook!"

"Well, it must be good to get a break from cooking, anyway. You must be running at top speed with your job and the kids and all. Aunt Evelyn said you and Mary have joint custody."

"Yeah, it's supposed to be fifty-fifty, but since Mary went back to school last year, I've tried to pitch in a little more. This summer, the kids are with me full-time. I'm not sure what's more challenging, keeping them busy while school's out or juggling all the stuff they're doing when school's in session. At least in the summer, there are fewer battles about homework. You're right, any break is welcome at this point, and for the kids too, I'm sure. Mom and Dad don't spoil them, but they do indulge them. You know Dad, though. He's a tough guy and expects them to play by his rules when they're at his house, and they do. At home with me, they gripe and moan, and split hairs about every rule. I'm not looking forward to spending the next few years with two teenagers. I've had a preview of coming attractions with preteen hormonal flashes from them both this year. Maybe they still blame me for the divorce."

Could Frank have kids on the verge of adolescence and only be a couple years older than she was? Jessica did the math. He had married his high school sweetheart, even before he finished college, and they didn't wait long to have kids. *Egads!* She thought. Frank's kids could easily be that old. Here she sat, sidelined, the body clock ticking, not even close to starting a family.

"I know it's not fair, but when my parents split, I wanted to make them both pay. It was like they had done me wrong, somehow. You must remember what a little witch I was."

"I do remember. You were cute, but you had a major chip on your shoulder. Hell, I wasn't the easiest kid to deal with as a teenager either. I did my share to help my dad grow old. And, I'm lucky my mom still wants to take care of me! Like I said, I'm not looking forward to what's in store for me as a single parent. Then, I guess we're both lucky just to be here, huh, considering poor Roger."

"Yeah, poor Roger," Jessica echoed in agreement.

"And poor Kelly, too. She's the reason I want to talk to you."

"Kelly? You mean *our* Kelly? Kelly Fontana?" All of Jessica's senses were immediately on high alert. Kelly Fontana was dead. Only nineteen years old at the time of her death, it had shaken them all. Why on earth would he want to talk about Kelly?

"That's right, *our* Kelly. Something's come up, and I'd like to get your input. Sorry to be so cryptic about this, but we should talk about it in person rather than by phone, on the fly. How about two o'clock? Is that okay?"

"Sure, Frank. I'll see you then." Jessica said goodbye and put down the phone.

"Let the ruminating begin," she announced to the empty patio as she dived back into the pool, letting the water envelop her in its silky embrace. Wondering: "cute," huh... "major chip on her shoulder," huh... "poor Kelly," huh? Jessica finally settled down as she struck up the beat and put in more miles in the water.

CHAPTER 3

Jessica finally dragged herself from the pool and into the house, using the sliders that led directly from the patio into her bedroom. Her huge bed hadn't been made. A copper-colored duvet, in a slinky, expensive fabric imported from Italy, hung half off the bed. Beneath the duvet, buttery soft Egyptian cotton sheets were adorned with a delicate paisley print in a paler shade of copper. The colors on the bed played off the earth tones on the walls, set at intriguing angles. Clerestory windows allowed sunlight to stream in, highlighting some surfaces and casting shadows on others.

Jessica's mother loved the look of "layered neutrals" based on a palette of creamy whites, taupe, and sandy beiges; browns that ranged from light toasty tans to dark espresso; and the blackest black. The neutral scheme was used throughout the Mission Hills house. It was made more interesting by varying the textures in each room. Stone tile, some polished and some unpolished; wooly woven rugs, grass cloth and silk fabrics; shiny mirrors and grainy woods set off the neutrals. So did pops of color in the art and accessories.

Jessica craved color. As a teen, she had insisted that more be added to the walls in her room. Her mother accommodated her request, with enthusiasm, and the walls were painted a rich golden hue. The fireplace surround, created by two interlocking L-shaped blocks of stucco, was painted in contrasting shades of a deep auburn-brown and a dark coral. She and her mother loved the way it looked so much that they'd added color to accent walls elsewhere in the house.

Pillows of various shapes and sizes were piled on a Kreiss bench at the foot of Jessica's bed. The whole house had been furnished in the plush contemporary designs custom made by Kreiss. It was another sign of the times that the company had declared bankruptcy. Jessica stopped to make the bed so she would be less tempted to climb back in it. *Did her mother know the design store she adored had gone belly up?* She wondered as she tugged and tucked the silky bedclothes.

She hadn't spoken to her mother or father in several weeks. When she filed for divorce, she felt obligated to let them know. Her mother, in Monaco at the time with her fourth husband, was casual about the news. Having been through the whole thing herself several times, she was able to assure Jessica that she would be okay, and she did. Her mother was trying to be helpful. Nevertheless, Jessica was bothered by her blasé attitude, and told her so, moving the conversation in a bad direction.

"What do you want me to say? You're *not* going to be okay? You can't live without Jim and you're never going to be happy again? It may feel like that right now, but it's just not true. You're strong, baby girl, and you'll get through this, trust me."

She didn't trust her. Her way of "getting through this" was to find another man, and that hadn't worked out so well. In addition to four husbands, Alexis Baldwin-Huntington-Cranston-something-Bortoletto had forged several less formal dalliances with men. How many wasn't clear. Too many, as far as Jessica was concerned, growing more irritated by the minute. She hated being called baby girl. It was so infantilizing.

"I hear you, Mom. It just doesn't feel okay, you know?"

"Yes, I do know." The tone in her voice had grown more serious. The moment passed, though, as her mother gushed. "Why don't you get out of California for a while? Don't even pack. Just grab your passport and get on a plane. Join us here in Monaco. We can get Giovanni to let us take the yacht out island-hopping. You haven't been to Greece in years. If you prefer, we could just tool around the Côte d'Azur, shopping. Giovanni is so busy these days, I'm sure he wouldn't mind, and I'd be glad for the company, baby girl."

There she goes again, Jessica thought. The offer had begun to sound tempting until she hit her again with that baby girl thing. That's how she felt around her mother, forever five years old. A force of nature, Alexis was like Sisyphus' boulder, flattening anyone in her path. She would want Jessica to meet people, some of them handsome, young, and not-so-young men. Before she could blink twice, her mother would have thrust her into the whirlwind that swirled around Alexis Baldwin-etc.-etc.-Bortoletto. Jessica

24

A Dead Sister

just didn't have the strength to hold her own right now, with her mother or her mother's entourage. But could there be any doubt about where the shopping habit came from?

"The offer is tempting, but I would be awful company right now. Maybe later in the summer, when the desert heat really sets in, I'll take you up on the offer. Who knows, by then I might even be in a better mood."

"Okay. Let Bernadette take care of you for a while. She'll know what to do." She had a wistful tone in her voice. "If you change your mind, the invitation is open. And, Jessica, you do know I love you, right?"

"I know. I love you too." With that, Jessica hung up the phone and called her dad. Unlike her mother, Hank Huntington had never remarried. As far as Jessica knew, there had not even been a close call. Occasionally, she would catch something on the news about a charity event or a groundbreaking ceremony involving her father or his development company. At those events, there were sometimes women on his arm or hovering in the background, smiling with admiration or affection. But he had never introduced her to any of them. If there was somebody else in his life after Alexis Baldwin, he kept it to himself.

Her father's reaction to the news about the split from Jim had differed from her mother's. Not so much in the content, but in the tone of his response and rather than *telling* her she was going to be okay, he *asked*. In that moment, she knew she would be, but sought his reassurance anyway. He confirmed that she was a tough cookie and would, no doubt, be just fine.

He also surprised her. "Jinx, can I tell you something?" He hadn't called her that in years. Not since she had figured out what the term jinx meant. As a befuddled "tween," she had come to regard it not as a term of endearment, but as one of the possible reasons her family fell apart.

Jinx was derived from her first and middle names, shorthand for Jessica Alexis Huntington. Her dad had come up with the name when, at four or five, she demanded to be given a nickname a name. That was after her parents tried to explain why some folks called her dad Henry and others called him Hank. The young Jessica had found the whole thing rather troubling until she had a nickname of her own. She liked the way it sounded and introduced herself as Jinx for the next few weeks to anyone who would listen. It wasn't until she hit the "terrible tweens" that she realized why so many adults had found it amusing when she had piped up with, "Hi, I'm Jinx, what's your nickname?" At eleven, she became convinced they heard

25

"Hi, I'm *a jinx*," which is what she felt like at that point, a jinx at home and school.

"Of course, Dad, go ahead."

"I never liked Jim Harper. I am not disappointed or even surprised that you've cut him loose, quite frankly." Jessica was shocked, since her father had always been amiable toward Jim.

"What do you mean? What didn't you like? Why didn't you say something?" She asked, pummeling him with questions, curious and incredulous in the same moment. Jessica considered her father guileless—an open book. She couldn't remember him ever lying to her or anyone else. Unlike her mother, he never seemed affected, pretentious, or out to impress. So, how had he kept his real feelings hidden? Why?

"It's hard to put into words, which is part of why I didn't say anything. He just seemed less, less than you, and less than you deserved. Jim struck me as shallow, maybe superficial, or phony. Honestly, I'm not sure. Besides, what father doesn't think something like that about the guy marrying his daughter? So, I gave him the benefit of the doubt. You loved him. I thought you saw something in him that I didn't. I can tell now that he's hurt you, and I'm sorry, Jinx." Jessica had not told anyone about Jim's betrayal yet. Something in her voice must have revealed the depths of her sadness.

"Thanks, for the support and for letting me make my own mistakes."

"It's one of the hardest things about being a parent. Trust me on that." She did. Then he surprised her again. "Your mother couldn't stand him, by the way. She was more adamant about him not being right for you than I was. More inclined to speak up about it too. You know how she is. I made her take an oath to keep her mouth shut. I didn't think it would change your mind and I didn't want to give you yet another reason to hate your parents." She was floored. Were they even on speaking terms at that point? Her mother had brought husband-to-be number three to Jessica's wedding. That was the guy whose name Jessica couldn't even remember. The marriage had come and gone in such a flash.

"I didn't know you and Mom talked things over like that anymore," Jessica said.

"When it had to do with you, we did. Still do. We made a pact to put our problems aside when it came to you. Even though we couldn't get along, we never stopped loving you." His voice trailed off. Jessica felt loved,

A Dead Sister

and thanked him for that as she hung up the phone. She also let him know she'd be "hiding out" at the house in the desert, and he was quick to offer her the use of the house in Brentwood. He wasn't there much. Most of his post-Great Recession business was outside the U.S., in China and elsewhere in the Pacific Rim.

Since then, she'd spoken to each of them again, but only briefly. She called to tell them about Roger's death. They knew who he was, of course, because he was married to her good friend, Laura. Neither could attend the funeral, but both sent flowers with notes paying their respects.

As she stacked the last pillow on the bed and headed into the bathroom to shower, a wave of nostalgia hit her. The conversation with Frank about his parents had triggered an avalanche of memories about their childhood. They were pleasant memories about Uncle Don and Aunt Evelyn, and the time spent with them and her friends. By then, she had worked through the worst of her tantrums about her parents' divorce, finding comfort and enjoyment in the friendships she made at St. Theresa's. She had also become a Catholic, making her conversion in a teenage sort of way. Partly, she did it to taunt her Anglican parents, but mostly to fit in with her peers. Maybe also to please Bernadette or to emulate her, hoping to garner the peace Bernadette found at Mass, or when saying the Rosary.

In college, where it was so uncool to be Catholic or a member of any other kind of religious sect, for that matter, she had let it slide. During a first quarter class on comparative religion, she dabbled in a variety of meditative practices, pursuing spirituality while eschewing religion. Enlightenment turned out to be a difficult thing to achieve. She let that slide too.

Barely into the second quarter of her first year in college, wham! Jessica was slammed by the news that Kelly Fontana was dead. That was the second terrible thing that had ever happened to Jessica as-yet-no-hyphen-Huntington. Uncle Don called her. It was the first time she had heard a grown man cry.

In shock, Jessica dropped everything to get back to the desert for the funeral. A memorial service was held for Kelly at St. Theresa's where the funeral Mass also took place. Jessica's parents had shown up too, and for a short time, they had been a family again, bound by the loss of such a young life in so deplorable a way.

Kelly Fontana had been found dead in a downtown Palm Springs hotel parking lot, the victim of a hit-and-run. Whoever hit her didn't have the

Anna Celeste Burke

decency to stop and help her or even call 911. Uncle Don had posted appeals for the driver to come forward, and the Fontana family had offered a reward to anyone with information about what happened that night. No one at the hotel had seen or heard anything, and no one came forward in response to the appeals. The investigation quickly ended, and Kelly's death was ruled an accident without ever identifying who had hit her.

After Kelly's death, Jessica ditched religion *and* spirituality for therapy, hoping to talk her way out of the existential dilemmas that hounded her. Nostalgia morphed into melancholy as she pondered Kelly's death and the prospect of talking about it with Frank. Jessica bowed her head in the shower and let the water run over her. The pain of that loss, mixed with the more recent losses, including her divorce from Jim and Roger's murder. She sobbed, remembering how she and Tommy had clung to one another at Kelly's funeral.

Tommy's father, Sammy Fontana, was Uncle Don's older brother. Sammy and his wife, Monica, were devastated by Kelly's death. Tommy's mother fell into a serious depression, and his father's physical health began to suffer. Even though they were only in mid-life, the death of their daughter propelled them toward a premature old age.

Tommy had always been a sweet-natured, free spirit who took an elfin delight in life. When Kelly died, it hit him hard, too, but he stepped in as best he could at sixteen to fill the void. There was only so much he could do to ease his parents' suffering. He must have been a source of great strength to his grieving parents. His auburn hair and delicate bone structure, so much like Kelly's, must also have made him a constant reminder of their loss.

Thinking of Tommy brought a smile to Jessica's face, even as she wept. His pale skin bore a spray of freckles on his nose and cheeks, something he'd disliked fiercely as a teen. They added a bit of roguishness to his features, especially when he smiled and his brown eyes twinkled. Jessica found it adorable, but treaded lightly, knowing how sensitive he was about his "blotches." He had gone through a phase when he tried to get rid of them, slathering all sorts of skin care products on his face to block the sun and fade the freckles. In his mid-twenties, he gave up and learned to live with them.

By then, he had also come to grips with his sexual orientation, an issue he had begun to address at sixteen when Kelly was killed. It was just a few weeks before her death that Tommy had found the courage to confide in her that he was gay. Retelling the story to Jessica later, he said Kelly had

28

A Dead Sister

embraced him. She told him how much she loved him, and that her only hope was that he would grow up to be a happy man, gay or straight.

Now, almost fifteen years later, Tommy was still tending to his parents, and living in the detached casita at their Cathedral City home. His young life had been marked by a series of ill-conceived schemes, false starts, and misguided occupational choices. Not to mention a capricious and sometimes even harrowing love life he experienced as a young gay man in the LGBT-friendly Palm Springs area. He had met his share of callous, self-centered, and even predatory heels while looking for love. On more than one occasion, Tommy had suffered the embarrassment and disappointment of walking in on a lover in flagrante. He tried to be nonchalant about such things, denouncing monogamy as the heights of heterosexist tyranny. Yet, he was wounded by his encounters with the gay counterparts to James Harper, dirtball par excellence.

Through it all, Jessica and Tommy had become close. She had tried to fill the vacuum left in his life by the loss of his older sister. He had become the little brother she'd wished for as a child. Their bond was a strong one. Of all those she had left behind in the desert, Tommy was the one she saw most often. He visited her in the OC, LA, and Cupertino. When Jessica paid a visit to Mission Hills, he was at the house in a flash, even when she had Jim in tow. Jim and Tommy tolerated each other, for her sake, but never forged much of a friendship of their own.

Stepping from the shower, Jessica dried her eyes and her hair. Her eyes were a little red from the shower and the tears. Otherwise, the face staring back at her from the mirror looked as good as new. Gone were the bruises, scrapes, and black eye she'd received tangling with an intruder at Laura's house. Jessica's skin glowed with good health, a consequence of keeping her promise to eat better, sleep, and exercise while allowing things in her life to settle down. Those facials at the Spa Grande in Maui didn't hurt either.

Jessica had also lost a few pounds and was more toned. Her sturdy little body was yielding to the discipline being applied to get rid of the "baby fat" she'd put on during fertility treatments. She was also hoping to be a little quicker on her feet, since she'd been forced into several situations where that had proved crucial. She was not only swimming but working out in the little room off her father's den where they had set up workout equipment years ago. She rode the spin cycle and lifted weights, too.

Her favorite thing was beating the living daylights out of a heavy bag. For now, she kicked it with her feet, since her wrist was still too iffy to risk a misplaced punch. She toyed with the idea of pasting a photo of Jim on the bag, but the image of him and the tramp was etched so indelibly in her brain that she didn't need to do it. The only real problem she had was remaining under control. She didn't want to pull a tendon in her efforts to obliterate that image by taking it out on the heavy bag. She was feeling the pain, but also a great deal of satisfaction from the pounding Jim, or any future bad guy, would get if they trifled with her again.

Jessica quit staring at the reflection in the mirror, and went into her large walk-in closet. The space had entry doors at either end, one from the bathroom the other from the bedroom. The walls were lined with clothes on hangers or shelves. At least a hundred pairs of shoes were arrayed neatly at one end of the room, near a full-length mirror. The center of the room was occupied by two rows of drawers, placed back-to-back so she could open drawers from either side. A bench sat at each end of the drawers.

On the bench in front of her sat a large suitcase. Jessica was hit by a surge of mixed emotions at the sight. She'd done it again. Gone on vacation and shopped so much that she had to buy another suitcase to get it all home. Bernadette and Laura had each come back with a new suitcase filled with treasures, too.

Between spa visits, they'd hit the shops. Jessica had insisted they let her buy them things while indulging her shopping compulsion. Popping open the suitcase, Jessica began pulling items out of it. She relished the riot of bright colors, the floral prints and soft textures of the fabrics in the clothes as she hung them up or stashed them away in drawers. They carried a hint of tropical fragrance that conjured up strains of the sweet Hawaiian music piped into the Spa Grande and elsewhere on the grounds of the Grand Wailea. Her black AMEX card had gotten quite a workout.

At one point, Bernadette, in true saintly fashion, had taken her aside: "Niña, thank you so much for this trip and the gifts. You know I love presents. This is such a beautiful place, so I'm glad to be here to share it with you." She reached out and cupped Jessica's chin in her hand, looking her in the eye. "You don't have to buy me things. I'm sorry this is such a hard time for you, thanks to that stupid man you married, but the best gift for me is having you around for a while."

Before they left for Maui, Jessica had spilled her guts to Bernadette about the circumstances surrounding her divorce. She described that awful day when she had caught him in their bed with another woman. Sad, angry tears had begun to fall before she could finish telling the story. The words stuck in her throat, the picture they painted was a vile and ugly one.

A Dead Sister

"Aye, que dios mio, Jessica! Demonio, malicioso!" She crossed herself as she spit out the words. "I figured something like that must have happened. He's no good. You must have someone much better, mi preciosa." She pulled Jessica to her, holding her tight as Jessica was racked by sobs. Rocking her gently, she murmured, "It's going to be okay! I'll say some prayers for el Altisimo to send you someone who will treat you right. A good Catholic boy, that's what you need. Like my Guillermo."

Guillermo was the young man Bernadette had married when she was still a teen. He had been killed soon after they married. Trust Bernadette to have found redemption in what most people would have regarded as an unforgivable tragedy. As far as Jessica could tell for Bernadette, like Hank, there hadn't been anyone else. Somehow, the loss had not left her bitter or caused her to lose her faith. Bernadette didn't talk about him often. When she did, it was with the conviction that her good Catholic boy was in heaven and with the hope that they would someday be reunited. If there was a heaven, Jessica felt certain it would be made better by Bernadette's presence.

How would she ever again be open to anyone, even a Guillermo? Jessica imagined Jim in a much hotter place. The fair-haired floozy too, slithering along behind, poking him with a pitchfork. Over a bowl of ice cream, she'd recounted the far-from-saintly way in which she had reacted after stumbling upon the fiends in her bed. Bernadette, looking somber at first, had started to chuckle. Finally, she burst out laughing as Jessica described how the two naked scoundrels fled, hiding in the bathroom while she ripped the bedroom to shreds.

"God didn't let you hurt anyone. Of course, you should tell Father Martin when you see him. He'll give you absolution so your conscience can be clean."

At Bernadette's urging, Jessica tagged along with her to Mass at St. Theresa's the following Sunday. The place had changed little over the years, and Jessica was awash in memories of the hours she had spent in that church. Somehow, Bernadette had engineered time alone for her with Father Martin after Mass. In a matter of minutes, Father Martin had Jessica talking, the anger and bitterness pouring out. After a few minutes, she stopped and apologized for her tirade. Father Martin called it a "lament" and reassured her.

"You're in good company. It's not surprising that the suffering and betrayal you've experienced would lead you to the occasional lament."

"The occasional lament, are you kidding? It's more like a perpetual rant. If there is a God, he's getting an earful!"

"God can take it. He's heard it all before." That's when he went to his shelf and pulled out several books for her to read. "Take these. They ought to challenge your intellect and appeal to the mystical nature you hold at bay with all your relentless activity. You might find answers to some of the questions you're asking. If not, you might, at least, take some consolation from the fact that you're not alone in your suffering. But, clinging to your love of natural wonders and your pursuit of costly, but transient things to ease your pain is a stop gap measure, at best."

She was dumbfounded by his pithy take on the status of her soul, shopping jones and all. And she nearly fell off her chair when he coached her through the Act of Contrition and then offered her absolution, post hoc. She hadn't quite realized that she had entered the confessional when she sat down to face him.

A little befuddled by what had just happened, she had to admit that her step *was* a little lighter as she left, even with the armload of books she carried: Thomas Merton's *Seven Story Mountain, Interior Castle* by St. Teresa of Avila; *Dark Night of the Soul* by St. John of the Cross, Hildegard de Bingen's *Book of Divine Works*, and several titles by Pierre Teilhard de Chardin. The books were stacked on a bookshelf in her room. She hadn't made much progress, even though she had taken a couple with her to Maui. Their physical heft was not as daunting as the mental and emotional challenge they posed. It was easier just to rant.

Jessica vowed to do more than hurl the books at the walls of her room as she pulled on a pair of colorful board shorts in a blue tropical floral print and added a matching tankini. Before leaving the closet, she slipped on a pair of comfy leather Rainbow-brand flip-flops. Her toenails, painted ruby red, reminded her of the time spent with Laura and Bernadette in Maui.

She was all over the place with her reminiscences today, a stream of consciousness carrying her along. Tugging at her, were memories she preferred to avoid. Not just Jim in flagrante with the bimbo, and poor dead Roger, but memories of Kelly Fontana. Her relationship with Kelly was marked by deep-seated ambivalence and unresolved conflicts brought up short by the abrupt end to her life. The prospect of talking to Frank about Kelly unleashed a wave of sorrow and regret. Maybe she should just take off again, head back to Hawaii or drop in on her mother in the Mediterranean. Did she really have to hear what he had to say?

CHAPTER 4

Showered and dressed, Jessica needed food. Before working out in the pool, she'd enjoyed freshly brewed black coffee and a glass of ice cold, hand-squeezed orange juice. Both courtesy of the resident wonder woman, Bernadette. She tried to guess what else Bernadette might have whipped up in her spare time. Bernadette was busy putting the house in order after returning from Maui and before taking off again for another trip, but something smelled wonderful!

Jessica opened the fridge and looked around, hungrily. "Aah!" A happy sigh escaped her lips when she spotted a container of Bernadette's fresh homemade chicken salad. Her mouth watered. Bernadette applied some sort of secret chipotle marinade to the chicken before it roasted. Lime juice and spices, like cumin and coriander were blended with mayonnaise. Then it was all mixed with the cold roast chicken, celery, diced avocado, and red onion.

"Bernadette," Jessica hollered, head tilted back. Was she in the house somewhere or had she gone out to run errands? Jessica decided to try again to rouse Bernadette from her suite in the wing of the house where she resided. "Bernadette, yoo-hoo," she sang out loudly.

"Cute shorts, Chica." Jessica jumped out of her skin. Bernadette was there at her elbow.

"Geez, don't sneak up on me like that."

"If you weren't bellowing at the top of your lungs, you would have heard me. What do you want?"

"I'm fixing lunch. Thank you, by the way, for making chipotle chicken salad. It's my favorite, as you know. Do you want something to eat or maybe a glass of wine?"

"I thought my mole was your favorite," Bernadette said, as Jessica took a bunch of grapes and a head of leaf lettuce from the crisper. She watched as Jessica rinsed the grapes and lettuce, then, patted them dry. Jessica scooped chicken salad on top of a lettuce base she'd made, then, placed a clump of grapes next to the chicken salad.

"That's my favorite too. So is your French toast. I have a number of favorites," she said, adding tomato slices and a hunk of bread to her plate.

"That looks beautiful, but I already ate. A glass of wine sounds good, though."

Jessica poured a glass of chilled Buoncristiani Chardonnay. She handed the glass to Bernadette and then poured another for herself. Bernadette was wearing one of the brightly flowered little muumuu dresses she'd bought in Maui. The deep rose-colored background in the ruffled sleeves of the dress set off Bernadette's dark eyes, and added a glow to the hint of mocha in her skin.

"That color is perfect for you. We're two good-looking wahinis, aren't we?"

"Yeah, I'm not bad for an old lady. But you, you're hot! That ex-husband of yours es un idiota!"

She and Bernadette moved from the kitchen to the nearby morning room. Their seats provided unobstructed views of the outdoors, and the meandering swimming pool. Beyond, sat the manicured golf course framed by mountains in the distance. Right now, the summer heat presided over an empty golf course. It was as if they had the Mission Hills Country Club all to themselves. That was an illusion, of course. The upscale community was rapidly becoming a year-round destination for the baby boomers that flocked to the area to retire.

For a few minutes, they sat in companionable silence while Jessica ate. "This ish sho gooooood," Jessica said, stuffing food into her mouth. "I love you sho musch!"

"Oh, stop talking with your mouth full," Bernadette clucked. "Haven't I taught you anythin' all these years?" Bernadette smiled, though, pleased by the praise.

A Dead Sister

Swallowing, Jessica took a sip of the chardonnay, perfection. "No kidding, this is *the* best. You could be a chef at any restaurant in town. And I've learned a ton from you. That doesn't happen to include the recipe for this chicken salad *or* your mole *or* your dreamy French toast, by the way. I could go on, but I'm too hungry." With that, Jessica shoveled another forkful of chicken salad into her mouth. Bernadette sipped her wine and gazed fondly at Jessica.

"What are you going to do while I'm gone to visit my family for the Fourth of July?" The question betrayed a note of concern.

"Well, I'm not sure. On Monday, I plan to call the insurance company again. I intend to keep the pressure on so Laura can get the benefits she's due as Roger's beneficiary. Laura's with her mom and dad, and the boys won't be back until the fifth, so I'll probably just hang out here for the Fourth. If I get too lonely, I can head over to Civic Center Park and join the crowd to watch the fireworks display. Don't worry. I have plenty to do. I've got to keep up with my workout regimen. Then, there are all those books Father Martin wants me to read. His idea of a workout for my soul, I guess. There is one other thing. This is kind of weird. You know Frank—Frank Fontana?"

Bernadette nodded, "¡Claro que sí! I'm getting old, but I'm not ditzy. Not yet anyway."

"Well, he called, and he's coming by tomorrow afternoon. Get this! He wants to talk about Kelly."

"Oh my, I got the chicken skin. You know, pimple gooses? That couldn't be good, could it?"

"Goose pimples not pimple gooses. I can't think of any reason, good *or* bad, that he'd want to talk to me about Kelly."

"She was such a gorgeous girl. Kind of like you, back then—a little wild, but a good heart. Terrible she died so young. It's such a shame when that happens." Bernadette had a faraway look in her eyes. Jessica reached over and took her hand. She must have been remembering another young person who died too young, her handsome Guillermo.

"I'm sure it's nothing. I'll tell you all about it when you get back from your visit. And you can catch me up on what's going on with your sister and her husband and their kids and grandkids." Jessica had lost count of how large the family was at this point. They had scattered a bit, as

Bernadette's nieces and nephews moved out and started their own families. Bernadette was, no doubt, an anchor in their lives just the way she was in Jessica's.

After lunch, Jessica could no longer avoid facing the memories that had nagged her since the call from Frank. Alone, in the sitting area in her bedroom, she picked up one of the books Father Martin had given her. Intending to read, she instead thought about what Bernadette had said about Kelly Fontana.

She was right about Kelly's appearance. Kelly was gorgeous, even at fifteen, when Jessica first met her. Taller than Jessica by three or four inches, Kelly had a lithe, willowy figure. Her naturally wavy auburn hair fell to the middle of her back. She had the pale skin of a redhead, without the freckles that tormented Tommy. Her features were delicate, set off by lushly-lashed, light blue eyes, so pale they sometimes looked gray. Jessica hadn't seen that shade before or since. They gave her an ethereal quality. If Tommy was an elf, Kelly was a fairy princess.

And she had the voice of an angel. Except for choir, drama, and art classes, school was a drag to Kelly. She could have been good at most any sport, but didn't like them. Dance was a different matter. Kelly loved to dance, and worked after school to pay for lessons. She belonged to a small ensemble group that performed at St. Theresa's, and participated in every school play or musical that took place during her stint as a high school student. Modeling was something she considered, but what she wanted to do was get into television or the movies. Her performances at St. Theresa's always received kudos. Reflecting on her ability, Jessica concluded that Kelly was at least as talented as the Hollywood blond about to become the second Mrs. James Harper.

Kelly was also wild. It was, no doubt, one reason she hit it off with her immediately. Although Jessica cleaned up her act once she got to St. Theresa's, she was no paragon of virtue. Kelly's angelic appearance allowed them to get away with a lot. Whenever Jessica was doing something she shouldn't do, Kelly was right there, aiding and abetting, if not leading the way.

Together, they filched their first drinks, pulling Laura and a couple other friends into their scheme at a sleepover. After Bernadette and her mother went to bed, Jessica brought out a bottle of Amaretto and five tiny glasses. The sweet liqueur was way too easy to drink. In a short time, they emptied the bottle. The more they drank, the sillier everything seemed, and the louder they got. Using her superpowers, or so Jessica had thought at the

A Dead Sister

time, Bernadette caught them red-handed.

Everybody got sent home in the middle of the night. Jessica could feel her cheeks getting hot with embarrassment even now at the scene the five drunken teenagers had created. One-by-one, disgruntled parents came to retrieve their wayward children. The scornful look given to Bernadette and her mother by one of the parents aroused feelings of shame to this day. Kelly was the last to leave. Drunk as a skunk too, she laughed uncontrollably as Jessica knelt on the bathroom floor, hurling into the toilet. When Kelly's father, Sam Fontana, arrived, he was more apologetic than annoyed with Bernadette and Alexis. He knew full well that at least some of the fault rested with his daughter. Wildness lurked behind that veil of seraphic beauty.

That incident, and the punishment that followed, didn't stop them from drinking. However, it did make them more discrete, or maybe the better term was sneakier. By the time Jessica turned twenty-one, she was bored with the whole idea of drinking to excess. Somewhere along the way, she'd figured out how many calories there were in a beer or a Piña Colada. A binge just wasn't worth the price she would have to pay when standing on the scale a few days later.

Kelly's take on the whole thing was different and became only one of the many conflicts that emerged between them. "You know you can eat and drink what you want if you barf it up. That's what dancers and models do." At first, Jessica laughed. Surely, she was joking. The whole idea was so gross that Jessica must have had a horrified look on her face. Kelly got ticked.

"*Everybody* does it. What's the big deal? It's not like you do it every day. Just if you want to have a little fun on the weekend and not worry about it, you know?" Jessica was not convinced. It just seemed easier to drink less. Besides, she was such a control freak that getting drunk scared her. After a few more minutes of fighting about it, Kelly brought the discussion to an end.

"Whatever be a stuck up little "b," I don't care. Don't blame me when you're at home by yourself because you're such a drag, or you're a fat cow." With that, she had stormed off. She and Kelly avoided each other for about a week, until Laura insisted they kiss and make up. They never resolved anything, but moved on after a teary apology.

She and Kelly had also smoked pot for the first time together. Hiding under the high school bleachers where they had tried cigarettes, and where Jessica had had her first kiss from a boy. Kelly was always way ahead of

Jessica when it came to boys. She practically had to fight the boys off who were drawn to her like bees to honey. If what she said was true, Kelly wasn't doing all that much fighting.

Kelly was so much more alluring than Jessica or their other friends. As Frank Fontana so aptly reminded her, Jessica was "cute," not stunning like Kelly. She was a "late bloomer" according to her mother and Bernadette, which meant nothing to Jessica as she threw a fit to wear a wonder bra. She wanted something that would add to her shamefully small bust right then; not later, when she was an adult and her life would be over anyway.

"You'll get your share, Chica. You don't want to go through life being false, a fake just to fit in." Bernadette advised, trying to admonish and reassure her at the same time. The thought of being false didn't really bother Jessica, fitting in mattered more.

Her mother had also encouraged her to be patient and not worry so much. "Besides, if things don't work out the way you like, there are plenty of good plastic surgeons around when you're old enough."

Bernadette and her mother were right, of course. In another year, Jessica had filled out nicely, getting more than her share, in fact. That had another set of drawbacks, as she quickly learned.

When the two of them were together, though, it was always Kelly, not Jessica, who drew the appreciative glances and comments from members of the opposite sex. Jessica tried not to let it bother her, but it did. Partly, it was envy about being overlooked. It was also a fear of losing Kelly as a friend. Her feelings were hurt when Kelly, enamored with some new boy, ditched her, Laura, and their other friends. During her absence, they would talk about Kelly as if she were a dog, vowing to never invite her to go anywhere with them again. Of course, they never kept that vow, and soon Kelly would be back.

The envy between them was not all one-sided. It was Kelly who first made Jessica feel self-conscious, and even a little ashamed, about being rich. The summer after their junior year in high school at St. Theresa's, she, Laura, and Kelly were all seated on the floor of Jessica's bedroom in Mission Hills. Jessica was griping about some injustice imposed upon her by the unholy trinity, her father, mother, and St. Bernadette, when Kelly suddenly let loose.

"Oh my God, what are you whining about? You have it all, looks, brains, *and* money! Give me a break!"

A Dead Sister

"I have it all? What do you mean?"

"Just look at this room. Do you really believe most people live in a palace like this? You've been in my room. Your closet is about as big as my whole room, isn't it, Laura?" Laura looked down at the floor, then, nodded yes, slowly. Jessica had never given the size of Kelly's room a moment's thought. But how was that Jessica's fault?

Kelly was just warming up, egged on by Laura's acquiescence. "How about the clothes you're wearing. You take us shopping on El Paseo, but do you know where I shop when I go by myself or with my mom? It's not Saks, I promise you. The underwear I have on came from Walmart, not Victoria's Secret! Does that shock you? I paid ten dollars for five pairs of panties sealed in a plastic bag, not ten dollars for one pair wrapped in pink tissue paper!"

Jessica was starting to get ticked. "What do I care where you buy your underwear, or how much you paid for it? What's wrong with you? I don't care about money."

"You don't care about money, because you don't have to. You just assume it's there because it is! You have no idea what it's like out there for real people like me and Laura, who have to work for everything they get."

Jessica was getting angrier by the minute. "What are you talking about? I am going to work. That's why I'm going to college!" By this point, Jessica's seventeen-year-old face was flushed, tears of anger welled up in her eyes, and her fists were clenched.

"Okay, so rub it in. I know, my grades suck and I'm not going to get into any college. I'm going to be lucky to even graduate from St. Theresa's with you two. If I did get into college, who would pay for it? Me! That's who! My parents don't have extra money lying around. When my grandma died, she didn't leave me a trust fund. I didn't even know what that was until you mentioned it. I had to Google it. So, if I did go to college, I'd pay for it." The truth of what she was saying got through in a ruthlessly blunt kind of way. A rush of guilt and shame flooded Jessica, warring with the anger she felt.

"I'm not trying to rub anything in, Kelly. I, I..." Jessica sputtered.

Laura had tried to object. "Shut up! You know what I'm saying is true. If you weren't trying so hard for a saint goody-two-shoes award, you'd say something too. You think you're that Laura Ingalls girl living in a 'Little

Anna Celeste Burke

House on the Prairie,' but you're not. You're Laura Powers living in a little house on the dump, not easy street like Jessica." Kelly turned back to Jessica and continued her tirade.

"How do you suppose I feel, knowing that I'm a charity case? How can I ever keep up, no matter what I do?" The steam finally ran out. Both Jessica and Laura were sobbing quietly. Kelly started to weep, too. The three of them sat in miserable silence for a little longer, until Laura got up on her knees and put her arms around them.

"It doesn't really matter," Laura had said over and over. "What matters is that we're friends, that we stay friends." That was Laura-the-peacemaker, doing her thing. She was the essential third leg, always propping up their unstable triad. Without her efforts, the three of them might have parted ways long before the end of high school.

Despite the intermittent drama, they'd been there for each other in important ways when they faced one teen trauma or another. At times they had fun, laughing until they couldn't get a breath. Once, they replaced the usual morning blessing broadcast over the intercom with Jon Bon Jovi's rendition of Keep the Faith. Another time, with other friends, they put all the picnic tables on the roof of the cafeteria. They toilet papered the campus on several occasions, and liberated the lab animals, some of which made their way, surprise, surprise, into locker rooms *and* the school cafeteria.

At least some of the good times they shared were brought to them courtesy of Jessica's prosperity. Whole days were spent at the spa. Alexis, who accompanied them on spa days and shopping trips, often coached them on how to use a product or accessorize an ensemble they'd bought that day. She also supplied them with first-run movies they could watch in the media room that Hank Huntington had built into the Mission Hills estate.

Bernadette fixed popcorn, made lemonade, and baked cookies. Even that sometimes provoked Kelly's intermittent tirade against Jessica's privileged life. The fact that there was a Bernadette, waiting on Jessica hand and foot, was another source of resentment. All that ambivalence hovered in the background as they finished high school at St. Theresa's.

It didn't get any better after that. Kelly did well enough in her senior year to graduate from high school with them. But she decided not to go to college, at least not right away, and opted to get a job instead. The fact that both Laura and Jessica started college the following fall put distance

40

A Dead Sister

between them. That distance was more than a matter of geography. UC Irvine, where Jessica enrolled to study environmental science, was only a couple hours away. Laura, who started college at the local community college, didn't even leave the valley. Laura tried desperately to cajole Kelly into taking classes with her at the College of the Desert. Kelly refused, adamant that there was nothing in it for her.

The last time Jessica had seen Kelly, they fought. On New Year's Eve in 1998, Jessica returned home, after completing her fall quarter in college. She and half a dozen friends, including Kelly and Laura, had gone out to celebrate. Jessica rented a limo with a driver who looked the other way while she and Kelly loaded it with food and drinks. They were all more than a little tipsy, having helped themselves to well-chilled Cristal as the limo driver took them from place to place that night.

On their way home, following a round of toasts to the last new-year of the twentieth century, Kelly's mood turned dark. "Let's not forget to toast our good friend, Jessica." A cheer went up. Jessica's friends, in their slinky party dresses and stilettos, raised their glasses.

Kelly wasn't done. "Where would we be tonight if it wasn't for you?" Her glass was still raised in a salute. "I don't know about the rest of you, but I would have been watching that frigging little ball drop on TV with my parents and my little brother."

Heads bobbed in agreement. "Ooh me too!" someone groaned. A ripple of nervous laughter followed as Kelly took a sip, and then held the glass aloft once more.

"Thanks, for taking time off from college to save us from that fate!" The others followed, raising their glasses again. But with less abandon this time. "What about next year? Are you going to do the same thing next year and the next?" Kelly paused, downed the champagne in her glass, and refilled it.

"How about tomorrow, what are you doing tomorrow? I've got to work to try to make up the tips I lost taking tonight off. You're probably planning to go to the spa tomorrow. I am too, but I won't be the one getting pampered. Are you coming to the Agua Caliente spa so I can wait on you? Will you leave me a big tip, Princess Jessica?" She bowed, spilling a bit of the champagne from her glass, which was filled to the brim.

"Oops! Sorry, don't want to waste the Cristal." She licked her fingers and giggled, sipping to lower the level of champagne in her glass.

Anna Celeste Burke

It had grown quiet in the back seat of the limo. Jessica was too mortified to speak. The others, stunned, angry, or embarrassed, were also mute. The silence didn't last long. Kelly lifted her head, wobbling a little in her drunkenness. She quickly refilled her glass again and drank it like it was water.

"You know what I think?" Kelly asked, slurring her words. "I think you like taking us along with you so you can throw your money around. You're just showing off again, like you always do."

"Kelly, shut up, you're drunk. You're embarrassing yourself and turning this into a downer for us." Kelly's head swung loosely in Laura's direction. She glowered at Laura who had made the comment. Then she turned toward Jennifer Cox, who had the temerity to utter a few syllables in agreement with Laura.

"Yeah, Kelly you're being rude," was as much as she could get out before Kelly's glare cut her off with a string of foul words.

Jessica, now past the initial shock of Kelly's attack, fought back tears. She was suddenly furious.

"Not this again! Kelly Fontana, I've had it. You are a mean, ungrateful wretch. I like doing things with my friends and I've got the money to pay for it. So, what? I'm sorry it upsets you that I have more money than you do, but that's the way it is. You can say no when I ask you to go places." Kelly said nothing, but glared sullenly as Jessica went on.

"If you've got to work tomorrow, that's your choice. I tried to talk you into going to college. So did the rest of us. If you want things to be different, *you* need to do something different. Otherwise, keep doing what you're doing and quit griping about it."

Kelly had mumbled something barely audible and almost incoherent about if I knew how hard she had to work to make a living, I wouldn't like it or tell her to keep doing it. I was so fed up at that point; I had just kept talking.

"Who cares what I think? Quit blaming everybody else. Get up tomorrow and come up with a plan. Do something besides feeling sorry for yourself and acting like an ass. That's not going to change anything, except make me believe our friendship isn't such a good idea anymore."

Kelly's mouth dropped open. Jessica had never spoken to her in quite that way before. Before Kelly could say anything else, Jessica hit a button

A Dead Sister

on the console and got an immediate reply from the front seat.

"Yes, is there a problem?" the driver asked.

"No problem, but a change of plans. We have someone who needs to get home right away. Can you take us to the address on the list for Kelly Fontana, please?"

"Sure thing, hang on a second. I need to pull over and get my bearings, okay?"

"No problem, do whatever you need to do." The driver pulled over, recalculated the route, turned the limo around, and had them back on the road again in no time flat.

Jessica never took her eyes off Kelly, who held her gaze at first, defiantly. She finally dropped her eyes. Kelly mumbled again, talking mostly to herself. "I know you don't approve of me. I have to make a living." Jessica hadn't said another word. Kelly continued to drink and mutter under her breath, "It's not my fault what I have to do," and "If you snooty college girls don't approve, that's your problem." When Kelly filled the glass again, she was still talking to herself, but Jessica was done listening. Kelly raised the glass, to no one in particular, before sucking down its contents.

That gesture signaled the end of the conflict. Several of the other girls ventured a little chit-chat in low voices. Laura gave Jessica a nudge with her foot. When she looked up, Laura gave her a reassuring smile with a nearly undetectable shrug. She was not going to try to fix this. Not tonight, at least.

When they got to Kelly's apartment and the driver opened the door, it was as though a wild, caged thing had been set loose. Kelly leapt from the limo, grabbing an unopened bottle of champagne as she left. Jessica marveled at how graceful she was. Even while drunk and breaking the hearts of her friends as she fled into the cool desert night air. Kelly did not look back, but wagged the champagne bottle up and down, like a town crier swinging a bell. There was no cry. It was two o'clock, and all was *not* well.

When the limo doors closed again, the relieved group burst into chatter. Jessica wasn't paying much attention to who was saying what.

"Thank God!"

"Good job, Jessica! She needed to hear that. Something is wrong with her!"

"You did the right thing," Laura said. "She's done that to you before, I know. She's done the same thing to me, more than once. Not about how much money I have, of course. How much I get away with at home. I don't have a younger brother; my parents make me babysit, blah, blah, blah. That's in addition to ranting at me about what a chump I am for going to college. If anybody is disapproving of others, it's her."

"It's about time somebody told her to shut up. She had no right to say any of that to you." That was her friend, Nicky, joining forces to support her.

"You're always happy to do stuff that doesn't cost a dime." Laura went on in a reflective tone. "Some of my favorite memories are of us sitting around eating popcorn and watching TV, doing each other's hair, or trying out some new eye shadow."

"How about those great parties at Uncle Don and Aunt Evelyn's house where we all brought something for the BBQ or a dish to pass?" Jennifer added.

"Those *were* great parties, especially when Aunt Evelyn made her Coca-Cola sheet cake. That was so good, wasn't it?" Shannon asked.

"Yeah, and it didn't cost a thing except for a few extra laps around the track or in the pool," Laura offered.

"A few, are you kidding?" Jessica interjected, finally climbing out of her funk. "You must not have eaten as much of that cake as I did! I had to run my legs off *and* swim like a maniac after one of those parties." Several of her friends giggled.

"You mean you didn't just puke it back up?" That question, from Shannon, evoked another round of giggles.

"Oh my God, did Kelly tell you to do that, too? That is so gross. There is definitely something wrong with that girl!" Jennifer said, with others nodding agreement.

"Maybe there's something wrong with me too, because I am starving." That was Laura again.

"Me too," someone else chimed in, "stop talking about that cake."

Jessica flew into action, hitting the intercom button again.

A Dead Sister

"Yes, what's up?"

"Sorry, but there's been another change of plans, we need food. We're desperate. Is there anything open this early on New Year's Day?"

"Nothing fancy, but maybe Denny's or IHOP. You want to swing by one of those places?"

"How does that sound?"

"Pancakes, yum!" Laura responded. The rest of the still-tipsy bunch agreed. Their long-suffering limo driver swung the car around again, heading for the nearest IHOP. He earned a huge tip that night. Joining them for pancakes, he turned out to be quite a storyteller. He held them spellbound with tales of even more bizarre evenings than their own. Some, which involved celebrities, seemed familiar to Jessica, the stuff of urban legend, perhaps. It was great to hear them told as eyewitness accounts, and in hilarious fashion. Near dawn, they had each returned home stuffed and exhausted. The memory of Kelly's tantrum faded away in the wake of pancakes and conviviality.

Less than two weeks later, Kelly was dead. Without the hope of reconciliation, Jessica was despondent, even when trying to console Tommy. Tommy tried to make her feel better by saying how sorry Kelly was about what had happened that night. He swore she intended to apologize. She planned on visiting her in the OC to hash things out if Jessica was willing to give their friendship another chance.

"She really wanted to explain," Tommy insisted.

"Explain what?" Jessica couldn't understand. "It was clear to me that Kelly just didn't like anything about me."

"You have got to be kidding. Kelly loved you almost as much as she loved me." Tommy's eyes, dark with sorrow and red-rimmed from crying, had started to fill with tears again. He was so distraught that Jessica accepted what he had to say.

"I'm sure you're right. You knew her better than anyone." Was that true? Did anyone know what was going on with Kelly Fontana? Jessica had done her best to forgive Kelly and herself for that night. She'd moved on, relegating it to the past. Here it all was again, after that enigmatic call from Frank. Now what?

CHAPTER 5

Sunday morning, Jessica awoke early. She surprised Bernadette by fixing coffee and an omelet for her. After breakfast, Jessica helped load Bernadette's luggage and a stack of presents into the huge Escalade that the petite Bernadette loved to drive.

Jessica was subdued, unhappy about those sad memories of Kelly Fontana. The prospect of being alone at the house for nearly a week also got her down. She even felt a bit sorry for herself. Of course, she had no hope of evading Bernadette's emotion-detecting superpowers.

"It'll be okay. A little quiet time isn't a bad thing." Bernadette stopped what she was doing and took both of Jessica's hands in her own. "You've got a lot to think about. Like whether you're going to go to work for that good-looking attorney, or date him. It's kind of hard to do both, you know. You have all that reading to do before you see Father Martin again, that insurance company to fight with, and all those laps to swim." She brushed Jessica's cheek with a kiss.

"I know you're right. I have plenty to do. After all we've been through in the last month, quiet *is* good. It'll be a blessing if the only fireworks in my life are the ones being set off by the city of Palm Desert. Don't worry St. Bernadette, I'll be alright."

Bernadette pulled herself up into the driver's seat of the SUV, shut the door, and started the engine. Then she rolled down the window. "I'll be back on Friday, and the boys will be back then, too. Why don't you plan a get-together for us? You're always so good at doing things like that. Why not get those caterers back here again? They did a great job last time."

A Dead Sister

Jessica felt like a ten-year-old being forced to stay home and do her homework or chores. She couldn't just invite herself along for a visit with Bernadette's sister's family. Scuffing the ground with the toe of her sandal, she finally agreed.

"Oh, all right, that's a good idea. You drive carefully, okay?"

"I promise! No distracted driving for me. No talking on the phone, no sexting like that Weiner guy," she said. That last comment evoked a little twitch from Jessica's lips, almost a smile. Bernadette put on her dark glasses, "See, no messing with my sunglasses while I drive. And Jessica," she paused.

Jessica looked up, "Yes?"

"I love you and I left something for you in the kitchen. Go see. It's something special for you and Frank when he visits this afternoon."

"I love you too," Jessica said. She stood on her toes and leaned in through the window to give Bernadette a kiss goodbye. Bernadette backed out of the garage, handling the gargantuan vehicle as if it was nothing. Jessica waved as the door started to shut again after Bernadette hit the button on the garage door opener. Jessica's mood had lightened in anticipation of what she might find in the kitchen. It hadn't been in the fridge, or she would have seen it when she fixed breakfast for them. Where then?

As soon as she stepped into the kitchen, she spotted it. Not in the fridge, but on it. It was cake, and not just any cake, but Bernadette's spicy, triple-layer chocolate cake. Made with Mexican chocolate, spices, and chili, it was rich, moist, and melted in your mouth. Topped with her fudge frosting, it was, by itself, a reason to live. Jessica held out hope that someday, Bernadette would share her recipe. That chipotle-roasted chicken was not the only fantastic thing that Bernadette had prepared while Jessica was working out in the pool or dilly-dallying in her bedroom yesterday. How she got so much done in so little time was a mystery—a blessed one.

Bernadette's recipe for life was as mysterious as her recipe for chocolate cake. Was the secret ingredient hidden in those dense volumes Father Martin had given her to read? Did they contain anything that might reveal the source of Bernadette's boundless kindness and joyous spirit? Jessica spent the next hour trying to figure that out. She found some of what she read intriguing. No "road to Damascus" experience, but there were a few moments marked by a thoughtful "hmm."

Anna Celeste Burke

She was struck by the sense of conviction shared by the believers who wrote so passionately about the desire to know God. A singular voice engaged in the pursuit of answers to the most terrifying questions about being human. Jessica came away from her reading without answers to those questions per se, but with a greater appreciation for the *process* of such inquiry. Perhaps it was true that not only the destination, but also the journey mattered too.

Jessica set the books aside and ventured out for a swim. She had some miles to put in if she was going to eat that cake. Still immersed in a reflective state induced by her reading, Jessica looked around at the paradise in which she lived. It was hot, extremely hot, for the last day of June. Saturday, the mercury had climbed to a hundred twenty-two degrees, and it was headed close to that again. When the heat beats full-on, the desert shimmers, creating the sensation that everything around you throbbed with life, even the inert matter. Odd in a place supposedly so bereft of living things.

Jessica had spent a lot of time hiking and riding on horseback in the surrounding desert. Beyond the reach of the synthetic Arcadia of country clubs and resorts, a realm of rugged desert terrain waited to be discovered. That realm hums with life. In a few natural oases, two-hundred-year-old Washingtonian palm trees shelter ponds fed by bubbling springs. The springs originate from a massive underground aquifer that supplies much of the drinking water in the Coachella Valley. The tall shaggy palms stand, like bearded old men, keeping watch over their desert refuges.

Even in areas rarely touched by water, desert life abounds. The desert is home to a surprising array of drought-tolerant succulents, wildflowers, scrub, and brush. Those habitats harbor wildlife, ranging from insects and reptiles to songbirds, roadrunners, wild cats, and bighorn sheep. The desert not only plays host to a stream of human visitors each year, but to birds and butterflies as well. Situated near the Pacific Flyway, the nearby Salton Sea serves as a rest stop for migrating birds, which also show up in water hazards on golf courses or water features at resorts. Monarch butterflies dance their way through the Coachella Valley on their sojourns to winter in Mexico and on their return north in spring and summer.

Much of the blow-sand desert has been destroyed by development, which blocks the movement of sand, halting dune formation and restoration. But the living landscape of dunes and hummocks can still be found in places like the Coachella Valley Preserve. It's also a stunning example of the natural oases that had sustained native Cahuilla for hundreds of years before outsiders discovered the valley. Hiking was

A Dead Sister

something Jessica looked forward to in the fall when summer yielded its grip on the desert landscape.

Maybe it was the reading she'd done, or just the early stages of heat stroke, but Jessica had the urge to fall in sync, somehow, with the living desert around her. Diving into the swimming pool, she found her rhythm, gliding through the water. Jessica imagined herself linked to the intractable durability of the desert, steadfast, and resilient under even the most extreme conditions. She would endure and rebound. Perhaps she might find what she was looking for after all if she just kept at it.

After finishing her workout, Jessica struggled to hang on to that hopeful mood as long as she could. The minute the doorbell rang, other emotions took over. In the lead was a ton of apprehension. Frank Fontana was right on time and Jessica went to the front door to welcome him. Accustomed to living in Riverside, where it was twenty degrees cooler, Frank was obviously uncomfortable in the heat.

"Come on in. Let me get you something cool to drink." Jessica had been inspired to make fresh-squeezed lemonade for the two of them. The tall frosty glasses were garnished with sprigs of fresh mint from the pint-sized kitchen herb garden that flourished under Bernadette's care. "I made us lemonade, and you won't believe what Bernadette left for us—chocolate cake! I hope you have room for cake, even though I'm sure Aunt Evelyn stuffed you." Jessica led him to the table in the morning room, where she had set out the glasses of lemonade and a pitcher for refills. In the center of the table was that cake. Three tiers high, covered with swirls of fudge frosting.

"That looks amazing. I haven't had Bernadette's chocolate cake in years, but I haven't forgotten how good it was. Mom and Dad eat lunch early. They're up at dawn and ready for lunch by eleven. My kids are still groggy at that time of day. That's more like breakfast time around our house if they don't have school. Anyway, Mom and Dad held off until eleven thirty when I rousted the kids into bathing suits and flip-flops so they could sit at the dining table. They both scarfed down food like they hadn't been fed in weeks! I have the grocery bills to prove otherwise. They must eat about ten thousand calories a day each, minus the ten percent or so that ends up on the kitchen floor after each feeding frenzy."

Jessica flashed for a moment on "feeding time" at the home of Laura's sister, Sara, who swore that as much food ended up on the floor as in her two toddlers. Ten percent on the floor was an improvement. She couldn't remember ever being that sloppy at their age. Maybe her memory failed her, since she had been oblivious to clean-up duties while growing up. Getting anything on her hands, face, or clothes, even by age five or six, had disturbed Jessica. The thought of leaving a trail of crumbs on the floor of the kitchen would have been unimaginable to the fastidious twelve-year-old Jessica.

"I'm sure it made Aunt Evelyn happy that they enjoyed the meal. And it sounds like it's been long enough since you ate to have plenty of room for cake and maybe a little ice cream to cool you off?"

Frank was guzzling his lemonade, and let out a sigh of approval as he put the glass down. "I'd make room for that cake even if I'd just eaten a horse," he said, smiling broadly. "This lemonade is doing a good job beating back the heat, but ice cream sounds too good to pass up." He smiled again, looking a bit shy as he spoke.

"You look great. Much better than you did at Roger's funeral." Frank picked up the glass and finished his lemonade.

As Jessica moved to the table and leaned over him to pick up the pitcher, she was close enough to feel the heat rising from his body. She caught a whiff of something fresh and clean like wood or sage and soap. His dark hair was a little shaggy, parted on one side, and combed back just off his forehead. Maybe the scent was from something he'd used on his hair, which looked like it had just been washed. He could use a haircut. With the long hours he worked as a cop, and raising two kids on his own, a haircut was probably not high on his "to do" list.

He was clean-shaven and wore a lightweight long-sleeved shirt in a camel color, which drew out the hint of olive in his complexion. It made his dark eyes seem even darker. His sleeves were rolled up, exposing an inexpensive watch that could use a new faux-leather band. He wore jeans and what looked like motorcycle boots. She couldn't remember ever seeing him on a motorcycle. Maybe he'd had motorcycle duty as a cop before he rose through the ranks to detective. Moving his glass closer, to pour him more lemonade, she brushed against his arm. A little tingle shot through her body.

Whoa, Cuz! She thought as she refilled his glass and stepped away.

Frank wasn't her cousin, but for many reasons, he'd always been off limits. Ahead of her in high school by two years, he'd been a big man on their small campus. On the baseball, tennis, and golf teams, he excelled at each sport. He was active in student government and, although not the top

A Dead Sister

student in his class, he was among them. Because of her friendship with his real cousin, Kelly Fontana, she and Frank mixed outside of school. Otherwise, their paths might never have crossed.

It wasn't just the age difference. By the time she got to St. Theresa's, where he was a junior in high school, it was clear that he wasn't available, anyway. Frank Fontana had a sweetheart. Like his father, Donato Fontana, Frank had fallen in love with an Irish girl, one Mary Catherine McNeil. Also like his father, who married his Irish sweetheart, Evelyn Mae Burns, when they were both young, Frank married Mary not long after graduating from high school. Unfortunately, Frank and Mary hadn't figured out how to make their marriage last like Uncle Don and Aunt Evelyn, who were nearing the end of their fourth decade as a married couple. Frank's marriage lasted only a few years longer than Jessica's had.

Flustered, Jessica started to walk away from the table, still holding the pitcher. It was her turn to look a bit shy, as she turned around and put the pitcher back on the table. She resumed her trip to the kitchen for the ice cream and a scoop. *What had gone wrong with Frank's marriage?* She wondered. Not that it was any of her business. She tried to shift her focus back to the subject that had brought him there. Kelly Fontana. When she came back to the table, she made sure to keep her distance. She strained to come up with something to say while she cut the cake and scooped the ice cream.

"I was trying to remember how old your kids are. It's kind of shocking that you'll soon have two teenagers on your hands."

"Evie is ten going on twenty-five, and Frankie is twelve. Those ten thousand calories a day he puts away are being put to good use. He's only a couple inches shorter than me." He picked up his fork, pausing as he gazed out the window.

"You're not the only one in shock about how soon they'll be teenagers. When I tell one of them to do this or stop doing that, I catch myself expecting to see this accommodating six-year-old say, 'Okay Daddy.' Instead, I get resistance, sometimes even belligerent questions asking me why! Half the time, I'm too tired to offer any reasonable explanation. Good grief! It just seems so obvious why you should put your dirty clothes in the hamper and your dirty dishes in the dishwasher. Or why you should get off the phone at ten when you've got to be up at six for school the next day. I hear myself saying, 'because I said so, that's why!' You can imagine how effective that is." He shook his head as he dug into the chocolate cake on his plate.

"That sounds grueling," she offered, as she took a bite of her own cake and ice cream. As expected, the cake was ambrosial! The rush of chocolate and sugar, with a hint of spice, sent a surge to Jessica's pleasure centers, still on high alert from that close encounter with Cousin Frank.

She stole a glance at Frank as he pondered the cake he was about to eat. He looked a lot like Uncle Don. Well, a lot like Uncle Don had when he was closer in age to Frank. His was a pleasant face, not exactly handsome in the conventional sense, but attractive. Maybe a little like Andy Garcia or John Cusack. *Good cop faces*, Jessica had often thought about Uncle Don and Cousin Frank. Honest, dependable, and direct, always able to look you in the eye.

Uncle Don and Aunt Evelyn's house had a whole wall covered with family photos. It was filled end-to-end with pictures from three or four generations of Fontana family members. There were baby photos, school pictures, and graduations. A picture of Uncle Don snapped when he first put on the uniform was positioned near a similar one of Frank taken decades later. Wedding photos and pictures from their honeymoons were there, too. One portrayed Uncle Don and Aunt Evelyn at the Grand Canyon, the photo faded with age. Cousin Frank and Mary posed in another, a blissful young couple somewhere in Hawaii.

Jessica was always envious of that wall with all those family memories on display. Her mother and the design divas she worked with over the years would have been appalled. Although Jessica rather liked it, her impulse to order things would have forced her to arrange the photos in a more systematic way.

"Yeah, kids are tough. Even the good ones can push you to your limits. And then there are the ones who lose their way." He put the cake he had been moving around on his plate into his mouth. You could tell the alarms were going off in his brain, chasing away some of the melancholy that had closed in around him.

"Wow! This is even more fantastic than I remembered." With that, he attacked the rest of the cake with gusto. Watching him eat, Jessica abandoned any attempt to be demure, and devoured her cake too. "That cake is amazing. Would it kill us to eat a second piece?"

"Let's find out," Jessica suggested, cutting more cake and scooping out the rest of the pint container of French vanilla ice cream. Spurred on by sugar and chocolate, they chattered away. He asked her for details about the events that had led up to the discovery of Roger's killer. Uncle Don had given him the run-down, but he wanted to hear the whole story. Her account of how she had eluded assailants with the use of her iPhone and Jimmy Choos, and what a headache she had become for Detective Hernandez, had him in stitches. Frank said that, according to Uncle Don, she was still a topic of discussion among police officers in the Coachella Valley. As the story passed from person to person, the number of bad guys the "classy lady lawyer from Mission Hills" vanquished had grown to more than half a dozen. They'd added to her ad hoc arsenal too, including stories about whacking bad guys with designer handbags and champagne bottles.

"The legend continues," Jessica said wryly. "I hope they let it go soon, although I do like the 'classy' part."

"Well, they have *that* part right. You are a class act, Jessica Huntington-Harper." Frank raised his glass of lemonade in a toast.

"Let's make that to Jessica Huntington-no-hyphen. How about to divorced women and men everywhere, struggling to do the classy thing?"

"Here, here," Frank said, as they clinked glasses. "So, I take it, then, that it's official. You and Jim are through?"

"Yeah, we're through. As soon as the State of California says so, that is. By Labor Day, for sure."

"Mom mentioned you were back in the desert without Jim. Are you here for good or do you plan to take off and start over somewhere new?"

"I'm just sort of drifting, taking things one day at a time. I don't trust myself to make good, long-term decisions right now. There are still times when I think it might be worth it to let some nice police officer like you arrest me for the pleasure of wringing Jim's neck with one of his two-hundred-dollar silk bespoke ties." Frank let out a whistle. Had she gone too far by revealing such a graphic fantasy of revenge?

"A two-hundred-dollar tie, are you kidding me? What a waste of money to strangle him with that." Jessica laughed, then, bounded out of her chair.

"I don't normally do this, but how about another act of indulgence? Want to chance a pot of coffee this late in the day, or will the caffeine keep you awake?"

"Are you kidding? I live on caffeine, round the clock sometimes. It never keeps me from sleeping any time I get a chance. Coffee sounds wonderful." Jessica picked up their dirty plates and hauled them to the kitchen.

"Another thing," Frank said.

Jessica looked up from where she was filling the burr grinder with black oily coffee beans.

"Yes?" She asked.

"I'm sorry, about the divorce. Divorce *is* a hard thing to do with class or grace. Mary and I have been divorced for three years now, and I am mostly civil when we have to deal with each other for the sake of the kids. That first year was the worst. You've got to go through a whole year, remembering all the things you did together and figure out how to do them by yourself, you know? I had the kids to take care of, but I was still a single guy instead of a married guy, and that just felt wrong."

"But it does get better, right?" Jessica asked, hoping the answer would be yes.

"Yes. Yes. It does."

Jessica used the sound of the grinder to give herself time to think. She trusted he was being honest with her, but she hadn't told him the whole story. Maybe at some point, she'd tell him about Jim and the strumpet and the baby on the way, but not today. Dumping the ground coffee into the coffee press, Jessica poured water over it and set the timer on the stove for ten minutes.

"How do you like your coffee?" She asked. She wanted to add, "And what went wrong with *your* marriage?" but didn't.

"Milk would be great."

Jessica went to the fridge and found a small carton of half-and-half. Jessica didn't quite understand why Bernadette preferred half-and-half in her morning coffee but two percent milk in her beloved lattes.

"How about half-and-half, is that okay?"

"That's terrific."

Jessica loaded a tray with the French press full of steeping coffee, two mugs, and a small pot of half-and-half. She carried it all to the table where Frank was sitting. They had a few more minutes before the coffee had steeped long enough to pour it. Jessica decided it was time to hear what Frank had come to talk about.

"So, what did you want to tell me about Kelly?"

"Well, this is sort of a strange situation. Did you know we have a cold case team at the County Sheriff's Department?"

"No, I didn't know that. I've heard that there's new interest in cold cases because of better DNA testing and better databases that track DNA profiles from convicted offenders like they track fingerprints. Of course, there's been some controversy among lawyers about their use like what constitutes probable cause, reasonable search, when using computers to match evidence to stored profiles. But I don't know much more than that."

"A lot of jurisdictions have added units like ours if there are enough resources in the department to run a team. Our team works cases for the whole county. And it's not just DNA evidence and information from databases that can reactivate a cold case. Sometimes it's good old-fashioned police work that gets a case going again like when a cop takes a new look at the case and gets a new angle. Or sometimes someone in the community comes forward and decides to confess or turns in an old friend for a past crime because they've had a row. Maybe a guy dumps his girlfriend and she gets even by calling the cops and telling them where the money or the drugs or the body is stashed. You know?"

"Yeah, I've got it." Jessica thought about Margarit Tilik and what she'd been willing to do to her boyfriend and anyone else who got caught in her tangled web, for that matter. Poor Roger Stone.

"A couple of days ago, I'm having a beer after work. I'm sitting with Art Greenwald, one of the guys in the cold case unit. He's going on about the kind of thing they've got to sort out when they're reviewing a cold case. Like some lowlife who gets nabbed by the cops, caught red-handed doing something he shouldn't do. What does he want to do? Play 'let's make a deal' by claiming he's got information about an old crime. They never know what to make of it. Does he have something legit, or is he just trying to snow us, or maybe recycling old news about a case?"

"Okay," Jessica said. "I'm following you. What has this got to do with Kelly?"

"Well, Art goes on and on about the latest bozo sitting in jail who claims he knows something about a girl who was murdered. The guy's a third striker. You know a guy who's going away for a long time unless he can make that deal? They caught him with a bunch of drugs and drug paraphernalia, and the clincher, a gun. It wasn't loaded, but it adds to the trouble he's already in." Jessica nodded, encouraging him to get on with the story.

"So, the public defender assigned to the case goes to the county prosecutor's office about his client's claims. The prosecutor asks Art to check it out. He pays the guy a visit but doesn't get very far because the old 'tweaker' is being cagey. Art figures he's pushing fifty, maybe. It's rare for a serious meth addict to live as long as he has. It's no wonder he doesn't want to spend what little life he has left locked up. Art is sort of mimicking the guy who says something about, 'It weren't no accident. It was on purpose.' I'm only half listening to all this until Art says something about this all happening so long ago near the casino in Palm Springs. Now he's got my attention. I ask him to repeat what he just said. The girl he witnessed being murdered was run down in a hotel parking lot at the casino in downtown Palm Springs."

A jolt of recognition hit. "When?"

"I'm not even sure. Art says he was about ready to let it go, but he can check into it a little more if I want him to. That's what I wanted to talk to you about. This guy claims she was murdered. If it was Kelly, does it make any difference how she died? It won't bring her back if they reopen the investigation. It *will* reopen old wounds. And there's no guarantee that this half-wasted human being can give the police enough information to find her killer. Or that they can make the charges stick, even if they dig up a suspect. Uncle Sammy and Aunt Monica have been through so much, I don't know what to do. Did it make a difference to Laura that you found out who killed Roger?"

Jessica's mind was in a whirl hearing the questions he asked and distress in Frank's voice. The alarm for the coffee went off and they both jumped! Frank must have been concentrating as hard as she was, or his nerves were as shot as hers. They looked at each other and burst out laughing, releasing the tension that had gripped them both.

"You think we need caffeine? Maybe I should be pouring a couple scotches!"

"If I didn't have to go home and face Mom, I'd ask you to add a little something to the coffee. She won't like it if I have a drink and then drive home, and if I stick around long enough to let the buzz wear off, I'll be late for dinner. So, there you go!" Jessica was back at the table after running to turn off the alarm. Frank had already pressed the coffee and was pouring it into mugs.

"Boy! Does that smell wonderful! The stuff I drink a lot of the time is strong enough to strip paint, and the taste is hard to take. There is a Starbucks nearby, so if I can, I'll make a coffee run to get a decent cup. I have to watch it, though, or I can go through a lot of money in a month on coffee. I just found out Evie is going to need braces." He took a sip of coffee after stirring in some half-and-half.

"Ah! Fantastic! Maybe I should get into the habit of making a pot at home and taking it with me."

"This is Peet's. It's not cheap, but you would save money if you fixed it yourself, and brought it with you. Another thing for you to do with all that spare time you have on your hands."

Jessica sipped her coffee, savoring the dark roasted Sumatran beans, which were flown in monthly. There weren't any Peet's stores in the Coachella Valley. In a pinch, she could buy a bag at one of the local grocery stores, but the selection wasn't always great. Sometimes all they carried was ground coffee, a taboo for her inner coffee snob. Soothed by the warmth of the delectable brew, Jessica ventured back to the topic of what to do about Kelly.

"Frank, it mattered to Laura that Roger's killer was brought to justice. In her case, though, she was on the list of possible suspects. Laura got closure on some pretty important issues. It's a matter of justice, too, in the larger scheme of things. There's also the fact that, if Kelly was murdered, that person is still out there and could do it again. I also get it that you don't want to stir things up unless there's a damn good reason. That's a judgment call, and it sounds to me like we don't have enough information right now to make that call."

"That brings me to the second reason I wanted to talk to you. You're a lawyer. You could talk to whoever's representing this guy in the public defender's office and get a better read on how far gone he is. Or maybe they'd let you interview the perp. If it is Kelly, I'm going to have to keep my distance, given that she's family. I don't want to create even the hint of impropriety. Or do anything that could be used later to claim that the investigation was tainted because a family member was involved. Uncle Don is in the same boat in Palm Springs. So, how about it?" He paused, watching Jessica intently as he went back to drinking his coffee.

Jessica wasn't certain. She picked up her coffee and sipped it, buying time. If she could do anything that would, even belatedly, help her friend, Kelly, then she should. Like Frank, she also wanted to protect Tommy and his parents from reliving that dreadful event. Or from false hope that someone might be held accountable for Kelly's death, whether an accident or on purpose. Jessica looked at Frank and knew she'd made her decision. She had to try to find out the truth.

"How about this? Let's do what we can without bringing the rest of the Fontana family into it, for the time being. I'll check it out, as you asked, while you get Art to go another round on his end. We'll take this a step at a time, and if it looks like we're getting somewhere, we'll break the news to the rest of the Fontanas. Does that make sense?" Jessica offered Frank more coffee.

"It does," he said, sliding his empty mug closer to her so she could refill it. Then she poured herself another cup. "Thanks. This just sort of dropped into my lap, so I feel compelled to follow up. How bizarre is that?"

Jessica's skin prickled, recalling that earlier conversation with Bernadette. "This is odd, I'll give you that. Not just the way you found out about it. But why on earth would anyone have wanted to kill Kelly?"

"I have no idea. We may find out some things about Kelly we'd prefer not to know. She was high-strung and gave her parents plenty of grief. I just presumed that was teenage stuff and she'd grow out of it."

"My last encounter with Kelly wasn't a very pleasant one. I feel bad about that, but it's also left me wondering what on earth was going on with her. I owe it to her as a friend to try to face the truth, even if it turns out to be unsettling."

"I had a similar reaction to her death. I had this uneasy feeling that something was not quite right with Kelly, but by then it was too late to do anything about it. I was so preoccupied with my own studies, and my relationship with Mary, that I didn't have a lot of time for other family members. She was hard to figure out: sweet and charming a lot of the time, but distant, and even hostile, at other times. She was so talented, and plenty smart, but never interested in my suggestions for how to use that talent or put her smarts to work. I chalked it up to immaturity, even though I was only two years older. You were closer to her than I was and probably knew her better."

"I wish I could say that was true. We loved each other, but we also fought like cats and dogs. I had so many of my own issues then, and it's still hard to sort out my problems from hers. I get what you're saying about her moodiness. Sometimes it was like this switch flipped and Kelly went from sweet to wild in a flash. Even that wild side was fun and kind of exciting at times. It was also scary depending on the kind of risks she was hell-bent on taking. I was a way bigger chicken than she was, and she just cut me loose at times. Why bring me along if I was just going to be a drag? Laura and I both got left behind, at times, usually when she had a new boyfriend."

Jessica paused and peered at the coffee in her cup. What she saw, instead of coffee, was an image of Kelly. Her auburn hair set in motion by the ripples in the coffee, a dreamy smile on her face, but a wicked glint in her eye. "She could turn mean, too. The last time I saw her on New Year's Eve, we went at it. She was drunk, so maybe it was the booze talking. There was so much anger toward me, mostly about things I thought we had settled. All our lives had changed so much. Making the transition from high school was stressful, and we were all flailing about, but Kelly most of all. I figured we had time to work it out later... and then, we didn't."

"So, let's say we're going this first mile for us, as well as for Kelly. We'll do what we can, even though it's too late to save her life. If she was murdered, she must have been in more trouble than any of us could have known, Jessica. She hid that from her parents and from Tommy, too, or they would have done something. Tommy would have gone to you or to me, if he didn't want to get his parents involved." Jessica nodded in agreement.

"Yes, that's true. Would your friend, Art, get me a copy of Kelly's file? Maybe something in the file will corroborate or disavow what this guy claims went on that night. Also, if it does turn out there's a reason to move forward, we'll be ready. We'll need to go back and talk to at least some of the people the police interviewed at the time. If I review the file, we'll know who to put on that list."

"Or, as you say, maybe there will be something in the file that can shut this down. If this is meth mania, or he's a lying little weasel, I'd like to bring this new chapter to a close as soon as possible."

"I agree. Does Art have the file?"

"You'd think so, but I'll ask. If he doesn't already have it, he can get it. Dad's in a different division of the Palm Springs Police Department, so Art should be able to get the file from the detectives without contacting Dad, directly. That's no guarantee Dad won't find out about it. His co-workers haven't forgotten how tough Kelly's death was on him, though. I'm sure they'll make efforts to keep this under wraps if Art is discrete. Back then, Dad wasn't a sergeant yet. He was the lead investigator with the traffic bureau, and got called to the scene by the patrol officers who found Kelly."

"Oh no! I didn't hear anything about that. He must have been horrified."

"Yeah, he was. And then he took it upon himself to be the one who gave Sammy and Monica the news. That wrecked him, too. It took him a long time to get over that. Uncle Sammy and Aunt Monica have never been the same." Frank grew silent, gazing off into space. "How do you want me to get that file to you?"

"I guess that depends on what you find out from Art. Once he gets his hands on it, if he doesn't already have it, he'll have to make copies for me."

Frank nodded. "Some of the stuff will have been saved electronically, but the file itself will contain things like the detectives' notes, which may be handwritten. I can get him to expedite things by picking up the file himself. He may need a day or so to do that and put a copy together for us."

"Okay, so let's say I'll swing by and pick it up on Tuesday or Wednesday at the Sheriff's Department. Which day depends on what sort of arrangements I can make with the Public Defender's office and the attorney assigned to this guy. There's something else you should consider."

"What?"

"You do know that criminal defense work isn't my area of practice, right? So, I'm going to do a consult with a colleague about this. Paul Worthington's a big-time defense attorney in LA, and he'll be a great help in cutting to the chase about what we're up against. I planned to give Paul a call tomorrow, anyway. His firm is opening an office in Palm Desert and he's waiting for me to tell him if I'm ready to be a lawyer again, or not. He doesn't know it yet, but I've decided to say yes, and take on a few clients. How do you feel about involving him?"

"We can use all the help we can get. This case is more than a decade old. For it to have gone cold, means that Dad's colleagues ran out of leads. They knew how distressing this was for Dad, so they wouldn't have given up if they had anything to go on. You're resourceful, but you have your work cut out for you. I'm just glad you're willing to put yourself out there and tap into your networks to give this thing a chance. Thanks."

A Dead Sister

"Don't thank me yet. We don't know if this is going to go anywhere. I may have nothing but bad news for you in a couple days. You might not have much to celebrate on the Fourth. Of course, not that finding out your cousin was murdered is a reason to celebrate, either. Don't listen to me. I don't know what I'm saying. I just don't want you to be disappointed."

"I'll take that chance. And that won't put a damper on a Fontana family Fourth of July celebration. The kids always have such a blast watching the fireworks. Mom and Dad are driving to our house in Perris for a barbeque. It'll be hot, but not like it is here. You don't even need to light the charcoal to grill something out here right now with a high of a hundred eighteen or something like that today! Listen, if you make that trip to Riverside on Wednesday, why not stay in town and celebrate with us on the Fourth? I can get you a discount on a room at the Mission Inn. We'll meet for dinner Wednesday night and you can bring me up to speed about what you've learned. That way we can decide what to do next, if anything." Before she could offer any objection, he rushed on. "If you come to the house for our picnic on Thursday evening, Mom will have someone besides me and Dad and the kids to rave about her potato salad and seven-layer dip. You'll make her so happy, unless you already have plans."

Jessica thought about it for a couple minutes. She was even less happy about the idea of being "home alone" for the rest of the week now that she might be pulled into another murder investigation. And she didn't have any plans. "Could you really get me a room at the Mission Inn this close to the holiday?"

"No problem. You're not the only one with connections. A friend of mine who manages one of their restaurants said renovations in a section of the hotel were delayed. They couldn't make the rooms available in time to fill all of them for the holiday. She was pushing me to get my parents to stay there, at a good discount! Mom and Dad won't want to miss a minute with me and the kids, so they'll stay at my place. But if you say yes, I'll call and have her save a room for you for Wednesday night. Thursday night, too, so you can go see the fireworks with us."

"Except for the fact that this is all happening because a close childhood friend may have been murdered, this sounds like fun. I haven't seen your mom and dad for a while and, honestly, I can't even remember what your kids look like! The last time I saw them, they were like five or six. Tiny, I remember, and moving at supersonic speed. They were part of a small herd of children running like gazelle."

"That sounds about right. Even if you could remember what they

61

looked like, you might not recognize them now. I do a double take every now and then to make sure they're my kids when I go pick them up at school. There are times I wish they weren't mine. Isn't that awful?"

"Hell, no! My parents were so fed up at one point, after I got kicked out of Palm Valley *and* St. Margaret's, they were going to pack me off to boarding school. Bernadette convinced them to give me another chance. St. Theresa's was my last stop before a convent or a boot camp, or the Swiss boarding school equivalent! Thinking about it now, I don't blame them a bit. I was out of control. Sounds like your kids have a way to go if you only *sometimes* wish they weren't around. And, I might add, moments ago you sounded enthusiastic about celebrating the Fourth of July with them."

Frank shrugged a little. "You're just trying to make me feel better, and it's working. I also feel much better about this thing with Kelly. I can't tell you what a relief it is to not be carrying that burden alone."

"Will you email me your address so I can map the route to your house? And do you remember the name of the man being held? I'd like to call and see if I can set up something with his attorney."

"I'm texting you the address right now." She heard that little "whoosh" as Frank sent the text. "As I recall, the guy's name is Chester Davis. I'll confirm that with Art Greenwald first thing tomorrow. The kids are staying out here in the desert with Mom and Dad until Wednesday, but I'm driving back tonight after dinner. Art is in by eight a.m., so I'll call you as soon as I speak to him in the morning. I'll tell Mom to expect you Thursday. She'll be thrilled." He stood up to leave. "Uh, you should be prepared for the possibility that Mom's going to jump to the conclusion that we're dating. I could tell her otherwise, but it would explain why, all of a sudden, we're hanging out together."

"I don't want to mislead her, but I suppose we don't have to go out of our way to prove things one way or the other. Just as long as your mom doesn't also jump to the conclusion that I'm some kind of a hussy for dating her son when the ink isn't even dry on my divorce papers yet." Jessica stood up to walk him to the front door.

"Mom thinks you walk on water and why not? You're kind and beautiful, intelligent, and well-educated. What's not to like?" He took a step closer. Jessica caught another whiff of that woodsy scent. It was like stepping out onto the deck area at the top of the Palm Springs tramway, and being hit square in the face by the scent of the Jeffrey pines that flourish at ten thousand feet. At the moment, it wasn't altitude that was

A Dead Sister

making her light-headed.

"Don't forget classy," Jessica added, nervously.

"How could I forget classy, Cuz?" With that, he chucked Jessica under the chin and turned to leave. Jessica was still struggling to clear her head. *What is my problem? No men, no men, no men.* Then another thought crept into her addled brain: *Chocolate cake, more cake, more cake.* She'd better get rid of it.

"Wait a second. Would your mom be insulted if I sent the rest of that cake home with you? I could put some of it in the freezer, so I won't eat myself into a stupor or let it sit there and get stale. What do you think?"

"Freezing that cake would be a crime. Trust me, I'm a cop. Bernadette's chocolate cake will bring back memories of so many good times, all those picnics and pool parties when we were growing up. Don't you want to save a little for yourself?"

"Okay, I'll keep another piece for me and send the rest home with you." With that, Jessica sprang into action, putting the cake into a carrier for transport, minus that piece for herself.

"You can pick up your carrier when you come to visit on Thursday night. Don't be surprised if Mom sends it home with something in it for you and Bernadette. She'll be inspired. Hey, maybe we can keep this going, with you and me, and my kids caught in the middle of a bake-off between Mom and Bernadette. How great would that be?" Jessica handed the cake carrier to Frank as they both walked from the kitchen to the front door.

"You and your kids can get away with that, but not me. I have to go hop on the exercise bike to work off what I've eaten already today!"

She reached past him to open the front door. Frank turned to face her as the blast of afternoon heat swallowed them both.

"You don't need to work off a thing. I meant it when I said you look great." His earlier shyness had reappeared. He bumped into the edge of the door before turning around, slipping out, and closing it behind him.

CHAPTER 6

Jessica rode the spin cycle like a maniac for an hour, sweating off the calories packed on by eating all that chocolate cake and ice cream. She was trying to discharge a different kind of energy, too. The whole encounter with Frank Fontana had left her charged up. Not just from the prospect that someone close to them might have been murdered. An unexpected combustibility between them had caught Jessica by surprise.

She noticed men in a different way than she had as a married woman. Why not? She was, after all, a healthy, red-blooded, youngish woman, suddenly single. Pedaling faster, she counted the days since she last had sex. Not days, but months had flashed by since her unanticipated entry into celibacy.

It wasn't just sex that was absent from her life. But all those small acts of physical affection taken for granted by partners in a committed relationship. The embraces and caresses, some fleeting, some lingering, were gone. Kisses too, passionate and affectionate, were missing and missed. How sad that the realization of so much loss was sparked by the briefest encounter with a flash of body heat and a hint of pine-scented pheromones.

Was it something about Frank, or was she just a slave to her own privations? Her wary female psyche rose up to shield her from having to answer that question. "Time," she whispered. She needed time to clear her head and to rid herself of the bitterness and disappointment that clung to her like a noxious cloud. It would surely taint any new relationship. She was not her mother. Not the kind of woman who could shed one man and move on to the next, was she? Jessica hit it harder, sending the spin cycle

A Dead Sister

into overdrive.

A mechanical ping signaled that her hour was up. She was sweating and her muscles were exhausted in a good way. Jessica downed the remaining water in the bottle she'd brought into the workout room. A shower would do wonders to put her in the right frame of mind to organize her thoughts, about Kelly, not Frank.

Their conversation had set her mind into high gear. Her compass was damaged, for sure, but it was still actively in search mode, the needle bouncing frantically. The more Jessica pondered Kelly's "accident," the more determined she became to find out what had happened. If it had indeed been an accident, why hadn't the culprit stopped to help her or call 911?

After showering, Jessica dried her hair so that the short, precisely cut bob sat in place as it was supposed to do. Her blond highlights, redone at the Grand Wailea, were shimmering. Sunlight streamed in from the clerestory windows above the large tumbled marble and glass enclosed shower. Conveying the characteristic golden hue of late afternoon, everything shone more richly. Jessica was overtaken by a powerful sense of well-being, a conviction that she was going to be okay without Jim or any man, for that matter. Committing that golden moment to memory, she hoped it would sustain her when the cyclones of anger, self-doubt, and recrimination swamped her later.

A year, she needed a year. She was going to put the calendar in her head down on paper. In March of 2014, she would be a new woman, a single woman without a grudge to bear against the man who so callously betrayed her. "... kind, beautiful, classy..." Frank's words drifted back to her. She stored those up, too, for the stormy days yet to come.

After slipping on a pair of short lounge pajama bottoms and a tank top, Jessica grabbed her laptop and climbed into her enormous bed. She propped herself up against the headboard upholstered in a plush, velvety fabric. Pulling up calendars for 2013 and 2014, she marked off the months since that awful confrontation with Jim and the floozy. She noted the month when her divorce would be final and highlighted March 2014 as the end of her year-long cycle of loss and grief.

Next, in a new folder called "Kelly," she created a file where she could make notes, recording today's date, June 30, 2013. She summarized what she could remember about the conversation with Frank. Then made a list of things she needed to follow up on.

The first thing was to call Paul Worthington. She remembered what Bernadette had said about figuring out if she was going to date Paul Worthington or work for him. At the time, she'd dismissed those words as an artifact of overwrought matchmaking. Once she had heard what Jim had done, Bernadette had been eager for Jessica to put Jim behind her: get up, dust herself off, and "climb back into the saddle" so to speak. Rather surprising coming from a woman who'd only had one true love.

Jessica was more convinced than ever that she was not ready to date. Not Paul Worthington. Not Frank Fontana. A tingle stuck, recalling Bernadette's prayer for God to send Jessica a good Catholic boy. Frank certainly qualified. "But I'm not ready," an inner voice cried out.

The job with Paul Worthington's firm was almost tailor-made for her current circumstances: a baby step toward a future in law. He expected no long-term commitment. Having a small number of clients would leave her plenty of time to recover from her divorce, but would also keep her from becoming a recluse. It would give her the opportunity to pursue the practice of law in areas other than environmental law, and with a well-regarded firm. It was a near-miracle as second chances go.

"So, okay, date Paul: no! Work for him: yes." Another decision made. *Ooh, and an office on El Paseo,* she thought. The desert cities' answer to Rodeo Drive, she'd be surrounded by her favorite shops: Saks, Escada, Between the Sheets, Tiffany's, Gucci, Louis Vuitton, Ann Taylor, Kate Spade, and a slew of local boutiques. Even with all that shopping on her doorstep, she'd do less damage to her black AMEX card if money was coming in as well as going out. Jessica picked up her phone to call Paul Worthington before she could change her mind again.

"Shoot!" She muttered. The ringer was still off. Two missed calls and a voice mail message were waiting. She listened to the voice mail left twenty minutes earlier.

"Jessica, this Paul Worthington. If you can give me a call, I need to ask for a favor."

She hit the callback icon and got an answer right away.

"Hey, Paul, this is Jessica. Sorry I missed you. Can you talk now, or is there a better time?"

"Now is just fine. I'm glad you got back to me so quickly. I know you're still trying to decide what to do about signing on with us at the El Paseo office. I don't want to pressure you, *but* I have a couple that I'd like you to meet as potential clients."

"Well, it's no pressure at all. I *am* interested in joining the firm at your office here in the desert. If you already have someone in mind as a client, that's good too."

"That's great news, Jessica. The client—clients—actually, are Nicholas and Nora Van der Woert. We got their daughter out of some trouble with the law a while ago. They're very nice people. Both in their late fifties, a two-career couple getting ready to retire and looking to buy something in the desert area. I immediately thought of you when they approached us for help in managing that transition. They may want your input about their housing choices in the area in addition to dealing with legal matters."

"I've been away for a while, but I do still have ties here, Paul. I have a pretty good idea about the range of communities and country clubs in the area." Before squatting in her family home, she'd looked at real estate on the internet. A familiar face or two remained among the realtors, still standing after the collapse of the local market. She'd also become reacquainted with the area's country clubs and gated communities. They run the gamut from moderately priced communities, targeting seniors and others of modest means, to super high-end settings catering to the needs of billionaires, with everything in between. In the end, she settled for mooching off her mom, overwhelmed by the decisions involved in buying a place of her own.

"I'd be glad to help with their search once I know what they're looking for in the way of amenities like golf or tennis. Do they want to be in a newer community, or a more established one with some history? What's their price range? Things like that," Jessica added.

"I understand what you're saying. You can ask them. They also have some estate planning needs. Changes to make to their wills, and they're looking for some guidance about setting up a trust of some kind. From what I gather, they have a longstanding track record of philanthropy that includes an interest in environmental causes. Given your background, you can be helpful on that front too. So, what do you think?"

"I suppose what matters most is what they think of me. I believe I can be helpful, and handle their legal services, as you've laid them out."

"I'll be your mentor, so you won't bump up against any problems with the firm. It will save the Van der Woerts money if you pick up most of the hours that I would have put in. You'll have not only me, but others in the firm on call to back you up, and we'll review the documents you put together, of course. You already met our office manager in Palm Desert, Amy Klein. She worked in this office for five years or so and knows more than I do about how the firm runs day-to-day. Amy will be around to show you the ropes, too."

"That all sounds just fine. Great, in fact, since I'll have a safety net while I get up to speed in areas where I have less experience."

"The favor I need from you is to have the first meeting here with us in LA, and soon. Ideally, we'd have a late afternoon meet and greet for an hour or so at the office. Then we'd all go out for cocktails and dinner after that. They're available on Tuesday. It's late notice, but they're under some sort of pressure to get things moving. I haven't asked, but maybe health problems are pushing them into retirement sooner than expected. I'd like to accommodate them if it's at all possible. Can you arrange to do this on Tuesday? I'd need you to meet with me first, around two or two thirty, so I can introduce you to people and show you around. That would also give me a chance to provide more background about the firm and the Van der Woerts. I'll ask them to join us at four or four thirty." He was speaking at a pretty good clip, finally pausing long enough for Jessica to answer.

"A Tuesday meeting will be fine." The wheels were turning as Jessica quickly calculated how this fit with what she had agreed to do in Riverside. If she could get hold of someone in the public defender's office, she would try to arrange for a meeting with Chester Davis on Wednesday, before checking in at the Mission Inn. So much for that week at home alone, it was filling rapidly.

"Two o'clock should be no problem. And I'd love to meet the Van der Woerts."

"Terrific, Jessica Huntington-Harper, I'll call them right away and then confirm all of this with you in an email."

"We should go with just plain old Jessica Huntington at this point, Paul." She tried to sound matter-of-fact as she added, "I've signed the divorce papers, and my divorce will be final by the end of summer. In the meantime, I'm going to go ahead and ditch the hyphen."

"Well, there's nothing plain or old about Jessica Huntington, I can vouch for that. How are you holding up? I gathered from our dinner that this divorce wasn't an easy thing for you. Of course, you were still

A Dead Sister

recovering from tangling with Allen Bedrossian then, too."

"Too many sleaze balls, for sure, but I'm fine, or I will be. I really appreciate the chance you're giving me to kick-start my career again. I've let that languish far too long. You've been a big help in getting me motivated to put things right, in that part of my life, at least. I won't let you down, Paul, promise."

"I know that. I'm a pretty good judge of character. I'm counting on the fact that once you decide to run, you're off the block fast and will be up to speed in no time flat. Unless you have other questions, it sounds like we're set for Tuesday at two o'clock."

"If you can spare a couple more minutes, I do have another situation I could use your advice about. I may need you to vouch for me with the Riverside County Public Defender's office."

"Not another dead husband, I hope."

"No, well a dead sister, actually. Not my sister, but the sister of a close friend. Kelly Fontana was my friend, too, when she was killed in a hit-and-run back in 1999. Nobody was ever tagged for the accident, and the case was put in mothballs."

"The statute of limitations was up for a hit–and-run long ago. So, what's up?"

"Apparently, some guy in custody in Riverside County says he knows something about a girl being killed in a Palm Springs hotel parking lot. He claims it wasn't an accident, but a murder. The family has asked me to check it out. I don't even know at this point for sure if it's Kelly he's talking about. Much less what leads him to believe it was murder, or if he's being truthful. I'm not sure how far I'm going to get as plain old Jessica Huntington if I start poking around asking the public defender to answer my questions. What I'd really like to do is speak to the guy they're holding. I thought it might help to drop your name as a reference."

"I can do better than that. Consider yourself an associate with the firm in our Palm Desert office at this point. Tomorrow, I'll email you a contract that will set out the terms of your employment for a year, along the lines we talked about over dinner. I can have business cards printed up for you with the El Paseo address and phone number and just Jessica Huntington, J.D., if that's okay? You can sign the contract when you come to the office on Tuesday, and you can pick up the cards then, too."

Jessica's head was spinning again, the gears whirring wildly. This was all happening so frigging fast... "Wow, that's amazing. That should get me in the door. Thanks."

"No problem. Get me the names of the principal characters, and I'll touch base with them if necessary."

"You've been more than helpful. I'll make a couple of calls tomorrow and see what sort of reception I get as Attorney Huntington, Associate with Canady, Holmes, Winston and Klein. Thanks again, Paul, for everything. I'll see you on Tuesday at two o'clock."

Jessica hung up the phone and tried to refigure where she was, and where she was going. She scanned the calendar on her laptop and started to put in the new appointments she'd made. The thought of battling traffic for three hours to make that two o'clock meeting on Tuesday was already making her skin crawl. Her inner stress engine revved a little. The way around that was to drive into LA tomorrow and stay at her dad's house in Brentwood. The concierge service that took care of the Brentwood property while her dad was out of town could let her in. Jessica called her dad to alert him first. The call went straight to voice mail. Who knew where he was, what time, or even what day it was?

"Hey Dad, it's me, Jessica. Hope everything's going well wherever you are. I'm calling to let you know I have a new job. That's good, I guess. It's with a law firm opening an office out here in the desert, but I'm going to be in LA for a couple days where the main office is located. I'm taking you up on the offer to let me hang out at the house in Brentwood. I hope that's still okay. I'll try not to trash the place. I'm going to call the service and get them to let me in. It'd be great to see you if you're coming back to town anytime soon. Anyway, love you! Bye!"

If Jessica got up early, she could get her workout done, and check in with the White Glove-whatever-it was-called concierge service in LA. She'd still have time to pressure the insurance company that owed Laura Stone a life insurance payout on the death of her murdered husband. Then she could call and set up a time to meet with Chester Davis' counsel on Wednesday morning. Maybe even arrange that face-to-face with Mr. Davis. It was a lot. By packing tonight, she could get all that done and still be on the road to LA by ten or so. If she could get to her dad's house and settle in by early afternoon, she would have plenty of time to swing by Rodeo Drive. That way she could buy a dress or two or three for all the lawyering duties in the queue for the week. The urge to shop was fierce, growing in tandem with anxiety about her burgeoning "to-do" list.

A Dead Sister

Jessica's fingers flew over the keyboard, pulling up information about her favorite shops on Rodeo Drive. Aha! Max Mara was having a sale! Her last Max Mara dress hadn't fared so well. Then, a lot of her clothes had taken a beating lately, along with the rest of her. She had to find something that would make a good impression on her new clients at the law office and that could handle the transition to dinner later. She also needed something for her visit to the public defender's office, the County Sheriff's Department, and the County jail, if that's where she had to go to meet Chester Davis.

CHAPTER 7

Jessica was energized by the prospects of making the trip to LA. She bounded out of bed, as she caught sight of the bags packed the night before. It was more than the prospect of shopping that had her psyched, although she was looking forward to that. The schlep into LA was emblematic of the fact that she had arrived at a turning point. A new job and an assignment in the works for that job signaled progress.

Her beautiful bed was made in a flash and, just as quickly, she donned a bathing suit for her workout in the pool. It took another minute to apply sunscreen, grab a pair of swimming goggles, and put on her flip-flops. Throwing on a robe, she darted into the kitchen and got a press pot of coffee going. The aroma of the freshly ground coffee sent her spirits soaring even higher. While she waited for the coffee to brew, she put in a call to the concierge service. Theoretically, someone was available to respond to her call any time of the day or night. Her call was answered on the second ring.

"White Glove Property Concierge at your service. How may I help?"

"This is Jessica Huntington and I'm going to be dropping in at my father's home in Brentwood today. I'm talking about Henry Huntington and he left my name with you as a permitted guest. I plan to stay for a couple nights. Will I need a code for the security system to get into the front gate and the house without setting off the alarm?"

"Well, Ms. Huntington, um, Huntington-Harper, uh..." Jessica interrupted before he could go any further.

"It's just Ms. Huntington at this point. I've dropped the hyphen, so no more Harper." Maybe she should have it printed on a banner across her chest. As soon as she signed those divorce papers, she started to play the name-change game with DMV and other businesses and bureaucracies. This morning she thought of half a dozen more places she needed to contact to update them. This was getting old fast, but it was a correction she would have to continue to make.

"No problem. I see your name on the list, and the room that you use when you visit. If you have an idea about what time you might arrive, I'll have someone at the house to meet you. We'll make sure the house is ready for you when you get there. What can we pick up for you for the kitchen or bath, Ms. Huntington?"

"I could use a pound of coffee. Peet's preferably, Arabian Mocha Sanani or Sulawesi, whole bean. Some bottled water, like Evian or Fiji. Fresh fruit, melon and berries would be great. A pint of Greek yogurt, please, plain, low fat, and honey, if there isn't already some in the house."

"Raw or pasteurized, Ms. Huntington, something local or do you have a particular product you prefer?"

"Raw, local is fine."

"Anything for the bath, or can we pick up theater tickets, a movie, or reading material of some kind? Or perhaps, we could make a dinner reservation for you?"

"No, thanks, but how about the pool, is it serviceable?"

"Of course, would you like us to heat it for you?"

"No, that won't be necessary."

"Will there be anything else?"

"No, that should do it. I'm hoping to arrive by one this afternoon. Thanks so much for all your help."

"It's our pleasure. Ms. Roberta Palmer will be at the house when you arrive. Please don't hesitate to call if there's any other way we can be of service. Enjoy your stay in LA."

With that, she hung up the phone and sprang into action. By nine a.m., Jessica had completed her laps in the pool, finished her coffee, and breakfasted on that piece of leftover chocolate cake. There was nothing like coffee and chocolate to put your day on the right track. She showered and dressed in comfortable clothes for her drive into LA.

Next, she placed the nagging phone call to the insurance company. The representative assured her that Laura would have her check within a week, even with the Fourth of July holiday delay. That would be almost one month since Roger's death. Jessica had called in credits from members of her network to get that quick turnaround. It had been worth it, giving her direct contact with the CEO of the insurance company via a member of their board of directors. That tactic cut a swath through the red tape that often swamps insurance claim transactions, especially those involving double indemnity payouts. Under ordinary circumstances, Roger Stone's murder might still have been under investigation, and Laura would have waited a lot longer for a check. Despite the terror they had all undergone, the matter was resolved. Jessica felt a modicum of relief after hanging up the phone, but wouldn't let up the pressure until Laura had that check in her hands.

While on the phone with the insurance company, Jessica received a voice mail from Frank Fontana. The person in custody was, indeed, Chester Davis. Detective Art Greenwald, was in his office and expecting to hear from her. Jessica dialed the number Frank had left for the detective.

"Hello, Detective Greenwald speaking."

"Detective, this is Jessica Huntington..." Jessica caught herself before blithely adding the Harper to her introduction. *Not again*, she thought, picking up where she left off. "I believe Frank Fontana told you I was going to call about Chester Davis."

"Yes, Ms. Huntington. I understand Frank already told you we were notified by the Public Defender's office that Chester Davis has information about an old case involving a hit-and-run. Mr. Davis didn't give us a name, but after talking to Frank, it sounds like the circumstances are a lot like those involving his cousin, Kelly Fontana. In particular, the fact that, according to Mr. Davis, the incident occurred in the parking lot of the Agua Caliente Hotel and Casino, which I understand is where Kelly Fontana's body was found."

"Yes, that's true. As I recall, she was an employee of the hotel and casino at the time."

"Well, I don't have the case file yet, just the incident report from '99 that I could pull up online. That report doesn't give me too much

74

information, but this afternoon I'm going to go pick up the case file. I should know more after I've looked at it."

"What do you make of Chester Davis?"

"I'm not sure how much stock to place in his story. He was arrested last week after some sort of ruckus at a local flophouse where he and two other males were apprehended. The police were called to the house because of the noise. They found the three derelicts going at it, fighting about somebody stealing something. Anyway, the police had to break it up, and when they went into the house, they found quite the little party going on. They confiscated small amounts of methamphetamine, oxycodone, and marijuana, as well as an assortment of drug paraphernalia, a few hundred dollars in small bills, and a gun. It was all laid out on the coffee table like a buffet. It's the gun that's going to get him in plenty of trouble. Possession of a weapon by a felon puts him on the fast track for more prison time. Of course, nobody at that little party will admit to owning the gun. Most likely, it'll turn up as having been stolen. They could all be in even more trouble, depending on the history that goes with the gun. Even if Mr. Davis and his attorney get the drug charges reduced from a felony to a misdemeanor, the gun is going to be a problem. Given his two prior felonies, he's facing a long stint in prison, despite recent changes to the third strike law in California."

This was virtually the same information Frank had given her. Kelly's death had been reported in newspapers back then. Chester Davis had plenty of motivation to dredge up an old story and use it for his own purposes. Surely, they could figure that out in short order, couldn't they?

"Okay, so is there any reason to believe this guy is doing anything *other than* throwing up a smoke screen, hoping to avoid spending the rest of his life in prison?"

"The public defender's office has assigned Richard Tatum to handle the case. He's an appointee, not on staff with the County. He's known the guy for years, and confirms Mr. Davis was living in Palm Springs when he claims to have witnessed the murder. That timeframe is consistent with the death of Kelly Fontana. We don't have the whole scoop yet since Davis wants some assurances they're going to make him a deal before he gives up the information he has. If he wants us to consider it, we've got to have more to go on than he's given us so far. We're waiting for the defendant's attorney and the prosecutor to play this out. I was ready to set it aside until I spoke with Frank."

"Where is Mr. Davis, now?"

"He's sitting in the County jail. He's been arraigned, but couldn't make bail so he's not going anywhere for a while. The preliminary hearing is set for two weeks, a little longer than usual because of the holiday coming up this week. His lawyer is fine with the extra time. Tatum's hoping he can work something out with the prosecutors so that the charges against Mr. Davis will be reduced or eliminated by the time the case goes back to court. Davis has already been through rehab a couple times. If he comes up with something of value in an old case, he might get another chance for treatment through the Drug Court. Prop 36 has created more interest in keeping a defendant like him from spending the rest of his life in a state prison. So, who knows? I've pulled the perp's old records but haven't gone through his file yet either."

"I presume Frank told you that I'd like review the records related to Kelly Fontana's case and that we're sort of keeping this low key for now. The family went through a lot. It would be a shame to bring up all that pain again unnecessarily. One thing that makes this trickier, too, is that Kelly's Uncle, Don Fontana, is in the Palm Springs office."

"I know all of that, and I get it. As I said, I'm going to go get the case file myself. We'll keep this between me and the detective at the other end, for the time being. He cares as much as you do about keeping this under wraps until there's a reason to do otherwise. Since you're representing the family, as their attorney, you can have a look at it. Most of what's in there is a matter of public record anyway. My guess is the file's pretty thin, given how quickly it went cold. I should have a copy for you by tomorrow afternoon."

"I plan to be in Riverside Wednesday morning and I'll come by and pick it up then if that's okay."

"That's fine. If I'm here, tell them to call me up front so I can say hello. If not, I'll have it ready and you can just pick it up."

"Thanks. I appreciate your help, especially agreeing not to arouse more interest than necessary right now. Sorry to ask you to keep this case in limbo."

"Limbo is a good way of describing where we all are for now. For anyone who's lost a family member the way the Fontanas have, limbo is an awful lot like hell. We want to avoid taking them there unless we have to." With that, they said their goodbyes.

A Dead Sister

Jessica immediately called the Riverside County Public Defender's Office and got a number for Richard Tatum. Her call to the attorney went directly to his voice mail. Not sure how much to say about the matter, she simply left her name and phone number and added, "I'd like to speak to you about Chester Davis at your earliest convenience." "Earliest convenience" was an odd turn of phrase when leaving a message about a murdered friend. It was an odd turn of phrase for an odd turn of events.

CHAPTER 8

Jessica reached her father's house around one o'clock, as planned. When she drove up, the gate to her father's estate was opened for her. She went through the gate and drove up the long brick-paved driveway to the house, which was set well back from the road. By the time she drove to the front entrance of the sprawling 1940s single story home, Roberta Palmer was waiting for her. She waved as Jessica pulled up, then, walked around to the driver's side window.

"Welcome Ms. Huntington, would you like to park in the garage?"

"No thanks. I'm planning to take off again. I'll just leave the car here for now." Jessica shut off the car and climbed out, extending a hand to Ms. Palmer. "It's nice to meet you, Ms. Palmer. I appreciate your arranging for my visit on such short notice."

"Roberta, please. It's really no trouble at all. Can I help you with your bags?"

Jessica had packed in a remarkably efficient manner, for her anyway. She only had one bag on wheels and a small overnight case. By the time she pulled it from the car, along with her laptop and purse, she was glad to have Roberta's assistance. They went into the front foyer, and a rush of childhood memories washed over Jessica. The house had a comfortable, casual feel to it, even though it sported the fine finishes and furnishings both her parents loved. Everything was a bit more traditional here than in the desert house. There were more curves to the furniture frames, buttons on the cushions, a splash of check or plaid. More wood was evident in this house, and brick rather than the stacked stone so prominent in the Rancho

A Dead Sister

Mirage estate. Something radiated the same sensibility as the desert house, though. A comfortable elegance, large expanses of windows, and sliding glass doors gave it the same light and airy feel. Like the desert home, those glass panel doors could be slipped back into pockets that opened up the whole place, blurring the lines between inside and out.

Her father already owned this house when he married Alexis Baldwin. An old-style California ranch, the house comprised several wings, each with a low-slung, gabled roof. It was adorned with white clapboard siding and a rambling white picket fence. Sitting on nearly five acres, it was surrounded by grass, shrubs, and trees that seemed lavish compared to the desert. Tall palms waved above the house along with Italian cypress, jacaranda, sweet acacia, and African tulip trees. They all bloomed at different times of the year. Clumps of manzanita bushes stood out with their thick, leathery leaves and cinnamon-kissed bark twisted into fanciful shapes. Ferns and giant-leaved elephant ears, lilies and wild roses, added to the lush feel of the place.

Jessica dropped her bags and rushed through the house to the patio area. Built at the top of a slope, the house had a view of the city in the distance, which was magical at night. An infinity edge pool created the impression that you would drop off and tumble into the gardens below if you stepped too close. The slope was, in fact, a gradual one. Jessica and her childhood friends had run up and down, playing hide and seek. They had all sorts of adventures on imagined jungle safaris, voyages to pirate islands, and escapes to fairy lands in those gardens.

Her mother loved this house and would have been happy to stay put when Hank Huntington got the urge to build his dream home in Rancho Mirage. After Jessica was born, they continued to shuttle back and forth between LA and the Palm Springs area until Jessica started school. Maybe that's when the trouble began between Hank and Alexis. Something changed that drove a wedge between them by the time Jessica had finished grade school, ending in divorce not long after that. They had seemed so happy here. Who knew what it was that turned an apparently good marriage into a bad one? Jessica was in no position to judge.

Stepping back into the house, Jessica spent a few minutes chatting with Roberta Palmer, who showed her where they had stashed the things Jessica asked them to purchase. She gave her the new pass code for the alarm system, and the device Jessica needed to operate the front gate to the estate and the garage door. As soon as Roberta left, Jessica settled into her old room in her father's house.

Anna Celeste Burke

After her parents' divorce, Jessica had continued to visit the Brentwood house but without her mother. She lost track of friends who had been with her throughout elementary school, once she was kicked out of Palm Valley. When she was expelled from St. Margaret's Episcopal School soon after enrolling, she hardly knew a soul. Riding, angry and alone, in the back of the limo transporting her from Rancho Mirage to LA, the dissolution of her family was painfully evident. Her father tried to make her feel better with outings to the zoo or the ballpark. She liked that he tried, but was too angry to tell him.

When she made the transition to St. Theresa's, she also made friends again. After that, she almost always brought someone along. Usually Kelly, Laura, or both friends accompanied Jessica on that limo ride to Brentwood. Relieved that she had companions, her father was often relegated to chauffer, sometimes delegating those duties to the limo service.

By then, Jessica preferred the excitement of Hollywood, shopping and spas to ball games or zoos. Hank tried to accommodate her changing interests. He surprised Jessica and her friends with tickets to the taping of popular TV shows at local studios. He bought tickets and pulled strings to get them backstage passes for an Alanis Morissette concert after hearing Jessica tell Kelly how much she liked her *Jagged Little Pill* album. He arranged special seats for Jessica and her friends at Fashion Week in LA, and red-carpet events like movie premiers.

Mostly, her dad remained behind the scenes, providing chaperones for Jessica and her friends but rarely accompanying them. Somehow, though, Hank had increasingly become the parent Jessica could talk to about her life and what she might do with it. He had encouraged and rewarded her efforts to get good grades in school, and inquired about the areas that interested her. Her father talked about his own work, sharing what he liked and didn't like about it. He showed her the designs in development and took her to the building sites. She had listened, attentively, as he spoke about the Huntington family legacy. That included telling her stories about their role in the development of California. It also included visits to places like the Huntington Library, tangible symbols of the family legacy.

At his urging, Jessica began to read books about architecture, design, and development. They discussed problems in cities, like sprawl, traffic, pollution, the loss of neighborhoods, and about the need for well-planned, livable communities. Whether intentional or not, their conversations about such issues greatly influenced her career choices. So did his passion for good design and sensible development, for fairness and doing the right thing even when it was difficult in business. When she finally decided to

80

A Dead Sister

pursue environmental studies and urban planning as an undergrad, she had a real head start from the hours spent discussing such things with her father.

She loved him most of all for trying: trying to make his life and the lives of others better, especially hers. Jessica was his daughter and cared as much as he did about figuring things out, solving problems, and making things right. It had shaken her to the core when Hank Huntington couldn't fix his marriage. Now, here she was in the same situation, no better able than he had been to mend the breach.

She was her mother's daughter, too. It was almost two o'clock and she had some serious shopping to do. Truth be told, she was more than a little nervous about her meeting at Paul's law firm tomorrow. She wanted to create a good impression, and that meant finding the perfect dress. She'd made a three o'clock appointment with an associate at Max Mara's on Rodeo Drive. Store hours varied, and she was taking no chances. Jessica also asked that they have a tailor on hand who could make minor alterations while she waited. Or while she shopped nearby for shoes and bags once she found "the dress." Max Mara was not the only designer Jessica admired. She'd come to trust the company's prêt-à-porter collection, shopping frequently at their Palo Alto store, when she lived and worked in that area. If time permitted, she could order from their fall collection as well.

Jessica cruised down Rodeo Drive, taking in the palm-lined street featuring a dazzling array of iconic designer names: Dior, Prada, Gucci, Armani, Versace, Cartier, and Harry Winston. Plus, newer, hipper names like Michael Kors, Etro, Juicy Couture, Jimmy Choo, Guess, and Bebe. She admired the architecture, set off by elaborate facades, expanses of glass, store names in bold lettering, and gleaming brass accents. She'd planned to use the valet parking near Two Rodeo Drive and walk to Max Mara's, strolling along the cobblestone pedestrian thoroughfare so often featured in the movies, but as luck would have it, a Bentley was pulling out of a parking space close to the Max Mara storefront.

She could feel the blood pulsing in her ears. The thrill of the hunt, and the challenge to find the perfect outfit, had her on point. She struggled to modulate her excitement, hoping to avoid the embarrassment she had experienced on several occasions in the past year or so. At times, exhilaration had morphed into anxiety and even panic. "Focus, Jessica. Relax and focus," she said to herself as she angled her white BMW coupe into the now empty parking space.

The first time her body betrayed her, she'd been in a doctor's office.

Anna Celeste Burke

Waiting for the results of yet another pregnancy test, Jessica was caught up in a familiar mix of excitement and apprehension. Suddenly, without warning, she was hit by a torrent of heart-pumping, head-pounding, throat-tightening adrenalin. She feared it was a heart attack. As she stood up to get help from medical staff, she became light-headed and saw stars. The next thing she knew, she was on the floor. She'd been aiming for her seat, but miscalculated and landed on the floor instead.

A slew of tests followed. They revealed nothing wrong with her heart: no brain tumor or any other neurological problem, no diabetes or hypoglycemia, etc. It took a few weeks to do the tests and get the results back. During that time, the same thing happened again, several times. Jessica's own careful review of test results, and a ton of internet research, finally led her to concede that she was experiencing an anxiety reaction.

Her physician made a referral and Jessica Huntington-Harper was officially given a mental health diagnosis by a psychiatrist: generalized anxiety disorder with episodes of panic. Since she was still earnestly seeking a baby at the time, she declined medication and pursued behavioral treatment.

It took her months to learn about the disorder and begin to acquire skills to manage the symptoms. That included learning to recognize the early signs that she was spiraling toward a loss of control. She developed a range of strategies: relaxation, thought-stopping, and self-talk to counteract the rumination that could send her body into overdrive. All the good things she was doing, exercise, healthy food, and sleep were part of her continued recovery. More than once, Jessica had wondered if her body knew her marriage was over long before she stumbled upon Jim and that minx. The unavoidable truth of that discovery still caused a surge of neurochemicals and unwanted emotions.

"Stop!" Jessica commanded in a whisper. She called to mind her morning swim: the soothing feel of sparkling water, buoyant and cleansing, the steady rhythm of her stroke propelling her through laps. She counted off the laps in her mind as she locked the Bimmer with a couple chirps of the electronic key, and fed the meter with coins from her purse. Much calmer, she observed that it was one-hour parking. She would run out and feed the meter if she had to, and hauling her purchases to the car would be a breeze.

Angela, the store associate at Max Mara, was waiting for her, and introduced her to Alfonso, the tailor who would be working with them. Based on their phone conversation, Angela had already pulled together a

82

dozen items for Jessica's consideration. The first thing that caught Jessica's eye was a short-sleeved sheath dress in a deep red, with a split neckline. Made of a wool stretch blend and fully lined, it had a smooth feel to the touch and draped well. When she put the dress on, it was too large. Working out and eating right had begun to pay off. She had them bring her the same dress, in a size smaller.

Jessica took a good look in the mirrors surrounding her. The smaller size was nearly perfect. The color added a glow to her complexion that made her green eyes look even greener. If she didn't find something she liked better, this dress would work. She slipped into the pair of black Jimmy Choo pumps she'd brought along from home. They worked, giving her the elegant, professional look she was shopping for. What a find, and on the first try!

Next, Jessica tried on a dress from Max Mara's studio collection that Angela had already swapped out for the smaller size. A gorgeous caramel color with side panels in black, the dress seemingly subtracted even more of the pounds she was struggling to lose. The sharp contrast of the inset panels added interest. Yet it had the same clean lines she liked, with short sleeves and a higher neck than the red dress. The concealed zipper and vent on the back of the skirt gave the dress an elegant look from the back too. She had found another dress that would work.

Angela had also chosen a couple sleeveless dresses for her. One, a wool-silk blend in a silvery gray, created a similar silhouette, but seemed a bit too casual for the work-to-dinner thing on Tuesday. It could be worn to the office in Palm Desert and she'd be grateful that it was sleeveless in the desert heat. A second sleeveless dress, in white with black color blocking insets and a detachable black belt, had a round neck. Pleats gave the line of the skirt more flare than the other dresses she'd tried on. The black insets were dramatic from the back, and the zipper inset in black created a vertical line that flattered her figure. The classic lines, flawless cut, and drape of the fabric in both dresses promised to make it easy to look pulled together. Even if she didn't always feel that way, Jessica intended to create that effect. In the fall when the weather cooled, she could add a jacket or cardigan, extending the usefulness of both dresses. She was on a roll.

That ended abruptly. The next three dresses did not work at all. One was too broad in the shoulders, another would have looked great if she were 5'7" instead of 5'4", and the third was in a shade of gold that somehow washed the color out of her hair. She was growing weary of the process when Angela brought her a luxuriously soft, beautifully tailored camel's hair blazer and matching pencil skirt. The suit fit like a glove. She disliked suits, but the color, fit, and luscious fabric won her over. Unfortunately, they didn't have a camisole or blouse to match in her size, but she could find one later if she didn't already have something in her closet at home that worked. They did have a simple cashmere wool-blend sweater in black with a V-neck, which fit well and could be worn with the pencil skirt, giving it a finished look without the blazer.

Jessica had been at it for nearly an hour, and she needed to feed the meter. She still hadn't looked at the fall collections to see what she might ask them to set aside for her or send to her in Rancho Mirage. She was about to call it a day when Angela handed her one more dress. A soft knit, panel dress in navy blue with a V-neckline and three-quarter length sleeves, it was form-fitting but tailored.

Angela sent someone to pump coins into the meter and urged Jessica to slip into the dress. A matching long-sleeved jacket with inverted notched lapels was also available in her size. The minute she put it on, Jessica knew that was it. The dress she was going to wear. It was an inch or so too long, but Alfonso assured her he could hem and press the skirt for her in a half hour or less. Comfortable and elegant, the dress would put her at ease at the office, and would be suitable for dinner later. Of course, she'd take the others too. By morning, she might change her mind, and wear that gorgeous red dress instead. They would all be useful as she forged ahead, rebuilding her legal career. A shopping buzz pulsed through her body.

While the tailor set to work altering her dress, Jessica went through a few remaining items Angela thought might be suitable as accessories. She bought a beautiful, classic pair of pumps in a deep caramel color with black heels, a wonderful roomy leather satchel in black, and a tote in navy. In addition, she purchased two luxurious multi-colored silk scarves that would add a bit of panache to the suit and dresses she'd selected.

Getting her second wind, she picked out a pair of Doppio stretch wool, classic crop pants, and a matching tunic of the same lightweight fabric. Both were in a deep red they called Bordeaux. She couldn't resist the soft allure of a scoop neck jersey tee in black. It was more than a little sexy when paired with sleek skinny black pants with zippered cuffs. Not that sexy mattered. For a split second, she flashed on Frank's appreciative gaze as he left the house on Sunday. Maybe sexy did matter. *Ay yi yi*, Jessica thought.

She was done. Ordering from the new collection would have to wait. When they rang up the total, Jessica experienced a brief bout of vertigo. Yet another symptom of her anxiety disorder, perhaps. Worrying about money didn't keep her awake at night. It did occur to her, however, that this tab

A Dead Sister

was all hers now that she'd signed those divorce papers. In only twenty-four hours, American Express had been happy to issue her a new card as Jessica Huntington, no hyphen and she'd wasted no time in putting it to use.

Jessica vowed to take a serious look at her finances before the end of the year. She was not nearly ready to buy a place of her own, in the desert or LA or anywhere else. If the contract she signed with Paul Worthington was extended beyond the year they'd agreed upon, then it might be worth making more permanent living arrangements. Of course, she might feel a great deal more urgency to find her own place if her mother, with husband-du-jour, turned up.

"I need a year," she cried inwardly for the umpteenth time, as that hyped-up feeling began to sweep over her again. She would have to start keeping tabs on the real estate market anyway if she and the Van der Woerts hit it off. What if they didn't—hit it off that is? Then what? The panic was creeping up on her. She had to get out of there. Maybe it would help to go for a walk while she waited for Alfonso to finish his handiwork.

Jessica hollered "back in a few minutes" as she rushed out of the store and into the waiting arms of a startlingly gorgeous afternoon in the 90210, Beverly Hills, zip code. The auric sunlight, vivid blue skies, and swaying palms on Rodeo Drive, beckoned. All the wealth and beauty of that street countered her anxiety with a big dose of the "anything's possible" spirit that pervades "LA-LA" land. The city of angels is, if nothing else, a city of dreamers. Despite her recent troubles, Jessica's life was about as close as you could get to the life so many Angelinos dreamed about. She stood on the street, trying to decide what to do as tourists and locals streamed by.

Suddenly, her heart sank. Out of a shop door, not half a block away, strode home-wrecker-Barbie. Having no baby bump yet, she wore tight, skinny white jeans and a sheer tank over a sports bra that left little to the imagination. Her wide-brimmed black-banded Panama hat teetered atop cascading, platinum locks, boosted by a surfeit of expensive hair extensions. As she made her way out of the store in strappy six-inch stiletto heels, she didn't wobble. Not even when stopping on a dime to smile for a member of the paparazzi. One hand carried shopping bags and the other held the leash for a large white standard poodle, all poofs and flounce, wearing a sparkly dog collar.

"Cruella De Vil, in person," Jessica sputtered to herself as the vamp ambled toward her. "I know, I know, wrong dog," she muttered nonsensically as she searched for an escape route before the creature could reach her. She wasn't worried about a soap-opera style confrontation of the cuckolded wife by the victorious younger woman. The Hollywood hussy might not even recognize her. What worried Jessica was how strong an urge she had to knock the silly skank off her tacky heels and onto her surgically enhanced derriere.

"Sprinkles, I need cupcakes." There was a Sprinkles cupcake store on Santa Monica Boulevard, not more than a few blocks from where she stood, amid the so-called "Golden Triangle" shopping district. Jessica was trying to remember exactly where the treasure trove of sugary delights was located when the bimbo-show began in earnest.

An officious older woman suddenly appeared, swooping down upon the photographer as though to shoo him away. Another blond, she had the teased hairspray-encrusted coiffure, and taut, overly-done face all too common among SoCal realtors or agents. Or, as in this case, personal assistants who used to be realtors or agents before the Great Recession. Of course, the photographer wasn't dissuaded from taking photos. Her actions drew even more attention to the top-heavy, red-lipped sex-pot.

As a crowd of tourists gathered to gawk, the dog became agitated and began to whimper. At the same time, a small gust of wind threatened to claim the Panama hat perched atop the starlet's head. When she reached up to grab her hat, the bags on her arm swung wide. She clocked the guy behind her who dropped the stack of packages he was carrying. That spooked the dog, which lunged forward, pulling his mistress with him. She collided with the personal assistant, and down they went, the stunned older woman cushioning the fall of the royally-ticked-off younger one. Dumping her shopping bags, the now furious actress reached up with long red fingernails. She swatted at the photographer who was still snapping pictures a few inches away from her angry face. He dodged her, took a step back, and continued to shoot. Still hanging onto the dog's leash, she was hurling epithets that would make a sailor blush. The guy she'd whacked stopped trying to pick up his packages and hurried over to try to untangle the two blonds, the dog, and the shopping bags. A moment of gut-wrenching revulsion overtook Jessica. It was her ex, Jim Harper.

"Cassie, are you okay?" He asked, sounding genuinely concerned. "Do you want me to call 911? Do you need a doctor?" He was practically dragging her to her feet as he spoke.

"Shut up! I don't need a doctor! I need a lawyer to sue that fat slob who's still taking pictures of me. Sandra, you clumsy cow, get up off the ground, now! Jim, *you're* a lawyer. Do something!" She ordered, stamping her foot. Sandra, still on the ground, moved, but didn't get up.

A Dead Sister

Jim looked around, perhaps tempted to just get the hell out of there. As he did that, he spotted Jessica and froze. Even though they were both wearing dark glasses, the mutual recognition was instant as their lens-clad eyes met. Jim blanched, turning almost the same shade as his beloved's platinum hair. Jessica gave him the tiniest salute as she turned on her heel and headed away from the scene, remembering exactly where that cupcake store was located.

"Oh, what a tangled web we weave," she said to herself, as she floated down the street toward cupcake heaven. "It would be wrong to skip," she babbled, a little maniacally. Having slipped out of those Jimmy Choo pumps and back into her Superga tennis shoes, she could have done it. But it would be wrong.

Behind her, the dog started to bark. The enraged diva was ranting again at the top of her lungs. "I want that camera! Give me that camera, you jackass!" Then, someone shouted.

"Look out! You're going to step on that lady on the ground." That was followed by a shrill cry of pain.

And a reply, "Sandra, get the hell out of my way. If nobody else is going to get the camera from that pig, I will!"

"Cassie, no, please, not in your condition!" Jessica recognized Jim's voice, even with the plaintive tone it had taken on. There was more, but Jessica's phone chose that moment to ring.

CHAPTER 9

"Hello, Jessica Huntington speaking."

"Ms. Huntington, Dick Tatum here. You left a message about my client, Chester Davis. How can I help you?"

Jessica had completely forgotten about leaving that message. In fact, in the rush of shopping, the call of cupcakes, and the fracas on Rodeo Drive, she'd put Chester Davis and Kelly Fontana out of her mind completely. *Some friend*, she thought as she hustled on down the street to get further away from the blond bombshell in mid-explosion. People were shouting, and she could still make out the strident cadence of the starlet's rant even as she increased her distance from the scene. The sound of police sirens could be heard in the distance.

"Mr. Tatum, thank you so much for returning my call." Jessica spent the next several minutes explaining who she was and why she had called. "I'd like to meet Chester Davis and speak to him, in person. Preferably Wednesday morning if that's possible." Dick Tatum, an affable sort of guy, had no problem with the idea of her speaking to his client if Chester Davis was willing to do so.

"In fact, I welcome your input. His drug habit is taking its toll. He's like a light bulb that flickers on and off, so it's hard to know how seriously to take him. I've known him for years now, but this is the first time he's ever made such a claim. Of course, he's in more trouble now than he's been in before, so I suppose he could have been saving this information for just such an occasion."

"Detective Greenwald mentioned that this is his third strike, and that

A Dead Sister

there was a gun at the scene. Sounds like his situation is dire."

"It is. Desperation can lead a man to do desperate things, but Chet's never really tried to pull the wool over my eyes. As far as I know, he's an honest low-level hustler, petty thief, and addict, if you know what I mean. He's always owned up to the fact that he's got problems, most of them, drug-related. His previous attempts at rehab were legit, as far as I can tell. They helped get him clean and sober for a while, a year or two. He knows he's in big trouble and he's scared. What I can't make out for sure is if he's scared because of the current trouble he's in, or because he's spilling his guts about a murder. Fear could be the reason he kept his mouth shut for so long, if what he says *is* true. He could be just as terrified at the prospect of being locked up for good, so I don't know. Anyway, if you meet me at the County jail Wednesday morning, say ten thirty, and he wants to talk to you, fine. If not, that's his choice, too."

"Thanks. I'll see you on Wednesday."

Just as Jessica hung up the phone, she reached the end of a line of people waiting to get into Sprinkles. Brooding while she waited, she went over the conversation with Dick Tatum. She didn't like the fact that Chester Davis was scared. That wasn't a good sign.

The line moved forward and Jessica stepped into the store. The scent of sugar and spice, the happy chirping of Angelinos getting a sugar fix, pushed the conversation with Dick Tatum to the back of her mind. Her eyes reveled in the sight of the scrumptious-looking cupcakes. She was glad she wasn't next in line yet. It took her a couple minutes to narrow down her choices, then, decide between the vanilla milk chocolate and red velvet bundles of bliss. She needed chocolate.

Savoring the rich, silky chocolate icing, laced with a hint of bourbon, Jessica strolled back down Santa Monica to Rodeo Drive. She tried to make the little confection last as long as she could, but finally polished it off. Doing the mental calculation of how many minutes she'd have to swim or cycle to work it off didn't lead to a moment of buyer's remorse.

Claiming her purchases from Max Mara was another matter. If she hadn't needed clothes for the very next day, she would have called and had them ship everything to her. Jessica strained her eyes for any remnant of the spectacle she had witnessed earlier. Her anger had morphed into sadness. This afternoon's encounter was too reminiscent of the last time she had stumbled upon Jim and the she-devil going at it. She felt ashamed of Jim. The Jim she'd fallen in love with would never have allowed himself to be humiliated like he had been today. She also felt like a fool realizing now that he was, as her father had said, so much less than she had imagined.

The street ahead seemed quiet, although a police car was parked at the curb across the street. Straining to peer into the back of the police car and seeing it was empty, Jessica picked up the pace and closed the distance to Max Mara's in no time flat. Angela rushed to greet her. Jessica's purchases were ready, and shop staff quickly loaded them into the trunk of her car. The relief she felt pulling away from the curb was enormous, as if she were fleeing the scene of a crime.

By six, Jessica had arrived at the Brentwood house, making a stop on the way for take-out sushi. She unloaded the car and hung up the new clothes, carefully, so there wouldn't be a wrinkle in them. Running her hands over the luxurious fabrics and smoothing the elegant lines soothed her, as images from the day bounced around in her head. That look on Jim's face today was haunting. How had this man, her husband, become a beast of burden for a screeching banshee? In all their years of marriage, she had never asked Jim to carry packages for her or even considered shouting at him in public. She almost felt sorry for him… the two-timing, unprincipled, dirtball.

She knew she should hop on one of the fitness contraptions her dad owned. In addition to doing penance for the cupcake, it might also stop the ping pong match going on in her head between pity and rage at Jim. It was such a nice evening in LA. Clear skies, a perfect temperature, and the sun would be setting within the hour. She could just sit on the patio, eat sushi, and watch the distant lights come on as the city began to sparkle. A breeze beckoned. Sushi and city views won out!

In the kitchen, Jessica picked up the stack of mail she'd brought in from the box near the front gate. The team caring for her dad's house had some rule they used about forwarding mail to her dad at selective intervals, tracking him wherever he was. A tray in the butler's pantry was used to hold the mail until it was sent to him. As she carried the stack to the tray, several pieces slid out and fluttered to the floor. Jessica bent to retrieve them and stopped short. One of the items was a postcard, written in her mother's hand. On the front was an idyllic scene of blue-domed, white stucco structures overlooking azure waters, with a golden sun hung low over the horizon. A little blurb on the back identified the scene: "Santorini, jewel of the Aegean." Her mother must have talked Giovanni into a yachting foray, or perhaps she had set out on her own. Far more stunning than the scene on the postcard was the brief message from her mother.

"Hank, thanks so much. See you soon. Ciao! Lexi"

A Dead Sister

For the second time today, you could have knocked Jessica over with a feather! That her parents were communicating was a bit of a surprise, but the casually intimate tone was more surprising, especially the use by her mother of the pet name, "Lexi." Jessica hadn't heard her dad call her mother that in years. What did it mean that she was going to see him soon? Who was visiting whom, and where?

Jessica, her head spinning, found a good chardonnay chilling in the large Subzero stainless-steel refrigerator. The concierge service must have had a record somewhere of her wine preferences, perhaps courtesy of her father. An intriguing Argentine Malbec was sitting on the counter, but the chilled chardonnay seemed lighter and more appealing as an accompaniment to sushi. Jessica opened the bottle and poured a glass, taking that and her dinner to the back patio.

Images of the day's first moments, cast so early in the morning by the landscape in Mission Hills, formed one side of a set of parentheses now closed by the LA cityscape before her. She could never have imagined all that had occurred in between. Father Martin's words, spoken in such an offhand manner several weeks before, drifted back to her as though carried aloft by an offshore breeze. "God is a God of surprises, Jessica."

"I'll drink to that," she said, tipping her glass to the sun setting before her. Questions poured out along the arc cast by her raised arm. What had possessed Jim to take up with such a repulsive woman? Would Jessica and the Van der Woerts hit it off tomorrow? Where was her mother, and why would she see her father soon? Had someone murdered Kelly Fontana?

CHAPTER 10

The offices of Canady, Holmes, Winston and Klein were everything you might expect of a Vault-ranked top-100 law firm. Located in a mega-city, they managed big deals and solved problems for members of the power elite. Given the firm's location, there was an entertainment industry bent to their work, although what garnered most of the publicity was their high-profile criminal cases. Many of those cases were honchoed by Paul Worthington, who had achieved junior partner status in near-record time after joining the firm right out of Stanford Law school.

Occupying a dozen floors of an historic building in downtown LA, the firm employed over two hundred lawyers plus many more staff members. They had a presence statewide, with offices in San Diego, San Francisco, and, of course Sacramento, the state capitol. They also operated smaller offices in wealthy enclaves like the one they were opening in the desert.

The LA "shop" had all the glitz and glamour portrayed in TV shows like "The Good Wife." Gleaming brass, expensive wood polished to show off gorgeous grains, fine art prints, and richly upholstered fabrics. Richly detailed conference rooms featured leather chairs and gleaming wood tables. Expanses of windows offered views of the city.

Even the elevators were stunning, Jessica noted, as she rode with Paul from one floor to another. The floors she visited with him housed the more senior members of the firm along with the waiting rooms, offices, and conference rooms where they brought clients. Things were likely to be considerably less glamorous behind the scenes, where staff and newly minted lawyers hung out. Many would occupy cubicles with standard-issue desks and file cabinets, not meriting an office with four walls or a window.

A Dead Sister

Those who supervised the work of others no doubt had private space, at least. Their offices were probably furnished with wooden desks and leather chairs. But it would not be an "exotic" wood, nor would the leather be as fine-grained as that on the chair she occupied in Paul Worthington's office. The view behind Paul was stunning, with windows on two sides of the elegantly contrived space.

He looked at ease. Jessica wondered, once again, about the amount of time and attention he was devoting to her. The practice of big law was always in a state of flux, but maybe more now than ever. The Great Recession had taken its toll on all sorts of firms at all levels of practice, and in most every area of the law. Only about half the graduates from law school last year had landed any kind of law job. Big law firms drew from the top ten or twenty percent of students in their class, at the top ten or twenty law schools in the country but even those firms had begun to recruit fewer students. Some deferred hiring or even cut loose students to whom they had already made offers.

Law school graduates hired by major firms were rewarded with high starting salaries and the promise of making a ton more as their careers took off. A heady sense of having arrived was common among newcomers to big law. Mega-deals, though, meant mega-mounds of documents and data to review. Tens of thousands, even on occasion, a million pages, according to Jim, who reveled in the challenges of the mega-deal.

Jessica had a good idea of what that meant. Even at a smaller, more specialized firm, she had done her time in "document review hell." Given her obsessive nature, and eye for detail, she had excelled at the task. She also had a talent for being able to scan documents, sifting through volumes of data to find the few facts that mattered, especially those that might make or break a project or win a case.

Despite the allure of the high life, fear or a close cousin dread, was commonplace in big law. Mega-deals were risky and mega-failure was a terrifying prospect. Keeping up with expectations to achieve two thousand billable hours a year, on top of all the other demands in big law firms, required a lot of sacrifice. Often referred to as the "misery index," it was the dark side of the high life. The mega-firm, and even a lot of smaller, boutique firms were twenty-four/seven operations, thanks to modern technology. The clients, who paid as much as a thousand dollars per hour to elite lawyers, expected to get attention from someone whenever they wanted it. Harried junior associates often fielded those late-night calls, shielding higher-ups from meltdowns by clients facing make-or-break legal outcomes.

Expectations of round-the-clock availability had begun to "trickle down" to smaller firms, and even solo practitioners could pay dearly if they didn't pick up their phone when a client called, or worse, didn't call back at an agreed upon time. In the legal profession, there was no room for a "slacker" mentality. That was true, at least, for anyone wanting a practice not run from the trunk of their car or a Starbucks coffee shop. Though lawyers generally held themselves and their chosen profession in high regard, the day-to-day life for many was more on par with a sweatshop.

Canady, Holmes, Winston and Klein churned like a perpetual motion machine. The activity was incessant everywhere she went with Paul that day and there were no slackers in sight. Everyone was hustling and bustling, phones were ringing and being answered on the first or second ring. The misery index must be relatively low at Canady, et al. because she spotted no hint of the existential angst that gripped many inhabitants in such rarified environments. In fact, the faces Jessica had encountered almost glowed as if lit from within by that can-do spirit, as bright as the California sunshine.

Jessica found herself emulating them, smiling back confidently, swept up by the almost pathological optimism of the place. She shook hands and exchanged niceties with a sizeable cast of characters, mostly at or below the same rank as Paul. They were deferential to Paul without being sycophants. They also showed an appropriate level of curiosity about Jessica with no expression of fear or loathing about the intrusion of this new competitor onto their hard-won turf.

The word may have already spread that she was being hired into an office in the desert resort cities. That's what Paul told them when he introduced her. She was not likely to be perceived as much of a threat. At least, not by those who loped through the expanses of the main floors at the firm. There might be more junior members hidden away in the dark recesses of document review hell or equally unglamorous nooks and crannies of the firm who coveted a foothold in the new ground being broken in Palm Desert. The desert was the antithesis of the sought-after mega-city habitat. No one "on the make" in big law would want to be too far from that center of action.

An ambitious newcomer might well perceive an office in the desert as the Gulag. Jessica could live with that. In fact, she preferred to think she wasn't stepping on anyone's toes. She loved the scaled down life she led in the desert and already felt a twinge of homesickness. It was fine with her if Palm Springs and the surrounding area served as a playground where LA go-getters came to rest up between scrimmages. Dropping wads of cash into resort city coffers, the desert area was disproportionately blessed by amenities not found in other communities of similar size. The arrangement proposed by Paul suited her just fine.

By four o'clock, when Jessica and Paul settled into the plush privacy of the conference room in Paul's office suite, she was ready for the espresso he offered her. Arranging to meet at two had been a great idea. She'd not only completed the tour but signed her contract and had been given a copy for her records. She also picked up the business cards printed for her, along with a key card to gain access to the on-site parking garage for future visits to the LA office. The key card also allowed her to enter the building after hours or on weekends, should she need to do so. Information about the firm's structure and organization, a brochure about employee benefits, the latest annual report, and an eloquently succinct account of the firms' history were provided in a hand-tooled leather portfolio with the firm's logo etched on it.

Paul had also given her a bit of background about the couple she was about to meet. This archetypal LA couple, he a plastic surgeon and she an executive at a public relations firm, was well-off and ready for retirement. They owned a house in Pacific Palisades, a condo in Maui, and an impressive portfolio of stocks and bonds, mostly in IRAs and 401ks, as well as substantial savings in cash accounts. Once Nick Van der Woert divested himself of his share of the clinic he owned and operated with several other surgeons, they stood to increase their liquidity considerably. They had few debts or liabilities, having paid off the mortgage on their house in Pacific Palisades, and purchased the condo in Maui outright. Their one child, Elizabeth Van der Woert, about the same age as Jessica, was out on her own, although it wasn't clear how she was supporting herself.

As Paul had indicated, their daughter was the reason they had first contacted the firm. In true Hollywood party-girl fashion, she had been arrested and charged with vehicular homicide after being involved in a serious automobile collision. The accident left her with minor injuries but the passenger in her car was killed. Elizabeth Van der Woert and her dead passenger were both "under the influence" at the time of the accident. The firm had been able to keep the report about her level of intoxication out of court based on some procedural error committed by the officers at the scene. Without evidence of gross negligence, the charges were reduced to involuntary manslaughter. By also getting a previous DUI expunged from her record, the firm had seen to it that she was given probation rather being incarcerated. Loyal clients for life after that, they had been invited to investigate what else the firm might do for them. That was two years ago, and here they were ready to forge ahead.

When the Van der Woerts arrived, the doubts that had been dogging Jessica vanished. She liked them both, instantly. They soon found, despite the difference in ages, that they had several acquaintances in common. Mostly people Jessica knew because of her father's business or charitable activities. She was also able to converse knowledgeably about life in the desert. They discussed the rhythms of the "season" in the desert and events on the charity circuit, initiating the conversation they needed to have about the causes and concerns that interested them.

Thanks to Paul, the Van der Woerts already knew that Jessica had excelled in her coursework at Stanford, a top ranked law school, and had passed the bar exam on her first attempt. They also knew she had sought out and been hired by a mid-size firm that accommodated her interest in environmental law. It was her expertise regarding environmental issues that had most interested them, given their desire to create a legacy around such matters.

Jessica spoke about the experience she gained at that firm and elsewhere, including two clinics sponsored by Stanford Law, where she handled a broader range of legal matters. She didn't add that, as a trust-baby, she had grown up learning about wills, trusts, and foundations. The Huntington and Baldwin families had both engaged Jessica in family business meetings once she turned twelve. They briefly discussed a range of options that they might use to protect and preserve their assets, convey gifts and bequests. Jessica admitted that, like most lawyers, she had never gone to trial, although she had been inside courtrooms or at the bench for pretrial proceedings on many occasions. Her role was to ensure that her clients never got into the kind of trouble that required litigation.

Their freewheeling conversation carried them along so pleasantly that everyone was a little surprised by the arrival of the limo driver who would take them to dinner. Paul had made a six thirty reservation at Providence, noted for their seafood, Nick Van der Woert's favorite. Like their meet-and-greet at Canady, et al., the rest of their evening was thoroughly enjoyable: good food, wine, and conversation. After the Van der Woerts said goodbye, Paul and Jessica lingered at the restaurant. They ordered a brandy and debriefed.

"That went well. Here's to what I hope will be a long and prosperous association between us." Jessica raised her glass and, after a little clink, took a sip.

"And, to you, Paul, for giving me this chance, I do not take it for granted."

A Dead Sister

"Let's just say the timing was right for both of us. I like you and I'm looking forward to getting to know you better, personally, as well as professionally."

"The timing is not so good on that front, I'm afraid. I'm far more ready for lift-off when it comes to relaunching my career than I am when it comes to sharing much about my personal life with anyone. I'm still in this obsessive phase about the end of my marriage. Where did I go wrong? I thought I was in love, and he loved me, or so it seemed. Then, I find him in a very compromising situation with a Hollywood celeb who, by the way, I stumbled upon making a scene on Rodeo Drive yesterday. I didn't have a clue about the guy I was married to for years. I'm still angry enough to kill him at times, although I think the new woman in his life may do that for me!" Jessica stopped talking to take a breath. It was like a dam had broken and all the concerns she'd been harboring about how to manage her relationship with Paul had surged in a deluge of disclosure that might or might not have been relevant to Paul's statement.

"Yeah, I know who and what you're talking about. The media has been having a field day with her, and, of course, Jim doesn't come off looking too great. You actually saw that?"

"That's my luck lately. There's a fiasco going on somewhere, and I'm right there in the middle of it. Here's part of my problem, Paul. My ex is an obvious ass. He's making a fool of himself, and I still feel sorry for him. Even worse, I start wondering what on earth *I* might have done to push him into the arms of that monster. That tells me I'm not even solidly on the rebound yet. I'm just praying I've got my act together enough not to let you down as a colleague. Case in point, the worst thing I could be doing right now is talking about my ex and my divorce and that disgusting psychodrama that took place today on Rodeo Drive. I think I need a year to get my head back on straight before trusting myself to tackle a new relationship. I'm sorry, Paul, you deserve better than to have to listen to me rail against my ex. How come you haven't married, if you don't mind my asking?"

"Well, timing is everything isn't it? There have been a couple of women who mattered a lot to me. They were important, but nobody that I felt the way you seem to have felt about Jim. Not only have I never been married, but I can't even remember thinking seriously about it. Now I'm at a different stage of life. Forty is right in front of me, and I'm wondering the same thing you are: why haven't I married? I'm sure the seventy to one hundred-hour workweeks are part, but not the whole answer to that question. I take responsibility for the fact that there hasn't been much time to invest in another person. I suppose that wouldn't have made me good husband or father material. If I *had* married, we might *both* be sitting here discussing the "ex." To friendship, Jessica! Let's toast that, and see if we can't figure that part out, along with building a working relationship. I don't know about you, but I could use a friend. I've even let that part of my personal life languish in pursuit of my career."

"To friendship," she said, giving his glass a clink. "Maybe that's why I'm so anxious to find out what happened to that friend of mine who was killed years ago. I've let friendships go too. It wasn't just my career, but my marriage and the crazy everyday life I lived trying to make two careers work. I'd like to chalk it up the dearth of friends in my life to the divorce, but I can't think of anyone I met, in all the time we lived as a couple, that I want to contact. My circle of friends in the desert is small, too. Although my family and I have lots and lots of acquaintances, I can count my close friends on one hand."

"Maybe that's all anyone has a right to hope for, Jessica, that you find four or five people in a lifetime that you can count on. Relationships take time and energy that are always in scarce supply under the best conditions. If you're fortunate, maybe one of those people turns out to be someone you can connect with in the way you hoped you had done with Jim, a soul mate waiting to find you."

"Paul Worthington, you are a true romantic. Thanks for being so understanding. It's a relief to be able to talk about all of this. I'd say that puts us well on the road to friendship. While we're at it, let's keep the dream alive. To soul mates!"

"I can be very understanding, and patience is a virtue I possess in scads. Let's give it a year and see where things stand, on all fronts. To soul mates!" They clinked glasses again and polished off the last of their brandy.

Their eyes met for a moment. She could see in them the openness that had drawn her to him that day at the office in Palm Desert when they first reconnected. Recalling what her father had said about Jim's lack of depth, she took stock of the man sitting across from her. This older, more reflective version of Paul Worthington than she remembered from law school was a man she looked forward to getting to know better. Add another surprise to the list accumulating in her unpredictable life, this one a pleasant one. In her mind, she made another toast: *"To surprises!"*

CHAPTER 11

When Jessica returned to her dad's house, it was nearly ten o'clock. She and Paul had lingered over a cup of decaf coffee after the brandy, engaged in amiable chatter about nothing much. The brouhaha on Rodeo Drive came up again, and this time they both had a hearty laugh about it. Shortly after she'd left for the cupcake store, a TV crew had raced to the scene in time to catch Hollywood's latest flavor of the month smashing the photographer's camera in a fit of unbridled rage. She and Paul both agreed the publicity couldn't hurt, given the crass nature of her most recent film. It might even help the tantrum-throwing diva. The incident, however, could play out differently in James Harper's life.

"How would you all handle such an incident if it was one of your associates?" She had asked.

"Speaking for myself, I'd be on alert about a guy like Jim, concerned that his judgment was as poor at work as it was in his personal life. Of course, not all of my comrades-in-arms would agree." He went on to explain. Jessica laughed as Paul described how each of the partners, the half dozen men instrumental in founding the law firm in the 1950s, would handle the matter.

That led to a conversation about the role the firm played, now and in the past, in relation to the film industry. From there, they moved on to talk about art and theater, more broadly. They discovered that she and Paul shared a passion for old movies, especially film noir. Paul had quite a collection. They even made a date of sorts. Setting a whole evening aside, they would watch a couple of their favorites, as well as a film Jessica had not seen before from Paul's collection. *He's serious about this friendship thing,* she thought as they planned their evening together. She felt a bit of eagerness, too, at the prospect of seeing him again. There was something so centered about the man. It was a pleasure to be around him.

After an hour or so, they'd called it a night. The town car dropped them back at the parking structure used by law firm employees. Paul walked Jessica back to her car, then stood there watching, with his hands in his pockets, as she drove away. She was sorry that he stood there alone and prayed, silently, that his soul mate was out there somewhere, as he believed.

Jessica had to be underway early to get to the County jail in Riverside by ten thirty. She was too wound up to sleep, so she went to work packing her things. Before midnight, she had the car all loaded up, except for the items she needed in the morning. The sleeveless gray dress hung on a stand in her closet, along with the caramel pumps and one of the paisley scarves that had hints of both colors in it.

It was odd how her work as a lawyer had come back to her, in a different form than she had ever considered. How odd, too, that this outcome had started with Roger's death and her desire to help her friend, Laura. Roger's death had not only led her to call Paul Worthington, but had rekindled her relationship with Frank Fontana. Sitting on the edge of her bed in her father's house, Jessica pondered the two men. They couldn't have been more different, at least superficially. What they had in common was more important. From what she could tell, both had pursued careers in law and criminal justice, led by an underlying conviction about the importance of fair play and playing by the rules. While it was too soon to know for sure, they both seemed to be decent, straightforward men. Jessica appreciated those traits after discovering her husband was a deceitful, coward, unwilling to confront her with the fact that their marriage was over.

When she got up at dawn the next morning, Jessica went through her routine. Coffee was followed by a half hour of laps in the pool. She took a shower after rinsing out her suit and putting it in the dryer so it would be dry for the trip to Riverside. Finishing the last of the yogurt and berries in the fridge, she dressed and did her hair and makeup. The scarf was the perfect accent for the gray sleeveless Max Mara dress, and those caramel shoes gave her a few extra inches of height. One last look in the mirror assured her that she was ready for another day of lawyering.

The drive to Riverside was as uneventful as sharing the road with about a million other cars can be. Most drivers were well-behaved on the freeways. Occasionally, some guy on a motorcycle sped by, driving between lanes when traffic backed up. That was legal in California. She'd never seen one of them get nailed, but it didn't seem like the smartest choice you could make when surrounded by F-150s and SUVs the size of tanks.

She was headed to the city of Riverside, the county seat where the courthouses and administrative buildings were located, as well as the County Sheriff's Department, where Jessica needed to pick up Kelly Fontana's cold case file. Chester Davis was being held at the Robert Presley Detention Center downtown, not too far from where he'd been arrested.

One of five jails, it was reeling from overcrowding, as were all the others in the county. Two decades of rapid economic growth in Riverside County had been accompanied by a commensurate growth in crime. The County jail had already added beds, but was still overcrowded. In 2011, local jurisdictions were mandated to keep non-violent, non-sex-offending felons out of state prisons and hold them in county jails. In the past, jails had held arrestees only while they were awaiting trial and/or sentencing, typically only for a few weeks or perhaps a few months. Now they were faced with burgeoning numbers of inmates needing to be housed sometimes for years.

Beds that would have "turned over" quickly remained occupied, so crowding and the shortage had worsened. A major expansion was underway in Indio, one of the easternmost desert cities in the county. Nearly three hundred million dollars was being spent to revamp the Indio jail and the complex of courthouses and administrative buildings surrounding that facility. Poorly equipped to house inmates long-term, jails were scrambling not only to find enough beds but to accommodate the inmates' needs for physical and mental health care, as well.

Jessica took the University Avenue/Mission Inn exit toward downtown and merged onto Mulberry Street. After a couple quick lefts, she was on Orange Street, where the Presley Detention Center was located. With ten minutes to spare, she found parking in front of the Riverside Courthouse across the street from the detention facility. When her interview with Mr. Davis was over, she could walk to the Sheriff's Department, nearby, on Lemon Street. The Mission Inn was only a few blocks farther away, so it would be a short jaunt afterward from where she was parked to the lot situated behind the hotel.

The street between the courthouse and the Robert Presley Detention Center was lined with palms. Built in 1989 to expand the old jailhouse, the detention center occupied a modern-looking, high-rise with tinted-glass windows. Well, maybe only a mid-rise by LA standards. At seven or eight stories tall, it towered over the gleaming white, more ornate Spanish-colonial courthouse. The lobby Jessica walked into was also modern and was more like a bank than a jail, with several "teller" windows operated by Sheriff's Department personnel. People were milling about, standing in line, or sitting, waiting for one thing or another. To her right was a sign leading to the restrooms, a locker room for visitors to store the things they weren't allowed to bring with them to their meetings with detainees, and an elevator.

Jessica was nervous. She'd visited a client in jail, but only once. The summer before she started law school, she had signed on for a prelaw community service course. It was intended to expose her to law practice as a generalist by shadowing lawyers and their legal assistants. What she remembered most about the jailhouse visit was the hooting and hollering of inmates. The smirking guard she followed had eventually led her to the visitation room where the lawyer she was "shadowing" was already meeting with his client. She discovered later that the guard had taken her the long way around. The second thing she remembered was the odor. Sweat and urine combined with the smell of peppermint from the gum the guard was chewing.

Jessica took another nervous look around. Before she could decide what to do next, a gentleman in a suit emerged from a door marked by a "staff only" sign. He smiled broadly, as he strode quickly across the lobby toward her. Of average height, fiftyish, he had just a hint of middle-aged spread around his waist. His face was round, with a slightly ruddy tone to his complexion, set off by a tangle of dark hair that needed to be combed. His round, wire-rimmed spectacles accentuated the roundness of his face. Something about him reminded her just a tiny bit of Columbo. Perhaps it was the air of disheveled amiability that induced her to smile as she reached for his outstretched hand.

The suit he wore was clean but wrinkled. In a medium brown color, it looked like it was made of a lightweight fabric, a practical choice for summer in Riverside. It was probably in the high 80s already this morning, and would top out somewhere in the mid-90s by late afternoon. His tie was a tad crooked, but it had a blue and tan stripe that went well with the light blue buttoned-down shirt he wore. The contrast was striking in comparison to the bespoke attire she'd seen yesterday at the big LA law firm, but a far more reasonable reflection of what a typical lawyer could afford.

"Ms. Huntington, I presume," he said as they shook hands.

"Yes, Mr. Tatum. It's good to meet you."

"I've spoken to Chet and he's willing to meet with you as you requested.

A Dead Sister

I explained that you want to hear what he has to say about this woman that he saw murdered in Palm Springs. I also explained she may have been someone you knew years ago, a friend, and that you want to find out what happened to her."

"Okay, that's right. I'm glad he's agreed to meet with me. Thanks for setting this up."

"Well, let's go. I've moved him to the old jail for now, where the inmates in protective custody are held. I thought we'd have more privacy, and he might be more comfortable telling you what he knows where it's more secluded. There's a tunnel in the basement that we use to move detainees from here to the courthouse. It will also take us to the old building. Follow me!"

On that note, he moved to the elevator, signaling to the guards responsible for securing its use where they wanted to go. Together, they rode the elevator down to the basement and made the brief walk down a well-lit corridor lined with security cameras. Another well-guarded elevator in the old jail building took them to the second floor where, after another round of security checks, they were ushered into a room with no windows, a small table, and several chairs.

"We might as well sit down, Ms. Huntington. This might take a few minutes."

"Sure, but please, call me Jessica." She sat down on a metal folding chair. The chair sat facing the door on the far side of the faux wood-grain, collapsible table. Dick Tatum pulled up another chair next to her and sat down.

"So, Jessica, you drove in from LA this morning. Is that where you live?"

"No, I'm sort of in transition right now. I grew up in the desert, Mission Hills in Rancho Mirage. That's not far from Palm Springs. I'm back there for the time being."

"That'll be quite a drive if you're going to be working in LA, won't it?" His head was cocked to one side, his arms folded over his chest looking at her with unabashed curiosity.

"Actually, the firm I'm working with is opening an office in Palm Desert. That's where I expect to do most of what they've hired me to do and it's where you can find me if you need to speak to me. Or you can just call me on my cell." As she spoke, she reached into her purse, a little sheepish at the thought that the bag she carried probably cost more than Dick Tatum's entire outfit. She pulled out one of the business cards Paul Worthington had given her the day before, removing it from a lovely, silver-clad business card holder engraved with the firm's logo. "My cell number is on here along with the contact information for my office."

Dick Tatum took the card and slid it into one sleeve of an inexpensive leatherette card holder. From the other sleeve, he pulled out a card of his own and handed it to her.

"Here, now you'll know how to reach me, too."

"Thank you. Mr. Tatum, I..."

"Dick, please. We're on a first name basis now."

"So, how is it you happen to be in Riverside? Is this home for you?"

"As a matter of fact, it is. I've lived here all my life... went to undergrad school here in town at UC Riverside. That's where I met my wife. I thought about going to LA or San Diego for law school, but then my wife got pregnant and wanted to be near her family. So, I got my law degree here in town, too, at California Southern." He had folded his arms over his chest again and that quizzical look had returned to his face. No, it was more intense than that. Sort of like Atticus Finch doing the Vulcan mind probe. Jessica found it mildly disconcerting, and was about to revise her view of the man as amiable.

"How many children do you have?" She asked, continuing their polite conversation. Before he could answer, there was a commotion at the door. Jessica looked up as a tall, heavy-set guard in the short-sleeved version of the Sheriff's Department uniform escorted Chester Davis into the room.

Jessica tried not to display the shock she felt at the sight of Chester Davis. The guy was probably only a few inches taller than she was and, possibly, weighed less. He swam in the bright orange jailhouse jumpsuit he wore. His forearms were nothing but skin and bone. He gave a nod of recognition to his attorney and then stared point blank at Jessica.

"Is this the lady lawyer what wants to talk to me?" He asked his lawyer, without taking his eyes off Jessica.

"Yes, Chet, this is Jessica Huntington." As he spoke, Dick stood, walked around the table, and stopped beside Chester Davis. A much smaller man than the guard, he still dwarfed the frail-looking inmate. "Thanks, Officer Burke, we can take it from here."

"Sure thing, Tatum. I'll be just outside if you need me. Ma'am," he said, acknowledging Jessica as he backed out of the room and shut the door behind him. Dick pulled out the chair on the opposite side of the table from Jessica.

"Take a load off, Chet. Shake hands with Attorney Huntington, why don't you."

Chester Davis bent over the table to shake hands with her before sitting down. For the first time, he smiled, and Jessica could see he was missing teeth and the ones he had left didn't look so good. There was no way to tell if the missing teeth had been knocked out, or lost through the ravages of drug use. Given his state of emaciation, he was lucky to have any teeth. A lot of drugs, but especially methamphetamine, could have done this to the man sitting across from her. Or maybe barbiturates, they did a number on your teeth, too. Even though Art had told Frank that he was in his fifties, Jessica had learned that Chet Davis was closer to her own age. The same age Kelly would have been if she had lived, about thirty-four or thirty-five. She could understand Art's mistake, though, since Chester Davis looked older than the fifty-something Tatum standing next to him.

Davis's hair, the color of wheat, was sparse and patchy. His bloodshot blue eyes were watering, and he was sniffling like he had a cold. Dick handed him a tissue. He was either sick or in withdrawal from whatever he'd been using. He gazed at Jessica, anxiety on his face. One eye twitched.

"You gonna help me get out of here?" He asked her, shifting nervously in his seat. He folded and unfolded his hands, wiped his nose with the tissue, then wrapped it around his fingers.

"I don't know, Mr. Davis. That's up to your attorney and the prosecutor."

"I thought you said she was going to help us. You said she was going to be on our team, Tatum. What's she saying?" His eyes were wide and blinked furiously as he asked those questions.

"It's okay, Chet. Ms. Huntington just wants to hear what you have to say. She's not going to repeat anything you tell her. She can't do that."

"What do you mean, it's okay? I'm not talkin' to no one who's not my lawyer."

"What Mr. Tatum is trying to say is that anything you say, with your lawyer present, will be a privileged communication. You know, private? That means it can't be shared, outside this room, without your permission."

"I know what privileged communication means." His eyes narrowed as he looked at Jessica, growing hard and stubborn. "He said if I talked to you, told you what I know, you was goin' to help make a valuation of what I said. That you mighta known who this girl was I saw get murdered and that could make me have more credibility. That's right, ain't it, Tatum?"

"Yes, that's right. But she doesn't have to be your lawyer to do that. She still has to go by the rules because she's sitting here in this room with us."

"Well, that ain't good enough. She's not my lawyer. I ain't sayin' nothin'." Chester turned toward the door. He was getting ready to call the guard.

"Wait. I can fix this if Mr. Tatum says it's okay." Jessica turned slightly toward Dick. "Have you got a dollar you can loan Mr. Davis?" She asked the attorney, who was already pulling out his wallet.

"If it's also okay with you, it sounds like Mr. Davis here wants to add me to the team. If you give him that dollar and he gives it to me, we'll call it a deal. What do you say?"

"That works for me. Chet is that okay with you?" Dick took the dollar bill from his wallet and handed it to the jumpy, wiry shell of a human sitting across from them. He slowly reached for the dollar, took it, and turned it over. He waited a moment longer, then, handed it to Jessica.

"Works for me," he said as she took the dollar. On a piece of paper, Jessica wrote out a receipt, speaking aloud as she worked: "Received, this the 3rd day of July, 2013 from Mr. Chester Davis, the amount of $1.00 for legal services to be rendered on his behalf in partnership with Richard Tatum." She signed it and created a space for him to sign it too. He scrawled his name unevenly with hands that shook.

"Do you want to keep that, or shall I?" She asked.

"You keep it." He handed the makeshift receipt back to Jessica, who folded it and placed it carefully into a pouch of the leather portfolio that was open in front of her.

"Okay, will do. Now, how about you tell me about this girl you say was murdered. This is very important to me, since it could have been a friend of

A Dead Sister

mine. Can you tell me what happened?"

"I bet she coulda' been your friend. She was real pretty like you. Only she had reddish-brown hair, an' it was longer, and the most beautiful eyes I ever seen." Jessica tried not to flinch. She was so glad it had been several hours since she'd had anything to eat. What she heard after that made her ill.

CHAPTER 12

"Can I buy you a cup of coffee? You look like you could use one. If it was later in the day, I'd suggest something stronger." They stood in front of the Riverside County Courthouse, across the street from the detention center building, near Jessica's car. She was shaken by what she had just heard.

"I could use some coffee, but you should let me buy it. I'll spend that dollar I just earned in there. I need to go to the Sheriff's Department next. A Detective Greenwald, in the cold case unit, went to Palm Springs and got Kelly Fontana's file out of storage or wherever it was in the police department. He left a copy for me to pick up this morning. I know it's nearby, but I'm sort of turned around now. Can we get coffee near there?"

A glimpse at her watch revealed it was still morning, but not by much. It was already eleven thirty. They had taken their time with Chester Davis, letting him tell his story in his own furtive, halting way. It spilled out in fits and starts, with long pauses in which he seemed to be zoned out or ready to bolt. Tatum was right that Chet was scared, terrified, in fact. At times, it was as if he was twenty again, and witnessing the event. The twitching and trembling in his drug-addled body amplified so that he shook like a leaf, and his tremulous voice was barely audible at times. He wasn't going to make the most credible witness if they ever got far enough along in an investigation to go to trial. Elements of his story were frightfully compelling, and mostly consistent, even when they got him to tell them the story a second and then a third time. The thought of eating made her stomach do a flip-flop, but it was probably bumping up against Dick Tatum's lunch hour.

"If there's someplace you want to go that serves lunch, I'd like to buy

A Dead Sister

that for you. You shouldn't have to give up lunch to babysit your co-counsel. I admit I'm shaken. Chester Davis tells a gruesome story about what sounds like the murder of a close friend."

He gazed at Jessica, thoughtfully. "The office you're looking for is right there on Lemon Street." He pointed just past the detention center building. "If you don't mind walking a couple more blocks in those shoes, we can have lunch at the Salted Pig."

"Hang on a second, will you?" Before he could answer, Jessica stepped off the curb and to the driver side of her car. She unlocked and opened the car door, tossed her scarf onto the back seat. Then she fished out a pair of black ballet flats. With one hand on the car door for balance, she switched from the pumps to the flats.

The whole thing took a couple minutes, max, and she felt lighter. The act of changing her external appearance discharged some of the contaminating stress she'd picked up listening repeatedly to the horror that Kelly had endured. It probably took longer for Chester to tell his story than for Kelly to have lived through it, or, more accurately, to have died from it. If he was to be believed, Kelly was running for her life, with two men in pursuit, as she fled into the parking lot where she was hit and killed.

"Okay, now I'm ready. Lead the way, if you don't mind," she said to Tatum, who waited on the sidewalk near her car. Without another word, he stepped out and dashed back across the street, and past the detention center building. The Sheriff's Department building was wedged in between Orange and Lemon streets. The entrance was in the middle of the block, facing away from either street. Once inside the building, while saying hello to acquaintances, Tatum hustled Jessica to the information desk in the Central Homicide Unit. She asked for Detective Greenwald. In less than a minute, out walked a tall, thin man in civilian clothes. He wore a long-sleeved shirt with slacks, and no tie or jacket. Art Greenwald was bald except for a fringe of dark hair that ringed his head. Heavy brows hovered above his brown eyes, giving his unsmiling face a stern quality. He examined them both carefully, letting his eyes linger on Jessica.

Still looking at her, he spoke. "Hey Tatum, how's it going?" Without waiting for a response, Art Greenwald addressed Jessica. "Nice to meet you, Ms. Huntington. How did it go with Chester Davis?"

Before Jessica could reply, Dick spoke up. "It went very well. Chet spilled the beans. As far as I'm concerned, we have ample reason to reopen that case. Jessica can tell you more."

109

"Yes, Detective Greenwald, I guess you could say things went well. I'd like to talk to you about what we learned. We were going to go have lunch. Dick suggested The Salted Pig. Did I get that right?" Dick nodded. "Can you join us? My treat, if you have the time, and there's no rule against my picking up the check."

"Sure, just as long as you're not trying to apply any undue influence with the offer of a free lunch." He stared at her for another few seconds, deadpan.

"No, no. Of course not, I wouldn't expect..." The detective broke into a smile for the first time. Laughing, he cut her off.

"I'm kidding," he said.

Was he trying to be irritating on purpose? Was this his usual manner or was he singling her out for some sort of special treatment? The crooked little smile that remained on his face could easily have been a smirk.

"Cut it out, Arty. Jessica's had a rough morning. She doesn't need you razzing her. I'm hungry as a horse. Let's go eat before she changes her mind and we miss out on a free lunch!" Jessica breathed a sigh of relief as the detective chuckled, with his brows moving up and down a bit, as he shook his head.

"Don't call me Arty, Dicky! So, Jessica, is it? Let me get that file for you, and we'll go to lunch. It's Art to you, too, not Arty or lunch is off, deal?"

"Deal," she muttered, not sure if he was still kidding or he meant that. He moved toward the back of the work area in which he was standing and pulled a large brown envelope out of a bin.

Dick leaned over and spoke to Jessica in a confidential tone, "Art's not as funny as he thinks he is, nor as smooth with the ladies as he imagines. You're bound to get some hazing as the new kid on the block around here. He's a dependable guy, though, and a good detective. We can count on him if he decides there's a reason to take another look at what happened to your friend."

Jessica thought about the difficult relationship she had developed with Cathedral City's cantankerous Detective Hernandez, who honchoed the homicide investigation into Roger Stone's death. He'd done more than just rib her. He was downright derisive at times and had threatened repeatedly to file charges against her for butting into the investigation. It wasn't too surprising that there was antagonism between the police who apprehended

A Dead Sister

bad guys and the lawyers who tried them. Especially lawyers charged with defending guys the police wanted to keep off the streets. Even a conviction didn't guarantee they'd be off the streets for long, though, at least not until they got to the end of their rope, like Chester Davis.

Art and Dick chatted with each other as they all walked to the Salted Pig. A crowd was already gathering, even though they arrived before noon. A self-proclaimed "gastropub," the place served a wide range of items. That included the proverbial pub fare, burgers and fries, but with a twist. Most everything was made in house, including the brioche buns and ketchup served with the burgers. Even the coffee ice cream and the time-honored favorite of police officers everywhere—donuts—were handmade.

Not surprising, for a place that had "pig" in its name, bacon and other "pig parts" figured prominently on the menu. The two guys insisted she try the bacon fat popcorn seasoned with maple sugar and sea salt they'd ordered as an appetizer. Dick's burger was made of ground pork, with Applewood smoked bacon and served with "filthy fries," which was a huge pile of fries covered with beer cheese, herbs, and roasted garlic. Slab bacon adorned Art's burger, along with Enoki mushrooms and Gouda, topped off with a fried egg and, on the side, a bucket of traditional fries.

Jessica couldn't handle a burger and fries, even though she felt much better after a few sips of diet Coke. There were plenty of alternatives on the menu, and she settled for a small plate of Brussels sprouts roasted with a kimchee spice, and a salad featuring labneh, tomato, basil seed, and a verbena vinaigrette. The salad was a new take on her perennial favorite, the Caprese salad.

"What is it with women and salads?" Art asked as they set her plate down in front of her. "Do you really like that, or is it some dieting thing, or what?"

Dick butted in before Jessica could respond. She wasn't sure what to say anyway. She couldn't get a read on this guy. "Hey, Art, it's got to be a lot healthier than burgers and fries, probably why they outlive us men."

"Yeah, maybe so, but what's the point if you have to pass up all the good stuff in life anyway?" He dipped a couple of fries in ketchup and stuffed them into his mouth. "They serve beer here, too. Their microbrews are great. Too bad we're all on the clock. What about beer, Jessica, is that also on your list of unhealthy foods?"

"I drink beer, but if I have a choice, I usually prefer wine. I'm not sure why, maybe the same reason I like salads. It just seems lighter, somehow." Jessica pushed the food around on her plate. She was preoccupied by the interview with Chester Davis, and this conversation was beginning to get under her skin. Staring intently at her fork, she willed herself not to poke the detective with it. Staying on his good side was probably the right thing to do. Putting her fork down, Jessica thought, *I wonder what his good side looks like.*

"So, are you two going to tell me what this guy said, or what?" Art asked, breaking an uneasy silence that had settled on them.

"Sure, Art. Jessica, why don't you start, and I'll jump in if I have anything to add. I've told him some of this already. It'll probably be better if you do it, since you won't be tempted to skip over anything."

"Okay, it'll help me to recap, too. Then, maybe, we can talk about where we go from here. What we learned from Chester Davis is that he saw someone fitting Kelly Fontana's description run down in the parking lot outside the Agua Caliente hotel and spa. He says he was twenty at the time. Dick says that works that works out, given Chet's date of birth. Kelly was killed in January 1999 the same year he turned twenty-one."

"Hang on a minute. Are you telling me that guy is only thirty-something?" Art Greenwald looked dumbfounded.

"Hey, he's lucky to be alive," Dick interjected. "He's been a meth addict for well over a decade, and it shows."

"That's for sure. I didn't mean to interrupt, Jessica. Go on." At first, it sounded like he was apologetic for butting in. Then, with that order to "go on," he slipped back into il comandante mode. Jessica moved ahead, hoping to get this over quickly.

"Chet says he had made a delivery to someone in the hotel. He claims it was a little weed and a few tabs of ecstasy, but who knows. At the time, he was a runner for a group of small-time dealers operating out of a house not too far away in North Palm Springs. Nothing big, a group of users like him, trying to make enough to support their own habit by selling to locals and tourists." She paused a moment, took a sip of her diet Coke and stole a glance at Dick. He gave her a little nod to go on.

"He'd just come out of the hotel and was about to get on a bike stashed near a back exit of the hotel. Chet claims there was construction or remodeling going on. The place has gone through multiple redoes over the years, but there's probably some way to corroborate that part of his story. Anyway, a line of dumpsters was sitting out there. His bike was leaning against one of them, hidden away so nobody would steal it while he was inside. Before getting back on the bike, he ducks behind the dumpster. He said it was to count his money, but with a little prodding, he admitted he was planning to get high before riding back to the place where he was living at the time. Apparently, when he had made his delivery to the hotel room, there were half a dozen young guys partying and already trashed. According to Chet, booze, joints, and pills were all over the place. While they were pulling money out of their pockets and putting it in a big pile to pay for his delivery, Chet helped himself to some of what was lying around." Jessica paused again, the story getting harder to tell. She took a deep breath and went on.

"So now he's in the parking lot with the drugs he skimmed and a wad of cash, and decides he's going to get high. He's about to light up when he hears the backdoor open and somebody running. That makes him nervous. Maybe someone from the party is coming to get the stuff he took, so he stoops down, hoping he's well-hidden. He peeks through a crack between two of the dumpsters and what he sees is a woman running, a young woman about his age. She looks as wasted as those guys he'd just seen, so at first, he thinks she's freaking out because she's so stoned. Or maybe she's had a fight with her boyfriend or something like that. The kind of situations he ran into often when he made drug deliveries. He's about to light a joint when he hears the door open again. The girl takes off faster as two men come into view, chasing her. They have jackets on so he figures it's hotel staff chasing a guest or employee who's done something wrong. She's running flat out across part of the parking lot that wasn't taken up by the old casino building that was adjacent to the hotel back then. Suddenly, he sees car lights come on, like somebody was waiting for her in a getaway car. The car accelerated and instead of coming to her rescue, it went straight for her. She tried to get out of the way, but never had a chance. The car hit her almost head on." Jessica's eyes met those of the detective's, her voice filled with misery and sadness as she continued.

"When the car hit her, she flew up in the air, hit the windshield, and landed on the curb near the bushes. Chet said there was a terrible sound when she landed on the ground, like something cracking." Tears welled up in her eyes, and her throat choked off her voice.

"That's enough. I can handle it from here. Let me tell Art the rest." He produced a tissue, as he had done for Chester Davis earlier, and handed it to Jessica.

"At that point, Chet says he's too scared to move so he keeps watching. The two guys who were chasing her stopped and just stood there until the driver rolled down the window. He was angry, and spoke loud enough for Chet to hear some of it. Something like 'What the hell happened?' and 'Where's the blankety-blank doc?' He couldn't hear their answers because they had their backs to him. They'd moved closer to the car window and were speaking more quietly. It's pretty dark in the parking lot, but there was some light from lampposts. The two men talking to the driver step back, and Chet sees the driver pounding on the steering wheel and pointing. One of them walks over to the young woman lying on the ground and then goes back to the driver. There's a couple more seconds of back and forth, then those two take off again. They head back into the hotel through the same door they'd exited. That time of night, they probably would have needed a key card or something to get back in, but Chet's not sure about that." Jessica could tell the story was getting to Tatum, too. He paused for a sip of water. Now that the restaurant was jammed with people having lunch, it was getting stuffy. Dick rubbed the side of his head, as if he had a headache.

"Chet says he wanted to leave, but he was frozen in place, sure if he moves they'll spot him. Anyway, a few more minutes go by with the car sitting there, the engine running. Then the two men come back out the door again. This time, they're lugging a third guy between them and they're moving quick, saying something like 'the doc's hurt,' and 'she got him.' The driver's screaming, telling them to 'put him in the car,' so they shove him into the back seat. They're starting to get in, too, when the driver says, 'what the hell are you doing? Get back in there and clean that place up. I want everything out of there, everything, got it?' The two guys slam the car door and the driver takes off. They go back into the hotel and Chet just sits there, waiting. He's not sure how long—half an hour—maybe longer. Finally, he gets up the nerve to move, and he goes to check on the girl, just in case she's not dead." He paused and looked at Jessica, rubbing his temple again.

"It was clear she was dead. Her eyes were open, but she wasn't moving, and he says nobody could have been alive with their head the way it was on her body." Jessica stared straight ahead, wanting to weep, but not here. Not in front of these men she barely knew. It was bad enough to have to share such a personal tragedy with strangers. She was not going to let them see her cry.

Art had been quiet the whole time, taking a few notes. He looked at them both before speaking in a low, steady voice. "Well, that last part seems consistent with the coroner's report. If it's any consolation, the report says her death was quick. She died the moment she hit that curb. Can I ask you a couple of questions before we call it quits?"

"I'm okay with that. How about you, Jessica?" Dick sat up, pushing the remnants of his dessert away. Jessica wished their waiter would come back and clear the table, but with the mob scene still underway, that wasn't likely. She would probably have to stand up and shout over the noise of the crowd to get their check.

"No problem. What do you want to know?"

"Well, first off, did he give you any details about the car?"

"Just that it was a big, dark colored sedan," Dick said. "Four-door, obviously. To Chet, it was 'new and pricey' but he didn't know or can't remember more about a make or model. No license plate numbers or anything like that."

"Okay, so how about the men involved. Did he get a look at any of them? Any sort of description, anything distinctive about the way they looked or sounded like height, weight, an accent—anything?"

Jessica replied first, "As I said, he did notice the men that came out of the hotel were in jackets or sport coats like hotel staff might wear. Not a uniform like a waiter or croupier, nothing like that. Sounded more like what hotel security or a manager might wear. He thought the two men chasing Kelly were..." Jessica paused ever so briefly, realizing that they were all now in tacit agreement that it was Kelly Fontana they were talking about. "He said they were big guys. Of course, you've seen Mr. Davis; a lot of men could seem big compared to him. But he said they were practically running when they came out of the hotel with the doc. That tells me they probably *were* big to be able to run with a couple hundred pounds hoisted between them. It sounds like the doc wasn't doing much to help, so they were hauling dead weight. Tell me if I'm wrong, Dick, but during one rendition of the story, Chet said the doc was a lot taller than the other two men were. When they put him in the back seat, they had to duck him down so he wouldn't bump his head."

"Yeah, that's right." Dick said, confirming what she said.

Jessica picked up where she'd left off. "So, let's say the two guys who chased Kelly are average or a little above average in height, then that would make the doc a standout in the height department. It sounds like he was injured badly, so maybe we can check ER and hospital admission records to see if anyone remembers an unusually tall man being admitted that night. That was a long time ago, so it's not likely, but why not check?" Jessica's voice trailed off as an image of Kelly, the last time she had seen her alive, flashed in front of her. What kind of a mess was she in that could have ended in murder?

"Who knows what sort of records might still be available about ER visits that night, or who might still be around who could remember what happened that long ago? Oh, there is one other thing, Art. Chet says the driver of the car had long, dark hair. In one version of his story, he says one of the guys referred to the driver by name, sort of, calling him Mr. 'P.' or Mr. 'B.,' most likely an initial of some kind. If you remember, Dick, Chet also said there was something familiar about the driver, maybe someone he'd seen before. Chet was a pretty regular deliveryman at the casino back then, so maybe the driver was a regular at the casino or the hotel. We don't have much to go on but somebody might remember a regular with long hair who went by the name of Mr. P. or Mr. B. or a similar moniker. Casinos make a point of cultivating regulars. They do what they can to make their stay memorable, so maybe that will make this guy more memorable, too. We need to talk to employees who worked the desk back then, a manager or a concierge, perhaps. There must be names of people the police interviewed in the case file. That would be a place to start. I suppose it's possible the driver and the men chasing Kelly were affiliated in some way with the hotel. Chet says when he went to see if Kelly was still alive, he recognized her. He'd seen her at the hotel before. He didn't know her by name, but he knew that hair and those eyes, and identified Kelly from a photo I brought with me."

Jessica looked up and was surprised at both men's expressions. They had stopped eating and were staring at her.

"She's not just a pretty face, is she Arty?"

"No, she is not, Dicky. That was a concise and perceptive summary of what we have to go on at this point. And using the photo to get a positive I.D. was a great idea. I've done a quick review of the old file. Ms. Fontana wasn't found until early the next morning. You're right that the police talked to whoever was on duty at the hotel that morning and went back later to speak to staff on duty the night before. We have their names. One of the grounds keepers found her as he was starting his shift at the crack of dawn. The coroner said she hadn't been dead long, a few hours at the most. She was dressed in the uniform that the waitresses wear, but that wasn't her regular job. She was officially on the books as a spa attendant."

A Dead Sister

"Chet didn't mention that," Dick said.

"It's not a very distinctive outfit—black tights, black skirt, and a white shirt."

"Not to mention the distracting condition in which he found my friend. Did anybody say anything about why she was dressed like that?"

"The investigators spoke to a couple coworkers who said she wasn't scheduled to work anywhere that night. They claimed not to know why she was there. Her supervisor at the spa said she didn't know what she was doing there, either. Your friend had missed her two previous scheduled shifts at the spa, and hadn't been to work for several days, since she was off for a couple of days before that. She said that was a bit unusual for Kelly Fontana, who was a good worker, but a lot of kids her age went AWOL for a few days, so she didn't make too much of it. It's possible she was wearing that other uniform because she was picking up extra shifts or filling in for someone, according to her supervisor. If she was covering for a coworker, it should have been put on the schedule, but it didn't always happen that way." Detective Greenwald flipped through his copy of the file that he brought with him, scanning the pages before continuing.

"Interviews with the hotel staff didn't turn up anything about the accident, nobody heard or saw anything. That's entirely possible, because that set of stairs leads directly outside, so they could have come and gone without being seen. The staff didn't use that exit much. It was routinely locked by ten p.m., so if Chester Davis entered the building that way without a key card, it must have been before ten." Jessica was adding to the notes she'd taken during the interview with Chester Davis.

"Chet said he used that entrance and exit for the very reason you indicated, that he didn't want to be seen. He wouldn't have had a key card, so it must have been before ten when he arrived. It could have been later when he left, though. I can't believe it was that easy to come and go like that. Wouldn't surveillance cameras have monitored those areas?" Dick asked.

"Casinos are super vigilant about cameras on the casino floor, but that may not extend to the places where guests eat and sleep, like the hotel. The casino is across the street now, but back then, it was so close you'd think that whole area would have been monitored," Jessica responded.

"I didn't see anything about surveillance photos or video in the case file, but I haven't pored over it. I'm sorry about that. I presume that if something like video had been available, the original investigators would have reviewed it. I don't know how long they keep film on file. It's been almost fifteen years, so I doubt we'd be able to get much now anyway. It would be nice if they had a film clip or big, glossy photos of those culprits chasing your friend into the parking lot, but that doesn't seem likely."

"Art, don't apologize, it seems to me you've done a good job looking through the file. It's too bad so much time has elapsed. If Chester Davis had only come forward, maybe the investigation would have gone in a different direction. Certainly, having some sort of a name and description of a couple characters like the long-haired Mr. P. or Mr. B. and his inordinately tall companion might have triggered recognition from employees at the hotel or casino back then. Incorporating that information into an appeal to the public might have made a difference, too. What on earth is wrong with someone like Chester Davis?"

"Jessica, he was scared to death, still is. You saw that. He already had a track record back then, so it's not clear how seriously his claims would have been taken if he had come forward. He would have had to explain why he was hanging around out there in the dark behind a bunch of dumpsters. Chet Davis was a coward. I don't condone it, but I do get it." Dick was doing his best for his client, but that didn't wash with Jessica or the detective. Art picked up where Dick Tatum left off.

"It sounds like there's reason to believe some of what he says. I must point out, however, that his track record isn't any better now than it was back then. It's worse, in fact. He's got us all going, but it's still possible that this is a tall tale he's cooked up to get out of the serious trouble he's in. I don't deny that he saw something that night involving the death of your friend, Jessica. His description of the way her body looked fits with the photos taken at the crime scene. We don't have a single bit of evidence to corroborate anything other than the fact that he found her dead and failed to report it. He may have witnessed somebody run her down, but right now all we have is his word for it that the car hit her on purpose. The stuff about a Mr. P. or Mr. B. and the doc sounds kind of screwy to me."

"What does this mean about reopening the case?" Jessica asked, her irritation with Art Greenwald stirring again. Her gut told her there was more truth to Chet's story than the detective was ready to acknowledge.

"I've already said that we'll go back through everything again. I'm taking his story on face value for the moment. But there's no way this will go anywhere unless we have more to go on. Who are we going to charge? Some mystery man with long hair, driving a dark sedan, nearly fifteen years ago, who may have a name that starts with p or b? I don't think the D.A. is going to cut Chester Davis much slack with that kind of info, either. But, what do I know? We're up to our eyeballs in lowlifes, no place to put them all, and as far as lowlifes go, your Mr. Davis is less offensive than some are. Heck, the biggest risk he poses is to himself. It costs a lot less to put the guy back out on the street than it does to put him up in jail for the rest of his miserable life."

"That may be true, but I'd like to see him get another go at treatment if I can get the D.A. to agree. Where there's life, there's hope. I'm sure Jessica would have preferred to have her friend alive, even if she was in bad shape like Chet." Jessica had to agree that was probably true. But the thought of her beautiful childhood friend looking anything like Chester Davis after years of being ravaged by drugs filled her with despair. She was ready to end this.

"You need to go through the file yourself, Jessica. Some of it's hard to take. I'll warn you, the crime scene photos and autopsy report are graphic. If you read through the case file, you can see why the police stopped pursuing the matter when they stalled out. Even though your friend was a lovely young thing, it's not such an unprecedented situation: an addict, who has been on a bender for a few days, is looking for a place to shoot up, gets spooked, and runs out in front of a car. Some drunk hits her and instead of stopping to help or call it in, runs for it. That's a crime, but it's not murder. Chester Davis could well have recognized your friend from bumping into her on one of his previous deliveries. There were track marks on her arms and a loaded hypodermic at the scene with her prints on it. A tox screen said she had a lot of drugs in her system, including heroin. If she had used what was in that needle, she would have turned up dead that night, anyway."

Jessica was aghast. "That can't be true. Kelly hated needles. She fainted at the sight of a needle getting shots at school one year. I don't believe it."

"Come on, you may not like the idea, but have a look for yourself. A drug binge would explain why she was missing in action at work for a couple of days. It's hard to face facts, but when you get to be as old as I am, you realize you just don't always know people the way you think you do. Let's say it was murder and not an accident, you'd still have to admit your friend must have had some nasty secrets if somebody wanted her dead. She wouldn't be the first pretty young girl involved in a dispute about drugs that got her killed."

"Check please!" Jessica hollered to the nearest waiter. She was getting that urge again to put her fork to use in a bad way. "I may not be as old as you, Art, but trust me, I do get it. I agree that you don't always know people, even those closest to you. Kelly Fontana obviously had secrets. I just don't happen to be convinced that she was an IV drug user." She stared directly at him until he looked away; her hand fiddled with that fork. For Kelly's sake, Jessica decided to end on a more conciliatory note.

"I'm glad that you're willing to do more investigating, Detective. I have some resources that I can put to work on that front, too. We'll just try to keep an open mind about all of this for now. It's clear to me, from what you've said, that we have a ton of work to do to convince ourselves, or anyone else, that my friend was murdered. Finding her killer is an even longer shot, but I intend to give it a try."

CHAPTER 13

The walk back to the Sheriff's Department building and to the detention center where she and Dick Tatum parted company was quick. Art and Dick chatted about office politics. Recent problems in the public defender's office had garnered unfortunate attention for the county. Jessica didn't care enough to pay attention to their grousing. Art thanked her for lunch, but had to engage in one last act of aggravation before he left.

"I know I don't have to tell you not to overreach with the investigating you plan to do. Poking around in other people's problems can be harmful to *your* health. That's especially true if we are talking about the type of problems that a long-haired Mr. P. or Mr. B. thought were best solved by murder."

Where's that fork when you really need it? Jessica asked herself. It was like déjà vu listening to another detective warn her about the dangers of snooping into a murder involving a friend. She *was* chastened by her experience with Roger Stone's murder investigation. Jessica had taken her licks for stepping into the middle of that free-for-all. That crime had still been underway, in a manner of speaking, when she got caught up in the maelstrom. But Kelly's murder was old news. What was it about her that irked detectives?

"I promise. I'll be careful. Whatever happened to Kelly happened a long time ago, Detective. Heck, for all we know, the long-haired Mr. P. or Mr. B. is now a balding senior citizen in a Sun City somewhere, driving a golf cart rather than a big pricey sedan. Or he might even be dead. If I learn anything of value, I'll pass it along. I trust you'll do the same and will keep us updated?"

"Sure. Dick is a fixture around here. He knows how to find me, and if he's trying to get information relevant to a client's case, he does not mind being annoying in the least."

He's not the only one, Jessica countered, with her mind, but not her lips. She looked at Dick Tatum, who was grinning at being told how annoying he could be. Okay, so maybe that was just the way it would be. Let them annoy the hell out of her and each other if that's what it took to get justice for Kelly Fontana.

"Whatever it takes to get to the truth, I guess. Thanks for all your help today, Art. I may have some questions after I go through the file. I'll get back to you both, if that's okay?"

"Sure," Art said with a little ambiguous shrug. Jessica bristled at the unintelligible body language, focusing instead on the one syllable response. Her brow was furrowed, though, her lips pursed.

"If you have questions you can call *me* anytime," Dick said, speaking loudly to the detective's back as he walked away. He was still grinning as he continued to speak to Jessica. Maybe he liked it that she and the detective were obviously antagonistic toward each other, a misery-loves-company kind of thing. Or perhaps he was glad not to be the good detective's only target.

"Art's on board. He mostly means well, and he's already paid you a couple compliments. I don't see that happen too often, so you can assume he's impressed. So am I. You're a good friend, Jessica Huntington, and Chester Davis is a lucky client to have you backing him up. A *luckier* client, I should say, since he already had me on his team." He reached out to shake hands.

"It was nice meeting *you*," Jessica said as she shook his hand.

"I'm going to go back on Monday morning and chat up the prosecutor, and sound him out about his willingness to get Chet into drug treatment while we sort this out. A new investigation is going to take some time. It's a shame to have him just cooling his heels in jail when he could be getting help. At least he'll continue to detox while he's locked up. I'll try to make sure they keep an eye on him, so he gets some medical help if he needs it. Maybe we can keep him in the old wing for now. How about we touch base Monday afternoon?"

"Monday, it is. I'll call you late afternoon. Have a nice Fourth of July."

A Dead Sister

She turned, stepped off the curb, and opened the driver side door. "Dick," she called out, causing the rumpled lawyer to pause for a moment, "thanks for giving a damn—about your client and about what happened to Kelly."

He smiled broadly, then turned and waved as he walked away.

Jessica drove the few blocks to the Mission Inn, deep in thought. She parked and rolled her bag across the street and around the corner into the lobby of the historic old hotel complex. A place that started out in the late nineteenth century as a twelve-room adobe boarding house had become an obsession of sorts for Frank Miller, son of the original proprietor, until he died in 1935. The first wing, built in the mission-revival style and opened in 1903, was reminiscent of the Spanish missions located throughout California. Frank Miller added three more wings by 1931, with a rather idiosyncratic strategy for integrating the wings as they were added.

An extensive traveler and compulsive collector with exotic and eclectic taste, he bought things. Lots of things he bought ended up installed in one area or another of the hotel. The place was a favorite of celebrities as diverse as Will Rogers and Paul Newman, but had a near miss with the wrecking ball when it fell on hard times after changing hands several times. It was rescued by being placed on the National Historic Registry, and by the current owners, who reopened it in 1992 after several years of renovation and extensive upgrades. Over the years, the Mission Inn had hosted ten U.S. presidents, including Richard Nixon and his wife Pat, who married there.

Portraits of the presidents who had visited the inn stared down at Jessica from the wall in the Presidential Lounge as she wheeled her bag past them to the check in desk. In no time, she was in her room, even though she had arrived well before the normal three o'clock check-in time. The reservation Frank Fontana made for her was in a stretch of rooms on the third floor called "Author's Row." The name of an author who had stayed at the hotel was written above each door. Her room, the Carrie Jacobs-Bond room, was a welcome sight.

Jessica kicked off her shoes, and stripped out of her dress and Wolford pantyhose. A robe hung in the closet where she stashed her bag and hung up her dress. In less than two minutes, Jessica had thrown herself down onto the comfortable bed, torn between crying and pitching a fit. She punched the pillow, but it was too plush to feel like she had accomplished anything. Instead, she shoved her face into the pillow and screamed. It was more like a growl or groan. At the same time, she kicked her feet like a child.

She couldn't decide who made her more upset. The antagonistic Detective Greenwald was high on the list. Not far behind was the weasel of a drug addict who might be putting them all through this trouble just to get back out on the street. If Chester Davis was telling some version of the truth, a long-haired scumbag was roaming around free as a bird after having mowed her friend down before her life had really begun. Of course, Kelly was on the list, too. She had finally gotten into more trouble than she could get out of on her own. Instead of asking Jessica for help, she'd picked a fight that last night they were together on New Year's Eve. A horrible fight that left Jessica feeling at least as angry with herself as she was with anyone else on her list.

What a nightmare! She needed this like she needed a hole in her head. She should be home right now reviewing the latest material she could find on estate planning. That included refreshing her knowledge of wills, health care proxies, trusts, and a dozen related topics stored away in her brain, all shrouded by cobwebs. Jessica punched the pillow a couple more times.

Jessica rolled on her back and stared at the ceiling in the hotel room. She really was jumping the gun, since the Van der Woerts hadn't officially given her the go-ahead to start working on their behalf. Once she did get the signal to begin, she would need more information about their financial situation and future goals before putting the elements of a plan together. The firm probably used a nifty tool to collect and retain information from clients like the Van der Woerts. She'd ask Paul about that the minute she got the word from him. As Dr. Nicholas Van der Woert the Third was no stranger to the use of health proxies and the like, not just a will, but a lot of other pieces were probably already in place and just needed to be updated. She had some time. Paul probably wouldn't get back to her until early next week. Amy Klein, the office manager could help her locate whatever background information was on file about the Van der Woerts. Paul was waiting in the wings to mentor her, just like Dick Tatum had her back with Chester Davis. It would be fine. It *had* to be fine.

Jessica felt herself calming down as she lay there recovering from the events of the day. The day wasn't over yet. Frank Fontana had left a message confirming that he was meeting her at the Mission Inn for dinner at six. Jessica had agreed to dinner with the understanding that he let her pick up the tab. A single father with two near-teens did not need to be buying *her* dinner. And he had saved her money on her room, getting the manager to give her a great discount.

Jessica had made reservations for dinner at Duane's, a high-end steak house on site at the hotel. It was a place she imagined that Frank would enjoy, but would never indulge in on his own. The cost of their meal would be equivalent to a down payment on the fee for Evie's braces. Tomorrow night, dinner at his house in nearby Perris would be on him, with a little help from his mother.

The restaurant also had a decent wine cellar, and she hoped a glass or two of good wine would soften the blow from the story she had to tell him about Kelly. A drug addict, could that possibly be true? Did Uncle Don know that back in '99 when they found Kelly's body? Had the police told Kelly's parents? What about Tommy, did somebody tell Tommy his sister was an addict? Or would Jessica have to be the one to tell Tommy that his beautiful sister was shooting herself full of drugs before some long-haired maniac ran her down?

Shoot! Shoot! Shoot! The thought of Tommy suddenly reminded her. She had taken Bernadette's advice and invited the Cat Pack to her house Friday night for dinner, but had not called the caterer. It was nearly four o'clock on the Wednesday before the Fourth of July. Why hadn't she called the caterer on Monday? How stupid and thoughtless could she be? She jumped off the bed and flew into action.

"Stupid, stupid, stupid!" Jessica muttered, as she dug out her phone and flipped through her contacts. Her breathing took off, keeping pace with her escalating heart rate. No number for the caterer. She was feeling a little dizzy and was going to need a paper bag to control her breathing any second now. The day's stress had suddenly crystallized around the urgent search for one phone number.

She was struck by how often she handled things this way. Slid over and around the big problems in her life, and then, one small mishap would send her over the edge.

"It's okay, it'll all be okay. We can just eat peanut butter and jelly sandwiches," she said aloud in the empty hotel room. She sat down on the bed and counted out the time between breaths. The exhales were the most important, according to her shrink. It wasn't just the big cleansing breaths that mattered. Fully exhaling expelled a backlog of toxins the human body was designed to get rid of. That is, if she hadn't lost the ability to do the most basic thing properly—breathe! A little giggle escaped as she imagined serving her friends a huge tray of peanut butter and jelly sandwiches with a case of cold beer. Brien would be in heaven. Even the vegan giant, Peter March, would be okay.

Not ten breaths later—a minute more—Jessica remembered the caterer was on her phone under the owner's name. In less than twenty minutes, it was all arranged. They would have a belated Fourth of July celebration on Friday, with a tiki twist, in honor of their recent return from the islands. Complete with grilled satay tempeh skewers, a minted fava bean salad, vegan double chocolate cookies, and pineapple-coconut sorbet, sure to be palatable to vegan and non-vegan alike. Kalua pig for the carnivores among them, along with Hawaiian sweet bread, rice, purple sweet potatoes, and braised cabbage. She smiled as she thought of the ever-hungry Brien feasting until he could no longer move.

Jessica reflected on the buoyancy she felt planning that feast for her friends. It wasn't the food. Well, not just the food. Living well was the best revenge for all the agony life had to offer. An extravaganza, entertaining those nearest and dearest to her, was a tried and true strategy for countering every form of darkness known to humankind.

How could Kelly have so misconstrued Jessica's efforts on that New Year's Eve so long ago? That celebration was classic Jessica Huntington. Her effort to face down the terror of what a new year might hold for her and her friends as fledgling adults. After Kelly's previous attack on Jessica's largesse when they were all still in high school, she and Kelly and Laura had all talked about it.

"I know I spend a lot of money, because I can. It makes me feel better when I'm freaked out about something. And it makes me feel better about myself if I think other people are having a good time because of me."

They had talked about whether she should stop, and concluded, in a fit of hysterics, that if she had to have a problem, it wasn't all that bad. Kelly and Laura both promised to tell her if they felt bad about not being able to keep up. They had cleared the air and Kelly seemed more willing than ever to avail herself of Jessica's inclination to party at the drop of a hat. Once Jessica had wheels, they headed further down the party girl track with Kelly taking the lead in their most outrageous escapades. Clearly, something had been wrong that New Year's Eve—very wrong and Jessica intended to get to the bottom of it.

Energized, Jessica moved into the bathroom, and splashed water on her face. The tiled walkway outside her room beckoned. A clerk at the front desk encouraged her to explore. Overlooking the Spanish patio, there was a clock tower with rotating figures and a glockenspiel, something akin to a carillon, when it worked! From behind her, at check-in, Jessica had heard the squawk of parrots. This was definitely one of the most unusual places she'd ever stayed.

A Dead Sister

There was also an onsite spa that she might have time to use in the morning, if she could bring herself to do it. By some strange twist of fate, it was called "Kelly's Spa," named for the co-owner of the hotel. What she *should* do, now or first thing in the morning, was carefully review the file Art Greenwald had given her. Depending on what all was in that file, she might need a massage or a facial, or more likely a head-to-toe scrub to rid her of the taint.

Jessica pulled on the Max Mara tunic and cropped pants she had purchased on Monday. The deep red gave her skin a rosy glow. She hoped she could conjure up a mood to match that would carry her through dinner. Before she could sink back into wallowing, she refreshed her makeup, ran a comb through her hair, and set out to walk off some nervous energy before it was time to meet Frank for dinner.

CHAPTER 14

At six, Jessica was sitting in the bar area outside Duane's, sipping a glass of chardonnay. When Frank walked in, he was carrying a single red rose, his face brightening when he spotted her. She was touched by the sweet, slightly romantic gesture, but it also made her nervous. Was she going to have the second I-need-a-year talk with a man this week?

"Hey, Cuz," he said, handing her the rose and brushing her cheek with a shy kiss. "You look great!"

"So do you, *Cuz*," Jessica said, trying to match his light tone. He did look great dressed in a dark jacket, with a deep burgundy shirt. A narrow tie, in the same dark color as the jacket, was held in place with a silver tie clip. His trousers were also dark, cut lean. In the scant lighting of the lounge, she couldn't quite tell if he wore a suit or sports jacket and slacks. His Italian heritage was evident, the colors accentuating the near-black of his hair and adding depth to his dark eyes. It felt as though he could read her thoughts. Not all of them, she hoped, as she shifted her eyes abruptly, focusing on the rose he'd handed her.

"Hey, don't sound too surprised. I'm Italian *and* I have a mother, an Irish Catholic one! I'd never hear the end of it if I showed up for dinner with Jessica Huntington looking like a slob. She and Dad are watching the kids tonight. I got inspected by them both before I left the house." He beamed at her, his mother's ironic Irish grin animating his pleasant features.

Jessica laughed and hopped down from the bar stool where she'd been sitting.

"Let's go eat. I'm starving!"

A Dead Sister

"I am too. Steak, I want steak!" He offered his arm as he escorted her the ten feet or so from the bar stool to the door of the restaurant.

"You clean up well *and* you're a gentleman!"

"I told you..."

"Yeah, I know, Italian and you have a mother." She added in her mind, *and you're a good Catholic boy.*

Dinner seemed to fly by, even though the meal was a leisurely one by most standards. The decision about what wine to order provoked a bit of discussion. At Jessica's insistence, they settled on an Italian red that Frank regarded as obscenely expensive. He was quite knowledgeable about wine, but not inclined to gratify his palate often.

"At my house, I drink 'two buck Chuck' a lot of the time and feel lucky to have that!" Frank said, referring to a Trader Joe favorite that many cost-minded Californians swore by. A tradition among aficionados was to go to the local Trader Joe store and buy a bottle. Then they take it out in the parking lot to sample, and if it's decent, go back in and buy a case.

Jessica had tried the wine more than once, since it was an affordable item that turned up at college parties. It was passable, as she recalled. A wave of sad sentimentality hit her, suddenly. She and Jim had once shared such delight, exploring and collecting wines.

When the wine arrived, they toasted the Italian vintage and Frank offered that perhaps he had been too hasty in characterizing the price as obscene. Jessica agreed with him that it was an outstanding wine. "But, I have to confess an almost patriotic allegiance to California reds. I swear, Officer Fontana, that I have more than one bottle at home as good, and at half the price." She raised her right hand as though taking an oath.

"Well, I'm afraid you're going to have to prove it to me, because this wine is amazing!"

"Prove it to yourself. Tommy, Laura, and a few other friends are coming over for dinner. Join us, Friday night, and I'll break out a bottle."

"Now that's an offer too good to refuse. Besides, what choice do I have? It's my sworn duty to serve and protect. Far be it from me to miss a chance to investigate your outrageous claims about a better bottle at half the price." He raised his glass and gave hers a little clink. Jessica gulped the wine in her glass. Seeing each other three nights in a row was likely to put them both to the test in a lot of ways. Would they run out of conversation? A silly question, really, given that they weren't going to be alone Thursday *or* Friday night. Getting a word in edgewise might be the bigger challenge.

Frank was being modest on Sunday when he told Jessica he could take care of himself and his kids in the kitchen. He was well-versed on the subject of cuisine. He had worked his way through college cooking in hotel kitchens and even considered a career as a chef rather than a cop, for about five minutes. The working conditions were about as bad, although you didn't have to worry about getting shot. Stabbed maybe, where, in mostly-male kitchens, a favorite insult was to say loudly, "You do that like a housewife!" often punctuated by stabbing the air with an enormous French knife.

Not surprisingly, his favorite dishes were Italian classics with recipes passed down from his grandmother and aunts to him. He had been much more successful at finagling secrets from them than Jessica had been with Bernadette. Tomorrow night, he acknowledged, dinner would be in his mother's hands. Comfort food was her specialty, having grown up in a large Irish family where meals were designed around stretching a dollar. Of course, she had done her best to be the dutiful daughter-in-law, and at least some of what Frank had picked up came from helping out at home when his Italian grandmother and aunts were tutoring his mother. His long-suffering mother had endured a lot at the hands of a well-meaning but overbearing mother-in-law. Both women could be caught crossing themselves and asking for divine intervention, calling on God and a litany of saints to get them through whatever was going on in the kitchen at that moment.

That had *not* been one of the problems Jessica had to face in her marriage. She and her mother-in-law were never close. Jim's parents had retired to Portofino soon after he and Jessica were married. They spent about as much time with them as they did with Jessica's mother and father, Jim's parents being as peripatetic as her own.

"I could probably count on one hand the number of times Jim and I visited his family, and I doubt we visited either of my parents much more often than that." A sigh escaped her lips as she took a sip of wine. Why did that matter, now? Her marriage was over. The profound sense of disconnect she felt at being newly divorced was somehow amplified by the loss of things that might have been.

Frank pulled her back to the present. "Families work in all sorts of ways. There's a price to pay for being part of a big, close-knit family. Mom can

A Dead Sister

tell you more than I can about that, I promise. While we're on the subject, you have to promise to give me a chance to prove what I can do in the kitchen. I'll fix dinner and you bring the wine, deal?"

"Deal," Jessica said, sealing the deal with another little clink of their glasses.

Food and wine was not all they had in common. They hardly spoke at all about family and friends, perhaps unconsciously avoiding the subject that had brought them together for dinner. Instead, they covered a range of other topics as they ate their meals of steaks with grilled asparagus. A twice-baked potato with gorgonzola cheese for him and garlic mashed potatoes for her. Finally, they were sipping decaf cappuccinos and finishing the last bites of a chocolate soufflé. Frank had ordered the soufflé but insisted that Jessica try it. She didn't take much convincing, since the operative word in chocolate soufflé *is* chocolate.

"It's been a fabulous dinner, a real treat. Thanks for picking up the tab."

"My pleasure, it was great to catch up a bit."

"I wish I didn't have to do this, but I would like to hear what you learned from talking to Chester Davis today."

"I wish we could put it off too, but I need to tell you so you can help me figure out what to do next. The first thing I need to do is apologize. I was so freaked out after my lunch with Dick Tatum and Detective Greenwald that I didn't do my homework. He passed along the file from the prior investigation of Kelly's accident, but I haven't looked at it yet. Before I get to your house tomorrow night, I will have gone through it, cover to cover."

"Geez, you don't have to apologize to me. This is all above and beyond, you know? You—we've got to take care of ourselves if we're going to do this. Whatever, '*this,*' turns out to be."

"There's a very good chance that *this* is a murder investigation. Chester Davis isn't all there. His thinking is jumbled at times, and he's a physical wreck from way too many drugs for way too long. He has plenty of reason to make up something that can counter the third strike he's earned, but... I believe he saw Kelly that night. His description of the awful way in which her body was contorted fits with crime scene photos, according to Art Greenwald who *has* reviewed that file. Whether it happened the way Chet says it happened is another matter. Kelly's file might shed some further light on that. If somebody *accidentally* killed Kelly, there should have been skid marks or some indication they tried to stop rather than plowing into her the way Chet describes."

"Does he say anything about who did that to Kelly or why?"

"Yes, Frank, although that's a little vague, too." Jessica paused to sip her decaf coffee. She'd only begun and her throat was already getting that dry, closed off feeling. By the time she'd gone through Chet's entire story once, she was in a funk. The sordid tale did not lose its effect by being retold again.

"Some of this sounds incredible—Mr. P. or B. and a huge guy that Kelly hurt bad enough that two henchmen had to carry him out of the hotel and to the car. How could Kelly have done anything like that to him if she was as messed up as Chet claims? Did you find him believable?"

"We had him go through what happened that night several times, and his story changed very little. A few new details emerged or he left out a couple of things when he told the story again. He was dodgy, at first, about what he was doing there, but soon admitted he was making a drug delivery to hotel guests. What he described each time was Kelly running for her life with two thugs chasing her when a car at a standstill, turned on its headlights and deliberately hit her, almost head on." Jessica paused again, taking a breath this time before going on.

"The impact sent her flying, up into the air. She hit the windshield, then the curb. I couldn't bring myself to look at the photos from the crime scene. Art Greenwald assures me they're pretty awful, and consistent with Chet's description of the incident and what he says it did to Kelly." Jessica gulped, trying not to think about it—about her, the way she must look in those photos. She suddenly felt tired. It had been a long, emotionally draining day and that was reflected in her voice as she continued.

"I'm not sure what to make about the man he says he glimpsed behind the wheel of the car. Kelly was running away, so maybe she hurt that doctor, or whoever he was, and that's how she got as far as the parking lot. She must have been so scared, and must have fought so hard to get the upper hand on a guy like that."

"Not to mention she got past the two guys who followed her out into that parking lot." Frank shook his head, obviously angry and disgusted.

"What gets to me is that she might have escaped except for that psycho waiting in the car to kill her." Jessica couldn't go on. She and Frank just sat for a few minutes in silence.

"He hit her so hard, Frank. Bits and pieces of the car must have been left at the scene. Trace material and fragments left behind might help us identify the specific make or model of the car that hit her. I mean automakers archive that kind of information so owners or body shops can match the paint on cars they repair. Could the fragments still be in evidence somewhere?"

"The log should list what was found at the scene, on or near Kelly's body," Frank said. "If the evidence log isn't in the case file we can get it, I'm sure."

"I think it is. I'm almost certain Art Greenwald mentioned it. I'll let you know for sure when I've gone through that file. Surely, the police ran anything they got against those archives."

"Maybe not. That accident happened fifteen years ago. I'm not sure what technology or databases were available then. Those archives get updated all the time. It's worth a shot to run the check again even if they did do it."

"I'm not sure what we would do with that information, but it's a connection of sorts to the dirt bag who ran her down." Jessica looked up to see Frank staring at her with a quizzical puppy-dog tilt to his head.

"What?"

"Well, I know about paint-matching at auto accident scenes. My dad's a traffic cop and has been for years. How do *you* know that, about paint color archives and the like?"

"You forget I was married to a master of the universe in training. The body shop got threatened with a lawsuit when they mismatched the paint once on his Bimmer after a fender-bender. Besides, you'd be surprised how much discussion there is about the use and disposal of paint and other toxic substances in environmental law, especially for real estate developers aspiring to 'go green.' Matching paint found at dumpsites and other environmental crimes involves forensic work is similar to accident investigation. Only some of the issues that kept me intrigued about environmental law and employed, for a while, anyway. The bottom line, Frank, is that if Kelly was murdered, why?" She made eye contact with him, his dark eyes set in a sad, grim face making it hard to deliver more bad news.

"I've been wondering about that, too. Before you had this story to tell me that Chester Davis saw a man behind the wheel, I thought she might have gotten involved with the wrong guy and a jilted lover was waiting outside the hotel to run her down. Now, I don't know what to make of what you've said as far as a motive."

"At one point, I might have been angry enough to take out Jim or Cassie. There's another horrible aspect to this sad story, though. I find it hard to believe, but Art claims it could be one answer to the question about why she was killed. Did you ever hear that Kelly was using drugs?"

"Drugs, like what kind of drugs? I'd seen her drunk on more than one occasion. In at least a couple of those situations, you were about as looped, I might add, and I wasn't so clear-headed myself. I caught her smoking dope once or twice, too. Are you talking about something else?"

Jessica nodded her head yes. She tried to hide the fact that she was getting choked up, but you could hear it in her voice. "It's another reason I couldn't bring myself to read through that file this afternoon. Art Greenwald claims Kelly was an addict. There were needle marks on her arms when they found her, and a hypodermic near her body had her fingerprints on it, like she was about to shoot up when she was killed. Apparently, it's all there in photos taken at the scene." Jessica looked up at Frank. "Art says heroin. How is that possible? Did your dad ever say anything to you about it during the investigation or later?"

"Not a word, Jessica. Not from Kelly, either. Of course, if she was in that kind of trouble, I don't suppose her cousin, the cop-in-training, would be the person she'd seek out for help. She would have been more likely to come to you with that."

"Not a chance. Remember what I said the other day about how things were between us? Kelly and I weren't getting along those last few months. New Year's Eve, when she got so angry with me, I just got mad back. She was loaded. We all were, even though none of us was old enough to be drinking, legally. That was my fault. I slipped a limo driver some extra bucks to look the other way while Kelly and I stocked the car with champagne that night." She paused to see if Frank was going to object in some way or call her out for doing such a thing.

"Hey, you were nineteen. Lots of college-age kids drink when it's not legal. Another of the many reasons I'm dreading having teenagers of my

A Dead Sister

own. So what are you trying to tell me?"

"She cussed me out and went on a rant about my being a spoiled, snooty, poor little rich girl. You said it yourself that she was hard to figure out. Kelly could be the most endearing person, vulnerable and sentimental, even a little wistful or melancholy at times. Then this wild thing took over. One of the reasons I was drawn to her. Sort of an alter ego to the part of me that was so anxious and shut down, always needing to be in control." Jessica realized she was probably revealing more than she should. This all suddenly felt too intimate; she felt her cheeks growing warm, and she stopped speaking. "I'm sorry this is embarrassing, too personal, and overly critical of my dead friend."

"You are one of the people who knew Kelly best. Maybe you had your own issues with her or your own issues, period. But New Year's Eve was less than two weeks before she was killed. So please, go on."

"Well, things started out fine. She seemed happy to see me and cheery enough as we loaded the limo with our contraband for the night. Everything went well until we were on our way home. Then, the Jekyll-Hyde switch got flipped. She was really drunk by then, so maybe that did it. Kelly, the fiend, suddenly went at it. That Kelly had a mean streak. She called it 'mischief,' I called it 'mean girl.' That night 'mean drunk' was more like it. I don't know, but when she went off on me, it hurt. I had the limo driver take her home and I just put her out, practically on the curb. Now I wonder if acting out like that, shoving me away that night was tied to the fact that she was in trouble."

"Did she say anything that night that made you think she was in trouble, more trouble than usual?"

"Most of her rant was about money and how hard she had to work to get it, unlike me. How I like throwing money around, making people feel bad about how much more money I have than they do." Jessica stopped, her cheeks growing warm again from a mix of anger and embarrassment.

"We both know that's not true. You do know how to spend money; I can vouch for that! You're like your dad, though. You know, down-to-earth, a solid-citizen who happens to have a ton of money. Hank would have kicked your butt if you even thought about becoming one of those 90210 brats."

"Thanks, that's kind of you. I've gone over and over that conversation on New Year's Eve. It was so long ago, but Kelly might have said something relevant. What I thought she said, at the time, was something nasty about how much I looked down on her because of what she did to make a living. I assumed she was talking about working at the spa and casino. Now I'm pretty sure what she said was more like 'If you knew what I have to do to make a living, you'd look down on me.' What if she *was* doing something illegal, Frank?"

"Like using drugs or selling them?"

"She was loopy that night, maybe loopier than booze alone could account for. Yeah, so maybe she was using. But that 'making a living' part sounds like it's more than *using* drugs. Working at the casino, she could have been involved in some gambling-related scam, I guess, like skimming. Or maybe she was stealing credit card information. The possibilities are endless! Screwing up an operation like that could have gotten her killed." Jessica stopped to collect her thoughts.

"Art's convinced it's about drugs. It's not just the photos of track marks on her arms or that hypodermic found at the scene. The tox screen produced evidence of drug use. On New Year's Eve, she looked so gorgeous. She had on this strapless party dress. It was a short, slinky thing that didn't cover much and there wasn't a needle mark anywhere on her. As I told Art, who happens to be a bit of an ass, by the way, Kelly hated needles. She got woozy, even passed out once, waiting in line for shots at school! How could she have been an addict—a dead one at that— not even two weeks later?"

"None of this makes much sense at this point. I don't know what to make of her comment about what she was doing to make a living. If Kelly was involved with drugs, it might explain how she got tangled up with the men Chester Davis saw chasing her that night. It's not hard to imagine guys like that running her down with a pricey sedan, either, if she got on their bad side." He grew quiet, thinking, while also studying Jessica's face. Eventually, he just shook his head.

"I don't understand this any better than you do. I'm sorry Art upset you. A bit of an ass is about right. He's a Larry David kind of guy, not always so good socially."

"If that's the appropriate comparison, it's way more than being socially awkward. Larry David calls himself a social assassin! That's all I need. I already have an ex-husband cavorting in public places with this floozy who's out to win a skank of the year award or something like that."

A Dead Sister

"I saw that!" The look on Frank's face was half amusement, half disgust.

"You saw it, too? Where?" Jessica knew the answer before he gave it to her.

"It was on one of the entertainment news shows. Isn't that what you're talking about? They ran video last night of her pulverizing some photographer's camera while the esteemed member of the paparazzi looked on in horror. The TV crew does this close-up of the reporter's face that's all scratched up and bleeding. He's bellowing that she's not going to get away with this! It's a free country, blah, blah, blah. Then they switch the camera around and there's your ex, trying to hold back this woman who's coming apart at the seams, literally. She's a few shreds of cloth away from a major wardrobe malfunction. Acting like a wild cat, elbowing Jim, stamping her feet, and screaming. The censors bleeped most of her shrieking. I almost felt sorry for Jim. Sometimes, you do get what you have coming to you." He broke into a rueful smile.

Jessica hung her head, shaking it back and forth. "Well, as fate or the shopping gods would have it, I was there. I had just walked out of Max Mara's when the she-beast appeared, claws at the ready." Frank was flabbergasted as she told him what had gone on before she got out of there and that TV crew arrived. That included the moment when Jim spotted Jessica witnessing the row. Frank went from disbelief about the timing of the event to out-and-out laughter about the tangle of blonds, shopping bags, and that poor poodle.

"I am so sorry. When I told you the first year of a divorce is the worst, I didn't imagine having to include embarrassing encounters brought to you by your ex and the other woman." Before she could stop herself, Jessica blurted out that she'd seen worse.

"Oh, you have no idea. This was more public, but not nearly as mortifying as my previous encounter with Jim and that bimbo at home, in my own bed."

"Are you kidding? You caught them?"

Jessica nodded yes, her eyes downcast. No way could she look at him—maybe not ever again.

"You may not believe this. The same thing happened to me." Jessica's head snapped up. She scrutinized him, putting her truth-o-meter to work.

"You walked in on Mary and some guy, at your house, in your bed?"

"I've never told anyone this before. Not my kids, not my mom, nobody. Yes, I walked in on them in our house. Not in bed, but that's where they would have been a minute or two later."

"No, that is so awful. I'm so sorry." She reached across the table to pat his hands, which were clenched in front of him.

"I knew we were in trouble, that she was struggling as a wife and mother, but I had no clue there was someone else. It wasn't a guy." He broke off for a moment, then, continued. "You know the worst part?" Jessica, realizing her hand was still touching his, let go, pulled her hand back to her lap, and shook her head, no.

"The other woman *wasn't* a skank or a bimbo. She was a colleague, someone I considered a friend. Until that moment, I thought the problems we were having in our marriage had a lot to do with my being a cop. Turns out not only was she fooling around, but with another cop!"

"She's a lesbian. It wasn't about your being a cop." She reached out and patted his hand again. "It wasn't anything about you at all. I know you felt betrayed, though, and that had to be hurtful. It had to be doubly hurtful since your friend betrayed you too. How did you get past that?"

"I didn't. I haven't. Just because the first year was the worst doesn't mean it's the last year you spend trying to figure out what the hell went wrong. That first year, I blamed myself. I honestly was so ignorant about the gay thing. I thought I had done something to push her in that direction. You know, turned her off to men? Mary confronted me about that. She took responsibility for the fact that *she* was confused about her sexual orientation, and that it had nothing to do with me. Why didn't she tell me that sooner? The lies and the sneaking around that went on right under my nose still hurts. I don't understand how she figured that was okay. I don't know if I ever will."

"Well, one of the more disagreeable things Art Greenwald said to me today had to do with the fact that someday, when I get older, I would realize you don't always know people the way you think you do. He was talking about Kelly, of course. I could have decked him, since I am dealing with *exactly that issue* as I continue to discover that the man of my dreams is an astonishing dirt bag. Your wife's confusion about her sexual orientation was not an excuse to betray you, Frank. That's on her, not you. That coworker you considered a friend doesn't get off the hook, either. I'm so sorry."

A Dead Sister

"I know. Thanks."

"This is so weird. Laura and I had almost the same conversation when she was wondering how she could have married a man in the sort of trouble that got *him* murdered. Here we are dealing with the same thing again. Not just with our cheating spouses, but with Kelly. Do you ever really know anyone? Is it even worth it to get out there and try?"

"You have to risk it or nobody would ever get married or have kids. That doesn't mean it's easy. Betrayal changes you. Divorce changes you. I'm not the happy family man with a beautiful wife and a couple great kids that I imagined I was. It's more than the fact that I check a different box when I file my taxes or fill out a form somewhere. I'm rewriting the story in my head about my life and who *I* am."

"And have you done *that?*"

"I'm working on it! By the time I get my head wrapped around the idea that I'm this single dad, juggling work and parenting, the kids will be grown. They'll walk out that door and I'll have to figure it all out again. I'd like to believe I won't still be alone when they leave, but who knows? Right now, there's not much time or energy left at the end of the day or the week, so I'm talking big when say it's good to keep trying."

"You *are* trying and I get how much courage and effort that takes. I hope I can do the same."

"You just need more time. What this conversation makes clear is that we need to keep an open mind about Kelly. Art Greenwald is correct, whether we like it or not, you don't always know people the way you think you do. It seems impossible to believe Kelly was a drug addict, but she was in serious trouble. Who knows, maybe it was drugs."

"Okay, I hear you. Here's the last thing I need you to consider. I want to put Jerry Reynolds to work digging into Kelly's past. You met him a couple times. You know, the P.I. who helped me with the investigation when Roger was killed? He's attached to Paul Worthington's firm in LA. I guess it's sort of my firm now too, since I've officially signed an agreement to affiliate with their Palm Desert office."

"Congratulations! You're taking on a lot, though: divorce, a new job, Chester Davis as a client, and reopening the investigation into Kelly's death."

"I know, it seems like a lot to me, too. The agreement I signed makes me an associate at the law firm on a contingent basis. The salary we negotiated for the interim isn't chump change, it's a good deal for them, and I'm grateful to have a place to hang my hat. A hat that's been in mothballs for several years, I should add. Paul Worthington has offered to provide mentoring. There will be lots of folks scrutinizing what I do before anybody signs off on anything. That kind of support is not easy to come by for junior associates these days. So, mostly, I'm not alone in any of this, except maybe the divorce part."

"You're not alone there either. Consider me your post-divorce tour guide, mentor, whatever you prefer to call it. There were times I was sure I wasn't going to make it that first year. More than once, I thought about just dropping the kids off on Mary's door step and making a run for it."

"I *did* run away. That's how I ended up in Rancho Mirage at Mom's house. At least I don't have two kids depending on me to stay sane!"

"Yeah, and the whole time they're nudging you closer to the edge. Look, what is it you wanted to ask me about Jerry Reynolds?"

"I already talked to Paul Worthington about using Jerry's services once he's back in town from his vacation in Hawaii with Tommy. When he and Tommy come to the house on Friday, I'd like to take Jerry aside and bring him up to speed, deploy him as fast as I can. The dilemma, of course, is what to do about Tommy. It's not a good idea, and maybe not even possible, to keep Tommy in the dark for long. What should we do?"

"That *is* a little tricky. It puts Jerry in a tough spot to hide things from Tommy. That doesn't sound so good, especially after talking about how painful it is to find out someone you trust isn't being open. If we tell Tommy, we sort of pass that burden along to him, because we're not ready to go to his parents with any of this."

"Not yet. We should give it another few days at least. Maybe see what Dick Tatum can work out with the D.A. If Art and his team start back to work on this in earnest, they'll have to go back to Sammy and Monica at some point and ask questions again. I'd rather they hear what's coming from you or your dad. I don't know. Maybe we can figure this out tomorrow night."

"Good plan. Let's sleep on it. Things may be clearer to one or both of us in the morning, who knows?"

"Yeah, I'll know more once I've gone through the old case file. Probably

A Dead Sister

more than I want to know..." Jessica said, letting her voice trail off as she signed for their dinner, charging it to her room. They headed out of the restaurant together, and paused before parting ways.

"Thanks again for dinner, and for the conversation. I'm so glad I'm not dealing with these new revelations about Kelly on my own."

"As tough as all of this is, I'd rather know the truth than live a deluded life."

"Me too, that's something else we have in common. Good night." With that, he swept Jessica into his arms for an embrace that left her lightheaded. She didn't make any move to break free, relishing the warmth and comfort of human contact. Surely, there was nothing magic about a year.

CHAPTER 15

The contradictions in Jessica's life hit her right between the eyes as she pulled on a swimsuit for a morning workout in the pool downstairs. Surrounded by luxury and comfort, she was engulfed by pleasant thoughts about dinner the night before with Frank. Nevertheless, she fought to stave off anxiety and dread. Those feelings whined and nipped, begging for her attention like a puppy shut up alone in a room.

"Not yet. I need coffee and a swim first," she muttered to herself, as she donned a robe and flip-flops and padded down the stairs, opting to skip the elevator. When she hit the lobby, she could smell coffee coming from the Mission Inn restaurant. A quick conversation got her a cup of coffee to go, with a shot of espresso added to mimic the extra oomph she extracted from coffee beans with her press pot at home.

The pool was nearly empty at this hour. Heated, it was warmer than her dad's pool in Brentwood. She quickly established a smooth rhythm, propelling through laps as she visualized the day ahead. A to-do list formed in her mind, growing longer with each lap.

She needed to check her voicemail and email to see if Paul Worthington had heard anything from the Van der Woerts. She was conflicted about news from him. If they said no, or even had reservations, it would be a setback. On the other hand, if they said yes, she was going to have to ramp up her efforts on their behalf, and soon. So, the good news is you have a client and the bad news is you have a client. Not having them as clients would definitely be worse. She and Paul hadn't talked about what that might mean for her new job, but it couldn't be good.

A Dead Sister

She also needed to run the address Frank had given her, mapping her route to his house to arrive on time for the family picnic. Under the circumstances, dinner with Uncle Don and Aunt Evelyn was another source of anxiety rippling through her. Should she bring something? She hadn't even thought to ask. It was Frank's fault for getting her all shaken up with that hug. There was a cupcake store on the hotel premises. All she needed was more cupcakes, but they might go over well with the kids. A bottle of wine would be good, too, if someplace nearby carried something decent. She tried to remember what Uncle Don and Aunt Evelyn liked to drink, with no luck.

The biggest task that loomed was reviewing Kelly's file. She had promised Frank she'd go through it. Staying on top of the investigation about to get underway meant organizing a file, starting with a list of individuals to locate and interview. Who knew what that would entail now that so many years had elapsed since Kelly's death?

The swim did what it was supposed to do, both relaxed and energized Jessica to face the day. She had planned to have breakfast in her room, ordering from room service so it could be prepared while she showered and dressed. But the clanking of dishes and the chatter of voices called to her from the restaurant. She preferred to be around people this morning. Poring over Kelly's police file in her room didn't sit well. Breakfast with happy, normal people won out over the prospect of facing the havoc wrought by her childhood friend's encounter with a long-haired misanthrope and his minions alone.

In a short time, Jessica was sitting on the beautiful patio at the Mission Inn restaurant, with breakfast selections from their wellness menu in front of her. More coffee, an egg white omelet with mushrooms, and other veggies, accompanied by fresh fruit set her on the right track. It was a virtuous breakfast following a decent workout. The waiter also spoke to the manager who arranged for a box of cupcakes and a couple bottles of good wine to be sent to her room. She would not show up at Frank's house empty-handed.

Waiting for her breakfast to arrive, Jessica checked, but there was nothing from Paul. It was a holiday after all. Even Paul Worthington and his firm might let things coast a little for the Fourth of July. The Van der Woerts were thoughtful people who weren't likely to make judgments about important decisions rashly. Still, they were the ones who had been urging Paul's firm to get things moving. Maybe things hadn't gone so well after all. What had she done wrong? Had she said something to put them off? "Stop!" She commanded her hyper-vigilant mind, scanning the environment for something to justify the dread that hovered.

Jessica soon had plenty of reason to be more than a little anxious. The photos from the crime scene were shocking. She fled the confines of the restaurant where the aroma of food made it impossible for her roiling stomach to settle down. What had she been thinking, taking such horrific images into a public place where some poor unsuspecting passerby might have glimpsed them? Up a flight of stairs, Jessica found an outdoor patio area with an elaborate fountain that made pleasant gurgling sounds. She sought courage in the blue skies above her and the delicate floral beauty of the small plaza in which she sat. So much for being around people, the babble of the water would have to soothe her as she pushed on through the carnage documented in Kelly's file.

The way Kelly's body was found, Jessica was more certain than ever that Chester Davis had witnessed her death. The horrific photos made her more determined than ever to find who had done such a thing, accident or murder. Someone *had* hit Kelly hard enough to throw her clear of the car, causing her to land with sufficient force to snap her neck, twisting her head in a grotesque way.

Kelly Fontana had been dead about eight hours when her body was discovered around six a.m. on Monday morning, January 11, 1999. That too fit what Chester Davis said he witnessed the night before about the timing of Kelly's desperate dash into the hotel parking lot. According to the coroner, as Art had told Jessica, Kelly's death would have been immediate. Still, Jessica was enraged by the succinct conclusion. Immediate! What about the moments of terror before she was killed by that snap of her neck? And where had she been for days? What had she gone through before making that frantic escape? Kelly had been running for her life. Those who chased her would pay along with the guy who had hit her.

The coroner noted contusions and abrasions on the lower left side of Kelly's body. The bones in her left leg and her pelvis were broken in several places, indicating she had been facing the car when it hit her, also horribly consistent with the story Chet Davis told. Although Chet said she moved to get out of the way, the driver still managed to slam into her. There was a blow to her forehead consistent with those sustained when a pedestrian hits the hood or windshield of a car before being thrown clear.

The photos of Kelly at the crime scene also left no doubt about the fact that Kelly had needle marks on her arms. There was no way to tell how old they were from the photos, and nothing was said about that in the coroner's report. Jessica didn't know enough about IV drug use to recognize scarring

A Dead Sister

if it was there. Mostly, it just looked like a lot of bruising on her arms, although she could see puncture marks too. She closed her eyes and recalled Kelly, as she had been New Year's Eve, before she started drinking that night. Laughing, bright, and beautiful, she had no marks or bruising anywhere on her arms. Of course, addicts chose other sites to hide their use. There was nothing in the coroner's report regarding needle marks elsewhere on Kelly's body. Surely, they would have checked. Jessica made a note to ask.

She could see how Art concluded that Kelly, party girl and addict, had been on one hell of a bender during the last days of her life. Without Chester Davis coming forward to cry foul play, it would have been hard to make a case that her death was more than a tragic accident. The autopsy report and toxicology screen told the same story. Kelly, the addict, had taken a lot of drugs in the days leading up to her death. Both heroin and fentanyl were found in her system along with THC and benzodiazepine, as well as traces of two substances Jessica had not heard of before: lamotrigine and risperidone. The last item on the list gave Jessica a jolt. Chloral hydrate. She *had* heard of that before.

It was the key ingredient in the infamous Mickey Finn, as in "being slipped a Mickey." Like that scene in the Maltese Falcon where Joel Cairo knocks private eye, Philip Marlowe, on his ass by giving him a drink laced with the stuff. Chicago saloon owner, Mickey Finn, who spiked patrons' drinks before robbing and dumping them outside his establishment, supposedly, invented the technique. Even the inimitable James Bond was a victim of such a ploy, his beloved vodka adulterated by the stuff. In her head, she could hear Sean Connery uttering the words "choral hydrate," as he passed out.

Bernadette, of all people, had recently brought up the subject of chloral hydrate. They were talking about Jim and the skank he was running around with, who was regarded by some in Hollywood as a rising star. Jessica had made a snide comment about the woman having about as much talent as Anna Nicole Smith with "most of it residing in her double-Ds."

"Don't speak ill of the dead. It's disrespectful." Bernadette had said.

"I don't mean to be disrespectful to the dead. I'm trying to disrespect the living. Anna Nicole Smith wasn't exactly a pillar of the community, I might add."

"Dios mio, Jessica," Bernadette said, crossing herself. "The poor woman died in a terrible accident. Let her rest in peace. Too much prescriptions and chloroform to help her sleep. You oughta be blaming the doctors who gave it to her."

"The doctors didn't give her chloroform, Bernadette. What are you talking about?"

"I read it in one of these magazines. They were talking about it again after Michael Jackson died."

"That wasn't chloroform, either. Propofol killed Michael Jackson..." Jessica was about to give up hope that she could sort this out. What was she doing arguing about something Bernadette found in a tabloid anyway?

"Here it is, right here. 'High amounts of chloral hydrate metabolites were found in her system.'"

"Okay, so did you mean to say chloral hydrate not chloroform?"

"Yeah, one of those chloro or chlora-somethings." Bernadette was getting annoyed and held out the magazine. "Why don't you read it for yourself?"

Jessica had glanced at the article in the magazine Bernadette held out for her. Sure enough, Anna Nicole Smith had been taking chloral hydrate to help her sleep. At the time, it was just one more on a long list of ingredients in a drug cocktail that killed the buxom blond. Who knew the drug was still being used as a sleep aid? Jessica hadn't really cared, until now.

Why would Kelly have that drug in her system? Could it have been prescribed as a sleep aid or used to knock her out? Why not Halcion or Ambien if she had needed something to help her sleep? Weren't they available by the end of the '90s? Of course, that begged the question about why Anna Nicole Smith was using it as a sleep aid when she could get anything she wanted. Jessica put it on the list of questions she was forming, this one for Laura, along with questions about all the other substances found in Kelly's system. That meant getting Laura in on what was going on, saddling her with more bad news about someone with whom she had been close. Someone close who turned up murdered, like Laura's dead husband.

Jessica gulped as she came upon the traffic collision report. Uncle Don's signature jumped out at her. He and other investigators at the scene asserted that there were no skid marks. No indication that the driver of the car had tried to stop or swerve to avoid hitting Kelly. The report also concluded that there were no apparent hazards or obstacles in the area that would have prevented a driver from seeing a pedestrian in time to stop.

A Dead Sister

Don Fontana had even gone back to the area to check on the lighting at the presumed time of death, somewhere between eight and midnight. He concluded there was adequate lighting in the area for a driver, under normal circumstances, to have seen a pedestrian.

As Jessica had presumed, paint chips were found on the ground nearby, along with fragments of chrome and glass from a headlamp. The chrome and glass shards provided no helpful information, but a paint data query run on the paint bits revealed the car that hit Kelly was a midnight blue, 1999 S class Mercedes sedan. That certainly fit Chet's notion that the car that hit her was a big, new, four-door sedan. The accident report also suggested the car was travelling at about thirty-five to forty miles per hour when it collided with "the pedestrian." That fact set Jessica's teeth on edge. It was hard to imagine a car going that fast in a parking lot, unless, as Chet claimed, the driver was intentionally trying to run someone down.

The small amount of paint collected from Kelly's clothes and wounds matched those found at what investigators determined to be the point of impact. Kelly's case file also contained information about other evidence retrieved at the scene, including that hypodermic found near her body. It had her fingerprints all over it, but also contained a partial print from an unknown person. The investigators ran the print through the Automated Fingerprint Identification System—AFIS—but produced no match.

The hypodermic was loaded with both heroin and fentanyl. Jessica paused long enough to look up information about fentanyl online. Used in operating rooms as an anesthetic, some addicts also used it to augment the high from heroin. It was, apparently, a dangerous mix. If Jessica decided to pull Laura in on the latest episode of murder and mayhem, she would ask about that, too, when she saw her on Friday. As a surgical nurse, Laura would certainly be familiar with the substance. Maybe both the on and "off label" uses for it.

A note in Kelly's file suggested the contents of that hypodermic, if injected, would most likely have resulted in death. Begrudgingly, Jessica acknowledged Art Greenwald was correct in asserting that Kelly might have ended up dead that night even if she hadn't been run down. True, only if she was an addict on the run, planning to inject the contents of that hypodermic. That was still an impossible scenario for Jessica to accept.

Investigators had visited Kelly's apartment, and found a small amount of marijuana, a few bottles of beer, some wine, and liquor. In her medicine cabinet, they identified ordinary OTC items, but none of the prescription drugs found in her system. Nor was there anything in the report about finding a sleep aid, no chloral hydrate, or anything else like that. There was no mention of barbiturates, heroin, fentanyl, or any illicit drugs other than the marijuana, and nothing in the report about needles or other drug paraphernalia in her apartment. "Odd for a flaming addict," Jessica muttered, resisting the urge to hurl the file and its contents into the fountain.

Jessica looked through the list of Kelly's personal effects logged in by the police. Nothing out of the ordinary there either: a large handbag, hairbrush, keys, lipstick, tissues, hand cream, gum, a wallet containing her driver's license, employee I.D., grocery store club cards, a library card, a few dollars cash, coins, and a couple casino chips retrieved from the bottom of the purse.

Where was her cell phone? She had one; Jessica was sure about that. She'd called Kelly to coordinate events on New Year's Eve. Perhaps she'd left it at home. Jessica checked again, but found no record of a cell phone anywhere in the investigators' notes about evidence collected at her apartment. She presumed the police would have checked calls to or from Kelly during the last week or so of her life, even if they hadn't found a phone. Jessica noted yet another question for Art Greenwald when she called him on Monday.

Police investigators had made the rounds, interviewing a lot of people about what went on that night. In addition to Kelly's supervisor at the spa, Bridget Potter, police interviewed those on duty at the front desk, a night manager, the supervisor of hotel security, the hotel food and beverage manager, and supervisors at the restaurants and bars in the hotel and casino where Kelly sometimes worked. Kelly had taken her regular days off from the spa Wednesday and Thursday. As Jessica already knew, that included Thursday night, New Year's Eve. She'd been penciled in on schedules for Friday, Saturday, and Sunday nights in different locations at the casino. She'd picked up extra shifts each evening in addition to working her usual shift at the spa.

Bridget Potter said she regarded Kelly as a good worker, and had last seen her on Monday, January 4th. She hadn't noticed anything unusual about Kelly that day. The next day, Tuesday, Kelly had called in sick. Since Wednesday and Thursday were Kelly's usual days off, it wasn't until Friday that Ms. Potter had any reason for concern. It was out of character for Kelly to miss work, especially without calling as she'd done on Tuesday. But Ms. Potter concluded that she was, after all, only nineteen, and a lot of her counterparts had lapses like that. By Sunday, she became concerned enough that she placed a call to Kelly but was unable to reach her. Jessica made

A Dead Sister

another note: "What number did B. Potter use to call Kelly on Sunday, January 10th?"

The police spoke to several of Kelly's co-workers, including a couple of spa attendants, as well as several servers in the bars and restaurants who wore the same outfit Kelly was wearing at the time of her death. None of them had seen Kelly that night or any night that week. She was someone they called on to fill in or trade shifts if they were sick or had an emergency of some kind, but none of them had tried to track her down that week. They generally regarded her as friendly and outgoing, but didn't know her well. No one seemed to have an unkind word about Kelly. Well, almost no one.

The police identified Robert Simmons as Kelly's boyfriend. He was also a co-worker at the time, a dealer in the casino. An interview revealed that he had last seen Kelly on the first Monday of the new year. He admitted they weren't getting along. She had "ditched him" on New Year's Eve to party with her "snooty friends," and had gone to work on Friday as usual. He complained that she had "ditched him" all weekend, in fact. She had picked up evening shifts, on Saturday and Sunday, in addition to her daytime shifts at the spa. On Monday when she was about to do the same thing again, he grew angry.

According to the boyfriend, some guy, a "whale," as he referred to him, gave Kelly a big tip at the spa that day. "The whale says he's going to have dinner that night at the hotel casino so there's another hundred-dollar tip in it for her, maybe more, if she shows up to work that night." The same thing had happened on Saturday *and* Sunday, and Bobby, as he called himself, was more and more upset about it. Monday, when Kelly came home just long enough to change from the spa attendant outfit to the garb worn by servers, he was waiting at her apartment to confront her face-to-face. That led to a shouting match and she stormed out, leaving him alone in her apartment.

Bobby Simmons claimed that was the last time he saw or spoke to her. When she didn't call or answer his calls, he figured she was still mad and needed time to cool off. When the officers conducting the interview asked if he had looked for her at work, he said "No way! I wasn't that hard up." Besides, when she was angry, he never knew what she was going to do, and he didn't want to run the risk of getting into it with her on the job. "She might've accused me of stalking her or something. Kelly Fontana was trouble when she was mad at you. I didn't want that kind of trouble on the job, or in my life."

Something was still nagging at Jessica. It wasn't just the missing cell

149

phone, even though she still wondered where that had gone. Why didn't she have it on her, in her purse or a pocket of her clothes? Jessica went back to take another look at those awful photos.

Kelly was sprawled on the ground. Her purse, and its contents, lay nearby, along with that hypodermic. Then it struck her. Kelly was wearing a soiled white shirt, a short skirt, and black tights, but no vest. According to the boyfriend, Kelly had been dressed for work in the restaurants or casino. Jessica went back over the evidence log carefully, and there was nothing about a vest or that cell phone. Another question to ask of someone involved in that investigation. As much as she disliked the idea, it was increasingly clear they were going to have to talk to Uncle Don.

The first thing Jessica did, once she had been through the file, was to create a timeline from all the reports she read. Her boyfriend last saw Kelly on Monday evening, January 4th, around six when he says she headed back to work. The last anyone had any contact with her was Tuesday morning, January 5th, when she called her supervisor at the spa to say she was too ill to work. Her body was found early Monday morning, January 11th. That left several days in which Kelly's whereabouts were unaccounted for. Had she spent that time partying her brains out somewhere, loading her body with drugs? If so, where? Had she been at the hotel all that time, or had she shown up there that night before the two men chased her from it? Had the two men chasing her been trying to deliver her to the man waiting behind the wheel of the midnight blue Mercedes sedan that killed her? Where were the cell phone and vest?

Jessica created a spreadsheet to collect the burgeoning number of questions. She also began entering the names and positions held by each of the individuals the police had interviewed. She wanted to speak to all of them, to hear from each what they remembered about Kelly. Of course, that presumed she could locate them. What were the odds that any of the hotel, casino, or restaurant staff would still be working in the same place more than a decade later? Turnover rates in hospitality and food service were notoriously high. Some of them might still be around, or might be found working at the newer "sister" casino opened just off I-10 in Rancho Mirage. Even if they had moved on, Jerry Reynolds, with his investigative skills might be able to track them down. Perhaps they could get a last known address from the police or someone in human resources.

By the time Jessica had finished, more than thirty names were on the list. The challenge now was figuring out where to start. The list of tasks was mounting. Mustering the courage to get back into the business of sleuthing, after the trouncing she had taken poking around into Roger Stone's death,

A Dead Sister

was no small matter. It felt a little like that upward climb on a roller coaster, with no hint about the twists or turns to come on the wild ride to follow.

CHAPTER 16

Jessica drove slowly and carefully to Frank's house. Anticipation increased as she got closer. Most of that anticipation was tied to the things she'd discovered in Kelly's file that she had to share with Frank. Some of it was the idea of sharing anything with Frank. Even more disconcerting yet was doing it under the canny watchful eyes of Don and Evelyn Fontana. They were sure to figure out that Jessica and Frank's liaison was a ruse, or was it?

Driving from downtown Riverside to Frank's neighborhood in Perris took just over twenty minutes, even with the commuter traffic at that time of day. Jessica pulled up at the curb in front of the home in which Frank and his family lived. It was one of the thousands of new homes built in the last decade throughout the inland empire. The California bungalow had a large porch supported by thick square columns, a sloping roof, and light brown stucco siding, trimmed in white to match the columns.

As Jessica headed up the walkway, the front door swung open. Frank invited her into the foyer, with a den on the left and a dining room on the right. Taking the box of cupcakes, and the bottles of wine she'd brought as gifts, he had Jessica follow him through the dining room into the kitchen where Evelyn was hard at work. Delicious aromas wafted toward her as Evelyn bustled around. She planted a welcoming kiss on Jessica's cheek.

"It is so wonderful to see you, Jessica." Jessica admired the vivacious woman, obviously in her element, as she moved around the roomy kitchen.

"It was kind of you to include me in your family celebration, Aunt Evelyn."

"My goodness, Jessica, there's no need to be so formal. You've been a

A Dead Sister

member of our family for a long time. I'm just sorry we haven't had a chance to invite you over sooner. That sad situation with Roger sort of caught us all off guard. None of us felt much like celebrating, or we would have had you over for a visit in the desert before now. We know what you did for Roger and Laura, Jessica. We're so glad you're okay after all you went through." She gave Jessica a big hug, whispering, "And we're sorry about that jackass you married. At least he's out of your life, and making a public spectacle of himself, too."

"Oh, ick, ick, ick! You saw that too, Aunt Evelyn?"

"According to little Frankie, it's gone viral, Jessica, whatever that means. Those entertainment news shows run it endlessly. There's a point where she elbows Jim pretty good while he's trying to hold her back. The look on his face says it all." She laughed impishly as she went back to preparing their feast. Frank had gone outside to the backyard where Uncle Don was busy with the barbeque grill, and the kids were swimming in the backyard pool.

"Jessica, why don't you take this plate of cheese slices out to Don, to put on the burgers? I'm sure Frank wants to introduce you to the kids, although you already met them at our house at some point. If you brought a suit, you're welcome to go for a swim yourself, although it will have to be a short one. Don will be growling about starving to death if he's not stuffing his face in a half hour or so."

"I have met Frank's kids, but it was years ago. I'm sure they don't remember me. A swim sounds wonderful, but I used the pool this morning at the hotel, so I'm probably already at my limit when it comes to sun and water for one day. Is there anything I can do in here to help you?"

"Not right now. When Don flips the burgers, you can come in and get the buns so he can toast them. Say, you should get something to drink. Grab a can of beer or pour yourself a glass of wine, if you want. Or we could open one of the bottles you brought. We have soft drinks in the fridge, too, if you'd rather have something without alcohol. That Frank! He should have offered you something before he ran out the back door. You know what, Jessica?"

"No. What?" Jessica asked, as she poured a glass of white wine from a bottle that was open on the table in the morning room just off the kitchen. Jessica took a sip. Not bad. The bottle contained a chardonnay from a winery nearby in Temecula. The area was trying to make a name for itself among the vastly competitive California wine-growing industry. It was cool and crisp, respectable as she rolled it around her mouth, bracing for whatever Evelyn had to say.

"You make him nervous. He acts sort of shy when he talks about you. He likes you... a lot." Jessica felt her cheeks flush. Evelyn was wearing that devilish smile again as she went back to work, slicing a huge tomato for their burgers.

Uh oh. She knows something's up, Jessica thought as she picked up the plate of cheese slices. "I'll take these to Uncle Don," was all she said as she passed the table laden with good things to eat in the morning room. Californians loved to build their houses with lots of places to eat. Like Jessica's house in the desert, this one had a large wrap-around bar in the kitchen with stools for informal meals as well as the family dining area in the morning room overlooking the backyard. The larger, more formal dining room was big enough to seat twelve for a dinner party. More than twelve if dinner guests were willing to squeeze in around the ample table in the dining room. In addition, there was a place for dining al fresco outside on the patio. That's where a table was now decked out in red, white, and blue, all set up for their burger bash.

When Frank saw her step outside, he glanced at her and smiled, then quickly looked away. Shy was right. Maybe he was feeling as disconcerted as she was about the deception afoot. Then she flashed for a moment on that hug the night before and felt that flush creeping up over her again. *Who was fooling whom?* She wondered.

"Hey, Uncle Don. How's it going? Are you about ready to put cheese on those burgers?"

"Wow, you look great. She looks great, doesn't she, Frank?" Frank nodded. "Get the cheese slices, why don't you?" He was grinning broadly, as he gave Frank a nudge with his elbow. Frank took a step in her direction.

Frank's parents are really enjoying themselves, Jessica thought. She wasn't sure if she should feel amused, irritated, or embarrassed by their reaction to the charade she and Frank were playing. Surely, Frank hadn't said anything to make them believe there was anything *really* going on. They couldn't possibly believe that she, a newly-minted divorcee, was a serious prospect as a partner for their son. Maybe Frank had caved and already filled them in on what they *were* up to, and they were all pulling her leg.

"You do look terrific. Dad's right about that." That shy grin remained on his face as he took her in with an appreciative look. She was dressed simply, in ankle-length skinny black jeans and a silky knit tank top that highlighted the curves she was working so hard to tone. The coppery color made her green eyes pop. She'd taken extra care to style her hair and apply her makeup just so, quite a bit of trouble for a non-date with a non-boyfriend.

"Thanks for the compliments, you two," Jessica said, trying to sound nonchalant. "Uncle Don, you're supposed to make sure I know when you flip the burgers, so I can go back inside and bring out the buns for you to toast."

"I hear and I obey," Uncle Don replied.

"And, Frank, Aunt Evelyn says you should introduce me to the kids." Jessica was suddenly aware that their shrieking had subsided the moment she stepped from the house. Both Frankie and Evie were watching her intently as they bobbed up and down in the pool. Frank handed the plate of cheese slices to his dad, who placed it on the stainless-steel counter built-in next to the grill where the burgers were sizzling away.

"Follow me," Frank said, as he walked across the patio toward the pool. Jessica did as she was told. When they were within a foot or so of the pool, Evie and Frankie swam over to the side.

"Evie, Frankie, I'd like you to meet an old friend of mine. This is Jessica Huntington. We went to high school together."

"Hi, Jessica," the two said nearly in unison. "Did you really go high school with my dad?" Evie inquired, eyeing Jessica with curiosity.

"That's right. I graduated from St. Theresa's in Palm Springs, just like your dad."

"What was he like in high school? Were you a girlfriend, or what? Did you know my mom? Were you rivals, or was she your friend, too?" Evie had let go of the side of the pool and was treading water as she peppered Jessica with questions. Frankie was rolling his eyes, but he didn't swim off. He was clearly waiting to hear what Jessica had to say.

"Well, your dad was a couple years ahead of me in school. He was kind of a big shot." Jessica pulled up a sling-back patio chair and sat down a couple of feet from the pool. She slid the sunglasses that were on top of her head down over her eyes so she could talk to Evie and Frankie without being blinded by the glare from the sun bouncing around on the moving water. Glancing sideways at Frank, she could tell he was uncomfortable. Jessica smiled as she continued.

"I had this huge crush on him, but so did a lot of girls." That got a reaction from Frank, as if he'd been hit with a bolt of electricity. Evie let out a giggle.

"For real?" She asked.

"For real," Jessica answered. "Let's see, what else can I tell you? Your dad was in student government and ended up being elected president of his class in his senior year. He was a good student, too, and quite an athlete, always winning games and tournaments, golf, tennis, and swimming. Because he was older than me, we didn't hang out that much. So, I guess I'd have to say we were friends, but not close friends. That goes for your mom, too. You know what I mean Evie, friends but not bffs?" She nodded her head, weighing what Jessica was saying very carefully as Jessica added, "I used to hang out a lot at your grandparents' house, but by the time that happened, your mom and dad were already a couple. Your mom didn't have any rivals, Evie."

"Yeah, I know my mom and dad fell in love in high school. Then they got married when Dad was in college. And then they had us. They're not in love anymore, Jessica. They're divorced." Frankie rolled his eyes again. He looked like he'd heard about all he cared to hear, and was about to swim off when Evie went on. "But if you weren't close friends with Mom or Dad, how come you were at Grandpa and Grandma's house?"

"Well, your dad's cousin *was* my best friend. Your grandparents and her parents, your Uncle Sammy and Aunt Monica, used to get together for all sorts of things. Like today, you know? Not just holidays, but birthdays and celebrations, graduations, things like that. We always had the best time with pool parties and barbeques and games like volleyball, music, and even dancing sometimes."

"Oh no, you mean Cousin Kelly, don't you? She's dead. Your best friend was killed in a car accident. That must have been hard to take!"

That was it! Frankie dove like a seal under the water. He was almost at the other end of the pool before he came up again for air. Not beyond earshot, however. As she spoke, she could tell that the older Frank was about to bolt, too.

"It was. Still is, Evie. I miss her. She was beautiful, and so much fun to be around. I wish she was here with us today."

"I'm sorry. I guess I shouldn't have brought it up. I understand what it

A Dead Sister

feels like to lose someone you care about. It makes you sad and angry and mixed up all at once." She had rolled onto her back, then flipped over abruptly and came up to Jessica at poolside. "At least that's how I felt when Mom left. Like this horrible accident had happened, and she was just gone. But she wasn't gone, really. And now I might have two moms, if she gets married again. Are you married? Do you have a new best friend now?"

That was the limit to what Frank senior could take. He was about to speak, but Jessica looked up and shook her head slightly, hoping to reassure him while waving him off. Then she bent over a little closer to Evie, as close as she could get without dumping her wine or tipping her chair over.

"Evie, that's a very good question. I did have, his name was Jim. I thought he was my bff, and I married him. Now I'm divorced too, so I'm sort of without a best friend at the moment again. I'm lucky, though. I don't have one *best* friend, but I do have several really good ones. Like Tommy, you know, Kelly's brother?"

"Of course, he's loads of fun." She'd folded her arms on the edge of the pool, resting her chin on her arms, as her legs, stretched out behind her, pumped the water.

"Well, he's a really, really good friend. And there's Laura Stone. She was friends with me and Kelly. She used to go to those parties with us at your grandparents' house too. Your grandparents, we called them Uncle Don and Aunt Evelyn, like Kelly and Tommy did—they're friends, too. Then there's my friend, Bernadette. My mom and dad are divorced, but they're both my good friends, too. Of course, there's your dad. We're good friends now, too."

"So, does that mean you're his girlfriend now, are you like, lovers or something?" Frankie dove under water again, and Frank, who was now at Jessica's elbow, sucked in a big gulp of air. That went down the wrong way and he started to cough. Even Jessica was caught off guard and burst out laughing.

"Evie, you ask the best questions! No, I'm not your dad's lover, but I am a girl and a friend. Not a girlfriend in the way some people mean. Right now, I'm still working through a lot of things that have to do with my divorce. Your dad is helping me since he's faced a lot of the same problems."

"Well, so have I. If you ever need to talk about anything, let me know, okay?"

"Okay. Your dad assures me that after a year or so it gets easier. Is that true?" Evie thought about that for a moment. Suddenly, Frankie popped up alongside his sister and answered for her.

"That's about right." He was sober as a judge. Then he was gone again. Evie nodded in agreement before taking off at breakneck speed, closing the distance on her brother in no time. Frank had stopped coughing but was just standing there with his mouth half open.

She wasn't sure how much Uncle Don had heard from where he was hovering over the grill, but he called out, "Jessica, I flipped the burgers. You want to go get those buns from Evelyn?"

"Sure thing, Uncle Don." Jessica stood up and grabbed Frank's arm as she stepped past him. "They're terrific, Frank. Thanks for the introduction." She gave the still stunned man a little yank, pulling him along after her. "Let's go see what sort of help your mom needs, okay?" He didn't say anything, but trailed after her. One look at Uncle Don told Jessica he'd heard plenty and enjoyed every minute of the episode.

"Uncle Don's ready for those buns now. What else can we do to help?" Jessica asked, as they stepped into the house.

"Not much, really. Frank, you should get those kids out of the pool and let them dry off. You don't want them to drip water all over the gorgeous new wood floors you just installed when they come into the house to fix their plates. It's nice enough to eat outdoors, but so much easier if we just leave the food in here. That way, we don't have to haul in the leftovers later." Frank hadn't said a word, still trying to recover from the poolside question-and-answer session. His mother looked at him quizzically.

"Here, Frank, I'll give you some bait to use to lure them out of the water." She came around from behind the kitchen island and handed Frank a small bowl of chips and a little shove toward the door. "If you crunch those loud enough, they'll probably climb out of that pool on their own." Frank wandered in the direction of the kids, eating chips and making crunching sounds as he was told.

Jessica trailed after Frank to the patio, and took the platter of burger buns to Uncle Don where he stood at the grill. Leaning in, he spoke to Jessica in a low, confidential tone.

"Just friends, huh? I see the way Frank looks at you. I'm glad to hear you're not rushing into anything. I don't want anybody to get hurt. He's

A Dead Sister

been through a lot and so have those kids." He carefully laid buns on one side of the huge grill.

"I get it. I told Evie the truth. Right now, I'm just hanging on and hoping things get easier. I need a year. At least a year, depending on what that slime bucket I divorced and his screwball media darling, are planning as a sequel to their latest melee on Rodeo Drive."

"I didn't see it. Evelyn told me Jim was splashed all over the television along with some out of control actress I've never even heard of before. I don't like the entertainment news. In my line of work, who needs to watch TV to see mug shots of some idiot getting arrested for doing something stupid on the street or behind the wheel of a car? I have to deal with that kind of stupid every day. It doesn't matter if they're celebrities or not when you're cleaning up the road after them." Don Fontana stabbed the burgers he was tending a couple times, for no apparent reason. Then he lifted the edge of one of the buns, which was turning a golden brown very quickly. Reaching for the platter that had contained the buns, he began to stack burger patties, piling a slice of cheese on each one, as he continued to speak in hushed tones.

"Scumbags and screwballs, the lot of them! I'm so sorry that ex-husband of yours has joined their ranks. I thought he was okay. Then again, I never thought my ex-daughter-in-law would be talking to my grandkids about getting married to her girlfriend. So, what do I know?"

Uncle Don began to layer the toasted buns onto the platter, too, stacking them haphazardly next to the cheeseburger patties. Once the grill was empty, he handed the platter to Jessica and looked her directly in the eye.

"Speaking of screwballs and scumbags, when are you and Frank going to tell me what's up with the guy in lockup in Riverside?"

CHAPTER 17

The next day, Jessica replayed events from the night before as she made the ninety-minute drive from Riverside to Rancho Mirage. Dinner had been delicious. She couldn't have imagined a more perfect Fourth of July barbeque: burgers and all the fixings; corn-on-the-cob; potato salad; red, white, and blue tortilla chips, and, as Frank had promised, Aunt Evelyn's 7-layer dip. The kids, having spent two hours churning around in the pool, were more than ready to tank up again. They must have come close to putting away the ten thousand calories Frank estimated they consumed daily.

Double desserts had helped. Aunt Evelyn had made a brownie flag cake. Brownies topped with white cream cheese frosting and decorated with blueberries as the dark background, with bits of white frosting showing as the stars, and red raspberry stripes. It was delicious, but so were the cupcakes. They went over well with the kids, who thanked her, more than once, for bringing the sweet treats to the feast. Evie oohed and aahed over how cute they were, while Frankie just wolfed them down. Jessica would have been convinced they were going to be sick eating so much, except that she'd seen Brien do the same thing, while washing it all down with several beers.

After dinner, Jessica would have been content to sit in the back yard for the rest of the evening. The kids were wired, mostly from sugar, but also from the anticipation of the fireworks. Frank had bought tickets for all of them to watch the fireworks from a cemetery in Riverside. "Best seats in the house," according to the locals. She would drive her own car to the fireworks display so she could return directly to the Mission Inn.

A Dead Sister

The more pressing issue after dinner was the talk she and Frank had agreed to have with Don Fontana. It was a relief to have the matter out in the open, ending the debate about whether to tell Frank's dad they were taking a new look at Kelly's accident. It felt so much better, too, not to delude Uncle Don about why she and Frank were suddenly seeing each other.

Her initial reaction had not been relief, however. Shock had shot through her, causing the platter of burgers and buns she was holding to wobble precariously. Fortunately, Frank had just walked up behind her and was able to whisk the tray out of her hands before disaster could strike.

"How did you know?"

"I may not be a detective, like Frank, but I am a cop and a good one. I saw Art Greenwald come in and then leave the building in Palm Springs, all hush-hush, no shootin' the-breeze with me or anybody else. That's not like him at all. Not everybody knows enough to hide his business from me, so I asked around. That's when I heard they've got some loser in the RPDC who says he knows something about a cold case, and Art wants the old file with all the case notes. If Art and his team are taking another look, it must be something worthwhile. I don't have to be Einstein to figure out it's Kelly. Otherwise, why would there be all this dodgy, under-the-table stuff going on to keep me out of the loop?"

"Sorry, Dad, we were trying to handle this without stirring up the past before we had to. I'm the one who got Jessica in on this, so I hope you won't blame her."

"I don't blame either one of you. I just want to know what's going on."

"Well, it would really help to talk this over with you. I'd like to get your take on the investigation and what you think happened the night she was killed. Then, maybe you can help us sort out what to do next."

"How about we talk about this after dinner? We'll all help Mom clear up and put the food away, then, maybe she'll supervise the kids so we can talk. They have to get out of those swimsuits, shower, and dress before we can leave for the fireworks."

"Your mom can handle that, no problem," He said with a cat-that-swallowed-the-canary grin.

"Can handle what?" Jessica and Frank both jumped. Evelyn had walked up behind them. His grin broadened as he spoke to his wife. How long had

161

she been standing there?

"The three of us need to talk after dinner about something that's come up at work. I was just telling them you could hustle the kids into showering and changing their clothes while we talk, so we won't be late for the fireworks."

"Of course, I can. You'll catch me up later, right dear? If there's something new about what happened to Kelly, I'd prefer to hear it from you." The three of them were staring at her, dumbfounded, as she took the platter of cheeseburgers and buns from Frank.

"What? I'm the wife of a cop—a good one. Let's eat before Don or the kids pass out from hunger." Evie and Frankie came bursting from the house where she had sent them to wash up. They were stuffing chips into their mouths, leaving a trail of crumbs on the ground like Hansel and Gretel.

So, after dinner, instead of taking a nap, which is what she felt like doing, Jessica sat with Frank and Uncle Don at the patio table sipping coffee. As she and Frank did their best to spell out what Chester Davis had to say, Don Fontana had a troubled look on his face, but remained quiet. Then Jessica lowered her voice a little trying to soften the words that followed, as though it would make a difference.

"I didn't know that you had been called to the scene that night. It must have been awful to find a family member like that. I am so sorry."

"It was. Hard on me, but so much worse for Sammy and Monica. At least I was able to I.D. the body so they didn't have to see her like that."

"This is hard for me, too. I looked at the photos taken of Kelly that morning when she was found. I'm convinced Chester Davis was there. His description of the way she looked was too horrifically like what's documented in those photos. Of course, that doesn't mean the rest of what he claims is true."

"Whoever hit her was going thirty-five or forty miles per hour, given the distance her body was thrown from the point of impact. That kind of speed makes no sense, considering the accident happened in a parking lot and not out on a street somewhere. And there were no skid marks like you'd see if the driver had tried to brake and stop before impact. So maybe someone did hit her on purpose."

"According to what's in the report, you revisited the scene later, after dark. When you went to the scene that night, you noted that there was good lighting, no road defects someone might have swerved to avoid, and no obvious obstructions that might have blocked the driver's view of a pedestrian. Is that right?"

"Yes, that's true. I was so upset when I realized the dead girl was Kelly that I had my guys take over at the scene, as any professional should do. I was afraid I might mishandle things or draw the wrong conclusions, since I was rattled. But I stayed there, made my own drawings, took my own measurements. I watched them take photos, bag and tag everything. I had them block it off and leave all the little markers in place. I went back again later when the lighting was closer to what it must have been at the time she was killed. We did that, trying to make sure we didn't miss anything. I wrote up that part of the report myself."

"So, what did you think had happened?"

"My thought was some jerk was stupidly drunk, stoned, or both. And maybe really ticked off about flushing a lot of money down the toilet at the casino, so he went tearing out of there and ran her down. The coward made no effort to help Kelly or call for help. Not that anybody could have helped her at that point, according to the coroner." He slapped the table, making the stone top rattle, shaking the whole table, in fact.

"I checked all the DUIs that night, hoping someone had been pulled over in a car that fit the description we had. All we had to go on at that point was the debris left at the scene. We put out an APB for a car painted a dark-blue, almost black color, make and model unknown, but with damage to the paint and the chrome on the front end. We found nothing from traffic stops that night in Riverside, San Bernardino, or any other of the counties nearby. Half a dozen dark-colored cars were being driven by drunks that night, but none with the kind of damage we were looking for. I checked accident reports as well as traffic reports just in case the loser got into more trouble somewhere else after running Kelly down. No luck there, either. It was all a long shot, anyway. It was probably some local dirt bag who just drove home that night and parked his car in his garage after killing a sweet, lovely girl like that." Don was choked up and stopped. Frank reached out and patted him on the back.

"It's okay, Dad. You want to take a break? We can talk more about this later, if you want."

"No, let's go on. What I'm telling you, Jessica, is that it never occurred to me that someone might have hit her *on purpose*. Why? Why would a nineteen-year-old girl have that kind of an enemy? Not that I necessarily believe what that lowlife, Chester Davis, says. He'd sell his own grandmother for a gram or two of meth. But given all the evidence, that someone hit Kelly on purpose makes as much sense as anything else about what happened that night."

"Okay, so you didn't get any leads searching the records for DUI citations made that night, or early the next morning, and nothing from the traffic stops or accident reports. The records say the paint chips were later identified as belonging to a midnight blue 1999 Mercedes S class. Did anybody go back and take another look at the DMV records to see how many cars of that make and model were registered in Riverside County at the time? I know Mercedes is practically the state car here in California, but that model was brand new, and one of the pricier sedans you can purchase. Another long shot, I know, but how many could there have been on the road in Riverside County or even in LA or San Diego counties, for that matter?"

"I don't remember if we ran a check like that or not, Jessica. By the time we got the report back from the PDQ, it wasn't likely we'd find a damaged vehicle anyway. Somebody deranged enough to kill Kelly and then just take off like that would have cleaned it up and repaired it right away. Even if we had tracked down a car fitting that description, you couldn't place it at the scene without a damaged front end to match with the bits and pieces we collected. I assume you're asking me about it because there's nothing in the case file, so maybe nobody did that." Don Fontana paused a moment and stared off into space before speaking again.

"Mostly, we concentrated on trying to find someone in the hotel or casino that saw or heard something the night she was killed. We put out alerts to the public. Sammy and Monica made an appeal on TV for anyone with any information to come forward. Meanwhile, we also did the best we could to backtrack and figure out what she was doing at the hotel. We tried to find out when she was last seen or heard from, who had contact with her before she died and what she said to them. As you can tell from reading the reports in the file, we talked to a *lot* of people that day after we found Kelly's body. Nobody had much to say that was of any use, and the trail goes completely cold after she called in sick Tuesday morning. Sammy and Monica didn't suspect anything was wrong, since they felt lucky to hear from her every couple of weeks or so. They expected to see her again on the sixteenth for Tommy's birthday, but not before that." He took a sip of coffee. His hand trembled. When he spoke, he sounded angry.

"Most of the people in her life didn't even notice, or care, that she was missing for days. The boyfriend said they'd had a fight and he was waiting for her to cool off or something like that. To her supervisors and coworkers, she was just one more immature, half-assed employee, acting like an irresponsible jerk. It's been such a long time, now. I'm sure I've forgotten a lot of the details about what went on. What I do remember, very well, is that even though I wasn't the lead investigator, I rode everybody about as hard as I could to get as much information as quickly as we could. Folks felt bad for me and my family, so I know they went the extra mile..." He peered into the dark cup of coffee in his hands, as if some secret were lurking at the bottom.

"Well, I know it was a long time ago, but I have a couple of more questions for you."

"Shoot."

"What about a cell phone? I didn't see anything about her phone being found with her that night or later when the police visited her apartment. I know she had one. I still have a mobile number for her in my contacts. I couldn't dump it... I..." Jessica's resolve to get to the bottom of things was floundering. She was on the verge of getting choked up herself and still hadn't raised the most distressing issue. "Kelly was missing for several days. There might be some hint about where she was all that time if her phone's in evidence somewhere."

"I don't remember anything about the phone. It must have come up during the conversation with the boyfriend. Her supervisor said Kelly called in sick on Tuesday, but I don't recall if she or anyone else said anything about where Kelly had made the call from. Somebody might have checked, but why? We didn't think we were dealing with a homicide. It's likely no one even pulled phone records for a hit-and-run accident investigation. Someone might have done it if Chester Davis had come forward back then. Even then, that probably would have required a warrant, right Frank?"

"Yeah, that's true, if you had some reason to suspect she was murdered. It's odd that her phone wasn't found in her purse. Maybe there's some way to track down what carrier she had, at least, and we can get something using that phone number you still have for her, Jessica. Sammy and Monica or Tommy might have a better idea about the phone."

"Remembering how Sammy griped back then sometimes, I wouldn't be surprised if he paid her phone bill part of the time, so he probably can tell you more. I'm not sure what good it will do after all these years. Who knows how long phone companies keep records. Ask Sammy."

"That brings us back to the problem we were grappling with previously. Should we dredge up all these sad old memories based on allegations made by a meth addict up against a third strike?" Uncle Don considered Frank's question before responding.

"Good point. If I were you, I'd try to get more to go on before taking this to Sammy and Monica. I probably sound like a hypocrite, since I was sort of wagging my finger at you two for holding out on me. But Jessica, you see Tommy all the time. Why not ask him about the cell phone?"

"That's another reason I'm glad to review all of this with you. I'm going to have Tommy and Jerry Reynolds at my house tomorrow night and I'd like to put Jerry to work trying to follow up on a few things. You know, he's the P.I. who helped with the investigation into Roger's death?" Uncle Don nodded. "It would make things easier to tell Tommy, too, since he and Jerry are close. That means he's going to have to keep our secret too, though."

"Yeah, I get it. We're passing the buck, aren't we? If this gets back to Sammy and Monica before we break it to them, I'll take the heat. So, yes. Tell Tommy and get him to promise not to tell his mom and dad."

I know we need to get moving soon, but I have a couple other things. One is simple. The boyfriend said when Kelly left for work she was wearing a black vest. In the photos, she's not wearing it. I didn't see anything in the record that says a vest was found anywhere near her. Does the matter of a missing vest ring a bell?"

"I don't recall. I was surprised by that fact that she was still wearing the same clothes after nearly a week. Hard to imagine that since she was always such a glamor girl. We used to tease her about that. Sammy complained she went through more clothes in a week than he did in a month, sometimes changing two or three times a day! She was in that bathroom of hers for hours, showering and primping. He says she was always asking for money for some new product for that gorgeous hair of hers. Sammy called her bathroom a shampoo museum with bottles lined up all over the bathroom. He never understood it, but it was one of the little things he missed after she moved out on her own. I'm guessing she left that vest wherever she was holed up for the last few days of her life. Maybe that's where she left her phone, too."

"Okay, I just wanted to be sure I hadn't missed something. One last thing, and that's the issue of drugs. Was she an addict? I thought I knew her well. She hated needles. Those pictures are hard to deny, but for her to mess her body up like that just seems impossible. Did Sammy and Monica say she was having problems with drugs like that?"

"I found it hard to believe, too. I heard early the next day that there was fentanyl in that syringe. That stuff is dangerous, even if you don't inject it. That's why I asked a couple of officers to visit her apartment. If Kelly had that drug stashed there, I wanted it found and her apartment cleaned before Sammy and Monica went there to get something to bury her in. I don't think they found fentanyl or anything else, as I recall."

"Did Sammy and Monica say she was having problems with drugs like that?"

"They were as shocked as you are, Jessica. Angry and hurt, embarrassed for Kelly, so we were careful not to go too far down that road. It didn't seem relevant to the investigation of a hit-and-skip. Sammy told me Kelly had been diagnosed with bipolar disorder, and had started taking prescription medications. They weren't sure what she had told the shrink that led to her diagnosis, and planned to talk to the guy after the funeral. Then Monica began having her own problems, and Sammy got sick. Both were seeing a lot of docs of their own. I don't know if they ever got around to talking with Kelly's shrink or not. I'm not sure what they could have learned by doing that, anyway. They were having such a hard time, I just let it go." He looked from Jessica to Frank and back again.

"What good would it do to look into Kelly's drug use or her mental problems when, as far as we could tell, she had been the victim of a terrible accident? Maybe she was so stoned or so crazy out of her mind, that she contributed to the accident in some way. But what difference did that make? That was no excuse to just leave her there like that. It didn't seem right to make a dead girl look bad or to put her parents through more by investigating that aspect of her life. Like I said, we weren't thinking about foul play beyond the fact that she was the victim of a hit-and-run accident at the hands of some douche bag. I suppose she could have stiffed some dealer. A guy like that might have been angry enough to run her down in his expensive Mercedes sedan paid for by selling drugs to young women like Kelly. Maybe we dropped the ball. I don't know..."

Don Fontana's voice faded out. His shoulders slumped, as he seemed to sink into the growing darkness around them. The patio light illuminating him from behind reflected off the gray in his hair and cast shadows that deepened the furrows in his aging face. At that moment, Jessica could believe he was a grandfather to two kids on the verge of becoming teenagers. It was the first time she saw him as an older version of the man they had all counted on while growing up. Everybody's Uncle Don, a sturdy anchor of a man, was showing his age.

"Dad, that's not true. You all did your jobs, and then some. You couldn't have done more without overreaching." Frank put an arm around his father's shoulders. That Uncle Don allowed such a public display of affection, such a reversal of roles, was a testament to how deeply disturbing all of this was to him.

"Frank's right, Uncle Don. You did as much as you could without Chester Davis or someone else coming forward with information to point you in a different direction. Frank and I will do everything possible to follow up on his story. If he's lying, we'll find that out, too. We'll do as much as we can without making Sammy and Monica relive this nightmare. I *will* talk to Tommy, though. Frank can help me do that, since he's coming to my house for dinner tomorrow night with Tommy and the rest of the Cat Pack."

"The what?" Father and son asked, almost in unison. They looked so much alike and were so similarly befuddled that Jessica's dark mood broke. She tried to explain what she meant by "cat pack," and how they had forged their little band fending off the bad guys involved in Roger Stone's murder. That included an effort to describe her role as cat herder or cat whisperer. The more she spoke, the sillier it all sounded.

Hopped up on sugar and giddy with stress, it took only a few more seconds for her to get a case of the giggles. They had all arrived at that point where you had to either laugh or cry. Huddling around the patio table in Frank Fontana's backyard, on a warm Fourth of July evening, should have been a lark. Instead, they pondered the fate of the dead auburn-haired girl, loved by them all. That she might have been murdered was too bizarre. Trying to explain about the Cat Pack had pushed the whole situation to the point of absurdity. Jessica laughed and they laughed with her.

When the laughing ceased, Uncle Don wiped tears from his eyes as he spoke. "Jessica, you still have to let Art and his guys do their job. Art Greenwald's been at it a long time, and he's a good cop, too. He'll go over everything again and again. Give him a day or two, then call or meet with him and ask him the same questions you asked me. They're all good questions. Sometimes, asking the right question is the most important part of getting the right answer, you know?"

CHAPTER 18

Jessica tried not to speed after she merged from State Highway 60 onto I-10. Whizzing past the outlet mall near Cabazon, she hardly noticed the fake dinosaurs hovering over the gas station not too far from the Morongo Casino. She was nearing the Banning pass. There is no more beautiful sight than the Coachella Valley coming into view on the other side of the pass, at least not to a "home girl" like Jessica. Well, maybe that wasn't entirely true. Driving or flying into the valley at night was perhaps more beautiful. All the desert cities lit up, glittered like jewels scattered across the valley floor.

The windmills dotting the landscape around the pass were unsightly and invasive to some. To Jessica, they were foot soldiers deployed alongside the guardians, Mt. San Jacinto and Mt. San Gorgonio, which stood watch on opposite sides of the pass. Windmills had proliferated in the Banning pass, one of the windiest places on earth, since Jessica went off to school at the end of the '90s. Their silent churning urged her on. She wanted to get home, unpack, and give Bernadette a head's-up about what was in store for them all this evening.

When she pulled into the garage of the estate in Mission Hills before noon, Bernadette's Escalade wasn't parked in the four-car garage. That meant Jessica would have time to unload and settle in before catching up with Bernadette. Settling in was one thing, settling down was an altogether different matter. She needed to do that, too, before speaking to Bernadette. Her superpowers would detect Jessica's hopped-up mood in no time.

Not all the fireworks the night before had been at the display put on by the city of Riverside. Jessica had tried not to think about it while she was driving, talk about distracted driving! Another of those goodbye hugs from

Frank had left her with buckled knees. She could barely remember arriving back at the hotel, making her way to her room or falling into bed. Her dreams had been vivid, to say the least, and she had no trouble at all remembering them or the encounter that had triggered them.

Jessica counted off the months again. First, the months *since last* March when she had filed for divorce... March, April, May, June. Then, she ticked off the months *until next* March when the awful first year would end. Nothing had changed since her last count, still four months down, and eight to go. Last night, and again today, Jessica heard Uncle Don's admonition echoing in her head.

She also heard Frank's voice, speaking to her as he had last night. They were standing next to her car in the dark, saying goodbye. Pulling her toward him, he had whispered in her ear, so close she could feel his breath as he spoke, "So, you had a crush on me in high school, Cuz? What am I supposed to do with that information, now that we're all grown up?"

Jessica had collapsed into his arms, giggling like a schoolgirl. A good Catholic one, of course. She couldn't stand the thought of misleading Uncle Don with her assurances about taking it slow, and being sensible. "You're supposed to help me clear my head, so I can get through the first year of my divorce and figure things out," she added, a little breathlessly, as his arms closed around her. "This isn't helping me do that at all." Instead of warding Frank off, those words only caused him to tighten his grip.

Jessica had to find out what he used to give him that scent that was making her woozy, giggling again as she realized her grip had tightened, too. Fortunately, his family was waiting for him to join them. Frank had ridden with her to the park. Since she was going straight back to the Mission Inn, he was riding home in the minivan with Uncle Don, Aunt Evelyn, and the kids. They were parked around the corner with the engine running.

"I'm being as helpful as I can. I heard Dad talking to you. I got the 'take it easy talk' from him, too. I promised I would. But this isn't going to be at all easy is it, even though a promise is a promise?"

"Yeah, a promise is a promise," Jessica agreed, releasing him ever so slightly. With that, he let go a little, too. As he did, his cheek brushed hers. A hint of stubble caressed, ever so lightly. Maybe it was whatever he used when he shaved that carried the scent she found so alluring. She breathed deeply, hoping to capture and hold onto it as he moved away.

Suddenly, a blast of nostalgia slammed into Jessica from out of nowhere.

A Dead Sister

Her body recalled, even before it registered in her mind, all the times Jim had caused her to laugh by tickling her when he needed a shave. Her head spun as she fought not to release a flood of bitter tears. She released her grip on Frank. "A promise is a promise," she muttered again. *Not to everyone. Not to Jim,* she thought, flashing for an instant on that scene in her bedroom in Cupertino.

Grasping, immediately, the change that had swept over her, Frank scooped Jessica into his arms again. "Trust me. It will get better, and that's a promise too." With that, he kissed her on the top of the head and let her go. He guided her around to the driver's side of the car and opened the door for her. When the interior light came on, she could see his dark eyes. They were filled with concern and something she needed even more than sex, understanding and compassion.

"Thanks. I mean that, too." She gave him a little peck on the cheek, and then slipped into her seat. As she pulled away from the curb, she could see him standing there, watching her drive off. It took willpower—lots of it— not to put her car in reverse, back up to the curb, and pull him into the seat beside her. She wanted understanding and compassion *and* sex! What was wrong with that?

It all still sounded good to Jessica, today too. Frank would be there for dinner and their discussion with the Cat Pack. Maybe she would have him stay the night, in one of the guest rooms, of course... just down the hall. She knew she wasn't ready to take the plunge. What if another of those sad bouts of reminiscence engulfed her as it had last night without warning? She could try to put the grief and betrayal out of her mind, might enjoy herself with Frank anyway, but why? What was the point? How did she really know he was any more trustworthy than Jim?

Trust mattered. Even more, now, after that kick in the gut by Jim. Sex was intensely physical, but way more than a booty call or some bodily function, like taking a crap. Not something you did to feign intimacy or a mere formality you got out of the way. Some loser in college had actually used something like that on her as a pickup line.

"Hey, Jessica, you're looking hot tonight. Why don't we go find someplace more private? We should get this sex thing out of the way so we can see if there's something real between us."

"Huh?" She had just stood there, looking at his eyes hooded from too much booze and the smirk on his face, as if he were trying to channel Elvis. Why on earth did he think she had any interest in him, sexual or otherwise, since she barely knew him? How could he possibly not know that was the buzz kill of all buzz kills?

It was still a buzz-kill, after all these years. Like a cold shower or a slap in the face. The recollection of that incident got her back on track, fast. She was in no shape to start a relationship of any kind with Frank, or anyone else for that matter. She had a career to re-launch and, oh yeah, a murder to solve.

Jessica had finished unpacking and was pondering what to wear when two things happened. Bernadette called out a "yoo-hoo, I'm home" as she came into the house from the garage. And her phone rang.

"Bernadette, I need to talk to you as soon as you're settled in. I've got to take a phone call. You need help unloading your car?"

She couldn't hear all of Bernadette's reply, but she did hear "no, I'm okay, Jessica. Take your call."

"Hello, Jessica Huntington speaking."

"Jessica, this is Paul Worthington. Have you got a minute?"

"Sure, what's up?"

"Not much, except that the Van der Woerts believe I'm brilliant. They absolutely loved you, *and* the fact that you live in the desert, *and* will be working at the office we're opening, so they don't have to come into LA after they retire. You'd think I had done it all just for them. They were impressed with everything about you. Not that I find that the least bit surprising. You do make quite an impression, Jessica Huntington, no hyphen."

"Thanks so much. That's such a nice thing to hear. What happens now?"

"I just got off the phone with them a few minutes ago, and agreed to call you and set a time for you to meet with them again. They'd like a block of time with you. Two hours, at least, so they can give you more specifics about their personal situation. That includes retirement, moving to the desert, estate planning, and the timeframe they have in mind. Tuesday worked for everybody last week. Can you do something like that again?"

"I can. What would you advise?"

A Dead Sister

"Well, it means driving into LA again, sooner than I had imagined, but we're trying to be accommodating. If you can plan on having lunch with the Van der Woerts, and then meet with them for two or three hours, that would be great. I'd like to join you for lunch and the first part of the meeting, and then turn it over to you. You can make whatever arrangements you want to make to meet with them from that point on. I don't see why the next time you meet, it can't be at the office in the desert. Maybe you can coordinate around their house-hunting plans. That's up to the three of you, and whoever is helping on the real estate side of things. So, how does this sound?"

Great and Tuesday is no problem. I'll just block out the whole day. So, whatever works for the Van der Woerts is fine with me."

"Wonderful! I'll get back to them right away, and let them pick a time and place for lunch on Tuesday. My administrative assistant, Gloria Crane, can make the reservations and email you with information about what time to meet at the office. It'll be easier if we all meet here. I can arrange for a car take all of us to lunch. I'll also have Gloria schedule one of the small conference rooms for the entire afternoon so you all can take as much time as you need. Staff will bring you coffee, tea, or other refreshments if the meeting runs more than a couple hours. What else do you need to get things moving?"

"Well, any more background information you can share about the Van der Woerts would be great. I presume, since they've been clients in the past, there's some sort of a portfolio that's already been compiled. I'd like to see that before we meet again, if that can be arranged. And if you have a standard template or checklist you use for an estate planning review, I'd like to see that too. If not, I can use one I'm familiar with. It's based on the one put together by the ABA." She didn't say she was familiar with it because it was the one her parents used or that she and Jim had used.

"No problem. We do have background information about the Van der Woerts in their file. That's basic, but a good place to start. They also have wills on file already. I have no idea when they were last updated. I'll make sure Gloria adds you as the attorney of record, and you can access the information we have about them from home or the office. As far as the estate planning review, we use a form that sounds similar. It's the ABA template, appended with information specific to California. You can get an electronic version that's fillable off our intranet. I'll have Gloria print copies so you and the Van der Woerts can all be looking at the questions together. We have a searchable database that contains all sorts of forms and templates, and document samples you can access on the firm's intranet. I'm sending you the link as we speak, and Gloria will send you a user name and password."

"That will be a great help. I really am happy to be working with the Van der Woerts, and grateful for your support."

"I'm happy it worked out, too. The last request I'd like to make is that you have dinner with me Tuesday night. That way, you can debrief about your meeting, and we can celebrate. I know we have a movie night planned for next weekend, but I don't think we should wait that long to toast your success. You're going to be in town, anyway, so we should mark the occasion."

He sounded ebullient. Jessica couldn't say no, even though the day's activities seemed daunting. She would have preferred to say goodbye to the Van der Woerts and make her way back to Brentwood for a quiet evening alone. He was so earnest, proud of her, and proud of himself for setting all this up.

"Sure. You know the area better than I do. If you have a place you like, I'm sure I'll enjoy it, too. Shall I meet you there?"

"No, I have a better idea. There's an exhibit I want you to see before dinner. It won't take long. Come to my office whenever the Van der Woerts leave. Take time to make notes. Do whatever you need to do so you can pick up where you leave off later, and then find me. We'll go to the exhibit and to dinner after that. I'll drop you off later so you can pick up your car from the lot. You're going to get a kick out of the exhibit." He was chuckling with delight.

How was it that she'd ever thought of Paul Worthington as standoffish or reserved? He was so likable and enthusiastic. His day would start before hers on Tuesday. God only knew how many clients he was juggling like he was doing with the Van der Woerts, or how many other associates he was mentoring like Jessica. He also had his colleagues and the partners at the firm to keep happy, too, and was charged with getting the El Paseo office up and running. Ay yi yi! Jessica was becoming exhausted just thinking about the hours he must keep. It was also inspiring. If he could do it, she could do it!

"I'd love to! Do I get a hint about the exhibit?"

"No, it's a surprise. A good one, though. I'll send out an email confirming our lunch with the Van der Woerts and the rest of the day will

A Dead Sister

flow from there. See you Tuesday."

Jessica got off the phone, and threw herself down on her bed. What did this mean for her plans to start digging into Kelly's case? She had better hit the ground running. That's what it meant. She hoped Jerry was ready to get back to work. They had to get this show on the road. The first thing she was going to do was print out the list of names she had culled from her review of Kelly's file so Jerry could get to work locating them. They had to start talking to people. That included the boyfriend and her coworkers, and the woman who had been Kelly's supervisor at the spa, since she was the last person known to have any contact with Kelly.

She wished that Tommy and Jerry were arriving before the others. That way, she could break it to Tommy, before it became a matter for discussion by their little group. Jessica looked at the time on her phone still in her hand. Maybe it wasn't too late to get Tommy to come over early, alone, or with Jerry. It was worth a try. As she zipped through her list of phone contacts, there was a knock on her door. Jessica had completely forgotten that Bernadette was home. *Thank goodness*, she thought. She needed to unload, spill her guts about all that had gone on since she and Bernadette had parted company Sunday morning.

"Come on in," Jessica said, as she pushed the call button on her phone. "I need your help."

"Aloha," a voice said on the other end of the phone.

"Aloha, Tommy, it's Jessica. How's it going?"

"Awesome! I'm totally stoked, amped!"

"Wow, you've been spending a lot of time with Brien."

"Yeah, well all the surfer dudes over there talk like that... so, really, what's up? Did you miss me so much you couldn't wait a couple of more hours to get the scoop on our absolutely delicious vacation?"

"Of course, I missed you. Something's come up, too, and I was hoping you could get over here sooner so we could talk before the others get here. Bring Jerry, of course. I need to talk to him too. How soon can you two get here?" She knew she sounded stressed out, even though she had hoped to strike a more casual tone.

"You're scaring the hell out of me. Are you alright? Is Bernadette okay? Don't tell me somebody's sick or dead or something?"

175

"I'm fine, and Bernadette's okay too. She just got back from spending time with her family for the Fourth. Nobody's dead. Well, nobody's dead that wasn't already dead." She sounded crazy. "It's about Kelly. I need to talk to you about Kelly."

Bernadette had been completely silent, just standing there. When she heard that, she sat down on the edge of Jessica's bed.

"Kelly? What about Kelly? Why do you want to talk to me about Kelly?" Tommy asked, his sunny mood vanishing, poof, all that Aloha spirit gone in an instant.

"There's this guy I interviewed in a Riverside jail who claims he was at the casino hotel parking lot that night, Tommy. He says he saw the whole thing. Can you get over here by five or so? Cousin Frank will be here by then, too. We can try to explain it to you. I'm sorry to dump this on you the minute you're back in town *and* over the phone. I just... it can't wait."

"Okay, we'll be there by five." He hung up.

Jessica looked at Bernadette and, like a big baby, started to cry. "It's m-m-murder, another murder. Can you believe it? Somebody killed Kelly on p-p-purpose." It wasn't until that moment that Jessica realized how truly horrific this week had been. Having to talk with her Uncle Don had been sad and stressful, but now Tommy. Wasn't there some way she could spare him? He'd suffered so much, and things were finally starting to look up for him. She felt horrible hearing the delight drain from his voice.

"So, I take it you didn't have such a good time at home alone this week? You want to tell me what happened?"

Jessica pulled herself up to a sitting position, leaning against the padded headboard. She did her best, between sobs and sniffles, to tell Bernadette all that had occurred since they had last spoken, starting with Frank's visit on Sunday, and the story about Chester Davis, her meeting with him and his lawyer, Dick Tatum. She even described her lunch with Dick Tatum and Riverside's answer to Larry David, Detective Greenwald. Then she backtracked, telling her about Paul's call, driving to LA, and staying at her dad's house in Brentwood. It was all such an overwhelming jumble, she wasn't sure she was even making any sense.

"I have a new job, and a real client—two c-c-clients. And I've got to find out who killed K-Kelly. And, oh my God, did you see that awful scene on Rodeo Drive?"

A Dead Sister

Bernadette nodded. "I wasn't going to say anything, but since you brought it up. That Jim Harper has gone la vuelta de la curva. You know, 'round the bend?" She was making little circling signs at her temple. "Completamente loco! Chica, you got rid of him just in the nick of time. You should start thanking God the first thing when you wake up every morning that he's gone and that you didn't make any babies with him. Those might be some loco babies, too." She was shaking her head and making the sign of the cross. Suddenly, she spoke again, "Dios mio, Jessica, maybe he's drogado! Could he be stoned on the weed or something worse?"

"I have no idea, Bernadette. He did his share of drinking, but he was always so critical of people who were sloppy drinkers or who used drinking as a crutch. I had a hard time getting him to take medications prescribed for him. At some point, he got a prescription for Ambien to help him sleep, but I don't know if he's still taking it or not."

"That could be it. Look what Ambien did to Tiger Woods. He was a good golfer one minute and the next thing you know, he's driving his Escalade into a tree in his yard, sleep crashing. Maybe Jim was sleep-shopping or something when that girlfriend of his went crazy. She was stepping all over that poor lady she knocked on the ground, and kicking that photographer in his cojones. I bet all that guy's screaming woke Jim up real quick, if that hit on the head and the elbow in the ribs didn't do it."

"He was awake enough to recognize me standing there watching him make an ass of himself. Bernadette, Tiger Woods' problems had to do with way more than Ambien. But what do I know? I'd have to take drugs to be in the same room with that platinum-dipped looney tune. Maybe Jim's a junkie, just like they claim Kelly was. I obviously didn't know either one of them as well as I thought I did. Poor Tommy, I wonder if he knew Kelly was using drugs. If not, this is going to upset him."

"I don't know about Kelly, but when it comes to Jim, que se pudra! Good riddance and be glad you found out the truth when you did. Tommy will want to know the truth about Kelly, too. You'll see. Truth, even the worst kind of truth, is better than the best kind of lie."

"Can I quote you on that St. Bernadette?"

Bernadette reached out, brushed Jessica's hair back off her face, and took her chin in her hand.

"Sure, if it will help you feel less sorry for yourself. A lot of good things happened to you this week, querida mio. Your lawyering job is back, and you have a chance to help some people who need your help. You've got friends who care about you, including a couple handsome men waiting for you to figure out, in your heart, what's already in your head. Jim is your past. You should go talk some more with Father Martin. He can tell you about the divorce rules. They can do that now you know, null it for you?"

"Are you talking about an annulment?"

"Yeah, that's exactly what I'm talking about. I don't know how they do it, but Father Martin does. He's like a lawyer, too. He helped my friend Meredith. She got a fresh start, and now she's getting married again." Bernadette leaned in and dropped her voice, "She's marrying a younger man—he's sixty-six and she's seventy-two—but Father Martin says that's okay, too. I'm going to be in her wedding in November. Maybe you can help me figure out what to wear, as matron of honor, once they decide on the colors they want to use."

"That's wonderful. I'd love to help."

"So, what do we need to do to get ready for tonight?"

"Not much, I hope. The caterers should be here about five thirty to set up dinner for six. They're bringing plates and all that. I wasn't sure what time either one of us would get to the house, so they're supposed to take care of it all—set up and clean up. I'll break out a few bottles of wine. I guess I should put the whites in the fridge to chill. I'm so spoiled, Bernadette. How can you stand me?"

"You have a good heart. You're a hard worker, and nobody cares more than you about doing the right thing. You just get swallowed up by your own worries. You gotta shake it off. Your mother has that problem sometimes, too."

"She does?" Bernadette just nodded in response, then, stood up. Jessica wasn't thrilled at the idea of being like her mother in that way, or any way, for that matter. One of the reasons she was so determined to take her time getting involved with other men was that she so disliked the revolving door in her mother's heart and her boudoir. As Bernadette was leaving the room, Jessica remembered that postcard she had seen at her dad's house. "Did you know that Mom and Dad keep in touch?"

"Of course, they do. Unlike you and Jim, they *did* have a baby together. Even though you're all grown up and they both travel a lot, they still keep

A Dead Sister

track of you." She started walking toward the door.

"But did you know they were *seeing* each other and soon? I found this postcard at Dad's house from Mom that said, 'see you soon.' Does that mean she's coming home, or is he going to visit her?"

Bernadette turned back toward Jessica. "I don't know everything that goes on between your parents. Things haven't always been easy. You know they're complicated. Your mother will tell us if she's coming home. Until then, dèjalo estar, leave it be, okay? You've got plenty to take care of already, chica." Jessica watched her walk out of the room. There was something in Bernadette's tone that she couldn't hide. Unspoken concern and "complicated," what did that mean? Nevertheless, she'd leave it alone, for now. "One mystery at a time," Jessica murmured, as she dug out Kelly's file so she could look through it again before she met with Tommy.

CHAPTER 19

Jessica used the afternoon to prepare as best she could for her meeting with Tommy and Jerry, and the rest of the Cat Pack a little later. She focused on the most tactful and succinct way to lay it all out for Tommy. There were several key things she wanted to ask him about. A lot of the same things she'd highlighted in her conversation with Uncle Don. She printed out the list of names the police had interviewed and put it in a folder for Jerry, along with copies of the reports from Kelly's file.

When Tommy and Jerry arrived promptly at five o'clock, she felt ready to deal with the whole matter. They both looked refreshed from their vacation, arm in arm as they came in the door. Clearly, they were making headway in their relationship. Jessica was glad somebody was doing well in that area. She rushed to embrace them both.

"Hey, you two, come on in and take a seat in the bar area, will you? Bernadette is going to have the caterers set up in the kitchen and morning room while we talk. I have wine and beer in the bar fridge, or I can pour you something stronger, if you'd like. We have a bottle of Macallan already open. I'm not sure what else is in the liquor cabinet, but I'll look."

"Oh, no, is it going to be so bad you're breaking out the single malt?" Tommy asked, joking but worried too. He and Jerry trailed after her into the huge great room, taking a seat in the comfy leather chairs at the bar. Laughing at Tommy's joke, a little uncomfortably, Jessica stepped down into the sunken area behind the bar.

"What'll it be, boys?"

"A cold beer sounds wonderful. It's not too hot out, but I've got to readjust after two weeks of tropical breezes." Jessica pulled a Pliny out of the fridge, popped the top off, and poured the golden brew into a frosty pint glass. Tommy eyed the cold drink as Jerry took it from Jessica.

"I'm going to have a shot of the Macallan, since you offered. I'll save the beer for dinner." He picked up a bottle of wine sitting on the bar, which was already opened so it could "breathe," then set it back down. "This looks tempting, too. How drunk am I going to need to be?"

"Well, I don't know. I guess a lot depends on how much of what I tell is new and how much you already know. You were such a baby back then, and this happened such a long time ago. I don't know how much you were involved in the investigation or what you remember about any of it. I don't even see any record in her police file that anybody interviewed you at the time. You were a minor." She poured two fingers of the Macallan into a sparkling crystal brandy snifter.

"Uncle Don talked to me. I was shook up about it, of course. It didn't seem like I had much to add or anything..." He stopped talking, realizing that Jessica was no longer paying attention to him, and followed her eyes to the entrance of the great room. "Cousin Frank, come on in. Jessica is plying me with liquor so I won't go all hysterical on her when she starts quizzing me about my dead sister."

"What are you drinking?" Frank was talking to Tommy, but he was looking at Jessica. She was gripping the sink around the bar area, trying to maintain her composure. She'd better have that talk with Father Martin, and soon. This was ridiculous. Jessica hadn't felt like such an idiot, even in high school, or when she met James Harper.

"I'm drinking the amber nectar of the gods. A twenty-five-year-old Macallan Single Malt from Hank's stash. It's the good stuff. It's probably a hundred bucks a shot or something crazy like that. Sit down next to me, and we'll pretend we're rich guys, living in this house, sipping something fine from our whisky cellar. Is there such a thing, Jessica?"

Jessica was staring off into space. At least she'd managed to break the eye lock with Frank. She didn't know where to look. Not at Frank, that was for sure. He was wearing a tailored pair of board shorts and an Aloha shirt with the top button open. That's what she'd told him to wear for the luau-themed dinner meeting of the Cat Pack. Tommy and Jerry were dressed the same way.

She and Bernadette had each put on one of their island dresses bought in Maui. Jessica wore a short, sleeveless tank dress, in an orchid color with a straight skirt and a rounded neck, a line of white ginger flowers streaming down the front and back. Now she wished she had told them all to wear more clothes. If she and Frank could stop undressing each other with their eyes, she'd feel a whole lot less naked.

"Earth to Jessica! What is going on, you two? How bad could this be?" Jerry gave Tommy a little nudge with his foot.

"Stop kicking me. Is this about Kelly or do you two need to get a room somewhere?" Jerry kicked him harder, and Tommy yipped, "Ouch! Now I have physical pain to go with my mental anguish. Can we get this over with, *please?*" Tommy's imploring tone finally got through to Jessica and she found her voice.

"So, Frank, do you want Macallan or the beer that Jerry's drinking? Or would you like something else?" He smiled as he sat down next to Tommy. That smile clearly said "something else," but what he asked for was the Macallan. Neat. *The man does have good taste,* Jessica thought, pouring a drink for him and one for herself. Tommy pushed his nearly empty glass toward her for a refill.

"Two hundred bucks a shot would be my guess. Mom keeps it around in case Dad drops by. The *really* good stuff is stored in cellar conditions at his house in Brentwood. Some may be warehoused, too, since he was quite a collector for a while. Always stored upright, no light, and you need to keep it around sixty degrees. When it's down to a third of the bottle or so, you might as well polish it off, with a little help from your friends, of course." She raised her glass to the guys seated around the bar and took a big swig, hoping it would knock some sense into her. It did.

"I have a list of questions for Tommy. Do you want to tell him how all this started?" Frank set his glass of Macallan down on the bar, reluctantly.

"This is terrific. Your dad knows what he's doing." Jessica saluted with another raise of her glass. She wished she could come out from behind the bar and sit down. Covered in a honey-colored, buttery-soft leather, the low-slung lounge chairs the guys occupied were *so* comfortable. But for the moment, Jessica liked the idea of having the bar between her and Frank.

She leaned in a little on the bar as Frank told Tommy and Jerry about Art Greenwald and the cold case team getting the nod from the D.A. to check out a guy's claim that he witnessed a murder. As Frank explained, there really wasn't any new physical evidence, but eyewitness testimony from a guy in lockup. For a price, he was willing to come clean about something he saw nearly fifteen years ago: A girl rundown at a Palm Springs casino. Tommy's eyes widened and a look of dread spread across his sweet features.

"It sounds like Kelly! Was it Kelly? Did he say it was Kelly?"

"Well, he didn't give us Kelly's name. The guy's a three-time loser with a brain cooked by years of drug use. But I had the same reaction. I asked Art to consider it, anyway. I also didn't want to get you and the rest of the family all stirred up, if it was nothing. So, I asked Jessica to follow up. Maybe Jessica can take it from here, since she was able to use her lawyer bag of tricks to get in and see Chester Davis right away."

"There wasn't much of a trick to it. You know I've been speaking with Paul Worthington about working in the office his firm is opening out here. As it turned out, he had a client he wanted me to take on, so I decided to enlist. I don't know if it was my affiliation with the firm or sheer desperation on Dick Tatum's part, but I was able to see Mr. Davis. Anyway, Chet's skittish, so I agreed to be co-counsel. Once I took him on as a client, he spilled his guts. There were some things he said that made me think he wasn't making it all up. Murdered or not, he saw Kelly after she was killed that night. I don't know how much detail you want me to go into. Some of what he said is gruesome, but backed up by the photos and the accident report in her case file. Later, when I showed him a photo of Kelly he said she was the girl he saw that night." Jessica had started to get the shivers. The air-conditioned space seemed chilly.

"Just tell me what I need to know. I'll do whatever you want me to do." Jessica came around the bar, drink in hand, and sat down, rolling one of the lounge chairs around in front of Tommy. "Okay, well the basic question is should we pursue this, given what a lowlife Chet Davis is? It might stir up a lot for you and your mom and dad. Is it worth that even if it's another dead end?"

"Hell, yes! If someone killed Kelly on purpose, you've got to do whatever it takes to get the disgusting degenerate."

"Okay, then, here goes. I'll give you the most cleaned-up version of what I heard, and then I have some questions for you." Jessica related the tale Chet Davis had told them, saying little about the condition in which Kelly's body was found, except to say her death was quick. Tommy sat quiet and wide-eyed, listening to every word.

"There are a lot more details, but we can get to those as the need arises. Anyway, my first question is: when did you last see or hear from Kelly?"

"That's easy. I talked to her on Monday, right after the New Year. She called me from work, upset because she had a fight with Bobby, that vile boyfriend of hers. He was hassling her because he thought she was dissing him. First, by hanging out with you and her other rich friends on New Year's Eve, and then working double shifts. It also made him mad that she was talking about going back to school. She was trying to figure things out for herself, and that reptile accused her of thinking she was better than him. I couldn't believe he was still holding New Year's Eve against her. They'd already had a fight about that even before she went out with you all. It sounds like she punished herself by being such a wench that night she got dropped off at home early." Jessica squirmed in her seat.

"That sounds about right. I didn't know she'd had a fight with her boyfriend. Hell, I didn't even know she had a boyfriend! She was drunk, mean, and nasty, so we took her home."

"Kelly said she picked a fight with you and said things she never should have said. I told you before she was trying to work up the courage to apologize. For what it's worth now, whatever happened that night was really a wake-up call. She made all these New Year resolutions. The truth is, even as messed up as she was, she was better than him. Way better than Bobby Simmons. He was up to no good. I don't know what kind of no good, but something."

"What makes you say that?" She asked.

"I'm not sure. I only hung out with him a few times, at Kelly's apartment. He was smug, thought he was going places, a big shot because he was a croupier and all that. He had this lounge lizard look going. Bobby was sort of good looking in an open shirt, gold chain, pinky ring kind of way. He didn't like me and I didn't like being around him, either. I asked Kelly once what *she* liked about him and she drew a blank. Can you believe that? I told her she needed to raise her standards so she could fill in the blanks on a question like that. I had such a fresh mouth. I know I hurt her feelings, but it was true. That was before your New Year's Eve bash that ended so badly. Oh, and another thing about Bobby the lizard. One time, he flashed a roll of cash. That made me *very* uncomfortable because dealers at the casinos around here don't make a lot. Not if they're legit, anyway."

"What do you mean by legit?"

A Dead Sister

"I was only fifteen, so I hadn't spent much time at the casinos then, but I considered becoming a dealer. One of many stops along the way to 'wtf do I want to be when I grow up,' you know? What I found out right away is the pay sucks. So, how does a loser like Bobby get cash like that? I was worried maybe he was into drugs or something worse. I didn't know then that dealers can get pulled into scams at the casinos. They cut deals with players to give them an edge at the table, and split the take from the games they win. That's risky, since everybody watches everybody all the time on the casino floor. He didn't seem all that smart to me, so maybe that's what he was doing. Sometimes, dealers can get big tips doing things like making referrals to off-site games around town or arranging things for players— especially the high-rollers who come to town. Kind of like a concierge, but shadier than the sort of things that get set up at that little desk in the lobby."

"Okay, so Bobby Simmons goes to the top of the list of people we want to talk to again. Can you find him, Jerry?"

"I'll give it a try. If he's not dead or in jail, it'll surprise me."

"I can ask around, too. If he's still local and into the sleazy side of things around here, I have connections." You could see the wheels in Tommy's head turning.

"Take it easy. I don't want you getting in over your head," Jessica said.

"Yeah," Frank chimed in, "we don't have a clue what we're dealing with yet, so we're all going to work at this around the edges. Art and his team will be stomping around soon. Let's see what kind of dirt they stir up. If you can ask around and keep it confidential, go ahead, but nobody sticks their neck out too far until we know more."

"Well," said Jessica, "I wasn't trying to sound the alarm and set off the police-detective-warning system. I don't want anybody to get hurt, but I don't see how we can avoid asking a bunch of people a bunch of questions. Like Uncle Don said, it's about asking the right question. Maybe by digging through the trash, the rats will scurry, but it's the only way we have a prayer of getting the right answer."

"I'm just saying... we should be a little cautious. That's all."

"Ooh, a lover's quarrel." Tommy was gloating at Jessica's growing agitation. This little bit of comic relief was helping him cope better than Jessica had ever dreamed he would.

"We're not lovers. I'm barely divorced. It'll be another month before the State of California even makes *that* official. This is just a difference of opinion—a disagreement."

"Let's not argue in front of the kids. That's one of the first things I learned when my marriage hit the rocks." She tried to glare at him, but his ear-to-ear grin melted her resolve. She couldn't help smiling back at him as she tried to get back to the matter at hand.

"Okay, the last time you had any contact with Kelly was Monday night after she had a fight with the boyfriend. Any idea what time that was, and was she calling you on her cell phone?"

"I have a *very good* idea what time it was, because she was complaining that fighting with Bobby might make her too late for a chance to fill in for no shows on the dinner shift. That would have been sixish. She got off work at the spa at five, ran home to change, and was on her way back. So maybe six thirty at the latest. I presume she was on *her* cell, since she was hoofing it back to work when she called. Can't you tell by looking at the info on her cell phone? It should still be on the SIM card, even if the phone is dead, right Jerry?"

Jerry nodded in agreement. "The police would have checked that, and it should be in the case file unless they didn't find her phone."

"You've got it. No phone and no one who spoke to her after you did, Tommy, except for her supervisor in the spa. Kelly called in sick Tuesday morning, so, officially, that was the last time anyone heard from her. We don't know what phone she used to make that call. The phone is missing, and so is the vest that the sleaze-ball boyfriend said she had on when she went off to work Monday night. There's no record that she worked anywhere in the hotel, bars, restaurants, or casino and no one remembers seeing or hearing from her that night at all. The phone call you got from Kelly jibes with what Bobby Simmons told the police about their fight and the time she left her apartment for work Monday."

"There's something else we have to ask you. It's about drugs."

"What do you want to know? If I don't already know, I can sure find out." Tommy was in a full-blown smart-alecky mode. No wonder, since he was nearly through that second glass of Macallan.

"What she wants to know, is how involved was Kelly with drugs?"

"Do you mean, like meth or cocaine or heroin? Hard drugs like that?"

A Dead Sister

"That's exactly what we mean."

"Uncle Don asked me if I ever saw Kelly using drugs back then and I told him no. Why? What does that have to do with anything?"

"The police were trying to be discreet, since it didn't seem to have any bearing on how she died, but Kelly had been using heroin, Tommy. There were needle marks on her arms, and the police found a loaded hypodermic close to her body, with her fingerprints all over it. The coroner said she had heroin and a bunch of other drugs in her system when she was killed that night." Tommy sat bolt upright and spoke as if in in utter disbelief.

"No, that can't be true. You know what a freak she was about needles. When she caught me with a couple pills and a little baggie of pot once, she went ballistic. She threatened to turn me in to Uncle Don! We had a mega fight about it and I accused her of being a hypocrite, since I knew she smoked dope. She hit me. That's the only time I can ever remember her hurting me like that." Emotion overtook Tommy, and his eyes filled with tears. "She said she was sorry and begged me to forgive her. I did, of course, but she made me promise to stay away from that stuff. I kept my promise, too. For a while, even after she died." Tommy had started to sob quietly. Jerry moved closer to comfort his anguished boyfriend.

Jessica felt like dirt. This is how she imagined the whole scene would play out. Frank had a crestfallen look on his face. The same one she wore, no doubt. Tommy, his face flushed and streaked with tears, sat up straight and gazed defiantly at Frank and Jessica.

"You've got to find out who killed her I don't believe Kelly was using drugs on her own account. You saw her on New Year's Eve, Jessica. She wasn't shooting up, right? It's that creep Bobby Simmons. He must have gone after her that night and forced her to go off with him. It's just not like her to disappear like that. She suddenly goes from working double shifts to ditching work; does that make sense? It's not like she was totally nuts, not like she was a mental case or something." Frank and Jessica looked at each other.

"What? Why are you two looking at each other like that?" He was dabbing at his eyes with a napkin from the bar. His eyes were red, his pale skin splotchy.

"There was something else we were wondering about. Did Kelly say anything to you about seeing a psychiatrist, or taking prescribed medication for bipolar disorder? Apparently traces of those were found in her system too." Tommy seemed like he was about to say no when he suddenly remembered something.

"This was way before she was killed, so I don't know why it matters. She *did* see a doctor. I never saw him, but Kelly said he was a big guy with a huge forehead, bad skin, these nasty teeth, and a scar of some kind. The way she described him, he looked like Boris Karloff. I asked her why in the world she was interested in seeing a doctor like that." Tommy had all of them on the edge of their seats.

"What did she tell you?" Tommy bit his bottom lip, struggling to recall what Kelly had said.

"It was kind of weird, but it didn't seem all that important at the time. Kelly said she was talking to some old rich guy who was one of her regulars at the spa. This guy tipped her *very well* whenever she worked at the spa or one of those extra shifts at a bar or restaurant. I guess he was a promoter or producer from LA, too. Anyway, he gave her his version of that 'you're a beautiful girl... you ought to be in pictures, yada, yada, yada' line. She said something like she had way too many problems to handle all the crap in Hollywood. He said he had plenty of problems of his own, and what she needed was a good head doctor. Kelly got this business card from him with a number on the back for some shrink."

"So, what happened?" Frank asked.

"At one point, she'd been having a bad day. I don't remember if she said why. Maybe she had one of those fights with Bobby. She called and set up an appointment. When she showed up, they talked for a few minutes, and he recommended prescription meds. He handed her free samples of Xanax and offered to write her a prescription for more right there on the spot. I suppose he could be the one who gave her the bipolar pills. I got the impression he would have written a prescription for whatever she wanted. Kelly never said anything to me about being bipolar and she never mentioned seeing him again."

"Can you remember the name of the doctor? Do you know when she saw him or where—a local clinic maybe?" Frank asked.

"No. All that old guy wrote on the card was a telephone number, and the appointment was at the hotel of all places. He met her there for lunch. Sounds real professional, huh? Kelly never mentioned a name, just called him the doc." Frank and Jessica both gasped and sat up straight.

A Dead Sister

"The doc, are you sure?"

"Yeah, I'm sure. What's the big deal?"

"That's what Chester Davis claimed the two guys chasing Kelly called the injured man they hauled to the Mercedes after Kelly was run down. This is very important. Did Kelly tell you the name of the man who gave her that card?"

"What do you mean? Who chased Kelly? What injured man, what card? What *is going on*?" They all looked at the archway that led into the great room. Laura Stone stood with her hands on her hips and a stressed-out look on her face. She was flanked on either side by Brien Williams and Peter March, the trio awash in Hawaiian fabric. The rest of the Cat Pack had arrived.

CHAPTER 20

Jessica got up to greet the three friends, Laura's questions hanging out there waiting to be answered. Bernadette came bustling up behind them. She wore a long red-ruffled muumuu, with a flower tucked behind her left ear. "The caterers are still setting things up. Dinner will be ready in a few minutes. It looks delicious. For goodness sakes, Jessica, invite your friends to sit down and offer them something to drink."

Bernadette was carrying a couple bowls of nuts. As she stepped around him, Brien reached out and grabbed a handful from one of the bowls.

"Who is Kelly?" He asked, tossing a nut up into the air and catching it in his mouth.

"Glad we weren't counting on keeping this too hush-hush," Jessica said to the guys seated at the bar. At least the question in her mind about involving Laura in this mess had been resolved. She walked over, hugged Laura, and then led her to one of the oversized sofas that were dwarfed by the huge room. The great room lived up to its name. Sprawling and voluminous, it could better be described in cubic feet than square feet. The vaulted ceilings and massive wall of cathedral-like, two-story windows paid homage to the glory of the desert resort landscape. Pocket doors could be opened, making the outdoor space available, too, for large gatherings.

Bernadette placed one bowl of nuts on the dark wood coffee table in front of Laura. In a flash, Brien was sitting beside Laura, reaching for another handful. Peter appeared to be a bit uncomfortable in the enormous, flashy aloha shirt he wore. Open, it revealed his usual tight dark t-shirt beneath, straining to cover his enormous pecs. He settled into a loveseat

A Dead Sister

adjacent to Laura and Brien, taking up most of it by himself. His thighs bulged in the shorts he wore as he sat down. Perched near one another, Peter and Brien could have been before and after pictures for some protein powder commercial. Even though the well-muscled surfer was probably more used to being the "after" photo in rooms full of men, next to Peter he was the "before" shot.

"Tommy, are you up for sharing the news about Kelly with our friends, here? If you'd rather, we can put this off until after dinner or another time altogether."

"If I don't have to do much talking. Hearing it all again might make it seem more real. Right now, it's like I've slipped through a crack into a parallel universe," Tommy said.

Jessica took the other bowl of nuts from Bernadette, placing it next to the guys at the bar, and then stepped back behind the bar to fix drinks for the newcomers.

"Whoa, you mean like one of those places where everything's totally flat? Like a day at the beach when it's all glass, no surf at all? Or someplace where everybody has special powers like Extra Sensatory Precipitation?" Everyone in the room was staring at Brien trying to figure out what on earth he was saying. "You know, ESP. Like how Bernadette just *knows* things?" He was nodding his head up and down solemnly, looking more like a bobble-head doll than a man in the know.

Jessica and Bernadette made eye contact. It didn't take ESP for Jessica to read her mind as Brien snapped another nut out of thin air. Clearly not all the nuts were in the bowl.

"The man does seem to know his parallel universes," Jessica said, speaking to no one in particular. She felt the urge to correct him about the whole ESP thing, but he was wearing that eager-to-please-golden-retriever look, made more dog-like by the shock of bleach blond hair hanging in his eyes. She just couldn't do it. The correction might trigger that "sorry I peed on the floor" look instead, and none of them needed to see that right now.

"Okay, so do you all want beer, wine, or something stronger?"

Jessica poured cold beer for Brien and Peter, a glass of wine for Laura, and another shot of the Macallan for herself. The men at the bar polished off the rest of the single malt between them, fortifying themselves against the retelling of the gruesome tale.

"Bernadette, you want something?"

"No thanks. I'm going to check on the dinner. When you get to that part about Mr. P. or Mr. B., call me if I'm not back. I just know I heard something like that before."

"Sure," Jessica said, as she sat back down in the swivel lounger that was still out in the middle of the floor. Once Bernadette left the room, Brien piped up again.

"Whoa, did you hear that? What'd I tell you? *That* woman knows things." He was doing the nodding again. Just like one of those little surfer dolls you see on a dashboard, with one arm around a surfboard.

"Frank, can you start once again from the beginning? I'll jump in when it comes to my conversation with Chester Davis. Tommy, Jerry, you've already heard a version of this, but if you have questions or comments on the second round, you jump in too, okay?" Jessica tried to listen as Frank told the story again.

Something *was* familiar about the man with a name that was just an initial. Elements of the story weren't all that original, especially the part about the whale. If he was indeed the same man who turned up in the Mercedes sedan later: aging producer on the make woos a beautiful, starry-eyed wannabe with hundred-dollar bills, offers to help her career, and hooks her up with his own personal "doctor-feel-good." That the doc happened to look like Boris Karloff was an odd twist to that old tale. It was a b-movie script for sure. One that resonated with real-life Hollywood tales of woe, however, all twisted up together. Like Lindsay Lohan meeting up with Michael Jackson's doctor at Phil Spector's house.

It only took Frank about ten minutes to get to the point where he'd provided enough background about Kelly Fontana, and the new cast of characters, to suggest something other than a hit-and-run accident happened that night. It was Jessica's turn to provide details about the horrible climax to that b-movie running in her head. The whole thing was narrated by the drug addicted, three-time loser, Chet Davis. Bernadette had returned to the room and listened, deep in thought.

Wrapping up her account, Jessica said, "It sounds far-fetched, but the case file backs up aspects of his story. And now Tommy says that Kelly *had* gone to see someone she referred to as the doc. Tommy doesn't remember Kelly mentioning a Mr. P. or Mr. B., but does remember some LA producer she met at the spa who left her hundred-dollar bills as tips and gave her a phone number for someone she called the doc. Maybe the producer's the long-haired mystery man behind the wheel of the Mercedes that night."

"That's it, Jessica! Now I remember where I heard about Mr. P. with the long hair. It's in one of my magazines—un momento." Bernadette was out of the room, moving at a speed that was remarkable at any age, but even more stunning for a woman pushing seventy. In a flash, she was back among them, bearing a raggedy old issue of one of her favorite entertainment news magazines in hand.

"Wow, that was fast," Peter said, a note of awe suggesting he was beginning to believe Brien's assertions about her superpowers.

"I may be old, but I'm bold!" Bernadette flashed him a sassy smile as she handed the article to Jessica. "Mira, mira esto!"

The title read: "That's *Mr. P.* to You!" A thin, short man in his fifties, with shoulder length dark hair, streaked with gray, stood smiling broadly among several rock and rap luminaries. He pointed a bandaged finger at the camera. Like one of those vintage "Uncle Sam wants you" posters. Jessica scanned the article quickly, passing along snippets of what she was reading. It announced "rap artists were not the only ones who used initials instead of their full names." In this case, for the record producer at the center of attention, it was partly "a matter of expediency," since his last name was difficult to spell and remember.

"There's also the fact that Christopher Pogswich makes him sound like a character out of a Harry Potter story. Not good, since he kind of looks like one too," Jessica commented, as she zipped through the article.

He also liked being referred to by the letter "P" because, "*p stands for pure platinum*," like the work done at his studio and the name of his label: *Pure Platinum Music Group*. Acknowledged by many as one of the best producers in the business, he was notoriously difficult to work with at times. Given to fits of frustration in his pursuit of perfection, he sometimes indulged in the studio equivalent of road rage.

Perhaps the rage was aggravated by his legendary capacity to go through fifths of expensive vodka between takes and still stand up in the control room. During one such tiff, he had shouted the now infamous line, "that's Mr. P. to you," while pointing his finger repeatedly in the artist's face. The artist, being as temperamental and no doubt as looped as Mr. P. was, bit the finger—almost completely through. It took stitches to reattach the offending digit. This was all deemed to be a hilarious mishap, and had since been forgiven. No criminal charges were filed, and all civil suits had been dropped. The producer and artist posed side-by-side. It had been written in 2003, so they'd have to investigate his whereabouts, before and since.

"Jerry, we need to figure out if we can place this guy at the spa or casino. Can you get us a clear photo, preferably one taken closer to the time of the hit-and-run in 1999?"

"I doubt that'll be a problem. I'll see if I can get a recent shot, too, so we have a better idea of what he looks like now."

"That's a great idea, Jerry, thanks. Frank, if we can get that old photo, I'd like to show it to Chester Davis, to see if it rings any bells. What do you think?"

"It's certainly worth a try. I'll see if I can get Art Greenwald to put together a photo lineup with a picture of our Mr. P. included. I'll call and ask him when he gets in on Monday morning."

"That's perfect. I have to drive back to LA Tuesday, so if Detective Greenwald can put a photo lineup together by Wednesday morning, I'll arrange to be there with Chet when he views it."

"How soon can you get us a photo, Jerry?" Frank asked.

"It sounds like Mr. P. is a media mogul who likes the limelight, so my guess is there are plenty of images on the internet. We'll need to figure out what pictures were taken when, but that shouldn't be too hard. Then we can print something off the web tonight. Is your laptop handy and do you have a photo quality printer, Jessica?"

"Yes, and yes. My laptop is down the hall, and there's a great printer in the study."

"If you go get it, Tommy and I can do a search."

"The other thing I want to do is visit the hotel, spa, and casino. A lot has changed, and it's not like we haven't been there before, but I want to see where she was killed. I'm going to call Uncle Don, Jerry, and see if he's okay meeting us there. I'd like him to do a walk through with us, recounting what he saw that morning when Kelly was found. Then, what it was like when he went back later, closer to the time of night she was killed. Can you go with me on Sunday if he's willing to do it?"

"No problem. I left the weekend kind of open to recover from jet lag."

A Dead Sister

"Sorry to ask you to do this, but I really want to get a jump on this. I've already spoken to Paul, so you're back on the clock with the firm. That'll be some compensation, at least."

"He doesn't mind. He knows this is important to me. I have scars from Kelly's death, and Jerry's already met what's left of my parents. I'll not only help do the search for photos online, but I can help track down the people who need to be interviewed. You don't even have to pay me."

"If you can handle the emotional stress and Jerry has work for you to do, you'll get paid too. That's the deal we worked out, and it still stands. In addition to the pictures, let's find out what we can about where Mr. P. lives and works now. Let's see what turns up by digging into Mr. P.'s property and business holdings, okay? We'll follow the money and assets and see where that takes us. That includes figuring out what kind of cars Mr. P. owns. I'm sure he doesn't still have a 1999 midnight blue Mercedes S class sedan, but maybe he's a loyal Mercedes customer and has a newer model. If we figure out where he purchased his current car, someone at the dealership may have been around long enough to recall if there ever *was* such a car in Mr. P.'s possession. I also want to know what kind of trouble he's been in with the law. Vodka and a nasty temper are two things likely to get him attention, not just from the media, but also from LAPD." Jessica was speaking at a good clip. Her mind raced as she considered all they needed to do. Before she could say anything else, Tommy spoke up.

"Why don't we *all* pay a visit to the casino, hotel, and spa? You and Jerry shouldn't have to go there alone. We'll make it a field trip—a sleepover! That way, we can get the complete experience by going undercover." A round of groans rolled around the room at Tommy's play on words. Tommy was back in imp mode. It was a familiar role, but couldn't disguise the pain in his eyes.

"Two rooms, Jessica; one for the boys and one for the girls." Those were the first words Laura had uttered since Frank had started talking about Kelly's death. Jessica eyed her friend, worried that hearing about another murder couldn't be easy for her. Especially the murder of another person with whom she had been close.

Still in the throes of dealing with her husband's death, she hadn't returned to work yet, so an overnight "field trip" to the casino wasn't going to be a problem on that front. She was overseeing repairs to the house where Roger was murdered, anxious to get rid of it as soon as she could. Not that it would be easy to sell a house in the desert during the summer months, even if it was on the market.

Once she had the double indemnity payout from the insurance company, Laura could afford to buy another house. She wasn't in a big hurry to do that either since living alone in a house felt too isolated to Jessica's newly-widowed friend. Laura claimed an apartment or condo seemed too close, almost claustrophobic. That closed-in feeling might have more to do with being back under the watchful eye of her parents. Laura was at loose ends, and growing antsy.

"I want to restart my life, but how do I do it?"

Tell me about it, Jessica had thought as she tried to find the words to support her friend. Jessica suggested she speak with a financial counselor to help sort through the financial issues related to her housing options. Figuring out her finances was one thing, dealing with the fear and loss she felt was another.

Soon after that conversation, the ever-conscientious Laura revealed she had taken a step on that front, too. She'd joined a bereavement group. Mostly older women who had lost husbands to aging or disease participated in that group and their issues weren't entirely the same. Still, she said she found solace and support hearing how others were coping with their loss. That didn't counter the deep sadness on her face as she spoke after hearing the news about Kelly.

Laura's face also bore a stubborn look Jessica had seen before many times. Her determination to go on that field trip was underscored by arms folded across her chest, as she sat on the couch with her legs stretched out on a cushy ottoman.

"That means me too," Bernadette said. She moved closer to Laura, mirroring her expression and folding her arms, too.

Jessica was silent as she considered the prospect of taking the whole Cat Pack to the hotel, spa, and casino downtown. They could certainly get the lay of the land quickly that way, covering a lot of ground in a relatively short period of time.

"With pictures of Mr. P., as he was then and is now, we could ask around and see if anyone recognizes him. Maybe someone in management or at the front desk or the spa will remember if he *was* a regular at the time that Kelly was employed. Heck, he might *still* be a regular, for all we know."

"Yeah, we can all ask around, talk to people, and get all the gossip. You shouldn't forget about the housekeeping staff. They clean up the mess. I bet they know plenty that goes on. I don't have to do the dirty work around here anymore, but I remember what that was like before I became the household estate manager. I can talk to them for you," Bernadette offered.

"That's an awesome idea, Mrs. B. I can talk to the pool guys and the guys who hand out towels and stuff like that. I can tell them about my experiences in the pool business, talk to them pro-to-pro, you know? And I'll hang with the maintenance workers too and see what they have to say."

"Ooh, that's a great idea. We can talk to the bartenders, too. We do know our booze, don't we?" Brien was beaming, nodding his head enthusiastically, as Tommy continued.

"Bartenders *always* hear things."

"Nurses do too. Spa attendants can't be very different. I'll bet they've heard plenty. I'm happy to chat them up while I get a massage," Laura added wearing a wicked smile.

"Brilliant! We can all take the waters at the spa and get treatments. That Mr. P. has a mouth on him. If he was there, he probably spilled his guts to his masseuse or esthetician about all sorts of dirt. You can chatter with the women on your side of the spa and we'll get the scoop from the attendants who serve male guests. Even if they weren't around back then, Bernadette is right about gossip. I bet there was a lot of talk *after* they found Kelly dead. Stuff that's still circulating years later and maybe never came up when the cops were asking the questions. Besides, I'm all tensed up from that long flight home. I could use a massage. Why don't we go tomorrow?" There was that twinge of pain in his eyes again. A quiet desperation hovered beneath his clownishness.

"Tomorrow? Are you serious?" Jessica asked. He was. She thought about the week ahead. It was either tomorrow or put it off until next weekend. Friday would be her dinner and film noir night with Paul, so that meant next Saturday night at the earliest. "Okay, I guess that actually makes sense. I can't figure out another night that will work. Not this week, anyway."

"What about you, Peter, can you join us? Maybe you could find out what sort of security arrangements were in place when Kelly was killed. How could Mr. P., or anyone else, have been in the parking lot at that time of night without being caught by a security patrol? Wouldn't someone have noticed and spoken to him if he was sitting out there in his car like that?"

"I was wondering about the same thing. That Chester Davis could come and go as he said he did is a little far-fetched, too. Granted, security wasn't as tight back in the '90s, when Indian gaming took in a hundred million a year rather than about thirty billion, like it does now." Laura gasped.

"Thirty billion? Are you kidding me?"

"No, I'm not kidding. That's the total for the entire country, but about a third of that is made right here in California or over the border in Nevada. That's the hardest thing for me to believe about what this Chester Davis character is saying. Casino operators are paranoid about cheaters. Surveillance is everywhere. They watch everybody, customers and employees, and the guys doing the watching even have guys watching them. No casino wants their players to get robbed in the hotel parking lot after winning a jackpot at the slots. His story seems odd from my point of view."

"The police did talk to someone in security back then. I can give you a name, if you want it."

"Sure, that would be helpful. One of the current security team members at that casino used to work for me. I'm sure he'll tell me as much as he can without giving away too many secrets. The other thing I was wondering about is all those comps casinos give out. Casinos climb all over each other to attract and keep the whales coming back. They must have a system in place to do that. Gaming commissions and casino operators keep an eye on who gets comps, how much, and for what. If he was in their system as a loyal customer or a member of a premium players club, those records might still be around. That's way more likely than video surveillance or other security records. Those probably got dumped long ago, even if they had them."

"That's great, we'll count you in. How about you, Frank? We'll even make you an ex officio member of the Cat Pack if you want to join us."

"Thanks for including me, but I have two kids at home. We have plans for tomorrow night. The only reason I got tonight night off is because Jessica was such a big hit at our Fourth of July picnic. I will take the Cat Pack membership, though, if that's an option."

"What about it, pack members? Paws up or down?" Tommy scratched the air and let out a round of meows. Jerry rolled his eyes and tousled Tommy's hair. All hands went up as Tommy pretended to lick his hand before smoothing his hair back into place.

A Dead Sister

"I suppose that means you're in," Jessica said, with those in the room nodding in agreement.

"Okay, thanks. After listening to Peter talk about Chester's story from the security angle, maybe we should all be more skeptical. As an addict who's been at it for as long as he has, Chester Davis is a practiced liar. He's been in and out of jail. He might have picked up what he knows about Kelly's death from talking to one of the officers or overhearing them talking to each other. When I talk to Art Greenwald Monday, I'm going to ask him to check and see if Chester Davis was arrested anywhere around the time Kelly was killed. Given that the dead girl was a police officer's family member, there was probably a lot of buzz." Jessica was a little irritated, not sure if it was Frank's unwillingness to accompany them to the hotel and spa, or the sudden onset of cop skepticism that chafed.

"Okay, I hear you. One way to sort this out is to follow up on this Mr. P. thing. There's nothing in the police record about a Mr. P., so he couldn't have gotten that from eavesdropping, right? If it turns out Mr. P. was a regular, that'll add credibility to his tale."

"That's true. I'm not saying we shouldn't keep digging. We might get more out of Bobby, the boyfriend. Maybe *he* can tell us if Mr. P. was a regular back then, by looking at a photo. More important than that is finding out if he can tag him as the 'whale' slipping Kelly hundred-dollar bills. How about finding Bobby Simmons, Jerry?"

"If he's still working for the tribal casino, it'll be easy to locate him. If not, I presume there's an address in the police record. There still might be a link to him online related to that old address. A driver's license number or a social security number would speed things up. He couldn't have been working as a dealer at the casino if he had a police record back then. If Tommy's right that Bobby Simmons was up to no good, it's entirely possible he's had a run-in with the law since then. Has the cold case team run a recent check on him?"

"That's a good question, but I don't know. I'll see where the cold case team is with all of this when I follow up with Art on Monday. I'll ask specifically about Bobby Simmons, his whereabouts and activities since Kelly's death."

"I need to talk to Art, too. I have questions from my review of the case file. I'll give you the first crack at him. If you could call me and let me know what you find out, that would be great. I'll wait until I hear from you before I contact the detective myself."

"I'm putting out my own query about Bobby-the-slug right now, using my connections to the looser side of life in the valley." As he spoke, Tommy's thumbs were flying, rhythmically punching out text messages on his cell phone. "If that guy's still around, or if he's been up to something slimy I'll find out quicker than you will, whether he's been tagged for it by the law or not. Especially if what he's been up to has anything to do with drugs, gambling, or sex. I'll hear about it."

"Let's go eat. After dinner, I'll get out my AMEX card and arrange our field trip. That's part of the deal, right?" Heads bobbed up and down again. "I'll go get my laptop, Jerry, so we can print out pictures of Mr. P. I'm sure we can find a couple pics to take with you, Frank, and I'll make copies for tomorrow night when we start asking around at the casino. There's a head shot of Kelly in the case file. I'll scan it so we can take her photo with us, too."

Hours later, when the others had left, Jessica was still pent up. Maybe from all the sugar and alcohol she'd consumed. She slipped out the sliding doors from her bedroom and stood on the patio. The night breeze curled around her, warm and comforting. After dinner, they had reservations at the hotel and set out plans to make the best use of their time. When the others had gone, she and Frank talked through everything once more. She could tell Frank still had doubts, but was as determined as she was to take the investigation as far as they could. A somber mood had gripped them both, putting a damper on the heat between them. When he stood to leave, she got up to walk him to the door.

"Jessica, I'm sorry about all of this. I wish we were sitting here doing nothing but watching the sunset and chatting. I'd rather be talking about wine or music, anything but Kelly and a bunch of lowlifes." He was as burdened as his father had been the night before. She couldn't ever remember Jim being moved so deeply by such a sense of responsibility for anybody or anything. How could she have missed that about him?

"None of this is your fault, Frank. Count your blessings. At least you don't have to listen to me go on and on about the lowlife I married. When this is all over, we'll have time to do those other things."

"You think so?"

"I know so. Heck, you're a member of the Cat Pack now. And, don't forget, you still owe me a home cooked Italian dinner. If all that comes of this is that we become better friends, Frank, I think that's good enough, don't you?"

A Dead Sister

"You're right, Jessica. It's more than enough, even if this is just so much ring-around-the-rosy." He draped an arm over her shoulders and she put an arm around his waist. The two of them stood there, side-by-side, in companionable silence as the last colors of the sunset faded away.

"Good night friend, thanks for the pep talk," Frank said, kissing her on the forehead.

Later, alone in the dark Jessica whispered, "Maybe all of this is a lot of ring-around-the-rosy." Even if they could make a connection between Mr. P. and the resort where Kelly worked, they still had no evidence that he killed her. Linking Mr. P. to the same make and model sedan that had run Kelly down wouldn't get them very far either. There still wouldn't be any physical evidence it was his car that hit her or that he was the driver. The statute of limitations had run out on the hit-and-run, so he'd be off the hook unless they could prove it was murder. The only thing that really made this any kind of case at all was the belated eyewitness testimony of a drug addict facing a third strike. If, as Chet claimed, Kelly's death was no accident, why? Why on earth would Mr. P. have done such a thing? Even if he had the means and opportunity to kill Kelly, it said nothing about a motive.

CHAPTER 21

When her phone rang Saturday morning, Jessica was still asleep. She did her best to get to the phone as quickly as she could, but struggled. Maybe scotch was more than she could handle, even an exquisite scotch. Or maybe it was the wine on top of the scotch. She did a quick tally in her head. A couple glasses of scotch before dinner, a couple glasses of wine with dinner, and another sitting on the patio after dinner. Officially, that's a binge and her body confirmed it. She wasn't hungover, but it was a close call.

"I'm getting too old for this," she said, as she answered the phone with a fuzzy, "Hullo."

"Jessica, this is Tommy. It's Bobby Simmons. You know. Bobby the lizard, Kelly's old boyfriend? The messages I sent out last night got a hit. Jerry's keeping an eye on him. He's serving food at a soup kitchen here in Indio. We can interview him if you'd like, but I thought you'd want to talk to him, too. You need to get down here, quick."

"You bet I do. Wait for me. I don't want to miss anything he says. What's he doing serving homeless people at a soup kitchen?" Jessica asked, as she dragged herself out of bed and into the bathroom.

"He's doing community service. He had legal trouble, and just got out after almost two years in the state prison. It's a condition of his parole. The community service, I mean. No way is Bobby-the-loser-lizard ever going to work in a casino again. He's toxic. Bobby Simmons does hair now, if you can believe that!" Tommy snorted.

"You two keep an eye on him. I'll be there in twenty minutes." The drive from Rancho Mirage to the soup kitchen in Indio would take ten, so that gave her less than that to throw on some clothes.

Jessica splashed water in her face, ran a brush through her hair, rinsed with mouthwash, and put on a couple swipes of deodorant. In her closet, she pulled on a pair of jeans, a t-shirt, and sandals. She scanned her bedroom for the essentials—purse, keys, phone, and a pair of sunglasses. In five minutes, she was dashing down the long hallway that led from her wing of the house, past the great room and to the open kitchen and morning room area.

"Please, God, let there be coffee, any coffee, made any old way!" Her prayer was answered immediately. Bernadette was nowhere to be seen, but Jessica could smell coffee, and spotted the thermal carafe on the counter. "Thank you, St. Bernadette," Jessica mumbled, as she dug through a cupboard for a travel mug with a lid that fit. She poured it half full of coffee and then added milk to the brim and drank it, still standing at the sink. The jolt of caffeine went straight to her brain and the milk soothed her acidy stomach. She refilled the cup, this time, mostly coffee with just a touch of milk.

"You're up! I thought you would sleep 'til noon after hanging around with Frank for hours." She had a wicked little smile. Jessica knew she was in no shape to go toe-to-toe with Bernadette this morning. She took a big swig of coffee from the cup, ignoring Bernadette's taunt about Frank. Instead, all she said was,

"Gotta go!" as she planted a big smooch on Bernadette's cheek.

"Go? Where are you going in such a rush?" Her eyes narrowed, sensing that Jessica was up to something. Jessica leaned in and gave Bernadette another kiss. This one made her giggle.

"Tommy and Jerry found Kelly's boyfriend, Bobby Simmons. I'll tell you all about it when I get back."

With that, she dashed from the house and hopped into her BMW. When she arrived at the soup kitchen minutes later, she spotted Jerry's pickup truck in a spacious lot in front of the complex. Feeding hungry people was only one of the many services offered by the charitable organization, so the parking lot was large, but it was nearly empty on a Saturday morning. The homeless were mostly carless.

The doors didn't open until eleven a.m., when a free hot meal would be provided to the public until noon. A variety of lost souls were already milling about, not exactly queuing up, but waiting for the signal that food was being served. They included the kind of folks you expected to see at a soup kitchen. Men with skin tanned and leathered by the desert sun, worn clothes, unshaven faces, and unruly hair. Several looked an awful lot like Chester Davis. There were also women. A small cluster included children, the little ones in their mothers' arms or clinging to them. A handful of older children played a game of tag, kicking up dust as they ran around on a playground off to one side of the building.

Jessica felt a wave of guilt wash over her, as she was reminded once again of how blithely she spent money. The clothes she wore, just jeans, a t-shirt, and simple leather flip-flops, probably cost more than what was required to feed everyone who passed through that line before noon. That was true without considering her Marc Jacobs handbag and sunglasses, which were a "steal" the day she had bought them for around three hundred dollars. She began to wonder how much cash she had in her wallet and whether the kitchen staff could accept it. Or maybe they would take a check. She was digging through her purse, adding a couple tens to the cash from her wallet, when there was a knock on her car window.

Jessica let out a little yip before she realized it was Tommy. He and Jerry hadn't been in the truck when she drove up, so she figured they were among the group waiting under a canopy near the front door. She rolled the window down and chided him.

"Tommy, please don't sneak up on me like that."

"Jessica, come on, will you? They're starting to feed people."

Jessica rolled the window up and shut the car off. As she glanced at the building, a thin man wearing a poufy white mesh hair net was standing in the doorway. He held the door open and directed the flow of down-and-outers. He stared at them for a moment as Jessica slammed her car door and walked toward the entrance, with Tommy at her side. Jerry met them as they entered the building, and they all followed the hungry throng into the dining hall that had a serving line set up cafeteria style.

"That's him," Jerry said in a low voice, nodding in the direction of the guy who had been staring at them earlier.

Bobby Simmons perused them warily as he took a place in the serving line behind the counter. In addition to the white bouffant hair net, he was wearing a large white apron hooked in a loop around his neck. Knee length, it covered much of his clothing. Jessica and her companions sort of hung

A Dead Sister

back, watching him as the hungry patrons, familiar with the routine, grabbed trays and moved through the line. Jessica hadn't given much thought about how to approach Bobby. She was about to confer with Jerry about what they should do when a woman dressed in similar food service garb approached them.

"Can I help you?" Jessica had pulled a business card out of her wallet while searching for cash earlier and handed it to the woman.

"We'd like to speak with Bobby Simmons. What would be a good time to do that?"

"Is he expecting you?" She sounded like his executive assistant. She had the officious demeanor to fit the question.

"No, he's not expecting us, ma'am. We're sorry about that," Jerry Reynolds answered, scuffing the floor a little. If he had been wearing a cowboy hat, he would have tipped it to her right about then. "The police department gave us this location as the best place to find him on a personal matter. It's awfully darn important, or we wouldn't have rushed down here this morning without calling first, Ms., uh... forgive me, but I don't think I caught your name."

Tommy's friend who supplied the info about Bobby Simmons *did* work for the police department, so what Jerry said was sort of true, but not exactly. However, even if they'd had a month of Sundays, they wouldn't have called ahead. No way would they have given a shyster like Bobby Simmons the heads up he needed to dodge them.

It didn't matter at that point. Jerry flashed a devastatingly handsome smile at their inquisitor, and then held out his hand to shake hers. She was obviously bedazzled, as she replied, "Ronda, Ronda Emerson." Smiling broadly up at him, she placed her gloved hand in his. Gay or not, the man had a way with women. Perhaps it was his leading man good looks, or his chivalrous behavior, mixed with that aw-shucks number he was running on her. In any case, Ronda Emerson was now putty in his hands.

"Let me take your card, uh," she let her eyes drop from Jerry's face long enough to read the name on the card that Jessica had handed her, "Attorney Huntington, I'll give it to Bobby. I can't make him talk to you, of course." Her eyes drifted back to Jerry, who was still smiling beatifically. "I'm sure he'll be right over. You all take a seat at one of those tables toward the back, will you?"

"Thank you, ma'am, we appreciate your help, given how busy you are." Jessica had to stop the impulse to roll her eyes. He was laying it on thick. Ronda Emerson bumped into two or three people as she backed away. Fortunately, none of them dropped their trays or spilled the food being dished out to them.

The three of them sat down as they were instructed, waiting while Ronda Emerson spoke to Bobby Simmons. Bobby took the card from her and put in a shirt pocket. For a moment, it looked as though he might run for it. His eyes darted from side-to-side, and he glanced over his shoulder into the kitchen. It was packed, so not a quick way out.

Next, he scanned the area between him and the doorway that led to the front entrance. She wondered if they could get to the doorway first. Probably, so she relaxed a little. Bobby must have figured out the same thing. His shoulders slumped as he handed his serving spoon to Ronda.

Ronda stepped into Bobby's place in the serving line. She smiled at Jerry, who gave her a little wink. Flustered, she missed the plate she was aiming to supply with what looked like sweet potatoes. She didn't notice, and the poor hungry man she was feeding didn't seem to care that it had landed on his tray. He just leaned in a little closer as Ronda Emerson doled out another spoonful, this time on his plate.

"You want to talk to me?" Bobby Simmons asked, in a sullen tone. Jessica spoke first.

"Yes, Mr. Simmons. It's nice to meet you." Jessica stood and held out her hand, as Jerry had done with Ronda earlier. She also tried out her own version of a ravishing smile on Bobby, with much less luck. He didn't return the smile, nor did he take her outstretched hand. "I'm Jessica Huntington and these are my associates, Mr. Simmons. Will you have a seat, please?"

Jessica took a closer look at Bobby as he sat down and pulled off the hair net. He was in better condition than Chester Davis but she still would have had a hard time believing he was about her own age. Nor did he have a swagger, or much of the lounge lizard about him that Tommy had recounted when describing the youthful Bobby Simmons. One reason Tommy may have found it so hard to believe he was doing hair was that Bobby had none of his own. Well, almost none. He had thin wisps around the sides and back of his head. A few strands combed over on top were kind of standing on end. Bobby reached up and swiped at the top of his head, patting down the restive tufts.

A Dead Sister

"This is Jerry Reynolds," Jessica said, gesturing toward Jerry, who sat across from her. Bobby cast a scowl in his direction but didn't say anything to Jerry. "And this is..." Bobby cut her off.

"I know who he is. You're Kelly's little brother, Timmy, right? I remember you. Hell, even if I hadn't seen you before, I would have known you were her brother from a mile away. You look just like her. Except for your eyes and except that you're a boy, of course." For some reason, Bobby thought that was funny, and chuckled. The glee fled as he leaned back in his chair and folded his arms, exposing tattoos as his sleeves rode up. Tommy said nothing, but clenched and then unclenched his jaw.

"So, what is this? What are you and your *'associates'* doing here during my community service, Attorney Huntington?"

"Some new information has come to our attention about the circumstances surrounding Kelly Fontana's death. *Tommy*, Jerry, and I have some questions, and are hoping you might be able to help us."

"Tom and Jerry, for real? Now that's funny. I love those guys. They're two of my favorite cartoon characters." Bobby still had his arms folded obstinately in front of him, but he was back in chuckle mode. He snapped out of it quickly and spoke very deliberately. "I didn't have anything to do with her death. That was a long time ago. I told the cops everything I knew. Ask them. They'll tell you I cooperated completely."

"We know that. We've gone through the record, and it's clear that you were very helpful. Especially what you told the police about the last time you saw Kelly and the fact that she was on her way back to work that night. I had a question about what she was wearing. I know it was a long time ago, but do you remember what you said?"

"That's easy, a no-brainer. I worked at that casino, off and on, for almost eight years. The girls all wore the same thing. Kelly wore black when she was working at the spa, black pants and a long black top. They called it a smock or something like that, but basically it was just a shirt, but longer. The ladies that served drinks and food on the casino floor or in the restaurants, they wore black, too, mostly. Black tights and these short little black skirts and tops that were just regular shirts, you know? Kelly had them in white and black and a light brown color, too."

"Okay, do you recall which shirt she wore that night?"

"White, I know for sure because I made her wear it. I told the cops we had a fight that night. I was mad because she was working all the time. She was my girlfriend and I hardly saw her. So, that night I was angry because she was going back to work again. I told her she didn't need to work that hard, that I could help with the bills. We could have saved a load of money if we moved in together, but nothing doing. She had a lot of reasons—excuses, really—for not moving in. She could be real stubborn, you know?"

"Yes, I do know, as a matter of fact. Please, go on. You said you made Kelly wear a white shirt that night, right? Why?"

"In the summer, when it's hot in the desert, the servers sometimes just wore a vest—no shirt. But it was January, and she was getting ready to walk back to work with just that vest on and no shirt under it. It was cold out, so why is she going to freeze all the way to work and back? Maybe she's trying to get some action from the men. Some old guy was slipping her tips, big ones, you know? I'm talking about hundred-dollar bills. Maybe she's showing a little skin to get that guy going. I asked her why this whale was being so nice to her, was there something she wanted to tell me?"

"What did she say?"

"She tells me I'm crazy, there's nothing going on. I told her to put a shirt on under the vest. What difference would it make, unless there something going on? She was furious at that point, but so was I. I can be stubborn, too. Kelly's eyes were shooting fire, but she got that white shirt and put it on. Then she put the vest on over it. It was a black one with the casino name and that little sign on the front of it in red. She flipped me off, stomped out of there, and slammed the door. Boy, she sure had that fiery red-headed temper, even though her hair was browner than red." Jessica watched him carefully. He showed little in the way of sadness. It had been a long time, but she had still expected him to express some sense of sorrow or loss as he described the last time he ever saw his girlfriend. All he displayed was a lot of irritation, even after all these years. He would be at the top of her suspect list if she hadn't heard that story from Chester Davis.

"Okay, thanks, Bobby, that's helpful. Do you know if she had a cell phone with her when she left the house that night?"

"Of course, she did. I told her to call me when her shift was over, and I'd give her a ride home."

"And did she call you for a ride home?"

"No, she didn't. I told the cops that back then, too. That was the last time I saw Kelly Fontana *or* spoke to her."

"Did you worry when she didn't call later?"

"Hell, no! I told you she was mad. As was leaving, I offered to pick her up later, you know what she said?"

"No, what?"

"She said, 'Bobby Simmons, drop dead,' just like that. Cold as ice."

"Okay, so Kelly went back to work that night because she was getting big tips from some whale. Did you know who she was talking about? Did she mention anyone by name?" Bobby shifted in his seat and glanced around him, as if to see who might be in earshot.

"That was a long time ago. How am I supposed to remember that?"

"There must not have been too many guests handing out hundred-dollar bills. I thought that might make the name stick in your mind."

"Not really. Guys would toss me a chip or two from their winnings all the time. I made way more in tips than I got in that puny check the casino deposited in my bank account."

"She never told you that an older man she met at the spa wanted to set her up in Hollywood, and that he was the one giving her those big tips?"

"No, she did not." He bristled and sat up, as if about to leave. Jessica reached out and touched his arm. That caused him to look at her. This time, her smile got a reaction. Not like the one Jerry had generated in Bobby's coworker, but enough that Bobby relaxed a little.

"We're almost done here. And speaking of tips, if it won't get you into trouble, we'd be really happy if you'd take something for the disruption we've caused in your community service." Jessica pulled out the wad of bills she had dug out earlier to use as a donation and laid them on the table. Bobby didn't hesitate. In a split second, he snatched the cash and slipped it into a pocket in the shirt he wore under the apron.

"We wondered if you ever saw this gentleman at the casino, in a restaurant or bar or anywhere else at the hotel or spa?" On cue, Jerry slid a photo of Mr. P. across the table, putting it in front of Bobby. In the black and white publicity shot from the late '90s, Mr. P. was wearing an unconstructed two-button blazer with rolled up sleeves, a dark t-shirt, and a pair of trousers with double reverse front pleats. His brown hair, streaked with gray, was shoulder length. Bobby looked at the photo, and a wave of recognition swept over his face. He shrugged a little. "He mighta' been there. I can't say for sure. Maybe I seen him, but it could have been on MTV or somewhere like that. He's a big shot in the music business. I'd be stepping over a line if I was to tell you for sure that I seen him at the casino."

Liar, Jessica thought, but did not say.

Bobby was squirming in his seat, again. With the money already in his pocket, they were about to lose him.

"Okay, thanks. There's just one last thing. Did Kelly ever tell you about a guy she might have seen once, maybe more? A tall guy called the doc, with a disfigurement like a scar or..." Jessica stopped without finishing her sentence. At the mention of the doc, Bobby had flinched, and then stood up abruptly.

"We're done here. I told you all I can remember about that last time I seen Kelly. I don't know why you want to ask all these other questions about Mr. P. or the doc. All of this was a long time ago, and I don't have anything to do with anything. Got that?" For the first time, Bobby had moved beyond wary to full-blown paranoia.

"Wait, you just called him Mr. P. I thought you didn't know the man in the photo."

"No, that's not what I said, *Tommy.* You trying to confuse things, or what? I told you I seen him before, and of course I know he's Mr. P. because I pay attention to what goes on in Hollywood and the music scene there. Anyone who doesn't know who Mr. P. is has got to be brain dead or something. I know who he is, I'm just not going to say he was at the casino handing out hundred-dollar bills, got it?" Realizing he had raised his voice, Bobby looked around, then nodded and smiled to a few of the patrons who had stopped eating.

"How's it going? The food good?" He asked an older man with a tanned face covered in white stubble, sitting at a nearby table. The old man nodded his head enthusiastically and went back to eating. Bobby was back in control. "Tom and Jerry, I can't get over that. Only you got the names switched. You should be the Tom cat and you should be Jerry the mouse." He threw his head back laughing as he turned to walk away.

A Dead Sister

"Hang on, Bobby. If you give me back the business card Ronda gave you earlier, I'd like to write my cellphone number on the back. That way, if you come up with anything else, you can give me a call even if I'm not at the office, okay?" He nodded and handed over Jessica's business card. When she'd added that phone number, he stuffed the card back in the pocket where he'd also stashed the money she'd given him.

"I'd like to show that guy a thing or two about what a mouse can do to a louse. I can get my Tomcat on anytime I damn well please," Tommy said, gritting his teeth. He clawed the air and hissed a couple of times once they'd left the building.

"Let's go, guys. Do you have time for lunch? My treat," Jessica said, hoping that changing the subject would make her feel less creepy about the encounter with Bobby Simmons. She didn't like the fact that there were moments when he was about as skittish as Chester Davis.

"Can we go to Inn-n-Out burger? I need junk food. There's one a few blocks from here on 111, please, please?" Tommy begged.

She would have preferred a salad and a good glass of wine somewhere. At least this would be a low budget, unpretentious lunch. "Sure, Tommy, a burger sounds good."

"I'm having fries, animal-style," Tommy said, pawing at the air and hissing again. Animal style fries was an item on the secret menu at the iconic west-coast burger joint. A load of fries served up with cheese and grilled onions, covered with Thousand Island dressing. It was more than Jessica could handle, especially after the scotch and pie and Kalua pig the night before.

By the time she arrived at the restaurant, the cloud of guilt swirling around her was more about gluttony than greed. Watching Tommy wolf down the animal fries with apparent abandon caused Jessica to contemplate a third deadly sin for the day—envy. How could he get away eating like that and stay so willowy thin?

She remembered sitting with Kelly wondering the same thing all those years ago. Kelly smiling and vivacious, full of life, as the two of them chattered about students or teachers at school. Kelly's words had tumbled out, each one practically tripping over the next as she filled Jessica in on the latest gossip. She was always the first to know who was planning to break up or make up, who was having a party or getting a hot new car, whatever. She was St. Theresa's answer to the Gossip Girl, but without the blog. *How*

Anna Celeste Burke

much of what Kelly had said was true, and how much was the figment of an overactive imagination? Jessica wondered.

She couldn't quite remember when Kelly had nonchalantly suggested that purging was the key to no more worries about eating all those animal fries. Did she have an eating disorder? Could her odd ideas, mood swings, and impulsiveness have been signs of bipolar disorder? Or was she wild and speedy, at times, because of some drug she was using, keeping that and other secrets from Jessica and her friends? And how in the world did she end up with Bobby Simmons as a boyfriend? When and why?

Over lunch, they agreed that, though he had shed a lot of his lounge lizard looks over the years, along with most of his hair, Bobby Simmons was still a creep. They also agreed he knew more than he was willing to say about Mr. P. and the doc. Like Chester Davis, Bobby Simmons was scared. It was hidden under a layer of belligerence, but it was there.

Jessica intended to go over everything again with Chester Davis Wednesday morning, whether or not Detective Greenwald had put together a photo lineup as Frank was going to ask him to do. *Had Chester Davis known Bobby Simmons when Kelly was still alive?* Jessica wondered. There was a lot of the small town in Palm Springs, obvious from the way in which townies had put the finger on Bobby Simmons' whereabouts so quickly once Tommy had sent out his inquiry. Maybe Chester Davis had crossed paths with Bobby Simmons. Now that she knew Bobby's name, she'd ask Chet about him.

Jerry and Tommy agreed to keep digging into Mr. P.'s past. There had to be a way to discover if the doc was hovering somewhere around Mr. P. A guy like that was hard to miss, and with his "doctor-feel-good" inclinations, it was difficult to believe he hadn't had some brush with the law. To check for a criminal record, though, they needed a name for the doc. If they could find a photo of Mr. P. with that hulk lurking in the background, they might get closer to identifying him.

Meanwhile, she'd get Art Greenwald and his team took another look at Bobby Simmons, if Frank hadn't already succeeded in getting them to do that. With whatever Jerry and Tommy could dredge up checking into Bobby since Kelly's death, perhaps they could turn up something linking Bobby to Mr. P. or the doc. They could at least find out what sort of trouble had landed Bobby Simmons in prison.

CHAPTER 22

A distinguished looking gentleman walks into a restaurant in downtown Palm Springs. The hostess asks, "Do you have a reservation, sir?"

"Why yes, I do. We're standing on it." This apocryphal story, widely circulated in the desert cities, reflects the unique arrangement of tribal lands in the Coachella Valley.

In the 1860s, the U.S. government made land grants to encourage railroad magnates to lay down tracks. In what was referred to as checkerboarding, alternating plots of land along the railroad corridor were given to rail companies to subsidize the cost of building the railroads. When it came time to square up with the native people who had occupied the Coachella Valley for two thousand years, checkerboarding served another purpose. Plots on the checkerboard, not previously doled out to the railroads, were awarded to tribal members.

After decades of wrangling with government authorities, the Agua Caliente Band of Cahuilla Indians ended up with more than thirty thousand acres of reservation land. About a third of that acreage was located within the Palm Springs city limits, often side-by-side with parcels bought and sold on the open market. It was the 1960s before the details of *tribal ownership* were worked out, allowing tribes to realize a profit from the land they owned by leasing it. Leasing land for both residential and commercial development began to bring badly needed money to the Agua Caliente, even before gaming took off.

In 1999, an agreement was reached with the State of California to allow expanded gaming on tribal lands. That included Nevada-style slot machines and card games. Gaming didn't pay off for all the tribes that pursued it, but for the Agua Caliente Band of Cahuilla Indians it did—big time. Half of the four hundred or so tribal members were living at or below the poverty level in 1993. Today, the tribe's wealth is estimated to be in the billions of dollars, including preserve land, real estate holdings, gaming, banking, agriculture, and a host of other ventures.

The Agua Caliente spa casino in Palm Springs was built on a square of the tribe's checkerboard reservation in the downtown retail district. That location encompasses the ancient hot springs the Cahuilla called "Se-Khi," or boiling waters. The area and the band of Indians occupying it were later given the name Agua Caliente ("hot water") by the Spanish. In the 1990s, the establishment in Palm Springs grew to occupy several square blocks adjacent to other commercial properties.

Jessica arrived at the downtown Palm Springs complex with Bernadette and Laura around six p.m., as planned. As they queued up to check in, Tommy and Jerry walked into the hotel and joined them. While they waited in line at the front desk, Brien walked by in swim trunks. He greeted them, saying he was heading out to do some "surveilling," as he called it, in the pool area. Somehow, he had already "scored" a beer and a bag of chips. He would meet the rest of them for dinner in the steakhouse at the casino, across the street from the hotel, at seven forty-five.

In the meantime, Jessica settled in and made their spa appointments for the next day. They'd decided to hit the casino, bars, and restaurants tonight, and then meet up at nine the next morning to have Uncle Don walk them through the area where Kelly's body was found. After that, they would visit the spa for their scheduled appointments, and then meet up once more to debrief.

Peter had arranged to meet his friend in security for a drink in the bar when his shift ended at six o'clock. By the time the rest of them made their way to the front desk, Peter had already stowed his overnight bag in his room and was headed to the casino for that drink with his friend, nodding to them as he passed. Tommy and Jerry planned to hit the lounge areas and bars before dinner. They all carried photos of Mr. P. and Kelly.

In no time at all, "the girls" were checked in, had dropped off their things, and scooted on over to the casino. Saturday nights were busy at the casino, even in the summer. Not crazy-busy like in the cooler months, but there was a lively crowd. A steady hubbub of voices undergirded the pulsing lights and mechanical sounds emanating from the slot machines. Even now, when not all the machines required players to pump them full of coins, they made a lot of noise. After a quick loop around the perimeter, Bernadette had abandoned them.

"I'm going to the bathroom and then I'm going to play the slots. I already spotted the machine I'm going to play."

"What? You're really going to pump money into one of these contraptions?"

"¡Claro que si! I'm undercover. I got to fit in, don't I? Maybe you two should try your luck at one of the card tables. Are you any good at blackjack or Texas Hold 'em? They got both in here."

Jessica and Laura looked at each other with their mouths open as though to speak. They eyed Bernadette. Maybe she was putting them on. The tiny powerhouse was chomping at the bit to get going. "I'm going to keep looking around. What about you Laura, are you feeling lucky?"

"Are you kidding? I've heard of blackjack and Texas Hold 'em, but I have no idea how to play."

"We'll have to leave the gambling to you, *St. Bernadette.*" Jessica fixed her gaze on Bernadette as she spoke.

"Don't give me your nasty nun look. I've played bingo since I was younger than you, Niña, and I haven't missed a casino night at St. Theresa's in twenty years. It's not a sin if you're not losing your grocery money or something like that, and if it's for a good cause." She seemed determined, so Jessica let it go, wondering how much there was about this precious creature she didn't know.

As Bernadette dashed off toward the restrooms, Jessica and Laura resumed their promenade around the casino floor. "Do I really have a 'nasty nun' look?"

"I wouldn't have put it quite that way. Stern, maybe, haughty and disapproving, more like a Mother Superior, I'd say."

Jessica frowned, as she took in their surroundings. Was Laura serious or was putting her on? Laura leaned in and spoke.

"See, you're doing it again. You don't like what you see around you and it shows! You've got that 'gonna whack somebody on the knuckles with a ruler' expression on your face."

Anna Celeste Burke

Jessica peered at herself in a nearby mirror. She did look serious, but haughty and disapproving? Well, okay, disapproving, maybe. "Go ahead, call me, Mother Jessica. At this point, I'm a practicing celibate so maybe I am channeling my inner prioress. Heck with the ruler, though. In this place, I'm going to need a yardstick. I just don't get the gambling thing."

Diehard gamblers did. They were hard at work, punching buttons on the slot machines, many of them puffing away on cigarettes as they perched on stools in front of one animated machine or another. The air filters in the place were going like gangbusters or the room would have been filled with smoke. There was a room full of slots designated as a nonsmoking area, but that room was nearly empty.

Apparently, compulsions were doled out in duplicate, smoking and gambling, two expressions of the same underlying drive. Or in triplicate if you also counted the steady stream of drinks being served to players. Women in outfits like the one Kelly had worn the night she was killed delivered those drinks. Jessica stopped and watched the players at card tables where rounds of poker and blackjack were underway. Gamblers, perched on tall stools, waited for each turn of a card with great anticipation.

"They're playing Texas Hold 'em here." As Jessica spoke, the dealer and a couple of the men sitting at the table looked up from their cards. They didn't shush her, but gave her their version of the nasty nun look. She moved away from the table, out of earshot, feeling lost.

"So, what's your take on all this?" She asked Laura, who had been quietly circling the room with her.

"Honestly, I don't get it either. It seems like some level of hell to me, but they seem so absorbed by it all. Kind of the way you look when you're in the zone shopping." Laura smiled at Jessica, taunting her.

"Ha, ha. I know you're right, but you don't have to be such a brat about it."

"I'm only teasing. Besides, you don't smoke while you're shoving items into a shopping cart as if you were feeding quarters into a slot machine. You may have given up sex, but you haven't taken that vow of poverty yet, Mother Jessica." Jessica stuck her tongue out at Laura.

"So, should we just walk up to one of these servers and flash the picture of Kelly or Mr. P.?" Jessica was eager to get on with it, hoping to speak to a couple servers before going to dinner at the restaurant, which was just off

216

the casino floor.

"We don't need to gamble to go 'undercover,' but let's order a drink first before we flash anything other than a credit card."

"Okay, that's probably a good idea." She and Laura hustled over to the bar area nearby, where several women were busy working. Most appeared to be twentyish, but one woman was considerably older than the others were. If they had any chance of finding someone who had been at the casino for a while, she was more likely to fill the bill than the younger women were. Jessica hopped up on the bar stool closest to the woman, Graciela, according to her nametag. Laura took the seat next to her.

"We'd like a couple drinks. Can you help us with that?"

"Sure can, what would you like?"

"I'll have a mojito."

"One mojito, coming right up." Turning to Laura, she asked, "And what can I get for you?"

"A mojito sounds great, actually. Thanks."

"No problem." Graciela stepped away and mixed their drinks. In no time flat, she was back. "You want to run a tab or settle up now?"

"We have a dinner reservation in a few minutes. I guess we should pay as we go. Can we take our drinks with us?"

"You sure can." Graciela told them what they owed, and Jessica paid with cash, adding a twenty-dollar tip. "Thanks. Where are you having dinner?"

"At the steakhouse," Jessica said, nodding in the general vicinity of the door leading to the restaurant.

"Good choice. Are you two in town for the weekend?"

"No, we're local. I'm Jessica and this is Laura. It's nice to meet you, Graciela." Jessica held out her hand and Graciela shook it.

"It's nice to meet you, too. I appreciate the tip. It's a little slow around here this time of year, so thanks. Let me know if I can get you anything else."

"Well, actually, there's a bigger tip for you if you have another minute to talk and can help answer a few questions for us." Graciela froze and looked at both women warily.

"What about? Are you, cops?" She asked.

"No, no. It's nothing like that. We had a friend who used to work here years ago and we're trying to find someone who remembers her. Have you been working here long?" Jessica asked the woman, who was still regarding them with suspicion.

"Long enough, I guess. I started with the casino right after the tribe bought the hotel back in the '90s. So yeah, I've been around about as long as anyone has. I like this job and I'd like to keep it, so I'm not sure how much help I can be."

"This is her picture. Can you tell us if you remember seeing her?" Graciela looked at the photo Jessica had placed on the bar in front of her.

"Could be, there's something familiar about her. Where did she work?"

"Her main job was as a spa attendant, but she filled in as a server on the casino floor and at the restaurants to make extra money. Until she had an accident, that is."

"Oh, now I know who you're talking about. She was such a pretty thing. They found her in the parking lot, right? That's why she looks familiar. I'm sure I saw her picture in the paper. I didn't know her, though. Back then, I wasn't working as a bartender. I started as a housekeeper and the tribal owners helped me get my training so I could do this job. The pay is a lot better, and it's easier on the back!" Graciela picked up the picture of Kelly and inspected it again, shaking her head. "What a tragedy. She was so young and gorgeous. I'm not sure what you were hoping to find out, but I can't help you. Sorry."

"We appreciate the time and the kind words about our friend. There's just one more thing," Jessica said, as she put a fifty-dollar bill on the counter next to the photo of Kelly, along with a photo of Mr. P. "We were wondering if you've ever seen this guy in here."

The wariness returned as Graciela stared at the new photo on the bar. Her eyes moved from Jessica to Laura and back to Jessica, trying to figure out what they were up to before she answered. She couldn't keep her eyes off that fifty-dollar bill, though, and eventually the call of the fifty must have won out over any reticence she felt.

A Dead Sister

"I don't know why you care, or what this has to do with your friend, but sure, that's Mr. P. He hasn't been around for a while, but he used to be in here all the time. Everybody knows Mr. P. He gives out Benjamins, not Grants—even better tips, and he doesn't ask questions. Break time, ladies! Thanks!" With that, she snapped up the fifty and fled.

"That was easy," Laura said, as she sipped her mojito. "Mr. P. is or has been a regular, and he hands out hundred-dollar bills. I'd say that takes care of that. The s.o.b. must have been the driver. That doesn't tell us why he would want to hurt Kelly, but I don't much care, do you? We have to get this guy." There was an angry set to her jaw as she took another sip of her drink.

"Yeah, I'm with you on that. I'm sorry Graciela got spooked. I would have liked to ask her more questions. She's got a good memory for faces. I bet she could tell us about the doc, too. Maybe I should go get some Benjamins and come back." Jessica peeked at her watch. "I guess it'll have to wait until after dinner because it's..." Her sentence was cut off by a sudden surge of noise in the place. Bells and whistles were going off; the lights were flashing along with a lot of hooting and hollering from somewhere behind them. Jessica caught one of the young women servers heading their way. "What's going on?"

"Oh, some itty-bitty granny just hit a jackpot—a big one. Why don't I have that kind of luck?" She rolled her eyes as she whisked on by.

Jessica and Laura looked at each other. "You don't think?" Laura asked.

"Nah, what are the odds?" Jessica responded.

"What's going on?" Jessica and Laura both started, turning to find Tommy and Jerry standing there with drinks in their hands. Behind them lumbered the giant Peter, with Brien in tow, hanging on to him by the scruff of the neck.

"Somebody just won a big jackpot. I should ask you the same thing, though. What's up with Peter and Brien?"

"We'll let them tell you."

Peter and Brien caught up to them at the bar. Peter released Brien, who looked less like a rag doll without Peter hanging onto him.

"Hey, man, was that really necessary?" Brien asked Peter, as he rearranged the Aloha shirt he wore with a pair of board shorts and closed toe sandals. He smoothed the collar on the shirt and ran his hands through his hair to get his blond surfer boy locks under control.

Peter fixed him with a flinty gaze. *Uh oh*, Jessica thought, *Peter's got a nasty nun look, too, and Brien was about to get that rap on the knuckles.*

As they stood there, an entourage of Agua Caliente big shots swept into the building and paraded by, heading in the direction of the jackpot hoopla. The noise had died down but hadn't stopped. The group was led by a well-groomed man, with a dark ponytail, in an expensive suit. With him was the hotel manager who had greeted Jessica and her party during their arrival. A young woman in hotel reception desk garb carried a super-sized check, followed by a photographer with his camera at the ready. Two men in the light brown jackets worn by security on the casino floor and elsewhere in the resort brought up the rear. One of the security men elbowed his companion as they passed. They both cast a grim look in their direction, nodding to Peter, who acknowledged them by returning the constrained gesture.

"What on earth is that about, Peter?" Jessica asked, as they all gathered around Jessica and Laura still seated at the bar.

"Our friend here set off the alarms a while ago, over at the hotel. Brien went out a back exit clearly marked as monitored and alarmed. The security guys on duty picked him up roaming around in the parking lot. He told them he was looking for clues. They figured him for a nut until they found out he was a hotel guest. Instead of calling the police, they called me."

"It was surfendipity, Jessica. I got turned around and went out the wrong door, but it turned out to be the right door, you know? I was in the parking lot where your friend got nailed. The pool guys showed me from up on the pool deck. When I looked up, they waved to me. That's how I knew it was the right place."

"More like surf-stupidity, if you ask me. What was your plan once the alarm went off?" Peter asked, gruffly.

Brien was about to answer when they saw Bernadette scurrying toward them holding the enormous check. The two security officers, who were hustling to keep up with her, were escorting her. They didn't look happy when they realized where she was headed.

"Hold this, por favor," Bernadette said, shoving the check into the hands of one of the gentlemen on her heels as she stepped close to Jessica.

A Dead Sister

"Mira! See! I won a jackpot. This undercover work is muy bueno, Chica." She lowered her voice as she spoke that last sentence. "I told them I wanted a picture with the manada de gatos—the Cat Pack." A photographer stepped out from behind the security men, who were glowering at all of them. Behind him stood the dark-haired manager with a grin on his face and the assistant at his elbow.

"Is this the rest of your party?" the photographer asked Bernadette, who smiled and nodded enthusiastically. In a matter of seconds, he had them all arranged for a group photo, with the "itty-bitty granny" standing between Laura and Jessica still seated on their bar stools. Jerry and Tommy stood on one side, Peter and Brien on the other. Bernadette held her check in front of her as they all smiled. Even Peter managed something more than a grimace.

A few minutes later, they were all seated in the steakhouse perusing menus. Security had accompanied Bernadette to fill out paperwork so they could issue her a real check and report her winnings to the appropriate authorities. After taxes, Bernadette ended up with more than thirty thousand dollars "por mi nietos, for their college fund," she said, as she went on to explain her strategy for winning the progressive jackpot.

Jessica didn't get it, nor did she think the rest of the Cat Pack got it. That is, except for Brien. "We know how you did it," he said, with a knowing nod of his head. "This is way more than surfendipity," he said, stuffing his cheeks like a chipmunk with bites of bread from a basket set on their table.

"Surfen-whatidy?" She asked. "Are you doing that beach talk again, Brien, and with your mouth full?" That shut him up instantly.

When a fresh round of drinks was served, Jessica proposed a toast: "To Bernadette, good friends, and good fortune." They all scarfed down well-prepared steaks, except for Peter. The chef, knowing a big winner was seated at their table, went out of his way to accommodate Peter. Acorn squash, stuffed with quinoa and topped with toasted pine nuts, finally put the still disgruntled Peter back in a better mood.

Sunday morning, "the girls" were up early, despite the late night. Bernadette was still buzzing about her jackpot, on the phone chattering in Spanish and English to her sister. They all planned to have breakfast at eight. Then Jessica, Laura, Jerry, and Tommy were going to meet Uncle Don in the lobby at nine. Peter's ex-employee in security had arranged for him to speak to someone about the comp program. Wanting to keep an eye on him, Peter decided to take his "not-so-mini-me" Brien along.

Bernadette was going to hang out and talk to the housekeeping crew, accompanying them as they made their rounds. They'd already discovered she was the big winner at the casino and that made her a star. Jessica wasn't sure if that was the hotel's doing or just the grapevine. By the time they got back to their room after dinner, there was a steady stream of felicidades and congratulations from staff along the way. The hotel had even left a congratulatory gift of spa goodies in Bernadette's room. News traveled fast. Perhaps someone did have information of value about Kelly, and might be willing to share it with the newly minted celebrity in their midst.

At breakfast, they had reviewed, once again, what they learned from their eventful evening at the hotel and casino. Laura and Jessica were not the only ones to discover that Mr. P. was a regular. How regular could be determined by checking his premier club comp history. His buddy in security set Peter up to do that on Sunday.

Given his high-roller status, security kept tabs on Mr. P. in several ways. They monitored and protected an array of expensive items Mr. P. brought with him when he stayed at the resort, such as jewelry, music-industry memorabilia, and, on occasion, film and recording equipment. There were luxury autos, too, of course. A Mercedes sedan was not Mr. P.'s only mode of transportation. Sometimes he drove to the hotel in a Bentley, showed up in a fiery red Ferrari, or arrived in a hired limo or town car. The records of autos associated with Mr. P. didn't indicate whether he owned them or not, but might hint at what he'd been driving and when.

Tommy and Jerry had spoken to a barkeep, Alex, who also knew who they were talking about when they showed him the picture of Mr. P. More importantly, when asked about a tall, unattractive man called the doc, their informant knew him, too. According to the bartender, "Unattractive is putting it mildly."

It wasn't his unusual height, which had to be close to seven feet. His hands were enormous, with long fingers and knobby joints. He also had a protruding brow, large cheekbones, and a massive jaw. The ridge of brow gave his eyes a hooded quality made more sinister by a raised zigzag scar on one cheek.

A mouthful of jagged teeth, in combination with his other features, conjured up an image of that villain in the Bond films with the metal teeth. That surprised Alex most of all, "You'd think a doctor would have the money and motivation to take care of his teeth." He also couldn't understand how the leviathan did it, but he was often in the company of beautiful young women. His lumbering gait and preference for undertaker-style clothing did nothing to make him seem less malevolent.

To Jerry, it sounded like the doc suffered from some sort of metabolic disorder. Like Richard Kiel, the actor who played that villain in the Bond movie. Kiel was only one of many well-known figures with acromegaly. That would account for many of the distinctive features their bartender friend had described. Not the scar, though, nor his bad teeth, or the preference for black suits, dark shirts, and string ties, like someone who had stepped out of an old western.

"Maybe he was going for the Doc Holliday thing," Tommy offered.

"Sounds more like Doc Holliday brought to you by Tim Burton, if you ask me," Laura countered. "It's got to be something to see the two of them together, given the difference in their heights. Our bartender, Graciela, took off before we could ask about the doc. Did yours make any kind of link between them?"

"Seeing the two of them together would stick with you, sort of like a carnival act." Tommy shook his head, as if trying to clear it of the image that was forming even without having witnessed the circus duo. "We asked Alex if the two men hung out together, and he said no. But he did say that the same hot-looking woman drinking with the doc was hanging out with Mr. P. later."

"Did he have any name for him other than the doc? Maybe from a credit card he used to pay for his drinks or a charge he made to his room?" Jessica asked.

"No. We asked him that question," Jerry said. "The doc paid with cash. He never charged anything on a credit card or to a room at the hotel. He did like to leave 'Benjamins,' though, like Mr. P. The doc was always flush, pulling bills from a stash in a money clip shaped like a miniature gold record."

"Whoa, dude." Brien, who had been silently stuffing his face with food from the breakfast buffet, suddenly spoke. He even put his fork down. "Mr. P. had the same one. The pool guys told me about it. They thought it was sort of advertising his studio." According to Brien, the "dudes" he spoke to told him the short, slightly-built, well-dressed man always carried a wad of bills bound by that money clip. Mostly easy-going, Mr. P. dished out those Benjamins, but he could also fly off the handle without warning when displeased. Of course, the way Brien put it was a little different: "It's like one minute, everything's grand. Then for some reason, he'd just get bent, turn into a hater, and go off on you."

The other thing Brien had learned was that Mr. P. often had a posse of attractive young men and women with him at the pool or elsewhere on the grounds at the resort. The pool guys figured they were Hollywood newbies or fledgling recording artists. At times, they said they were in town to do a "shoot" or scouting for a location to shoot a music video. Just because a bevy of beauties accompanied Mr. P., didn't mean he wasn't on the lookout to add to his troupe of pretty people. Pool boy scuttlebutt held that the older man hit on their co-workers at the hotel, spa, and casino. None of Brien's informants admitted that they had personally witnessed or experienced Mr. P. putting the moves on anyone, but "like Bernadette said, word gets around."

Brien had shown Kelly's picture to the pool boys. They agreed that she was the old guy's type, but none of them had been around long enough to have met her. They did know the story about a girl's body being found in the parking lot. That's when they took Brien to a maintenance area near the roof. From there he could view the site where the body had been discovered years before. That was when Brien took it upon himself to check it out, using the back stairs to get down to the lobby floor as Kelly might have done, if Chester Davis' story was true.

"Those guys said, back in the day, it was wacked what you could do using those stairs. I figured that's how Kelly could have gone up and down the stairs and in and out of the hotel without anybody seeing her, except the dudes who chased her into the parking lot." He looked at Peter, "Not anymore, I guess." He kind of winced as if Peter might swat him.

Peter didn't take a swing at Brien. He did tell them that there wouldn't have to be another security breach because Don Fontana had already arranged for security to accompany them to the parking lot this morning. The security representative expected them to show up in the lobby on time, and follow protocol.

Spa appointments started at noon. Taking the waters at the spa sounded a whole lot better to Jessica than traipsing around the hotel parking lot with Uncle Don and a cranky security guy. There seemed little to be gained, at this point, from revisiting the site where Uncle Don found poor Kelly's dead body in that parking lot. They'd learned enough already to shore up Chester Davis' story. There was, indeed, a Mr. P. and a large, skulking character known as the doc. Both had frequented the resort on a regular

A Dead Sister

basis when Kelly was alive. With testimony from Tommy and Bobby Simmons, they could even make the case that Mr. P. knew Kelly. That ought to be enough to keep the prosecutor interested. Chet Davis would likely get another round of treatment instead of jail while they continued to investigate the cold case that was getting warmer by the minute. Jessica was boiling mad. Uncle Don was as angry as Jessica was when he heard what they'd learned. They still had too little to get anything in the way of justice for Kelly. So now what?

CHAPTER 23

Uncle Don was more despondent than angry as he stepped into the role of crime scene tour guide. By the time they met up with him in the lobby, he'd already had an earful about the fiasco with Brien. He was grim-faced. The updates from Jessica made him grimmer still, but he had committed to doing the walk through and agreed even though his jaw was clenched in anger. Anger at Brien, anger at Kelly's killers, maybe at himself and Kelly, too, Jessica imagined. He wasn't talking so who knew for sure?

Their surly hotel security guard seemed almost as disgruntled as Uncle Don. He quickly escorted them to the parking lot where Kelly's body had been found. The space was cordoned off and restricted to hotel vehicles and valet parking only. Self-parking was on the street or in a lot that took up an entire square block across from where the casino now stood. No one could lie in wait for an unsuspecting nineteen-year-old, running for her life.

Perhaps hoping to get the worst part over first, Uncle Don took them to the spot where the groundskeeper had discovered Kelly's body. Jessica felt a little light-headed as the photos she had seen of Kelly's dreadful death came alive. That spot was eerily similar to the way it had appeared in the photos, as if no one had wanted to disturb Kelly's last resting place. Silence fell upon them and their little group huddled close together as Uncle Don began to set the scene.

In an almost robotic voice, Don Fontana pointed out where they had found the few personal items logged into evidence, and the loaded hypodermic. Then he walked them to the point of impact where they'd collected bits of debris from the vehicle that had hit her. Looking around at the largely empty lot, he described what it had been like back then. There was only one point of entry and one exit for the vehicle that hit Kelly. Lampposts and security lighting on the hotel building were almost the same today as they had been then, and would have provided adequate visibility to the driver that night.

A single dumpster, shielded from view by fencing, was all that remained of what had been a row of dumpsters, according to Chet. Uncle Don confirmed that there had been several dumpsters there that night, with no fence in front of them. Given their location, it seemed entirely possible that Chet could have seen what happened to Kelly while remaining concealed from view.

Tommy must have wanted to see that for himself. Maybe he was just trying to release the tension that had to be nearly as unbearable for him as it was for Uncle Don. He flew over to the dumpster and walked around it, peeking out from various locations. He squatted down, too.

"Uh, I checked that out already," Brien called out to Tommy. "You can see everything that happens from over there—right through the slots in that fence they put up."

"Can you see me?" He called out.

"Of course, we can. It's broad daylight," Jerry responded. Tommy dashed back, a little breathless from the short jog.

"Chester Davis wasn't lying about being able to see what went on." Jerry opened his mouth as if about to speak. "I know, I know, it would have been dark."

The still irritable security man accompanied them into the building, and out again, through the only door that led from that wing of the hotel to the parking lot. That door now served principally as an emergency exit, although hotel employees sometimes used it to haul materials and supplies in and out of the building. He acknowledged that the current system of alarms and surveillance cameras around that exit were probably installed ten years ago.

Uncle Don assured him that they were not there at the time of Kelly's death. Because Kelly was dressed for work when she was found, investigators had initially assumed she was working somewhere in the hotel or casino, exiting by that door. Since no one reported seeing her anywhere at the resort that night, the police also considered another possibility.

"Somebody at the hotel made the point that Kelly could have walked from some other location to the parking lot or someone could have dropped her off there. At the time, it seemed like a reasonable option since we didn't have Chester Davis or anyone else claiming she came out of the hotel. Guys canvassed the area, but it was late at night, and no one claimed to have seen or heard anything. No one came forward after Sammy and Monica offered the reward."

Entering through the side door from the parking lot into the hotel stairwell, Jessica quickly took the steps up to the second floor and back down again. "Kelly could have fled from a room in the hotel and down the stairs without anyone seeing or hearing her. The exit doors to the stairs weren't armed and not even locked before ten o'clock, right?"

"That's right. The stairways weren't under video surveillance at the time, either. The fact that we couldn't keep tabs on this area is why surveillance was added and this exit was armed."

Jerry stepped from the stairwell out into the hotel corridor, looked both ways, and then turned to the guard as he spoke. "I take it this corridor leads to the hotel lobby, but it's not a straight shot. It would have been impossible to see what was going on in this corridor from the front desk or lobby area. It probably still is." The guard walked past Jerry and stepped into the corridor.

"That's why we added surveillance cameras at strategic locations along the corridor and in the stairwells. There was a camera or two already in place back in '99 but most have been added since then." He gestured as he spoke, pointing to cameras as Jerry looked on.

"I couldn't remember for sure, so I checked with a colleague who worked on the investigation," Uncle Don said. "We were told that the video cameras in the corridor had been installed but weren't operational that night. A contractor involved in the renovations had damaged a switch or something like that. No one even tried to get video since they were still in the process of making repairs on several floors in this wing." Their escort was visibly uncomfortable under Uncle Don's gaze but merely shrugged.

"Hey, it happens," was all he said.

When Uncle Don took his leave, Jessica had another moment of regret about stirring the pot, and dredging up such sad old memories for the man. He tried to be stoic, but he and Tommy had both wiped their eyes after a goodbye hug.

A Dead Sister

"It's okay, Jessica," Tommy said. "Uncle Don's sad, but grateful that we're trying to get to the truth about Kelly's death."

"I'm amazed at how much investigating they did at the time given that this was a hit and run accident," Jerry added. "He's got to be reassured that they did everything they could under the circumstances."

"Crummy circumstances," Laura groused.

Jessica and her little band of friends bemoaned those missing video tapes when they held their final debriefing at the hotel over drinks. If only the cameras had been operational, they might have caught images of Kelly, running for her life, and the two men chasing her. Small compensation since that wouldn't have saved Kelly's life, but the investigation would have gone in a completely different direction, even without Chester Davis coming forward.

They were all more than ready for their spa visits after that ordeal in the parking lot. Unfortunately, the spa attendants had provided little new information about Mr. P., the doc, or Kelly. No one recognized the auburn-haired beauty, or had a clue about who she was. Nor had anyone ever seen a man fitting the description of the doc.

They did know Mr. P. "You mean the little man with the big tips," the woman had said as she escorted Jessica and her women friends to their treatment rooms. She repeated, almost verbatim, what Graciela had told them, "It's too bad that he hasn't been around much lately. Not like he used to be when he used to hole up here for weeks and party hearty. I heard he sometimes had an entire floor for himself and his guests."

"Wow, it sounds like something out of Palm Springs Babylon in the Hollywood heyday out here. When did all that partying stop? Any idea why?" Jessica asked.

"Those parties are legendary, but they were before my time. I've been working at the resort and casino almost ten years. I'm not sure why, but we opened another casino out closer to 'the ten.' It could be he likes the newer accommodations better, or it's easier to get on and off the freeway to get back to LA. Why don't you ask him?" *We will*, Jessica had thought. That and a whole lot more, too.

Tommy had cajoled his masseuse into revealing that Mr. P. could be a lunatic in the spa, too. "It's the same story Brien got from the pool guys. He could be nice as you please, flashing all that cash, and then just lose it.

229

Before I could even ask if the guy was on drugs or something, Jewel told me that once when he was loaded, Mr. P. went on a rampage. He tore the place up and stomped out through the courtyard and into the lobby, buck naked. Some spa attendant was running behind him with his robe."

"Apparently, Mr. P. could afford to pay to clean up any mess he made here or at the other casino," Peter said. "The guys who monitor the comp program wouldn't let me look at any of their records, but he is a whale! Once they opened the new casino in Rancho Mirage a few years back, he did start spending more time there than here. He never balked when they added the costs of cleaning up his messes to the tab for his visits."

"That's a good thing for the hotels. He left the rooms he occupied like garbage dumps, too," Bernadette added. "The women I spoke to in housekeeping say that the P in Mr. P. stands for puerco as in pig. He left big tips, too, though, so puerco rico was a secret name for him when he was around."

"Rich pig is too good a name for Mr. P. I could give him a few of my own," Laura added.

"One of the pool guys told me the P stood for party."

"The bartender mentioned the parties, too. He said they went on for days at a time, with beautiful, young, very drunk, or stoned people roaming the halls. Word about a party would spread like a wildfire, and the rooms packed with more partiers than just the people traveling with Mr. P.," Tommy said.

"Management must have known that was going on, right?" Jessica asked.

"Yeah, but if no one complained about the noise, and Mr. P. was willing to pay up later, why interfere?" Jerry responded.

"Sometimes he left a few of his party guests behind. Housekeeping would have to get security to run them out before they could even clean up."

"Maybe he was hosting one of those parties and that's where Kelly was for the days she went missing before turning up dead. Is there a way to find out if he and his entourage were registered at the hotel around that time?" Jessica asked.

"I don't think so, but I can try. I've pushed hard to get as much information as I could. With a warrant, the police could find out, though," Peter replied.

"I hear you. I guess we can't expect to wrap this all up in a weekend, can we? Did anyone happen to mention if someone fitting the doc's description was spotted at those parties?"

"My contacts in housekeeping knew right away who I was talking about when I called him el doctor. They have a name for him, too. 'El doctor maligno.' He was not a nice man. No one ever saw him in the same room with Mr. P., but he was in and out of there."

"While the nasty little king was holed up with his courtiers?" Tommy asked.

"Si! That's what they told me."

"I know they had that maligno name for him, but did they ever get his real name?"

"I wondered that, too, Laura, but they said doc was all they ever heard anyone call him." Laura sighed so loud it almost sounded like a growl.

"I need to tell you another thing I found out. When I showed Kelly's picture around, one of the old-timers around here said she saw her. She noticed because Kelly was so beautiful. Even with all the pretty people around Mr. P. and dressed in her server outfit. She also remembered because she was just chatting and laughing with Mr. P. and they went into his suite together. Employees aren't supposed to hang out with guests, especially not in uniform, but it happens." Bernadette shrugged.

"Was she partying with that twisted little freak?" Tommy asked.

"She said she didn't know for sure. Kelly could have been on an errand for the hotel, so she thought it was good to mind her own business."

"Can she remember when she saw Kelly go into Mr. P.'s suite?"

"Nah, she wasn't sure, but she said she recognized Kelly right away when the story hit the news, so it must have been around the same time, don't you think?"

"Maybe her memory will get better if she's testifying under oath." Tommy was close to speaking with a growl or a hiss in his voice, now.

"We'll speak to her again once we get this investigation back on track in a formal way. I've got a ton of work to do to get all this written up for our detective friends." *So they can rip it to shreds no doubt,* Jessica thought. She could already hear Frank and Art whining about nothing but circumstantial evidence, hearsay, and wishful thinking.

Bernadette had one more tale to tell from her discussion with the housekeeping staff. This one they considered to be the weirdest one of all. "After one party, when Mr. P.'s rooms were trashed, one was clean. The bed had been stripped down to the mattresses. All the garbage was gone, and the dirty sheets, too. Everything in the room like towels, pillows, and comforters, even the mattress covers had disappeared. Room service had left a tray. That was gone too, along with all the drinking glasses and the ice bucket. Even ordinary stuff that guests don't usually steal like toilet paper and tissues. It was all gone." Bernadette paused to cross herself. "Everything in the room—all the furniture, the TV, the counters, the tub, and toilet—it was sparkling clean.

According to Bernadette, the housekeeping staff got the chicken skin just recounting the story. Management sent someone to inventory the missing items, and put the cost to replace them on Mr. P.'s tab. Chester Davis' assertion that Mr. P. had ordered his minions to go back and clean up the place after hauling the injured doc to the car sure made sense out of that apparently inexplicable event. When Jessica told them about what he'd said, they all got a round of the shivers.

CHAPTER 24

As Jessica turned her car onto El Paseo Monday morning, she experienced a rush of exhilaration at the prospect of working as a lawyer again. It felt good to focus, for a while, on something besides the dismal circumstances surrounding Kelly's death. True to her nature, the excitement was paired with a lot of anxiety. Jessica walked quickly in her caramel pumps with the black heels and the color-blocked short-sleeved dress. She could have dressed more casually for the brief visit to the office, but wearing grown-up clothes, including panty hose in one hundred ten degree weather, signaled that she was a professional woman. Meeting with the sharply-dressed office manager, Jessica was glad she had donned full-on professional garb.

With Amy Klein's help, Jessica pulled together the materials she needed for her Tuesday meeting with the Van der Woerts in less than an hour. Amy also spent nearly that much time on a sort of "who's who," from the point of view of a firm insider, and an insider she was. Amy Klein was a Klein, as in Canady, Holmes, Winston and *Klein*. She didn't go into the details about how she ended up working for her uncle, Albert Klein, one of the founders of the firm. Her perspective was very illuminating and it gave Jessica a much better lay of the land, and greater clarity about the cast of characters inhabiting it. Amy also confirmed Jessica's notion that they were holding down the fort at a wilderness outpost. Despite the long list of designer names that emblazoned the path to their door, Palm Desert was the hinterlands to those in the main office in LA. She and Amy agreed that was just fine.

Satisfied that she had accomplished what she intended, Jessica left her office, ready for that drive to LA. She'd parked her car on a side-street off El Paseo, near her office. The spot had been open, and since she only planned to be in the office for a couple hours, street parking seemed fine. Besides, she wasn't quite ready to park in the nearby structure, where she had tussled with one of the goons involved in Roger Stone's murder. As she stepped off the curb across the street from her parked car, she could see the taillight was broken on the passenger side of her car. As she got closer, she could also see a scratch along the full length of her car.

How could this have happened? Were the shopping gods trying to tell her something? First, Rodeo Drive and now trouble on El Paseo, *again*. Jessica scanned the area. Was there anyone around who might have witnessed what happened? Not a soul that she could see and there were no shop windows that looked directly out onto the street. She bent to inspect her car wondering if she could have been sideswiped. No dents or dings, just that long, jagged scratch, like it had been keyed. Jessica froze. A little shiver zipped down her spine. Who would do that to her car?

A piece of paper tucked under the windshield wiper on the driver's side caught Jessica's eye. *Ah, someone did hit me*, she thought, feeling a little foolish about getting the willies. The note must have contact information or insurance information so they could settle this. Jessica froze again as she walked around her car and reached for the note.

"Shoot, shoot, shoot!" She muttered. The driver side was scratched too. The heebie-jeebies were back as she read the note.

"*Back off before it's too late*," was scrawled on the slip of paper.

"Shoot, shoot, shoot!" Jessica said louder. She stomped her foot, too, shuddering again when she saw that the tire she was about to kick was flat. The back one was flat as a pancake, too.

"Now what?" Clearly, the car wasn't drivable. As much as she dreaded it, she needed to call the police and file a report. It wasn't likely that the police could do anything. At least it would be on record for the insurance company and for the accountant when she took a loss at the end of the year. The car would have to be towed to the BMW dealer, or wherever her insurance company wanted it taken, for repairs, and she was going to need a rental car. No way was she going to get on the road before noon as planned.

Jessica had promised Father Martin that she would try not to react to every bad thing that happened by putting up her dukes or seeking oblivion in a shopping binge. Squaring off for a fight felt like the right thing to do, but it wouldn't help. She tried, instead, to find something closer to acceptance. The deed was already done, and there was no one around to fight. Nor could she run away and shop 'til she dropped, since a week's worth of obligations stretched out before her.

"This is what I'm being asked to deal with in this moment and in this place," Jessica whispered, struggling to remember the remaining words Father Martin had used. All that came to mind was, "I'll do my best and forget the rest." Somehow, that didn't seem too poetic or spiritual, but it would have to do for now. The tightness in her chest and the lightheadedness that had begun to creep up on her as she fumed started to retreat.

It was close to lunch time and her morning workout and a light breakfast were catching up to her as she stood in the summer heat. It was already a scorcher. Getting help was going to take a while. Where could she make a round of calls, have lunch, and wait more comfortably? A nearby Starbucks would do: AC plus coffee and food, too.

Jessica sat down with a venti nonfat latte and a sandwich. She stuffed an apple and a bottle of water into her purse for later. First, she called the police and reported the vandalism to her car.

"No, it's not an emergency," she assured the woman who took the call. She *was* going to have to get her car towed, so the sooner they could get an officer to the scene, the better. The dispatcher was polite, but didn't seem moved by Jessica's plight. She put Jessica on hold for less than a minute, though. When she came back, she said a squad car was on its way. Jessica thanked her and hung up.

Scooting her chair around, she finally found a spot that made it possible to view her car. She could catch the police officers the moment they arrived. Next, she called her insurance agent, who advised her to have the car towed to the dealer for repairs. The dealer arranged for a tow and a loaner, but that would take a half hour, or so, to reach her.

"No problem. The police aren't here yet. Once they get here, they'll have to make out a report."

Jessica wolfed down the sandwich between calls and drained the latte. The infusion of caffeine was a real boost. She dug out the bottle of water and was about to drink that too, when her phone rang.

"Hello."

"Jessica this is Frank, how's it going?"

"Not great." Jessica told him about her car.

"That's more than a little scary. Maybe you *should* back off, Jessica. My news isn't any better." She was getting that prickly feeling again.

"What does that mean?"

"Chester Davis is dead."

"Dead, in his jail cell? What are you saying?" Jessica felt faint. All the work they had done to validate his story and their key witness was dead.

"No, he was released sometime over the holiday weekend. Apparently, he went back to the flophouse where he was living before he got busted. This morning, 911 got an anonymous tip about a dead body at that location. The officers responding to the call didn't find any obvious evidence of foul play at the scene, but *lots* of drugs. The working assumption is that he overdosed, like a lot of addicts do when they get back out on the street. They pick up where they left off, using the same drugs they were using before they were busted, and it's just more than they can handle."

"Hang on a second, can you? I have another call coming in." Without waiting for a reply, she put him on hold and took the incoming call.

"Jessica Huntington speaking," she said quickly.

"Jessica, this is Dick Tatum. I wanted to give you an update about Chester Davis." He sounded despondent. "He's dead."

"I know. I have Frank Fontana on hold. He just told me Chet was released over the weekend. How did that happen? I thought he needed to put up a couple grand to get out on bail. Where would he get that kind of money?"

"One of the guys in the holding tank with Chet put up the money for him on Saturday night. His name is Arnold Dunne. He has a rap sheet as long as Chet's and includes a bunch of low-level drug-related charges. He did a couple years in the state prison after trying to bring drugs back from Mexico through LAX. He was picked up for a parole violation. That's about all I know at this point."

"Listen, I've got a situation of my own I need to deal with. I'll see if Frank can get a run down on Dunne, even though nobody's calling this a homicide. If they can locate him, they can ask him how it is he happened to have that kind of money to bail Chet out. Will you keep digging to see what else you can find out?"

"Sure, I'd also like to know what Dunne can tell us about what happened to Chet after he was released. Unfortunately, none of that will help us with our cold case. Our star witness, if you want to call him that, our *only* witness, to the murder of your friend is dead." Before she could respond, she caught sight of a police car pulling up alongside her car.

"I'm on my way to LA and I'll be tied up all day tomorrow on business. I should bring you up to speed about our investigation into the circumstances surrounding Kelly's death. I'm not sure what any of it means either, now that Chester Davis is dead. Can you meet me for lunch Wednesday and discuss it?"

"That's fine. Call me, and we'll set up a time and a place to meet. I feel awful about this."

"I know you do. You were really pulling for Chet. And I know you wanted to get to the bottom of things for my friend, Kelly, too. Thanks for that. I'll call you tonight." Jessica looked out the window of Starbucks as the police officers were getting out of their car. "It might be late before I can call you, is that okay?"

"No problem."

She stood up and moved toward the door. As she left the Starbucks, she picked up that call to Frank, who was still on hold. She waved at the police officers, trying to get their attention.

"Hey, Frank, I'm back. Do you have another minute?"

"Sure."

"That was Dick Tatum. He said some guy in lockup with Chester Davis put up his bail, two thousand dollars. His name is Arnold Dunne and he was in jail on a parole violation. That's a lot of money for somebody to come up who hadn't been back out on the street very long."

"I suppose Chester Davis could have been holding out on you. Maybe he had cash stashed somewhere. The money he used to by the drugs to kill himself had to come from somewhere. If a drug overdose *is* what killed him. The preliminary autopsy should be able to rule out other obvious factors that might account for his death. In the meantime, I'll see if we can find Arnold Dunne and bring him in for questioning." Frank suddenly sounded very tired.

"Hang on a second longer will you Frank? I'm back at my car. The police are here to take a report."

"Hello, officers. I'm glad you're here."

One of the officers, a young woman, was walking around the car, already snapping photos. The other, a black man of medium height and build, looked up.

"So, Ms. Huntington-Harper, we meet again." He smiled ruefully as he spoke, entering information into a handheld device.

"Officer Parker, that's *just* Jessica Huntington now, if you please. How are you?"

"Obviously, a whole lot better than you are. I thought they got the bad guy responsible for attacking you in the parking garage here last month."

"They did." Jessica was a little uncomfortable by the directness of his gaze. She remembered his kindness to her that day when she'd been attacked by a would-be purse snatcher in an Armani suit and Bruno Maglis. His kindness had been meted out with plenty of skepticism. The skepticism was back.

"I take it the trashing of your car is unrelated, right?"

"Yes, I presume it's unrelated since the guy who attacked me here last month is dead. I've got to wrap up a call and then we can take care of this, okay?" He nodded, as he continued to enter information for the report he was putting together.

"Frank, I need to talk to the police officers about the damage to my car. Then I've got to drive to my dad's house in Brentwood. Can I call you tonight?"

"Sure, but none of this sounds good. You have good security at the Brentwood house in LA and you'll use it, right?"

"Of course. The service taking care of my dad's house is top notch. They know I'm coming, and will have someone at the house to meet me."

"Someone you already know, I hope." Jessica turned away from the police officers and lowered her voice a bit. She didn't want to give Officer

A Dead Sister

Parker more reason to be suspicious. She was as concerned as Frank was about the events of the day. A dead Chester Davis and a trashed car bearing a threatening note were too coincidental to be taken blithely.

"Yes, someone I know. I'm more than a little freaked out by the fact that somebody is paying enough attention to me to find me, savagely attack my car, and leave a nasty note under my windshield wiper. I get that it is *not* a love note." The exasperation she felt had seeped into her voice.

"Alright. Would it be too self-serving to say that I'm *glad* to hear no one's leaving you love notes under your windshield wiper?"

"Hahaha, very funny."

"I wasn't trying to be funny, well, maybe a little. I have to fix dinner, but the kids are off with Mary and her gal pal this week, so call whenever you want."

"Will do! I did learn from the circumstances surrounding Roger's murder. I am on high alert, promise."

She hung up and gave Officer Parker, and the officer with him, her complete attention. He bagged the note now laying on the seat of her car. She explained that she had touched it before reading the message it contained. Jessica set out the timeframe surrounding the visit to her office, and gave him her business card. She wrote Amy Klein's name on the back so he could corroborate the timeline she gave him.

"I didn't know you were a lawyer. Does the hate mail have anything to do with your employment?"

"I didn't know they let you drive a police car," she snapped. The last time they had met, the officer had been on bicycle patrol. "Sorry to snap. No, I can't blame my clients. I've only been on the job a week. They don't hate me yet."

She could go on the record about the fact that she was poking around into an old friend's murder, but shades of Roger Stone! That would go over like a lead balloon. Bringing up Chester Davis' recent demise also seemed like an open invitation to extend the conversation with Officer Parker and his dutiful, but quieter partner, Officer Smythe.

"So, who wants you to back off from what?"

"If I knew that, I'd tell you. I'm as curious as you are. If you ask around, maybe someone saw something and can give you a description of the person who did this. Or it could be there's a print on the note that I didn't destroy when I fished it out from under the windshield wiper. Maybe some guy has me mixed up with the divorce lawyer his wife has hired to put the screws to him."

For a moment, Jessica wondered if Jim or, more likely, his crazy she-beast, thought she needed to be warned off. Could they have sent someone to leave that warning? Her gut told her this was related to Kelly, and had nothing to do with Jim or Cassie.

"Okay. If you think of anything else, you know how to find us."

It took another half hour, but Jessica was finally on I-10, driving a nearly new pearly white BMW sedan. It was less sporty than her own, but a gorgeous thing with all the bells and whistles. The tow truck driver helped transfer her packed bags from her battered Bimmer before loading it onto the flatbed truck and hauling it off to the dealer.

As she drove to LA, Jessica tried to rethink her plans for the evening. Originally, she had hoped to get into town with plenty of time to go over the file that Amy Klein had helped put together about the Van der Woerts. Jessica managed to catch up with Roberta Palmer and let her know she was running a couple hours behind schedule, and might be delayed further if she couldn't get into LA before rush hour.

"I'll get there when I get there," Jessica sighed, trying to put herself in a state of acceptance per Father Martin's exhortation that she could learn to find more equanimity in even stressful situations. At least she still had the option to try. She could juggle her schedule, put a couple more phone calls on her to-do list for tonight, get her BMW repaired, and otherwise deal with all the unforeseen hassles of the day. Not so for the unfortunate Mr. Davis, whose pitiful excuse for a life was over.

Why had he left the relative safety of protective custody to go back out on the street? The urge to get high may have overcome him. Where had he or his confederate come up with two thousand dollars? Had Chester Davis been holding out on them? If so, what else had he been holding back?

A growing sense of dread crept over Jessica with every mile she logged, bringing her closer to LA, home to the disturbed and disturbing Mr. P. An old prayer she had learned in high school popped into her head. She had come across the prayer again recently while reading the books loaned to her by Father Martin.

A Dead Sister

Tradition held that St. Teresa of Avila carried the prayer with her everywhere, using it as a bookmark. Father Martin had included it as an actual bookmark with his copy of St. Teresa's *Interior Castle*.

"Let nothing disturb you. Let nothing frighten you. All things are passing away. God never changes. Patience obtains all things. Whoever has God lacks nothing. God alone suffices."

At that moment, Jessica knew what she was going to do. Her foot pressed down on the accelerator, she reset the cruise control a little closer to eighty. The car sped up to close the distance between her and the city of angels.

CHAPTER 25

On her way to LA, Jessica had impulsively decided to pay Mr. P. a visit. She wanted to look him in the eye as she showed him a picture of Kelly. Two pictures, in fact. One, the head shot of Kelly as the lovely young woman she had been at nineteen. The second, Kelly with her head horribly askew after Mr. P. had run her down.

When Jessica arrived at the offices of Pure Platinum Music Group Monday afternoon, it was a little before five o'clock. The glass-enclosed building comprised five floors. A security guard sat on a high stool behind a polished stainless and wood information desk that was molded into an oval shape. A sign indicated: "guest check-in here." Framed art from album covers hung on the gleaming wood walls behind him. In a case to his right, guitars and other memorabilia were on display. On the left, a similar case contained vintage recording equipment and a vinyl record pressing machine. On all the walls were pictures of Mr. P. at different ages, standing among icons in the music and film industry.

Jessica gave the security guard her card and indicated that she would like to speak to Christopher Pogswich. The beefy, fifty-something black man momentarily looked befuddled, and then smiled jovially. He looked at the card, then at Jessica, staring over the spectacles sitting about halfway down his nose. Shaking his head, he spoke.

"I take it you don't have an appointment with Mr. P., Ms. Huntington. A word of advice: no one, absolutely no one, calls him Pogswich. Don't do it. I'll see if he's in. Is this business or personal?" Before she could respond, he answered, shaking his head again. "Business—it's just gotta be business."

A Dead Sister

Jessica wasn't exactly sure how to take that. Perhaps anyone who had personal dealings with Mr. P. would already have known better than to use his given name. She figured this was going nowhere, but she stood there and waited as "Lil Dwayne," according to the nametag, called upstairs to see if Mr. P. was in. He explained that a Ms. Huntington was there to see him.

"Yes, that's right, Huntington, Jessica Huntington. Says here she's an attorney with Canady, Holmes, Winston and Klein. Uh huh, uh huh, sure will." He hung up and, to Jessica's surprise, said, "Mr. P.'s assistant will be right with you. Please have a seat." He pointed to a seating area that didn't seem like it got much use. Copies of music industry magazines were neatly arrayed on a glass side table set between L-shaped rows of block-like chairs with leather cushions and metal frames.

She sat beneath a large picture of a much younger Mr. P. with shorter, darker hair, combed down Beatle-style. He sported a mustache and long sideburns, wore a burgundy Nehru jacket, and held up two fingers in a v-shaped peace sign. He looked a little like Peter Sellers, or maybe Jimmy Fallon playing Peter Sellers. His eyes in this picture, as in others, were somehow unsettling, maniacal, like a cult leader. So maybe more like Peter Sellers in the role of Dr. Strangelove. The longer she waited, the more she kept thinking about how scared Chester Davis had been and the fact that the man had turned up dead.

Jessica had changed her mind about meeting Mr. P. and was going to tell Lil Dwayne she had to go, when the elevator opened. Out stepped a retro-looking young woman with shoulder-length, jet black hair, teased to give it a bit of a bouffant, accentuated by a headband. Dark eyeliner was drawn out into wing tips over heavy lashes, accompanied by deep red lipstick. She wore a navy sleeveless form-fitting shantung silk sheath, dark silk stockings, and stiletto heels. She might have stepped off the set of Mad Men, except that she had a Hindu goddess tattooed from shoulder to elbow on one arm. That gave her a bit of a Bond-girl vibe. A bored Bond-girl, apparently, from the deadpan mien and the tone in her voice.

"Follow me, please." No introductions, no amenities, nothing.

Lil Dwayne turned in his seat, looking Jessica up and down as she passed by on the way to the elevators. When he shifted in his seat to watch her go by, Jessica noticed that, in addition to a wolfish grin, Lil Dwayne was wearing a gun. Stashed in a shoulder holster; she caught a glimpse of it as his jacket fell open.

Anna Celeste Burke

The ride up to the fifth floor was silent. When the elevator stopped, it opened into a plush outer office. As in the lobby on the first floor, the walls here were covered, too. In addition to the ubiquitous photos of Mr. P. with this or that rock or film star, there were also signed concert posters, gold and platinum records, and blown-up versions of covers from Billboard, Rolling Stone, Music Connection, and other industry publications.

The room was dominated by large windows that let in the afternoon sunlight and provided views of the city. A large, dark wood desk with modern lines sat in front of the window, accompanied by a white leather chair. The wall that separated the outer office from Mr. P.'s was made from a jigsaw of expensive woods. White leather loveseats were set out to accommodate those who waited for Mr. P. A sheet of silvery glass seemed to float above the white base of the coffee table set in front of the loveseats.

"Sit," the zombie ordered, pointing to the white loveseat. She tapped so lightly on the door to the inner office that Jessica could barely hear it. From inside, a man's voice responded.

"Come in, please." Zombie-girl opened the door, but only a crack. She slithered through a space too small for any mortal female to pass. In another minute or two, the door swung wide and Mr. P. made his grand entrance. His hair, now snow white, had been sheared short, a mid-length flat top in the front. He sported a trimmed mustache and beard, also white.

"Ms. Huntington, welcome. Sorry to keep you waiting. Please come into my office and have a seat." He didn't offer to shake hands but directed Jessica toward another white leather chair that sat opposite his enormous desk. Jessica did as she was told. Her heart skipped a beat at the sight of this odd little man, and did a little jig as she entered the inner sanctum of his private office.

A wall of windows dominated this room, too. The light streaming in sparkled off a glass conference table that was surrounded by half a dozen white leather, high-backed chairs. Mr. P. whispered something into the zombie girl's ear as she towered over him. Even without the five-inch stilettos, she would have been taller than Mr. P. who couldn't have been no more than 5'2" or 5'3". In a flash, the vamp moved to a spot on the wall behind Mr. P.'s desk. His desk was a larger version of the one in the reception area and was also accompanied by a white leather chair. This one was more the size of a throne than any ordinary chair.

The wall behind him mirrored the jigsaw pattern of that in the outer office, also a composite of gleaming exotic woods. Jessica thought she recognized rosewood and maybe a maple with a distinctive burl. A panel on the wall opened, revealing a bar area from which Mr. P.'s assistant retrieved two bottles of baby Bling H_2O and two frosty crystal goblets. Without a word, she placed a bottle and a glass in front of each of them. Then she exited the room, closing the door silently behind her.

Jessica opened the bottle of water and poured it into the glass as Mr. P. sat down and did the same. "So, Ms. Huntington, I have only a few minutes before I have to make a dash for the airport. How can I help you?" Jessica took a sip of the water before answering, then, picked up the Bling bottle, examining it more closely. "Swarovski crystals, if that's what you were wondering." The word Bling spelled out on the bottle was encrusted with them.

"I asked for a few minutes of your time in hopes you might help clear up a matter for me. It has to do with this young woman, someone you may have known years ago." Jessica slid the head shot of Kelly across the desk and watched Mr. P. as he picked it up. His reaction was immediate, not simply recognition, but a kind of wistful look came into the man's eyes. He ran his hands over the image, almost fondling it. Jessica's fought the urge to snatch that photo back.

"I believe I have seen her before, but who knows where or when?" That last part came out sing-song, like the lyric that it was from some old standard. "Should I know her? And how might that help you, if I did?"

"From what I understand, you knew her quite well. To refresh your memory, her name is…" Jessica paused as the aged man fixed her with his gaze, "her name *was* Kelly Fontana. She was killed in a hit-and-run accident more than a decade ago." She slid the second photo of Kelly across the table. That photo jarred him. When he picked it up, his hands trembled slightly, and his skin blanched. "She was only nineteen years old."

"I *don't understand* what this has to do with me. She looks familiar to me, but I've seen hundreds, maybe thousands of beautiful auburn-haired girls in my lifetime. With my ties to the music and film industry, there's always some nineteen-year-old knocking on my door, looking for a leg up. You can't expect me to remember them all, can you?"

"What makes you think she had auburn hair? That head shot is black and white, and you certainly can't get a clear view of her hair color from that photo taken at the scene of her, um, accident." Jessica had intended to press him while he was still a little off balance from seeing that awful picture of Kelly, dead. She took another sip of water and noticed that her own hand had a slight tremor. This cat and mouse game they were playing was growing old quickly.

"I told you, she looks familiar to me. I, I..." Jessica interrupted him. She was wary of the man sitting across from her, but the way he was dancing around the fact that he obviously *knew* Kelly was making her more angry than afraid.

"Mr. P., what if I told you that an eyewitness has come forward? He puts you at the scene of that accident years ago where Kelly Fontana died."

"I'd say, so what? The statute of limitations for hit-and-run was up long ago." The cold, calculating frankness of his statement was unnerving, but Jessica went on.

"There is no statute of limitations on murder. That eyewitness I referred to says that Kelly Fontana's death was no accident. He saw you waiting in the parking lot when Kelly ran out of the hotel, being chased by two men, your men, Mr. P." Fidgeting with his glass of water, he was obviously becoming agitated. "It's at that point, according to our witness, that you floored it. You drove your 1999 midnight blue Mercedes S class sedan at Kelly and slammed into her, almost head on. You can see the outcome of your handiwork in that photo of Kelly taken at the scene."

With that, he dropped the façade, and the full-blown fiend emerged. There was something of the trapped animal in his rage at being cornered. Perhaps a bit of surprise in the details she had reeled off about the car that had hit Kelly. He rose, sweeping the bottle of water and the expensive crystal goblet onto the floor.

"How dare you! What is this, a shake down? I let you in here because you have a job with a prominent law firm in LA. That firm has an impeccable reputation, Ms. Huntington. At least it did, until now. I thought we might chat about my legal needs and your need to establish yourself as a rainmaker at your new job. Instead, I get falsely accused of committing some heinous crime." He paused, perhaps trying to regain control or trying to gauge the impact he was having on Jessica.

"Let's say I did know this Kelly Fontana all those years ago, so what? If you have an eyewitness, produce him, and I'll challenge every lie that drug-addicted cretin has told you." He slammed his fist on the desk for emphasis.

A Dead Sister

Jessica was stunned. Not just by the tantrum, but also by Mr. P.'s frank disclosure of what he knew. He was clearly a step ahead of her. More than one step, in fact. She had said nothing to indicate she was new to the firm identified on her business card. Nor had she said anything about the eyewitness being a drug addict. His challenge to produce the witness sent a chill through Jessica. *He not only knew who the witness was, but that he was dead.*

Interview over. Time to go! What had she been thinking coming here alone and without telling a soul about her plan? Jessica fought for control as she considered the potentially dire consequences of her impulsivity. Clearly, the guy was rattled; otherwise, he wouldn't have revealed so much of what he knew. She decided her best bet to get out of there was to exit quickly, while he was still off balance. Adopting a sad, bewildered tone as she spoke, she leaned over and picked up the picture of her dead friend that had been swept onto the floor. Reaching into her purse, she took out a tissue and dabbed at her eyes, even though there were no tears in them.

"Mr. P., I certainly am not here to shake you down. Kelly Fontana was my friend, and I care about what happened to her. I obviously have reservations about the eyewitness testimony, or I wouldn't be here, speaking directly to you, would I?" With that, some of the tension drained out of the man leaning on his desk. His shoulders slumped a little, but he maintained eye contact.

"I am not here representing my firm. I apologize that I didn't make that clear from the very beginning. In fact, I'm not here in any capacity other than that of a caring and concerned friend to someone lost so young." Jessica stood up to leave. The thought of touching the man was almost more than she could bear, but she extended her hand, willing it not to tremble.

"I've taken up enough of your time, and I don't want you to miss your flight. Thank you for meeting with me without an appointment. I should have been more delicate with my inquiry. It's just that I was so distraught after hearing this disreputable man's claims. I apologize for waylaying you. Please do go, so you can catch that plane."

Mr. P. took her hand, shaking it perfunctorily. "I won't miss my flight. It's my own plane. They won't go anywhere without me. I meant what I said about steering some business your way. Who should I speak to on your behalf?" The rage and fear had receded and an almost convivial wiliness took over.

"Paul Worthington is the person mentoring me. He's charged with overseeing the opening of the Palm Desert office where I've hired on. You can reach him at that number on my business card. I'm sure he'd be glad to hear from you. Of course, it would help me out, too. I'm just grateful you're still willing to do that after such an awkward first meeting." Jessica mustered the closest thing she could to an appreciative smile.

Mr. P. looked like the cat that swallowed the canary. He must have pushed a button or something, because the near-catatonic assistant in the slinky dress and spiked heels materialized in the doorway.

"Please show Ms. Huntington out. We're done here." With that, he turned his back on Jessica. It was "game over," as far as Mr. P. was concerned: check and mate.

Let him think he's won, please God, Jessica thought, as she retreated from his malevolent conceit.

The silent ride down to the lobby gave Jessica ample opportunity to observe the young woman standing beside her. The operant word was young. She surely must be eighteen, or Mr. P. wouldn't have her on public display, but she couldn't have been much older.

He still likes them young, Jessica thought, recalling how he had run his hands over that photo of Kelly. What might this taciturn subordinate have to say about Mr. P.'s inclinations if she could somehow break through that stoic façade?

"I'm sorry Mr. P. forgot to introduce us. I'm Jessica Huntington. I don't think I caught your name."

"I know who you are. I gave Mr. P. your card, remember?" She didn't turn toward Jessica, or otherwise acknowledge Jessica's overture. With her head down, she spoke again. "My name is Kim Reed, not that it's any business of yours. If I were you, Ms. Huntington, I'd mind my own business."

Jessica casually looked around, presuming from Kim Reed's demeanor that there was video surveillance on board the elevator. As the elevator came to a stop, Jessica dug around in her purse, pulling out her keys, making sure the image of her keys was caught on film. She also palmed a business card.

Stepping from the elevator, Jessica reached out and took Kim Reed's hand in both of her own, slipping the card to the startled young woman. "Thanks so much. Please thank Mr. P. for me again, and tell him I hope he has a safe trip." With that, Jessica turned and walked quickly past Lil Dwayne, waving jauntily as she stepped out of the lobby and back onto the street.

She'd parked close to the Pure Platinum Music Group building and wasn't far from her car when a very tall gentleman strode toward her, basketball player tall. He was thin, with long, lanky arms, and large hands and feet. A pronounced forehead and angular cheekbones dominated his countenance, as did a jagged slash on his right cheek. Jessica forced herself to keep moving to her car. She looked both ways before stepping into the street and opening the driver side door. The hulk lumbered on. He hadn't glanced up or acknowledged Jessica in any way as he passed. Slipping into the car, she adjusted the rearview mirror in time to see the doc entering the building she'd just left. Where had he come from?

CHAPTER 26

It was nearly seven o'clock by the time Jessica settled in at her father's house in Brentwood. The traffic from downtown LA had been brutal. She was so distracted she made a couple wrong turns that cost her twenty minutes more on the clogged streets. A lot of things disturbed her about the raging Mr. P. and the unpleasant-looking man fitting the doc's description. Unpleasant-looking, who was she kidding? The women Bernadette had spoken to in housekeeping had it right. He was just plain ugly. It wasn't merely his physical appearance. There was something in the way he carried himself, something sinister or "dis-eased."

"El doctor maligno," was right, Jessica muttered. Even though he had not looked at her, Jessica sensed he was keenly aware of her presence as he passed her on the street.

The dutiful Ms. Palmer had been waiting patiently at the Brentwood estate for nearly an hour, even after Jessica had pushed back her expected arrival time. Roberta Palmer very obligingly accepted Jessica's apology, before taking up an attenuated spiel about the use of the house. Jessica had heard it the week before. This time, she paid close attention to everything she was told about security at the Brentwood estate.

She was still on edge. Mr. P. and the doc knew more about her than she knew about them. How had he learned about her or Chester Davis? Two thousand dollars was a lot of money. Had Mr. P. put up the bail money for Chet using Arnold Dunne as his emissary? Was it really an overdose that had killed Chet so soon after his release?

After a salad and a glass of wine, Jessica found herself pacing. She'd changed into a bathing suit, hoping a swim would ease the tension that held her taut like a guitar string wound too tight. Too soon after eating for that swim, she sank into the bubbling hot tub. Jessica called Dick Tatum to confirm their lunch meeting on Wednesday.

He didn't answer his phone, so she left a voice mail, suggesting that they meet at the Mission Inn. Unless she heard otherwise, she would plan on meeting him in the lobby of the hotel at eleven thirty, and they could choose to dine at one of the restaurants on site or go elsewhere. The bubbling water soothed her. Still, she felt vulnerable outside in the dark, even with all the security systems on at the house, and lights blazing from every room. More than once, she would have sworn she heard movement in the bushes or on the slope below the house. Real or imagined scraping and clanking sounds soon drove her inside behind locked doors, without ever taking that swim.

A phone call to Frank Fontana made matters worse. During that phone call, Frank had come about as close as anyone had come in a long time to calling her an idiot. Maybe it was a cop thing. Once they'd been given a badge, they were the final arbiters of what was sensible or not sensible in the pursuit of justice. That did not sit well with the lawyer in her. Playing devil's advocate was one thing, laying down the law was altogether another matter.

Jessica had to admit what had seemed like inspiration on that drive into LA now seemed more like desperation. Idiot was about right. She came close to saying as much to Frank, who reluctantly agreed that she was already on Mr. P.'s radar, even before the confrontation in his office. She was not the only one. Mr. P. knew all about Chester Davis. Frank agreed there was a good chance that the bail money came from him via Arnold Dunne.

Preliminary evidence from the autopsy turned up no sign that Chester Davis had been injured or otherwise involved in a struggle before his death. He had vomited, not an uncommon occurrence among addicts who overdose. It would be several more days before they had findings from the toxicology screen to determine what all he had in his system at the time. At this point, the coroner had concluded that asphyxiation was the cause of death, from aspirating his own vomit during a drug overdose.

Neither Frank nor Jessica was entirely convinced that Chester's death was an unfortunate accident. It seemed a little too convenient to be purely accidental. They reached an impasse almost immediately about what to do about the situation, however. Still furious with Jessica for making that visit to Mr. P., Frank was adamant that they had done all they could. Any further investigation into Kelly's death ought to come from Art Greenwald and the cold case team.

"You need to lay low. Pray Mr. P. was convinced by the mea culpa song and dance you did on the way out of his office. Let him believe you can be bought off by that offer he made to send a little business your way. The best way to do that is to stay out of it! You're lucky to be alive. What if you two had still been going at it when the doc got there? Have you thought about that?"

"I have, thank you very much. I don't need you to add to my anxiety. What I need you to do is help me figure out how to get that crud. Both cruds, in fact, so there aren't any more dead girls like Kelly. Do you think they just gave up all their bad habits, or whatever it was they were doing that got Kelly killed? That creep's already been at it again. You and I both know he put someone up to killing Chester Davis. For goodness' sake, Frank, you're the homicide detective. Surely you're not going to let him get away with murder again?"

"When I said, 'we've done all we can for Kelly,' what I really meant was *you've* done all *you* can do for Kelly. I want you to leave this to me and to the rest of us who are paid to take the kind of risks you took today. You no longer have Chester Davis as a client, so there's no official reason for you to be involved in any sort of police investigation. His murder happened on my watch, and I'm on it! And Jessica, before you blow your stack at me again, I want you to ask yourself one question: How *did* you get on Mr. P.'s radar? You've been out there asking lots of people questions about Kelly's death. If this Mr. P. knows so much about you and Chester Davis, there's a good chance he knows a thing or two about the company you keep. Not just me and your pal, Dick Tatum. I'm talking about Tommy and the rest of your Cat Pack friends. Please, do what the psycho who trashed your car and left you that note told you to do: just back off."

"Great. Now you're siding with the psychos. No problem. I'll back off, alright." With that, she hung up the phone. She shuddered from a mix of rage and fear. *Had that been only this morning?* She wondered, as she tried once again to reach Dick Tatum. Her anger was still blazing hot. It wasn't that Frank had pulled rank on her, as he and his colleagues were wont to do. It was the fact that he was right. Here she was again putting herself and others in harm's way. She left Dick another message. This time she included a warning that the men Chester Davis believed to be responsible for Kelly Fontana's death were on to them. "Please call me, Dick, and be careful."

CHAPTER 27

As Jessica tried to maintain her focus on meetings at the LA law firm, that argument with Frank intruded. Mostly because of the dreadful circumstance she, and maybe her friends, were in. It also bothered her that she cared as much as she did about what Frank Fontana thought about her. As willful and determined as they both were, their clash was too reminiscent of the disputes she'd had with Kelly. She wasn't ready for that kind of Huntington-Fontana volatility, even when her own impulsivity had contributed to the turmoil. The attraction between them was undeniable. Nevertheless, she was not willing to take up with a guy she couldn't get along with outside of the bedroom.

She was thinking that very thing when Paul Worthington stepped out of his office wearing a crisp white shirt with a red tie, and khaki slacks. He looked remarkably refreshed for a man who must have been working on knotty problems since early morning. His blue eyes sparkled and he was smiling as he ushered out his client, an attractive woman in professional attire.

Jessica recognized her, not from the tabloids, but from some business show Jim loved to watch. She was an executive at a studio involved in film production featuring computer-generated animation, like Pixar, but smaller and less prominent. The company had made a big splash a while back hiring this woman away from Google or Apple or someplace like that. Jessica strained to recall the woman's name.

"I'll be right with you," Paul said, in a very formal way, as she remained seated in the outer office of the suite he occupied. The administrative assistant usually at her desk must have stepped away or had left for the day.

Gloria was nowhere to be seen and her desk was tidied up and neat as a pin.

"Thank you so much. I can't believe this can all be handled so easily. It is such a relief. The man's a genius," Paul's client said, speaking to Jessica.

"She knows that," Paul said. "I just hired her for our new Palm Desert office. Leslie Windsor, this is Jessica Huntington. I cleared up a little matter for Leslie, but I'm hoping she's going to let us handle some of her other legal concerns. Leslie is interested in finding a place in the desert as a weekend getaway."

"Property is still such a steal out there. Not like LA or the Silicon Valley, where I live and work. It's irresistible."

"If there's anything I can do, Ms. Windsor, I'd be happy to assist. I grew up there and recently returned after an extended absence. I'll be checking things out for another client, so if you have an idea about what you're looking for, I'd be glad to do a little scouting for you, too."

"Really, where do you live?"

"I'm in Mission Hills. That's in Rancho Mirage, if that's an area you know."

"Do I ever! I've rented a place there for the Kraft-Nabisco Open several times. I love, love, love golf! If I could get away with it, I'd trade places with any of the great ladies on the LPGA pro circuit. I'm nowhere near good enough to do that, so I'm not giving up my day job any time soon. Second best is to have a place to go and play all the golf I can squeeze in."

"You have plenty of choices on that front, a hundred and twenty courses in the valley. More, depending on how you count them."

"Let's set up a lunch once it gets a little cooler. There are probably a lot of issues I should consider before I plop down money for a house, even at a bargain price."

"True. Does it matter that you're on a private, semi-private, or public course? How challenging a course do you want, how much you're willing to pay for an equity stake, and what other amenities are you looking for? Or you could forget about all that and just go with your gut. Buy the house you fall in love with, like a lot of happy people do, Ms. Windsor."

"No thanks. I prefer to do things more systematically. Paul is trying to clean up one of the muddles that love, or something like it, left on my

A Dead Sister

doorstep. But please, no more with the Ms. Windsor thing. It makes me feel old. It's Leslie, Jessica. Please, give me your card. When I see a window of time open, I'll call and we can find something that works for you, too, okay? My latest run-in with a lothario also makes me wary about how I own what I own, so maybe we can chat about that too." Jessica dug out a card and handed it over.

"I'd be happy to talk things over whenever you have the time. I look forward to hearing from you." That was the polite thing to say, but Jessica really meant it. She liked the woman. Smart, thoughtful, and direct, she could probably make a decision when the time came about whatever legal matters required Jessica's assistance. It was easy to understand how she became a CEO. She couldn't have been much older than Jessica was, maybe forty. *Good for her*, Jessica thought. It was inspiring to see a woman making her mark and being so upbeat about it.

Paul came back after seeing his client out to the elevator. He was ecstatic. "I am a genius. You've got yourself another client. Let's get out of here." He stepped back into his office for a moment and came out wearing a navy blazer. "I presume all went well with the Van der Woerts. I caught a glimpse of you all with your heads together after I left and everybody was smiling."

"It did go well. We got through the interview. I have a much better idea about documents that need updating. They have a lot of ideas about a legacy, but no clear plan for how to realize it. I get the feeling that whatever's going on with their daughter is putting pressure on them to act, but also keeping things up in the air. I gave them an overview of their options to consider until we can meet again. They're coming out to the desert Labor Day weekend. A realtor is taking them to look at homes. I'll arrange for dinner, maybe at my house, if that sounds like a good idea to you."

Paul had been listening carefully while scurrying around, turning out the lights in his office, and closing and locking the door. He scribbled a note for Gloria, leaving it on her desk. "That would be a very nice thing to do. That sort of personal touch really would put them at ease, and build trust. There is definitely a problem with the daughter, but they should tell you about it rather than hearing it from me." He stepped closer and smiled down at her. "You're the antidote to the grief their daughter is giving them. Just about the same age, but the daughter they deserved, not the one they got."

He shook his head, thinking about whatever it was they were going through. "All ready for your surprise?"

"I guess so."

"Can you walk a few blocks in those shoes?" He asked, looking admiringly at more than her shoes. She was wearing the red Max Mara dress and black Jimmy Choo pumps with sensible two-inch heels.

"No problem. Let's go!"

Paul took her by the elbow and steered her from the outer office, locking the door behind them. They ran the gauntlet of inquiring eyes and friendly hellos as they made their way to the front desk and elevators to the ground floor. At that time, in addition to the exchange of salutations, Paul took a call and placed a call on his cell.

Along the way, "hey Jessica" was tossed at her from people she'd met during the whirlwind of introductions on her previous visit. She acknowledged their greetings, but couldn't respond in kind by using their name. Names *and* faces were still such a blur. Once they were outside the building, she confessed her inability to recall the names of those who greeted her.

Paul set off down the sidewalk as he addressed her concern. "You should be able to recognize and greet the more senior people if you bump into one of them. Our website can help you with that. Amy is planning a kind of open house at the Palm Desert office in the fall. We'll coordinate that event with our annual meeting, probably after Thanksgiving. That will give you a chance to mingle and meet more of the members of the firm. We're talking about a couple hundred lawyers, Jessica, and twice that many legal assistants, interns, and support staff. Give yourself a break."

He was moving at a good clip. The LA streets were bustling with foot traffic, as well as a constant stream of cars. Rush hour was building to a pitch. Jessica hustled to keep up, chatting a bit more about the ground she had covered with the Van der Woerts. When they had travelled several blocks, making a turn or two, Jessica was lost until a recognizable storefront came into view. The A+D Architecture and Design Museum, she knew, of course. Her father had taken her there on more than one occasion since it opened in 2001. As they reached the front door, Paul held it open for her.

"In you go," he said. Once inside, they met up with a middle-aged man, casually attired in an arty mix of nerd and hip. "This is Jessica Huntington, Jeff. Jessica, Jeffrey Stark is working on an exhibit that will open the end of

A Dead Sister

July, and there are a few things you just have to see while you're in town."

"It's nice to meet you, Jessica. Follow me." He was smiling pleasantly as he led them through a maze of space in the process of transformation. "Watch your step," he cautioned, "and your head!" He added, ducking through a doorway with a partially hung banner slumping in the door opening.

"Here we are," their escort announced. The three of them came to a halt in front of a long glass enclosed display case. In the case were architectural renderings and blueprints. There was something familiar about the artist's drawings and the graphic designs set out side-by-side in the case. The soaring lines and bold angles were classic mid-century modern but infused with the love of the outdoors, and something fanciful or romantic. It suddenly hit her. She knew where she had seen them, or something similar.

"Dad's, these are Dad's designs. How did you find these?" Jessica was fascinated as she peered at the items in the case. There, on one of the prints, was her father's signature. It was Jeff who answered her question.

"The exhibit is going to be called 'Never Built,' Jessica. It will pay homage to the Los Angeles imagined but never realized by artists and architects like your father. We'll mount an enlarged image of one of his designs on the wall behind this display case, and there will be a brief bio and photos of the things he *has* done in LA and elsewhere. That will include your family home in the desert, by the way." He walked her down to one of the last exhibits at the far end of the display case. There was an exquisite rendering of the house in Mission Hills. A drawing just like that, penned in ink by her father, was hanging in a frame in his office. This had to be a copy, or an earlier draft, perhaps.

"But how did you find out about this, Paul?"

"Paul is on our board. When he saw your dad's name on the list of individuals we were including in this exhibit, he offered to foot the bill for the whole thing. He was thrilled. He's been a fan of your father's work for years. Now I see he's a fan of his daughter, as well."

Jessica spun about and threw her arms around Paul, tearing up as she thanked him. Swept up in a rush of gratitude, she fought to regain her composure as she clutched at the fine Italian wool in Paul's blazer. There was something so completely disarming about the thoughtfulness of this gesture that she was overcome by emotion. Inexplicable, unanticipated kindness was a powerful thing. A potent antidote to the dark revelations about Kelly and the malevolence that had killed her.

Paul had put his arms around her, holding her close as she recovered from the impact of his surprise. Both men were smiling, pleased to have made her so happy. Taking a step back, she was finally able to speak again.

"Actually, I'm his fan, Jeff, and yours now too. This is such a wonderful thing you've done for my father. Does he know?"

"Oh yes, we've told him. There will be an opening night gala on the thirty-first. Your father and several other living architects will be there. Others will be represented by their families. We hope you'll join us too. You'll get a formal invitation, by mail, but now you can go ahead and put it on your calendar."

"Of course. I'll be there. This is just so amazing. I'd like to donate to the museum, too, in Dad's honor. Will you take a check?" Her head was still spinning as she wrote out a large check to the A+D. The place not only served as a museum but also did outreach and education, identifying and nurturing the next generation of Hank Huntingtons.

Jessica was awash in a glow all evening long. Paul was happy too, charming and animated. He regaled her with tales about his childhood, growing up in California amid an odd assortment of family members. He had a brother and two sisters. From what Jessica gathered, they were more invested in spending the family money than preserving or adding to it. True to Andrew Carnegie's adage, "from shirtsleeves back to shirtsleeves in three generations," meaning the first generation makes the money, the second holds on to it, and the third squanders it. Paul was fighting to hold the line on his share of the family fortune. That fortune had its roots in the California gold rush. Not gold per se, but a fortune made in the sale of pick axes, dried beans, coffee, and other supplies sold to the droves of treasure hunters who flooded into California in the nineteenth century.

Paul was the only member of the family's current generation to pursue a legal career, though that line of work was well-represented among his ancestors. An uncle was a sitting member of the California Supreme Court and his great uncle had been a lawyer who moved into politics, as many do. That great uncle was a member of the United States Senate for a couple of decades, serving in an era when a long tenure in Congress was considered a virtue rather than a vice.

They talked about where the practice of law was heading, at the firm and elsewhere. Paul detailed some of the specific issues that firms like theirs faced handling high profile cases while dealing with the peculiarities of the entertainment industry, especially Hollywood celebrities.

"You never know what you'll face next when representing the rich and famous when they're in trouble."

"Tell me about it. I'm getting a lesson of my own in the peculiarities of Hollywood celebrities courtesy of my ex-husband and his glamour girl."

"You have much yet to learn," he said, speaking in a mock guru voice. "If you stick around here for any length of time, you'll see plenty. Consider what you're going through with your ex and his wife as experience you may well have to use dealing with one of our clients." He launched into a series of stories about some of the more outrageous antics they had dealt with at the firm. In no time, he had her laughing, convincing her that Jim had better get used to bizarre public and private upheavals now that he was linked to a Hollywood diva.

"The claim to an artistic temperament is cover for a lot of things that are mean and stupid. Throw in a gigantic dose of narcissism, and you've got a recipe for a wall full of mug shots to go with all those glamour-girl shots." He knew all about the latest episode in the sad saga. Jim's succubus had been arrested, and a defiant mug shot was now being broadcast on the entertainment news channels.

An image of the tantrum-throwing Mr. P. flashed through her mind. *His is one mug shot I'd love to see*, she thought. She didn't linger long on the dreadful man, but returned to the subject of Jim's bride who had been hauled off to jail.

"At least she's got herself a lawyer," Jessica added, ruefully. Other than their discussion about Jim and the she-beast, and that fleeting vision of Mr. P., she thoroughly enjoyed the evening. When Paul dropped her back at the firm's lot, he got out of their limo and sent it on its way. As he walked her to the door of her loaner car, she suddenly realized how little she'd thought about the distressing events of the previous day. Paul's kindness had staved off thoughts about Kelly and her horrible death. Nor had she fretted about where the investigation, her encounter with Mr. P., or where her relationship with Frank might be heading.

Saying goodbye, Paul thanked her for a lovely evening and very debonairly kissed her hand. Maybe it was the joy he exuded by doing such a nice thing for her father or the pleasant conversation. She found herself looking forward to their movie night. She told him that, pulling him toward her, and stepping on her tiptoes to place a kiss on his cheek. He pressed her to him as he said good night. The tautness in the muscles of his arms gave way as he released her, leaving Jessica a little breathless. He opened her car door, waiting as she shut herself in and locked the door. As he sidled back to his car, he whistled a happy little tune.

"Amber and bergamot," she said to herself, finally recognizing the scent that tantalized her in this man's arms. Jessica drove home a little perplexed by the fact that, in the matter of a week, two men had nearly swept her off her feet. Could she offset becoming too involved with one man by seeing another? Was such a thing possible, and was it fair? They were both decent men, neither of which deserved to have their hearts trampled.

Jessica hadn't ever really dated. Dating was an archaic notion in college. She had a group of friends with whom she did a lot of studying, but fun things too. Some paired off at the end of an evening, or after several outings with the larger group. Once that happened, it was generally assumed you had "hooked up" and were having sex. That's when things got tricky. A kind of "one man at a time" rule prevailed against the old conventions of dating several men.

Casual sexual liaisons had the potential to wreak havoc on your life and reputation, at least for her women friends. Returning home in the same party clothes you wore the night before was risky business. Being seen taking that "walk of shame," as some called it, one too many times, with one too many men could earn you the slut label. Hook-ups and booty calls also took another toll on many of the young women she knew. They were sometimes deeply disappointed when casual sex didn't lead to something more.

Their male friends, however, seemed to suffer much less. Less invested in sex as a pathway to relationship-building, and she wasn't even sure there was a male counterpart to the term slut. "Player" was about the closest thing that came to mind. That moniker was the kiss of death, as far as Jessica was concerned, and no guy meriting that label would have remained on her list of friends for long.

Neither Frank nor Paul seemed remotely inclined toward "player." Jessica worried more about "playing" them by getting too involved, too soon, or leading them on in some way. There were all those questions hanging out there: why hadn't Paul ever married, and why had Frank's marriage ended in divorce? She now had short answers to both, but there was more to learn.

A Dead Sister

What the heck? She still couldn't answer the question about why her own marriage had turned out to be such a disaster. She owed it to herself and the two new men in her life to get a better understanding of her own situation, as well as theirs. It was those hugs that were causing all the trouble, with Frank and now Paul, too. That had to stop.

As Jessica neared her father's house, alone and in the dark, her uneasiness grew. Was it the unwelcome third man, occupying center stage in her life, who had called to mind the male-as-player motif? For the time being, the tantrum-throwing Mr. P. had passed up Jim Harper as the most detestable man in her life. Of course, she hadn't yet come face to face with the prescription-wielding doc, who had sashayed into the Pure Platinum Music Group's building yesterday. Had she done enough to forestall such a meeting?

CHAPTER 28

Wednesday morning, Jessica awoke feeling challenged by the prospects for the day. She had to face Dick Tatum and whatever new revelations he might have obtained about the demise of Chester Davis. There was no longer any doubt in her mind that the attention-seeking Mr. P. and the elusive doc were involved in Kelly's death. Frank's concerns for her safety reflected that he shared her conviction.

Despite sinking deeper and deeper into the muck and mire that surrounded the two despicable men, they had nothing to link either man to Kelly's death. Nothing, that is, other than the eyewitness testimony of a now dead drug addict. Dick Tatum had recorded their interviews with Chester Davis, but she wasn't sure they would be of much value or even admissible as evidence. Surely, not enough to get an indictment of either man even with the work she and her Cat Pack buddies had done to corroborate parts of his story.

Tommy and Jerry were still digging up as much background information as they could about both men. Jessica considered calling and telling them to back off. There was so little to go on anyway, especially when it came to finding background information about the doc. No name and no history, other than his tentative association with Mr. P. It was hard to believe some lurid tale hadn't surfaced somewhere about the unsightly character hanging around Mr. P.

Lil Dwayne might know the doc's name. Fat chance getting anything from that cagey guy, Jessica thought.

"Good grief," Jessica muttered, "the doc stands out!" The women in

A Dead Sister

housekeeping had attested to that. Jessica could too, now, after catching a glimpse of the man. Wandering in or out of Mr. P.'s workplace, as he had done Monday, should have provoked a curious-minded Hollywood reporter to inquire about his connection to Mr. P. or the studio. Where was the scintillating scuttlebutt about the doc?

Given his propensity to write prescriptions for Mr. P.'s friends and associates with apparent abandon, it was also impossible to believe he had avoided legal trouble. To track him down, they needed a name. Perhaps some link to the doc could be discovered by a more careful review of Mr. P.'s legal troubles. Jessica put more digging into Mr. P.'s legal dealings on her own to-do list, not wanting to encourage Tommy or Jerry to get in any deeper than they already were.

After swimming, tanking up on caffeine, and eating breakfast, Jessica decided to track her father down. Paul Worthington's surprise was a ray of sunshine in the growing storminess surrounding the investigation into Kelly's death, punctuated by that bolt of lightning signaling the end to Chester Davis' pitiful life. She was bursting with pride and happiness for her father, and wanted to congratulate him. After several attempts to locate him, Jessica gave up. Voice mails and a text message would suffice for now.

She was disappointed that there was no message from Frank. Didn't he feel some remorse about how he handled that last conversation? Jessica certainly did. So why didn't she call and leave a message communicating that to him? The answer was simple. She was as stubborn and prideful as Frank Fontana was, if not more so.

There was nothing from Dick Tatum, either. That was odd. He was, no doubt, as upset as she was about Chet Davis' demise and their stymied investigation. *He doesn't know the half of it*, she thought. They had a lot of ground to cover at their lunch meeting. Perhaps, when he heard all that she and her Cat Pack friends had discovered, he would come up with a fresh angle they might pursue. Or maybe he'd ward her off too, and lay the matter to rest along with his now dead client.

By ten o'clock, Jessica was pulling out of the driveway leading from her dad's estate to the street. As the gates closed behind her, Jessica inched forward, checking to see that the street was clear of traffic. Suddenly, something caught Jessica's eye. She gasped in disgust. A large doll lay in the street, its head on the curb, horribly contorted. The doll had long auburn hair and wore what looked like a shorty pajama top that might have fit a real three or four-year-old.

A wave of nausea grabbed her as she called security. In less than three minutes, a team arrived at the house. The two men initially looked at her like she was a crazy woman when she pointed out the source of her concern. That reaction was the main reason she'd called them, and not the LAPD. The shortest way to get her point across was to pull out that awful photo of Kelly, as she explained that the cold case she was working on was no longer cold.

That did the trick. Jessica asked them to take photos at the curb, and then go through the house and grounds making sure the culprits hadn't left similar mementoes elsewhere. She also asked them to review every bit of surveillance footage from the night before, and pass along information about any vehicle that had stopped nearby or passed the house more than once in the past several days.

"Call in extra help if you need to. I'll pay you triple your usual hourly rate if you turn around a report in twenty-four hours. The bill goes to me, not my father, okay?"

The team on site called in her request to management. They were having the same sort of trouble explaining the problem at the house until Jessica had the guys on the scene send a photo of the doll and the crime scene photo of Kelly to the manager at the home office. All the arrangements were made quickly after that.

Jessica also called the concierge service, and in minutes, Roberta Palmer pulled into the driveway. She stopped only long enough to check out the scene at the curb, to speak to Jessica, and glimpse that photo of Kelly. Roberta Palmer paled ever so slightly before continuing up the drive and entering the estate through the gates. She, more than any of the security guards, would know if something was awry anywhere on the property. Jessica also asked Ms. Palmer to bill her directly for a day's work, at triple her usual rate, as security had agreed to do.

She wasn't just interested in whatever they might dig up that could help figure out who'd left the latest message to back off. Jessica was determined that her father was not going to get sucked into whatever trouble she'd stirred up. Nor was he going to come home to find his property had been desecrated in some way by thugs.

The whole situation took much less time to manage than any police report would have taken. Jessica asked Roberta Palmer to report the incident to the LAPD once she and security had completed their own inspection. Not that she had much hope that the police would find any evidence linking the doll back to her tormentor, but the incident would be on the record. It would be a real stroke of luck if security got a license plate number and a vehicle description from reviewing all the surveillance footage.

"Give the police my card, please, with my name and phone number. That way they'll have a way to reach me if they need to speak to me later about the incident." Roberta agreed and secured the gate as Jessica turned out of the driveway.

Still jittery as she sped along the highway from LA to Riverside, Jessica pushed up against the posted limits when she could. Traffic and roadwork made it impossible to sustain anything close to the speed limit at times. Congestion also made it difficult to determine if anyone was following her. With wall-to-wall cars stretched across several lanes, all jockeying for position, who could tell who was stalking whom? She felt sure Mr. P. had someone tracking her. How else could they have known where, and when, to leave that horrible doll?

She remained vigilant until she spotted the exit to downtown Riverside and the Mission Inn, almost two hours later. As she moved into the right lane to take the exit ramp, the check engine light came on.

"Are you kidding me?" Jessica said, as the engine missed. She pulled off the road, onto the shoulder of the exit ramp, as the engine seized up and the car coasted to a stop. No way was she going to get to that lunch meeting with Dick Tatum now. She pounded the steering wheel a couple times before trying to restart the car. No luck.

As she was preparing to make a round of phone calls for assistance, a low rider taking the exit to downtown Riverside slowed. The two young men in the car leered at Jessica as they passed. One of them flashed a toothy grin, loaded with the bejeweled grill so popular among rappers and their followers. The car hopped up and down a couple of times, seemingly in sync with booming music being played from speakers that shook the ground. Jessica was preparing to dial 911 when they moved on.

She got out of the car, raised the hood, and set out a flare she found in the trunk. Satisfied her actions would keep her from getting hit by a passing motorist, Jessica called the BMW dealer. Roadside service was dispatched immediately from the location closest to her in Riverside. They apologized profusely that the nearly new loaner had malfunctioned. She could ride to the dealer with the tow truck driver and pick up another car, or the driver would drop her somewhere else, if she preferred. Jessica wasn't sure what she wanted to do until she spoke to Dick Tatum, and told them as much.

"No problem," they assured her. "Just tell the tow truck driver what you want to do when he arrives."

Next, she called Dick Tatum, who picked up, this time on the first ring. "Dick, it's me, Jessica. I'm so glad to get you on the phone. I tried to reach you several times last night and this morning about our lunch today. You're not going to believe this, but my car died. I'm sitting on the exit ramp to downtown, waiting for a tow. Actually, it's not *my* car. My car was trashed Monday while I was at my office in Palm Desert. The one I'm sitting in right now is a loaner."

"I believe you, Jessica. I've had some car trouble of my own. I didn't get your voice mails until I picked up a new phone a little while ago. My phone was in my car last night when somebody torched it."

"Somebody set your car on fire?"

"Yeah, that's right. This guy in a hoodie and sunglasses lobbed a Molotov cocktail into the window of my car. I was talking to a colleague in the parking lot at Applebee's after dinner. If I hadn't walked away from my car to look at my friend's latest pictures of his kids, I don't know what would have happened."

"I'm so glad you're okay."

"It took me hours to file the police report, make a claim with my insurance company, and pick up the rental car I'm driving. I got a license plate number for the car the perp was driving. That didn't do much good since the car had been reported stolen. They found it torched, too, late last night. When I picked up your messages, I figured I'd just meet you at the Mission Inn and explain it all. I'm only a few minutes away. Why don't I come pick you up?"

"Okay, if you don't mind fighting the lunch hour traffic. That would be great. I've already called the dealer, and they've got a tow truck on the way. They have my cell phone number if they need to find me later. Maybe after we talk, you can take me to the rental place you used. I'll see if I have better luck in something other than a BMW."

"No problem. I'll be there in ten minutes. Stay put."

"Ha ha! You can count on that." Jessica tried to be as good a sport as Dick Tatum but the number of traumas was mounting rapidly. Frank's words were pounding in her ears. She called the dealer to tell them a friend was picking her up, and that the keys would be under the mat on the driver's side of the car. They seemed fine with that. It wasn't as if anyone could drive off in the car. The flatbed truck was already in route. Jessica leaned back, grateful that it was barely ninety degrees in Riverside. The battery on the BMW wasn't dead yet, so she lowered the windows to get a cross breeze in the car.

It hadn't been more than a few minutes when Jessica felt, even before she heard, the beat of oversized speakers. She looked in her rearview mirror. The low rider had pulled off the road maybe ten feet behind her with the top down on the vintage Chevy Impala. The passenger with the mouth jewelry was climbing out of the car without opening the passenger side door. She didn't see anything resembling a Molotov cocktail in his hand, but he was wearing a hoodie and sunglasses. With only ten feet separating the two cars, he wasn't likely to do anything to blemish the sunburst paint job or the polished chrome on the well-cared for low rider.

That didn't mean this was going to go well. Jessica punched 911 into her cell phone and prepared to hit send, calculating in her mind how long it might take for the police to respond. She also reached into her purse for a can of police grade pepper spray. A definite upgrade since her last murder investigation when she'd gone into a tough situation with nothing but hairspray and a hatpin. By then, she'd already acquired experience using everyday objects as defensive weapons.

"Hey yummy mummy, you need some help?" the slouching young man asked, as he approached with some caution. Perhaps he was trying to figure out whether she was armed. He slid the sunglasses up onto the top of his head as he took another step closer, and peered at her.

Was she safer staying in the car with the doors locked and the windows rolled up? Could she get them rolled up before the guy decided to make a move? Or, should she get out of the car and spray the scuzzball? Stalling for time, she shouted out a reply to his question.

"No thanks. Help is on the way." From the rearview mirror, she could see the driver jack the low rider up and then down again. The ground was rumbling from the booming speakers.

"We got something for ya, Jessica." She caught a glint off the grillwork in his mouth as he smiled and grabbed his crotch at the same time. Several things occurred to her. First, she had waited too long to make that 911 call. No way would the police reach her before the punk ambling toward her did. Second, she did not want to find out what he had for her. Third, he had called her by name. Her name had rolled off that tongue and those lips that had been who knows where!

Before he took another step, Jessica whipped the car door open, and hopped out. In a flash, she sent a stinging spray that blasted the still smiling young man right in the face. Thank goodness—and Peter—she had practiced for such an incident. She knew exactly how to direct the caustic droplets.

"I've got something for you too, Eminem!" Jessica shrieked, spraying him again. She had hit him squarely in his gaping grillwork. The scrawny gangster wannabe was squealing. The sound was somewhere between a greased pig at the county fair and a twelve-year-old girl at a Miley Cyrus concert. He was twerking like a Miley Cyrus concert goer, too. He spun around blindly, gasping for air, and spitting. Off flew the sunglasses from atop his head. Out popped the gem-studded grillwork. The driver was shouting, dropping f-bombs and telling him to "do it," "just do it, sucka!"

It was like listening to some demented, X-rated Nike pitchman. Jessica wasn't sure what "do it" meant, but she did not intend to find out. She aimed and shot at the driver, who ducked even though he was behind the windshield. He finally shut up as a second spray, aimed higher, shot up above the windshield, and then, showered down on him. She took a step forward and let loose more sprays, saturating the head and neck area of the writhing young man still pulling at his hoodie. He yanked it off, exposing a lemon-colored buzz cut on his head, a concave chest, and pale white, spindly arms. Red splotches were popping up here and there. As he spun back around, facing her, she let more blasts go at twenty-second intervals. He shed the wife-beater t-shirt next. The young man was now half-naked as he hopped around on the side of the road. Items were falling from the clothes he discarded, or maybe from the pockets of his baggy pants. Among them was a gun.

Jessica made a mad dash for the gun before the half-blinded man, now flailing about on his knees, could locate it.

"Get in, you mother. She's got the gun," the driver hollered. "I'm gettin' the hell outta here wit' or wit'out you, Gomer." He gunned the engine of the car. The baggy-panted young man on the ground rose. He did a Frankenstein's monster walk in the direction of those engine sounds. When he reached the car, he fell forward, tumbling head first into the passenger seat of the car. The driver revved the engine again and glared right at Jessica.

A Dead Sister

"Oh no you don't! Don't even think about it!" She shouted, as she emptied the gun into the front end of the car. With that, he took off. Steam was rising from under the hood. Two cars slammed on their brakes to avoid ramming the low rider as it burned rubber, leaving a trail of fluid from somewhere under the car. One of the two cars that had braked pulled off onto the shoulder of the road. It slid into the space vacated by the vintage Chevy.

"Don't shoot, Jessica. It's me, Dick Tatum." Jessica dropped the gun and sat right down on her backside. Her legs no longer providing support. The sound of police sirens could be heard in the distance growing louder by the second. Dick was at her side a moment later, helping her get to her feet.

"You need to get out of the sun. I've got the air conditioner running in my car. Come on, you're okay. It's okay."

"I'm probably going to need a lawyer."

"That's okay too, Jessica. You've got one."

Dick guided her to the front seat of his rental as a patrol car pulled off the road behind him. Two minutes later, another marked car arrived, followed a few minutes later by the tow truck. The shoulder of the off ramp was now too crowded to accommodate the arrival of an ambulance and the EMTs. A passing motorist had apparently called 911 with information that there was an altercation taking place on the side of the road. A second caller had said there were shots fired. The first officer at the scene waved off the ambulance on assurances from Jessica that she wasn't injured.

One of the officers from the second patrol car was directing traffic. He tried to keep the looky-loos moving, while a third officer set up a perimeter and began taking photos of the scene. They set out markers next to the gun where Jessica had dropped it, and her now nearly empty pepper spray device nearby. The hoodie, t-shirt, and grillwork left behind by her would-be assailants were also marked and photographed where they had fallen. There were dark streaks on the pavement left by the driver of the Chevy Impala. The quick-thinking Dick Tatum had noted what he could see of the license plate as the vehicle fled. It shouldn't be too hard to find the decked out low rider painted in a bright yellow-sunburst pattern and riddled with bullet holes. Besides, how far could it get far in that condition?

Jessica did her best to describe the incident to Riverside's finest. She sipped from a bottle of water someone had handed her as she went through the now familiar routine. She answered an endless stream of questions as another police officer collected information for yet another police report. The whole scenario had played out in less than ten minutes. The telling and retelling of the story took much longer.

As she recounted events, an officer swabbed her hands for the presence of gunshot residue. The officer who had been taking her statement asked her to "hold on a sec." Recognizing Dick's name, he ran it, and quickly discovered that Dick had been involved in a car-bombing incident the night before. Did they think the two incidents were related?

Jessica wanted to shriek "hell yes" but let Dick responded with a more taciturn "most likely." They were discussing what the two of them were up to, and how the incidents were "most likely" related, when the officer taking photographs asked if Jessica could join her where she was standing. Jessica walked a few feet and stood next to the policewoman holding a camera.

"Any idea what these might be? Did you have them with you, or did your gentlemen callers drop them?" Jessica was hit by a bout of nausea. On the ground was a pair of panties, the print matched the top worn by that doll found outside her dad's house. That sight was eerier to Jessica than being accosted by ruffians in a low rider. Creepier even than the mouth jewelry or seeing that gun fall out of the young thug's pants. She knew who had sent them.

"They're not mine. Maybe if you send them to the lab, you can get fingerprints or something from them, but I wouldn't count on it." Jessica walked dejectedly back to the car. Any fingerprints would no doubt belong to one of the lowlifes in the low rider. They'd be no closer to Mr. P. Not unless they could catch up with the punks and get them to turn on the schemer who had sicced them on her.

As Jessica sat back down on the edge of the seat in Dick's car, a call came in to the police. They had found the Chevy on a back street, not more than a mile away, abandoned, and on fire. One of the officers pointed to a pillar of smoke rising into the sky just south of their location.

"There she goes," he said, as a flash signaled that the car had exploded. Who knew what all was under the hood along with the hydraulics used to raise and lower the car on command? It was ablaze now.

Having finally finished collecting evidence, the police stopped traffic so the tow truck driver could move around in front of the BMW. The man had been waiting in his truck for nearly an hour. When he was finally able to inspect the car, he had another tidbit for those at the scene.

"Uh, Miss, did you notice that the gas tank access door is damaged? I'd say it's been tampered with." Jessica stepped over to the car and looked. The panel was dented and scratched, and no longer sat flush with the body of the well-crafted sedan.

"What does that mean?" Jessica asked, wearily.

"The way the car up and died on you, I'm guessing someone put something in the tank."

"You mean like sugar?"

"Sugar and water, possibly, water's harder on a car than sugar. At least you were close to town when it conked out on you. A shame to do that to a fine car like this one, if you ask me. The mechanics will be able to tell you more after they look it over."

The officer made another note in the record he was keeping, including the name and address of the dealer where the car was being towed. The shock of the ordeal was taking a toll on Jessica. Dick didn't look so good, either. It was well past the lunch hour, and they were running on empty. They were both in for one more surprise as they heard another car drive up. Frank Fontana stepped out of a four-by-four, his personal car. A police beacon, attached to the top of the car, flashed.

"If he says I told you so, I'm going to get into the driver's seat of your rental and run him over, two, maybe three times."

"Nah, you don't want to do that, Jessica," Dick said softly. "That's the kind of depravity that got us all in this mess in the first place."

Frank did not say a word. Instead, he rushed to Jessica and swept her into his arms. *Damn hugs*, she thought, as she hung on to him for dear life.

CHAPTER 29

When the phone rang Thursday morning, Jessica was still unpacking. It had been late by the time she arrived home the night before. Bernadette was waiting up, even though Jessica had called and told her not to do so. She took one look at Jessica and insisted on being told the whole story. It was midnight before Jessica rolled her suitcase into her room and fell into bed.

The discussion with Bernadette was a good thing, since it put them both back on high alert about using the security systems at home. Bernadette also insisted she call Peter and get him to put his guys back on the job. She would ask that they take up their post out in front of her house, as they had done when Roger Stone's killer was stalking Jessica and her friends.

She left Peter a message, making her request for help. When she hung up the phone, she noticed a voice mail of her own. Her father had called: "Hey, Jinx, it's your dad. Sorry I missed your call. Thanks for the good wishes, sweetie. I'm going to be back in LA in a week, and I am looking forward to the exhibit. It's great you'll be at the reception opening night. Can you come into town the night before for dinner? Okay, well, see you soon. Love you."

Jessica threw herself down on her bed and wept. "Sure thing, Dad," Jessica said. "I'll see you soon, if some maniac doesn't mow me down like poor Kelly. Or have somebody do it for him." Maybe she *was* a jinx *or* jinxed *or* both. Most dreadful was the prospect of becoming one more episode on one of those true crime shows. That doll-on-the-side-of-the-road thing would be too salacious to pass up along with the fact that the panties showed up later at another crime scene. There was that shoot-out on the exit ramp, too, and cars being torched. Nancy Grace would have a

A Dead Sister

field day with that.

She cried herself to sleep and woke up still in her clothes. Things didn't look quite so dire this morning, once she cleaned herself up. One of Peter's guys was already on duty outside. Still, she flinched when her phone rang.

"Well, Ms. Huntington-Harper, I hear you're at it again."

"At *what* again, Detective Hernandez? And, please, it's Jessica Huntington, no more Harper." She recognized the crusty detective's sardonic tone of voice immediately. She knew exactly what he was getting at, but decided to play coy.

"Running law enforcement ragged, that's what. I heard you were involved in another incident on El Paseo Monday. Apparently, that's becoming a favorite spot for Jessica-Huntington-centered calamity; Harper or no Harper! Word is you're branching out and creating crime scenes elsewhere in our fair county. You and your colleagues made quite a stir with the Riverside County Sheriff's Department, *three* crime scenes in a twenty-four-hour period. As I recall, Ms. Huntington, that ties your previous record."

"Yes, someone vandalized my car, Detective, two cars, actually. One on El Paseo and the other in LA that managed to get as far as Riverside before it gave up the ghost. And yes, after a couple of gangster wannabes finished terrorizing me, they torched their own car, creating another site for the police to clean up in Riverside. Imagine that, lowlifes acting like lowlifes! It's not my fault. Besides, I don't know why it matters to you. None of the so-called Jessica-Huntington-centered calamities were in your jurisdiction."

"That is true. But imagine my surprise when I get called out to investigate a shooting that *is* in my jurisdiction, and the dead man has your card in his pocket, Attorney Huntington. When I'm arranging for the county coroner to process the body, I do a little research about our dead guy, and I come across not one, but two reports of incidents involving Jessica Huntington and the Riverside County Sheriff's Department. No, wait, there's more. One of the reports indicates there *might* be a connection to yet another act of vandalism, involving the firebombing of a car. Richard Tatum, who just happens to be a lawyer, owned that car. A friend of yours, I presume. You want to tell me what's going on? Or am I just supposed to be grateful we actually had a few weeks without running into you at a crime scene?"

Jessica sat down on the side of her bed. That "things-seem-less-dire in the morning" feeling had fled. "Who's dead?" She knew before he answered her question. There weren't many people in the area with one of her new business cards in their possession.

"A parolee recently returned to the area, Robert Simmons. Does the name ring a bell?"

"Yes, sadly, it does. He was my best friend's boyfriend at the time she was killed years ago. I can explain: my place or yours, Detective Hernandez?"

"Have you got coffee?"

"I can make some by the time you get here, no donuts, though."

"Very funny, that's stereotyping you know, and not very PC of you."

"Touché," she said, as she hung up the phone and hauled her weary carcass to the kitchen to make coffee. Maybe caffeine would help. She already had her usual "dose" with her morning swim. She was ready for more, though, caffeine, that is, not more repartee with churlish detectives.

Frank Fontana's face floated before her, as he had looked the day before when arriving at that scene in Riverside. Ragged with worry, his countenance had been instantly transformed when he caught sight of Jessica. Rushing to embrace her, the relief was palpable.

"I heard the dispatcher mention your name, and something about 'shots fired.' I know you're not ready for a relationship. Please, you've got to promise me you'll live long enough to give me a chance when the time comes!"

Not only had he refrained from chastising her after that, but Frank had actually apologized for being so pig-headed about the situation they were in. He conceded that what she and the others had done was basic investigative work. In fact, it was at his urging that she was involved in this mess at all. Jessica acknowledged that, while she was already on the psychopath's radar, she had aggravated the situation by walking into Mr. P.'s office. Confronting him point blank about a situation that could put him behind bars was like tugging on Superman's cape. A deranged, self-designated Superman, with a depraved prescription-wielding hulk at his side.

Frank did not back down about the need to stop and let the professionals take over. Dick Tatum had jumped in to back him up. He was as horrified as Frank by Jessica's decision to go into the lion's den alone.

A Dead Sister

Not only was it risky, but her confrontation had been rather pointless, given how little tangible evidence they had.

Even if they couldn't hold Mr. P. responsible for Kelly's murder, Frank hoped they might be able to make a connection between him and Chester Davis' death. It now looked more like a homicide than an accident. Someone had been with Chester at the time of his death. That someone was Arnold Dunne, the guy who put up the money to spring Chester from jail. He had left his fingerprints at the scene and on Chester's body.

They now had the rogue in custody. Using the GPS on his cell phone, they located him at a sleazy motel near the border with Mexico. At Tecate, not Tijuana, a smaller, less-traveled entry port. If he had crossed the border, they might have lost him for good. Instead, he had stopped and holed up for several nights. It wasn't clear why. Perhaps he was trying to figure out how to get across the border with his stash of drugs. He may have been overcome by the urge to party, since he had been doing plenty of that during his three-day layover at motel hell.

In any case, the local police had nabbed Arnold Dunne. He had nearly fifty thousand dollars in cash and a variety of drugs with him at the time of his arrest. Plus, a suitcase full of illegal porn in both print and video formats. Found in a semi-comatose state, Arnold Dunne had been taken to the forensic ward at a hospital in San Diego. He would be transferred to the County jail when he recovered from his binge. Frank and his partner planned to make the hundred-mile journey to interview Mr. Dunne about his connection to Chester Davis. They were waiting for word that he was alert enough to speak to them.

Mr. Dunne was lucky to be alive. Included in his stash were several syringes loaded with heroin and fentanyl. Some contained large quantities of fentanyl; when he got around to partying with one of them, it would have been his last hurrah.

Dick was totally blown away by Frank's news, and by all Jessica and her friends had uncovered in so short a time about Kelly and Mr. P. Especially the similarity between the contents of the hypodermic found with Mr. Dunne and the one in Kelly's possession so long ago. It was another of those maddeningly elusive links that suggested, but did not confirm, that both Chester and Kelly had met with foul play. Nor did it provide any direct evidence about the malefactor responsible for the deeds.

Making headway on unraveling the mystery of Chester Davis' death made it worth a drive from Riverside to San Diego to interview Arnold

Dunne. There was no guarantee, of course, that he wouldn't clam up or lawyer up, but he was in a world of trouble. Given all the charges piling up, there might be a deal to be made. Especially if they could get him to understand that he was under investigation for the murder of Chester Davis. The flophouse was a forensic investigator's nightmare. Prints, bodily fluids, and trace of all kinds were everywhere in the house. It would take days to sort out and catalogue, much less process, all the evidence recovered at the scene.

Even though Arnold Dunne's fingerprints weren't the only ones found at the scene, they were notable because they were found on Chester's person. Apparently, Dunne had rolled him over. Perhaps checking to see if he was still alive or, more likely, making sure that he was dead. His fingerprints were found in the vomit trailing down Chester's sleeve.

"I'm counting on getting to the bottom of this whole sorry tale by having that heart-to-heart with Arnold Dunne. Once he's able to think clearly, Dunne has got to figure his best chance is to cut a deal given all the trouble he's in with the law."

"Yeah, but does he realize it might also be his best chance to stay alive?" Jessica asked.

CHAPTER 30

Detective Hernandez must have already been in his car when he called. The Cathedral City police department was fifteen minutes away; he was there in ten. The coffee was ready by the time the doorbell rang and Jessica let him in. They sat in the morning room off the kitchen, sipping coffee as she laid it all out on the table for him. The detective was reasonably quiet as she spoke. He gasped when she talked about her chitchat with Mr. P., but merely shook his head and continued to drink his coffee. "I'll admit it; I've been out there stirring the pot."

"Stirring the pot, huh? I take it that means you've added a new tactic to complement your reliance on kismet as the key to sleuthing. That's what you called it, right? Wasn't it kismet that drove you into the clutches of Roger Stone's murderer? Walking into Mr. P.'s office and informing the man that you have an eyewitness who saw him murder your friend qualifies as stirring the pot, alright!" He set his mug down loudly. Jessica envisioned steam pouring from his ears, like a character in an old Saturday morning cartoon show.

"I've already had this conversation with another detective friend of mine. I was on the man's radar before that confrontation in his office. My car was trashed earlier in the day, and I presume the 'back off' message left on my windshield was from Mr. P. or one of his friends. He was already tracking me, and that poor deadbeat Chet Davis, too, apparently."

"Add Bobby Simmons to the list of guys on Mr. P.'s radar. He also turned up dead within a few days of you stirring the pot. I'll tell you what we know so far about the end to Bobby Simmons' so-called life. Maybe you can help me make the connection between his murder and the newest

277

psychopath in your life."

"The ne'er-do-well was out on parole after serving two years in state prison for felony drug possession with intent to sell. That was a second drug-related offense for the loser who lost his job with the casino several years before because of a drug bust. He did a stint in prison and a round of drug treatment," Hernandez said.

"You said Bobby Simmons didn't die from a drug overdose, though," Jessica said.

"No, he did not. He was found dead with a bullet hole in his head, sitting in a used car he'd recently purchased with cash. There was no sign he'd struggled with his assailant, who shot him at close range. His lap was full of drugs, including an array of pills, a balloon containing maybe a gram of black tar heroin, and a baggy full of marijuana."

"If he was there to buy drugs, something went horribly wrong," Jessica said.

"With the car parked in a secluded spot near an abandoned house high up in Cathedral Cove, the scene sure had all the markings of a drug deal gone wrong, but who knows for sure? His wallet was missing and he had no money on him, even though he had just cashed a meager paycheck from the Super Cuts where he worked. Maybe he came up short paying for all those drugs and his dealer shot him." The detective shrugged and took a big swig of his coffee. "Excellent, as usual," he said, raising his cup a little before going on with his story.

"His boss at Super Cuts thought Bobby had one of those pay-as-you-go cell phones, but if he did, that was missing too. So maybe it was a drug deal that turned into a robbery, but I don't think so. The back seat of his car was loaded with bags and boxes, a pricey pair of sneakers sitting right there in plain view, alongside an Xbox or some such thing, and a stack of CDs. Why not take that, too, and maybe clean out the car? Why leave the drugs with a dead guy? The whole thing could have been staged. A clean, execution-style hit with a little bit of drugs and a little bit of robbery thrown in to confuse things." Hernandez downed the rest of his coffee and then pushed his empty cup toward Jessica without asking for more coffee. She refilled the mug as he continued to speak.

"Mr. Simmons may have been planning to hit the road, despite the repercussions for his status as a parolee. The car he bought last week was loaded with what must have been all his worldly possessions. That included

A Dead Sister

fairly new household goods I figure he bought to set himself up after his release from prison. You know, pots and pans, dishes, sheets, and towels, ordinary stuff, but kind of new?" The detective paused, seeming reluctant to continue.

"There were personal papers too, and what could only be described, as the crud's putrid scrapbook. Lewd pictures of young-looking females. Some of those photos featured the man himself. I'm not talking about do-it-yourself Polaroids. These were professional. If you can call trash like that professional. There was also an old VHS tape starring a youthful Bobby Simmons letting it all hang out, so to speak. Apparently, Mr. Simmons aspired to a career in the theater and had at least one gig of the X-rated variety. Now that I've seen your photo of Kelly, I'm sure she was in some of the still shots. She looked younger than nineteen. It could have been the hair and clothes: pigtails and those little shorty pajamas. I'd guess more like fourteen or fifteen than nineteen."

Jessica felt like she might heave: too much coffee on an empty stomach, but also too much filth in too short a time. She placed her elbows on the table in front of her and rested her head in her hands.

"Can I get you something to eat? I need crackers or chips, something."

"If you've got them handy I could eat," Detective Hernandez replied.

A tub of Bernadette's homemade salsa sat on a shelf in the fridge. She'd made enough of the scrumptious spicy dip for an imminent meeting of the Cat Pack. Jessica had summoned the group to her house to debrief one last time. After that, she planned to call them off the trail of Mr. P. and the doc. Bobby Simmons' death had tipped the scales. One too many bodies, too close to home. It was time to abandon their efforts to solve the mystery of what had happened to Tommy's poor dead sister. She didn't want one of them to be added to the mounting body count.

Besides, what they had learned so far was hard to bear. Whether she was a drug addict or not, Kelly clearly had ties to loathsome characters like Bobby Simmons and Mr. P. Jessica felt sucker punched. Like she was fifteen again, caught following blithely along behind the wild and out of control girl, right into the hands of Mr. P.

Jessica set a tray with a bowl of salsa and a bag of chips on the table in front of them. She also brought them water to drink. With Bernadette's salsa, they'd need it. She picked up the conversation where they'd left off, dreading where the conversation was headed next.

Anna Celeste Burke

"Did I mention the fact that among the possessions found with Arnold Dunne at the border was a substantial quantity of illicit pornographic material? Apparently, underage women figured prominently in the triple X flicks and rags. That might mean there's a connection."

"It might. Guys like Bobby Simmons dabble in a lot of raunchy activities. I'm not sure why. It could be a general fascination with corruption or maybe it's hard to satisfy one vice without picking up another one." He dug into the bowl of salsa with a chip, his eyes brightening as he took a bite of the fresh, savory concoction.

"Your friend, Kelly, and her boyfriend were both mixed up in the kind of modeling that's tied to the porn business. Unless Bobby Simmons and Arnold Dunne knew each other, there's no reason to believe they were dealing with the same producers of that smut. More than a decade has elapsed since those photos were taken of Bobby Simmons and those girls. So, the fact both sleaze balls have porn in their possession doesn't necessarily connect back to your Mr. P. and his sidekick, Doctor Death."

"He's not my..." Jessica began wearily.

"I know, I know. He's not *your* Mr. P. My point is, you've got nothing, and he seems intent on keeping it that way. If Bobby Simmons had something on Mr. P., it's too late for him to do anything about it now. Even if this homicide does somehow lead back to him, you do get that the 'p' in Mr. P. stands for psychopath, right?" Watching her intently, the detective scarfed down another chip loaded with salsa, then took a gulp of cool water as a chaser.

Jessica nodded in agreement, as she forced herself to chew and swallow the chip she had put into her mouth. Her throat was bone dry. Her stomach was in knots. Here she was again, toe-to-toe with a mad man. Terrified, she also raged at the idea of backing down. Mr. P. had gotten away with murdering her friend and was at it again.

"This is primo salsa, by the way. Will you give up the recipe if I offer to go through everything that degenerate Bobby Simmons left behind and identify anything that has to do with your friend?"

"No." That sounded rather abrupt. "I'd welcome any information you can come up with by going through that deadbeat's belongings. As much as I dread seeing them, I should get copies of those pictures of Kelly. You can skip the ones of her dead boy toy. As for the salsa, I honestly don't know the exact recipe. It's one of St. Bernadette's many secrets. Yet another mystery I'm not likely to solve in my lifetime." Just then, they heard the door from the garage into the house open, and the lady herself bustled into the room.

"Speak of the devil," Jessica said loudly enough for Bernadette to hear.

"That's not nice to call Detective Hernandez the devil. He's not *that* bad." Bernadette set bags of groceries on a counter, and then walked through the kitchen to the morning room where they sat. "Nice to see you again, Detective," she said, looking from him to Jessica and back again. "Isn't it?"

"Bobby Simmons is dead. He was killed just a few days after Tommy, Jerry, and I spoke to him at the soup kitchen. We must have spooked him, because Detective Hernandez tells me he was packed and ready to hit the road when someone put him out of his misery."

"Not another murder, ay que Dios mìo! On top of all the trouble you've been having, Jessica. Thank God Peter has his guerrero, that warrior man, sitting in the front yard again." She crossed herself as she spoke. "Did she tell you about her trouble, Detective? Those gangsters with the pistol she had to take away from them."

"Oh, I heard about it. The way I heard it, she didn't just take that pistol, but made sure all the bullets went away, too. Right into the front of that sweet low rider they were driving." He abandoned his stern demeanor. "Okay, I admit it. I wish I could have been there to see that."

"Better you than me. Our detective friend here loves your salsa. He wants the recipe."

"¡Claro que si! Of course! I'll have Jessica send it to you." She bent toward them and lowered her voice, "The key is good tequila." She smiled angelically as she made her way back through the kitchen and out the door to the garage. "You going to help me with the groceries or do I have to go drag that big guard man away from his post?"

Jessica sat there with her mouth open. "You'd better go help the little lady. I don't want her to change her mind about giving me that recipe." He stopped talking and shoveled the last of the salsa into his mouth with gusto. Besides, I've got to go. I'll get those photos to you as soon as I get back to my office. I'll send you a copy of the evidence log once the miserable slob's belongings have been inventoried. You can tell me what you want to take a closer look at, okay?" Detective Hernandez asked.

"Sure. I'll talk to you later."

"Go! Go help Bernadette. I can find my way out."

The detective gave her a jaunty wave as he moved toward the front of the house. Jessica headed out to the garage, stunned by what had just transpired. She wasn't sure which was more startling, the detective's sudden burst of charm, or Bernadette's willingness to give up the secret to her salsa. Jessica felt a surge of hope that someone could stop the scurrilous Mr. P. and his still elusive ally, the doc. Preferably before they could kill again. Or order up another murder, as seemed more their style. At this point, there still was no clear evidence for their involvement in Kelly's death or anyone else's murder, for that matter. Yet she was keenly aware of their presence. Mr. P. and the doc hovered like dark, misbegotten shadows.

CHAPTER 31

Friday night with Paul was a bright spot in an otherwise distressing week of fights and frights. Jessica was distracted, but Paul was so thoroughly engaging, she soon felt lifted out of the malaise that had settled in after meeting with Detective Hernandez. The down-and-out around her were dropping like flies: two dead and one in the hospital within the week. The reprobate who lost his hoodie by the side of the road was probably in need of some medical assistance, too. She wasn't sure what that much pepper spray might have done to his scrawny body, but it couldn't have been good.

Frank called Friday morning to let her know that Arnold Dunne was stable, but the doctors had asked that he give the man another day to recover. Frank and his partner agreed and were driving down to San Diego on Sunday to interview Mr. Dunne. If they found out anything interesting about how he happened to put up that money for Chester Davis, Frank would be back in touch. Especially if they learned anything that led back to Mr. P. or his elusive partner-in-crime, the doc.

Meanwhile, Frank and his colleagues at the Sheriff's Department had identified one of the punks with whom Jessica had the run-in in Riverside. He was a small-time hustler by the name of Justin Baker. His last known address was actually in LA. Frank asked his fellow officers to see if Baker was tied to the other investigation involving Jessica Huntington, undertaken at the Brentwood estate. Lo and behold, they found a link. The low rider turned up in the video surveillance tapes.

In addition, they found blood on the fence surrounding the house, along with a few fibers from torn clothing, indicating someone had tried to scale the fence. Not realizing, until too late, that the spikes were more than

283

ornamental, they had left a bloody mess behind. The fibers on the fence matched trace on the doll's clothes at the curb. More importantly, preliminary analysis of DNA from the blood at the Brentwood estate led them to Justin Baker. As did DNA taken from the saliva on the mouthpiece he left behind on the exit ramp into Riverside. They could place him at both scenes. Like Chester Davis and Arnold Dunne, Justin Baker had a long rap sheet of low-level misdeeds. Rather prolific for a twenty-two-year-old, but nothing that had landed him in the kind of trouble he now faced.

The police in Riverside and surrounding counties had orders to pick up Baker for the attempted B&E and vandalism at the Brentwood site, as well as attempted kidnapping using a firearm, and arson for torching the low rider in Riverside. He also fit Dick Tatum's physical description of the man who had lobbed a Molotov cocktail at his car. If Dick could I.D., him they'd nail him for that incident too, and for driving the stolen vehicle torched later on. Frank was hopeful they'd catch up with the scurrying rat, and by asking him the right questions, might get closer to Mr. P.

That night, it was a relief to watch murder and mayhem rendered in vintage Hollywood style. No booming beat of psycho rap or a dead friend's face in sight. The images of a teen-aged Kelly intruded. Detective Hernandez had scanned and emailed them to Jessica after leaving her house on Thursday. In all, there were nearly a dozen shockingly licentious photos of her gorgeous young friend.

Adding to their shock value was the fact that several were indeed taken of Kelly as a young teenager. In some, she sported the same maniacal glint in her eye that Barbara Stanwyck flashed at Fred McMurray in Double Indemnity. In those shots, she was Kelly the teenage femme fatale. Some of the photos taken later, when Kelly was eighteen or nineteen, revealed something else. In them, Kelly appeared weary and lost, less defiantly sure of herself. The light shone less brightly in her pale, languid eyes. She stared blankly at the camera lens, as though some part of the life inside her had already fled beyond its grasp.

Was Kelly, by then, deeply addicted to a drug that was sucking the life out of her? How could Jessica have missed the loss of that light in her friend? Could that loss have gone unseen by all those who loved her, even Tommy?

Jessica flashed again on that last New Year's Eve with Kelly. She was struck by how hard Kelly had shoved Jessica and her other friends away in a drunken rage. Perhaps, by that point, no one could get close enough to see what was happening to her.

A Dead Sister

Between films, Paul and Jessica talked again about a lot of things. That included another round of discussion about how to manage their business relationship and a personal one. Should she be concerned about the fleeting glances from colleagues as she and Paul left the building together on Tuesday evening?

"I'm sure there's a lot of curiosity about who you are. The rumor mill will churn away when a junior colleague and a senior colleague are seen dashing off together somewhere. We could try to be more discrete, I suppose. My intentions are above board, and my reputation is squeaky clean. It's squeaky clean because I've worked hard keeping it that way. Integrity matters to me, and that's not going to change."

"I know that, Paul. That's why we're having this conversation. I don't want to mislead you about my intentions, since they are virtually incomprehensible to me at times. I feel overwhelmed by your kindness and generosity toward me. I'm so needy right now. I don't want to respond inappropriately to the attention you show me. I'm afraid *I'll* cross a boundary that I shouldn't cross because I've been knocked on my behind by my soon-to-be ex-husband."

She gazed into his blue eyes, which fixed her with an amiable twinkle. He was such a good sport, so balanced and judicious in his interactions with her and others. Maybe it was that stolid even-handedness, and his directness that appealed to her. Or maybe it was just those piercing blue eyes and the little crinkles in the corners around them. It could be the handsome set of his jaw, the sensuous lips, and the engaging smile.

"Well, I won't deny that I'm drawn to you, Jessica. I've told you that already. I've heard every word you've had to say about your struggle to make a new life for yourself. I hope I can be part of that new life in some way. Let's leave it at mentor and friend for now. I'm no fool, though, *and* I'm a lawyer. If I do or say anything that makes *you* feel uncomfortable, you need to tell me. I'll do the same if you do something I find troubling. I'll try to keep my wits about me, even when you throw your arms around my neck. Deal?"

"Deal," Jessica said as a rush of emotions engulfed her just thinking about those hugs. *Mm. Bergamot and amber*, she thought, hoping she could hold up her end of their bargain.

"Speaking of deals, guess who called me and wants to make one—involving you, by the way?"

"Let me guess, a gentleman by the name of Mr. P. Am I right?" Jessica asked, cringing as she uttered the man's name.

"Yes, as a matter of fact. How did you know?"

"I should have updated you about my latest encounter with psychopaths at dinner the other night. After that wonderful surprise about the exhibit honoring Dad, I didn't want to ruin things by bringing it up. I figured I'd find a better time to fill you in on my latest foray into sleuthing. I guess now's the time."

Jessica spent the next twenty minutes bringing Paul up to date on the cold case involving her friend, Kelly, whose boyfriend had recently turned up with a bullet in his head. She included the fact that her "pro bono" client, Chester Davis, had met his maker. Perhaps at the hands of a former cellmate, only one hypodermic needle away from the same fate. She detailed her admittedly impetuous visit to the man himself, their tumultuous conversation in his office, and the string of incidents involving the destruction or near-destruction of numerous autos before and since that visit.

"Wow, things have taken a few twists and turns, haven't they? I guess it's good that Mr. P. made that call. I presume that means he still sees you as someone he can woo with the promise of billable hours. While also still trying to scare the living daylights out of you. I'm not sure what to make of the work he wants us to handle for him. It's not really my bailiwick. They want the firm to tackle copyright and licensing issues related to a video archive the studio has in its possession. Some still shots and music videos they've produced. Also, older, more valuable films purchased with film preservation in mind. In addition to sorting out ownership, he also has a concern about putting the collection into a charitable trust with provisions for maintaining the archive long-term. That's as far as we got during our initial conversation. I could steer the man toward others in the firm, except for his expressed intention to include 'that stunning young woman newly in your employ, Jessica Huntington.'"

"I'll defer to you on this. The man is loathsome, and I dread the thought of working with him. I suppose it's probably smart not to disabuse the man of his belief that I can be bought off. Is there a way to say yes and no at the same time?"

"What I can do is stall. It doesn't sound like there's any urgency about Mr. P.'s plans for the archive. I'll have Gloria put him on my schedule two or three weeks out. That'll allow more time for law enforcement to carry out their investigations. You've got a horde of police detectives in at least three counties hard at work. If he's behind even a small part of the trouble spinning around you, especially the deaths of Chester Davis or Bobby Simmons, your trouble with Mr. P. may soon be over."

"I hope that's true. I'd like to get justice for Kelly and Chester but I'll settle for getting enough on him to bring an end to the murder and mayhem."

He was right. There *were* a lot of people working on a lot of angles. According to Frank, even Art Greenwald and the cold case team were still at it. They were chasing down a couple of new leads of their own as well as following up on the information Jessica and her friends had dug up. If they could connect the dots, there might be a way to stop Mr. P. *and* get belated justice for Kelly. The missing piece was still the matter of a motive for killing Kelly. Perhaps she had pushed him to his breaking point as Jessica had done. It wasn't hard to imagine the tantrum-prone Mr. P. acting on his rage from behind the wheel of an expensive luxury sedan transformed into a lethal weapon. *What did you do, Kelly?* Jessica wondered as she went back into hostess mode for her movie night with Paul.

CHAPTER 32

Saturday, Jessica gathered the Cat Pack, determined to deliver the news that their investigation into Kelly's death was over. They were silent and wide-eyed as Jessica detailed recent events. The toll of misdeeds was astonishing: Chester Davis and Bobby Simmons dead, two cars in Jessica's possession vandalized, and three others torched by the punks who apparently pursued her from LA to Riverside. Or maybe even from Palm Desert to LA and then to Riverside, if it turned out they were also the ones who left that first warning for Jessica on El Paseo. With Arnold Dunne in custody, and the police on the hunt for Justin Baker, Jessica tried to sound optimistic about the chances of nailing Mr. P.

Two things had alarmed members of the Cat Pack seated in a circle on the patio, after cooling off in the pool: First, Jessica's confrontation with Mr. P., in which she had learned he was so far out ahead of them.

"It's like déjà vu, Man," Brien had said. "You know, the same thing all over again?"

"Yes, I know what you mean. It is a little like what we went through with Roger's murder, isn't it? In this case, it's clear he's had me followed. Frank's rounding them up. The good news is that one of the goons Mr. P. hired is bound to squeal on him."

The second thing that spooked them all was that doll left at the Brentwood estate. It was clearly meant to terrorize and disgust by being posed to mimic the way Kelly's body was found at the scene of her murder.

"That alone ought to be enough to establish a link to Kelly's death, don't you think?" Laura asked. "That monster is mocking what he did to

A Dead Sister

her. Who else but her killer would consider doing such a thing?"

"You won't get any argument out of me. It's plain as day. The courts will want more though. The testimony of that weasel I doused in pepper spray, especially if he's got texts or phone numbers or money that can be tracked back to Mr. P."

"Frank and his guys will get something, I just know it," Tommy said. "They just have to, now that the investigation is so close. If only Kelly had told me about him. I can't believe she kept her connection to that little creep a secret!"

Jessica reluctantly revealed yet another secret about Kelly. She kept the details to herself, but told them about the raunchy photos found in Bobby Simmons' possession. "She was mixed up with Bobby Simmons and probably Mr. P. too much longer than you might think. In some of those photos she might only be fifteen or sixteen." Tommy was obviously distressed.

"It's upsetting, but gay culture has the same problems as straight culture when it comes to a preference for young and pretty. It's a cover for pervs looking to exploit the young and dumb, pretty or not. No kid is a match for one of those freaks. I've got a ton of damage from trusting the wrong people for the wrong reasons, you know?" Tommy's face wore such an earnest expression.

"Tell me about it." Jessica sighed. How did you ever really know who you could or couldn't trust? She was in her twenties when she fell for Jim Harper. Certainly, no fifteen-year-old should have been put in the position Kelly had been placed by the likes of Bobby Simmons or Mr. P. Or, whoever it was that had lured the lovely, mixed-up, young girl into posing for those photos.

"Could anyone have spared you any of that? Could I have done more for you or Kelly to prevent you from getting into those situations?" He thought about it for a bit before replying.

"Probably not. I was so angry, confused, and needy."

"Kelly was involved with Bobbie Simmons for years. Some of those photos look like they were taken while she was still in high school or maybe even junior high. She never mentioned him to me. Did she ever say anything to you about him?"

"Not a word. I thought they hooked up once she started working at the casino. Getting connected to that slime ball might make more sense if it had happened when she was younger. You know, more easily impressed? I could totally see the creep conning her into modeling. She could have been mixed up with Mr. P. before she even knew it, given what we found out. Do you want to tell them what we dug up, or should I, Jerry?" Tommy asked.

"Go ahead. You start, then, I'll jump in."

Tommy and Jerry had unearthed a studio of another kind owned by Christopher Pogswich: Pure Porn Studio Group. The activities of the small adult film studio weren't illegal, and it was a lucrative endeavor. They had released a stream of low budget films with suggestive titles, many of them tawdry twists on the names of mainstream Hollywood hits.

"Here's what we think is most important," Jerry interjected. "California mandates that adult film companies have physicians who certify the health of their *actors*. I'm using that term loosely, of course. In any case, we have a name. The physician of record for the porn studio, since they opened their doors in 1989, has been a Dr. Maxwell Samman." When he spoke that name, Laura sucked in a breath of air.

"I heard that name, too, or something like it. I went to lunch with one of the women in the grief group I'm in. I knew Angie before Roger died. She worked at Eisenhower hospital for thirty years until she retired a couple of years ago. I don't know exactly how we got onto the subject, maybe I was trying to avoid talking about Roger and me." Laura paused for a split second and then went on.

"Anyway, I started out asking Angie about her work in the ER, sort of curious about the records they keep, stuff like that. Then, I told her why I was interested. The whole story tumbled out. When I described what the doc looked like, she knew immediately who I was talking about." Laura leaned in speaking excitedly.

"Angie says this guy came into the ER, covered in blood, with a scrape on his head and a gaping hole in his throat. His companion was doing the talking, because the big guy was nearly unconscious and couldn't speak with his throat like that. He claimed the man had choked while eating dinner and then fell, hitting his head. Someone had tried to perform an emergency tracheotomy. He didn't say who had done that. This gigantic mangled man was just lying there in the ER, weak, and nearly unconscious. While examining him they found he had fractured a couple of ribs and one had punctured a lung, so they admitted him to the hospital." Laura paused

A Dead Sister

longer this time. Like she was trying to remember all she'd been told.

"Angie says she remembered his name because more than just his name had sounded fishy to them. According to my friend, his name was salmon, 'like the fish.' The young guy with him gave them cash: no insurance company, no check, no credit card, just a lot of cash to pay for the bloodied goliath's care. They thought something was suspicious about them and their story."

"Why didn't they report their suspicions to the police?"

"It was really odd, but nobody was accusing anyone of wrongdoing. This nice-looking young man, sucking up to this repulsive older man in such bad shape, had them all wondering. Not so much about foul play. More that something involving sex, money, or drugs had gone terribly wrong."

"So, what happened to him?" Tommy asked anxiously.

"Well, she wasn't sure, exactly. He recovered and the young man came back a few days later to pick up the beastly man. By then, they were all glad to see him go. He was not only big and ugly, but nasty, too."

"Did she remember the name of the young guy with him?" Tommy asked.

"No. I asked her that too. They all thought he looked like that friend of OJ's, Kato Kailin. A slick wheeler-dealer type with blond hair, and an Aloha shirt, complete with open-neck and gold chain. His name didn't stand out so she couldn't remember it."

"Her description fits the young Bobby Simmons to a tee. Sounds exactly as you described him, Tommy. He was holding out on us about Mr. P. and the doc, if they called him in to help that night. I wish I'd pressed him harder, or gotten Art's men to pick him up. He knew a lot more than he told us about what happened to Kelly. We must have scared the heck out of him with our visit to the soup kitchen and asking all those questions."

Tommy and Jerry had also traced Dr. Maxwell Samman to an address in the Hollywood Hills, to a house he didn't own. The house *was* owned by none other than Mr. P., or more correctly, by Mr. P.'s recording company. The place was a well-known party house. Dozens of cars were parked there at times, including paparazzi on the hunt for shots of celebrities who frequented parties held there. The police had been called to the address on numerous occasions. The owner and partygoers were cited for violations of noise ordinances, disturbing the peace, and public drunkenness, as well as infractions of public safety and traffic ordinances tied to the wanton disregard for parking restrictions in the area. Despite all the trouble over the years, the doc had never been arrested and there were no prints, mug shots, or DNA on file for the wily culprit. None for Mr. P., either.

Jessica was riled up after everyone left Saturday night. She had agreed to play it cool too but really, really wanted to do something. She even toyed with the idea of storming into Mr. P.'s office and confronting him once again. What good would that do? Except maybe get her killed.

The hospital might have a record of the doc's blood type. Laura agreed with Frank and the other detectives that they ought to quit poking around for the time being. Nevertheless, she volunteered to check the hospital records to see if she could retrieve information about Maxwell Samman's blood type. A match to the sample on Kelly's shirt might add a little fuel to whatever fire was keeping Art's team from putting the case back in cold storage. It might be enough to subpoena DNA samples from the man.

It was late, but she decided to call Frank anyway. She wanted to give him the news about Maxwell Samman and that house in the Hollywood Hills. He had declined to attend the latest gathering of the Cat Pack, spending time with his kids instead. He would give up his Sunday with them for that trip to San Diego and the interview with Arnold Dunne. He offered to pass on information about the doc's name, the porn studio, and the party house to Art so she didn't have to call. That was a good thing. Apparently, Art Greenwald, like Frank Fontana and George Hernandez, was in utter disbelief at the trouble Jessica had managed to get into in so short a time. She would be spared another lecture.

She didn't need it. The lengths to which Mr. P. had gone to stop Chester Davis and to put the fear of God into her had already worked. That bullet in Bobby Simmons' head, so soon after their little chat with him about Kelly, was also unnerving.

Terrified, she was also infuriated that he was pumping the world full of filth. Worse, was the fact that he was making a bundle from it, and mowing people down in the process. Surely, there had to be somebody who knew the man for what he really was, and who was as angry as she was about it.

As Jessica readied herself for bed, she picked up her phone and found a missed call from a number she didn't recognize. A voice mail message revealed the identity of the caller, but not much else.

A Dead Sister

"This is Kim Reed, Ms. Huntington, please call me."

The image of the mod-looking, black-haired girl came back to her. Silent and motionless as they rode down the elevator together. Jessica had identified the female figure in that tattoo she wore. Saraswati, the Hindu goddess of culture, learning, and art, was set out in bold colors running from shoulder to elbow. Kim Reed had to be a thoughtful young woman to have chosen so stunning a figure to emblazon her body. Perhaps she was the key to putting this whole ordeal behind them.

It was too late to call her back tonight. Giving Kim Reed that business card had been another impulsive act on Jessica's part. It was prompted by her sense that a furtive defiance oozed from the pores of the automaton. Perhaps it was the boldness of that body art. The image was resoundingly reproachful of the luridly self-indulgent world in which Mr. P. presided as a perverse overlord, a sham petty deity.

Excitement fought with foreboding as Jessica tried to sleep. Finally, Jessica got up and pulled out her laptop. Eventually, she dozed off while scanning the collections of several favorite designers. She had searched for something to wear to the opening night at that exhibit paying homage to her father. His accomplishments, his vision, and vitality, were soothing counterforces to the cesspools created by the Mr. P.'s of the world. When she finally fell asleep, she dreamed of Kelly. Adorned in a headdress like that worn by the Hindu goddess, she danced joyously, and sang in that lyrical voice of hers.

CHAPTER 33

"Are you insane? You walk into the studio and start a fight with Mr. P. That's after digging up a bunch of dirt about your long-dead friend who was no innocent. In fact, she was a real pain in the ass, just like you. You do not get who you are up against. These guys have been at it a long time. They're good at what they do. If they overlook some detail when covering their tracks, they hire lawyers like you to clean up after them. I called to beg you to let it go, please. You're going to get yourself killed."

There was wretchedness in that young voice that wrenched Jessica to her core. Despite the tough words, the woman was frightened, using anger as her shield. "So, why does that matter to you, Ms. Reed? And how do you know what Kelly was like? Mr. P. murdered my friend long before he met you. He used her, and then, ran her down like a dog. It sounds like you know all about that."

"Please, no more. Just let it go. I know what he's capable of, better than you can ever imagine. I'm mute around here a lot of the time, but I'm not blind or deaf. I know way more than I care to know about what happened to your friend."

"Then you have to tell somebody so whoever hurt her can be held accountable. Tell *me*. I *can* help you. You're right that I am a lawyer. I have friends and money. If you need a place to go, I'll come get you. I'll take you where you'll be safe." If only someone had spoken words like those to Kelly.

"Then what are you going to do to get him out of my head? Can you erase the things I've seen and done? You can't help me, nobody can. I've

A Dead Sister

sold my soul to the devil. Your friend is dead. Nothing you can do can change that. Save yourself."

"The way to do that is to stop him. You've got to help me. I can do it."

"No, you can't. He's *the* Mr. P., music mogul and studio wizard. Who's going to believe a gutter rat like me?" She asked, sounding more like a ten-year-old than a grown woman as she hung up that phone.

Jessica tried to call back, but her call went directly to voice mail. She marched around her bedroom, making the bed, cleaning the room, even scrubbing the bathroom top to bottom. Growing more distraught, she was about to call Peter to see if there was some way his security firm could trace the location of that call from Kim. If he could locate her, Jessica would go get her. Her phone rang. Jessica grabbed for it, hoping it was Kim.

"Jessica, it's Frank. We've got him. We've got him, or will have him soon. Arnold Dunne has copped a plea. What finally did it was telling him what was in the remaining hypodermics he had. Those came straight from the doc. Man, was he scared and angry when he learned how close they had come to killing him. Now he can't stop talking. Not just about Chester Davis, but a ton of his other dealings with Mr. P., and the doc, too. He's an eyewitness to enough heinous acts to put both men away for a very long time. The other good news is that there are a lot of other folks interested in what Arnold Dunne has to say about Mr. P. LAPD is here, as well as the San Diego County Sheriff's Department, Border Patrol, and DEA. Apparently, the FBI has had the weasel in their sights for a while now. They've got a team here now, hanging on every word Arnold Dunne has to say, Jessica."

"What a relief. I can guess about the DEA, but what's the interest from the FBI about?"

"That suitcase of smut Arnold Dunne was carrying wasn't the first. He's a regular distributor for the products Mr. P. churns out. I'm not talking about the above board garbage his adult film studio produces. I'm talking about the illicit material Arnold Dunne had with him at the time of his arrest. It's sick stuff, mostly child pornography. Turns out Arnold Dunne has had a hand in procuring the girls in some of those videos. The scumbag says he's helped dump them once Mr. P. decided it was time to get rid of them. We're talking about sex trafficking, moving back and forth across the border with drugged-up young girls. Most of them were from Mexico, but the traffic also moves the other way. It sounds like that's another fate Kelly might have faced if she hadn't been killed that night. The police in San

Diego County have already started to round up a few of the characters involved on this side of the border, courtesy of information provided to them by Arnold Dunne. At one of the locations, they found several girls being held for transport out of the country."

"Does Mr. P. know what's up?" Jessica was thinking about that phone call from Kim. She had sounded desperate, but the message to Jessica was about backing off, as if Mr. P. thought he was still out ahead of the game. Surely, she wouldn't have called Jessica with another warning to back off if he had any real inkling about the juggernaut heading his way.

"I don't know. A warrant has been issued for his arrest, and for the doc, along with separate warrants to search both the music studio and the porn studio locations, the house in the Hollywood Hills, and Mr. P.'s beach house in Malibu. The FBI and the LAPD are in the process of coordinating a raid on those places even as we speak. If they do locate them and make an arrest, I don't know who's going to get the first crack at them, in terms of filing charges. I'm sure he'll lawyer up, hoping to get back out on the street as soon as he can."

"Surely that won't happen. No court is going to believe the man poses no threat to the community or that he's not a flight risk. The guy has his own private jet. He could take off and head out of here anytime he wants."

"Hey, you're singing a song I know all the words to. You never know what sort of case a crafty lawyer might be able to make. Well, actually maybe you do, Attorney Huntington."

"Ha! You know I'm not that kind of lawyer. Can you do me a huge favor?"

"I can try."

"Is there any way you can get the LAPD to pick up Kim Reed, Mr. P.'s assistant? She called me last night out of the blue. When I called her this morning, she seemed distraught and barked at me to butt out. She's scared, and I'm scared for her. She knows something about Kelly, too. Kim has been up close and personal with the freakish Mr. P. Can you put her into protective custody or hold her for questioning somewhere safe? If we can convince her that Mr. P. is going to end up behind bars, she'll have at least as much to say as Arnold Dunne, and she'll be even more credible."

"Do you know where we can find her?"

"No. I have a cell phone number for her. There's probably an address

A Dead Sister

on file for her at Mr. P.'s music studio where she works. Can your guys put a trace on the phone, locate her with GPS?"

"I'll do what I can to find her. Also, I presume somebody has already done it, but I'll make sure that Mr. P.'s plane is grounded."

Even as she spoke, Jessica had decided to call Peter. She felt certain there was no time to lose. She would have *him* track Kim, too, using the GPS in her cell phone.

"Thanks. This is such good work. Not just to locate Arnold Dunne before he could get away, but to get him talking like that. Kelly will get justice out of this and Chester Davis too."

"Hey, you and the rest of our Cat Pack have helped too. I hate to say it, but I believe stirring things up put Mr. P. into panic mode and caused him to screw up, big time. Not that I'm endorsing the risk you took confronting him. There's a good chance this is finally going to bring down that maniac, once and for all."

As she bid Frank goodbye, Jessica hoped that was true, and that it could be done before Mr. P. could get to Kim. She would try to get to her first. It was too late for Kelly but maybe not for Kim.

"Peter, this is Jessica. I need your help." As soon as she had explained, Peter did not hesitate. He promised he'd track Kim down.

CHAPTER 34

Jessica resumed pacing as she waited for Peter or Frank or someone to get back to her. She tried a couple more times to reach Kim Reed on her cell phone, but with no luck. When her phone rang, a couple hours later, she hoped beyond hope that it was Kim.

"Jessica, this is Amy Klein. I'm sorry to bother you on a Sunday, but I need to see you right away at the office on El Paseo."

"Now?"

"As soon as you can get here, yes."

"Of course, Amy. Is Paul okay? What's this about?"

"Paul's fine. It's not that. There's been a break-in. Your office is a wreck and the police are here asking a lot of questions about what's missing. It'll be easier for you to answer those questions."

"I am so sorry. I have a good idea who's behind this. Tell the police I'll be there in twenty minutes, okay?"

"Sure. No problem."

Jessica grabbed a pair of Tahari slacks and slipped them on. She added a sleeveless silk shell, topped off with a Michael Kors blazer in a lightweight fabric with three-quarter length sleeves. A pair of comfortable ballet flats completed the outfit, hoping she'd be presentable at work on such short notice. She took a swipe at her hair, put on a little makeup, and checked her bag to make sure she had the essentials.

A Dead Sister

On Friday, Jessica had gone to pick up her BMW from the dealer, and it looked as good as new. As she hustled out the kitchen door, she scrawled a note for Bernadette on a pad on the counter: "Gone to my office. Back in a while. Got news!"

Jessica waved at the security guy who was sitting in his spot out in front of the house. She stopped for a second, rolled down her window, and shouted out her destination. He nodded in acknowledgement, then, typed something on his tablet. Jessica wasn't sure why she'd left that note for Bernadette, or bothered to announce where she was going to the guy from Peter's firm. She felt uneasy about the call. Amy sounded a little rattled, but who wouldn't be when confronted by a mess like that, especially on her day off? Talking to the police was no picnic either. She was not relishing the idea of another round with the officers assigned to duty on El Paseo.

She sped to I-10 and took the Monterey exit, anxious to get to her office as soon as possible, but without breaking the speed limit on Monterey. There had also been a tone of urgency in Amy's voice that caused Jessica to push the posted limits. She pulled into one of the parking spaces that had recently been set aside for the Palm Desert branch of Canady, Holmes, Winston and Klein, directly behind the building that housed their offices.

As she climbed up the stairs and reached the entrance to her office, she stopped for a minute to dig out her cell phone, which had started ringing. The summer heat was oppressive. It added to the stress-induced sweating that followed on the heels of the news delivered by Amy Klein. As she stepped through the doors into the cool air-conditioned space, she took the call from Peter.

"Jessica, we've located the cell phone you asked us to find. It's nearby, as a matter of fact."

"Nearby, as in here in the desert?" She asked, adjusting to the darker light in the office. Amy was not sitting at her desk in the reception area. She and the police officers must be in the back where Jessica's office was located.

"Yes, that's exactly what I mean. And, in one of your favorite places— El Paseo. We're a few minutes away, zeroing in on her, and should have her location soon." Jessica sucked in her breath as Amy stepped out from the back, pushed toward the reception area by the doc. On the surface, Amy appeared calm. The woman, usually impeccably groomed, hadn't fixed her smudged makeup. Nor had she retrieved errant strands of hair that had pulled free from the chignon she wore. Next, Kim Reed appeared, followed by Mr. P., who had something between a grimace and a smile on his face. Jessica considered bolting out the door and down the steps, but they had Amy. It was Jessica, not Amy, who was responsible for the current predicament.

Without skipping a beat, Jessica picked up the phone conversation "Well, I can assure you, Mr. March, it is *not* okay. I understand you're already in the area and feel it's an emergency, but I cannot possibly drop everything here at my office right this minute. I have people waiting for me." She paused as though listening to someone on the other end of the line. Peter got it right away.

"Jessica, are you in trouble?"

"Yes, I know you are a good client. I would be happy to meet with you later. Come to my office in an hour or so, and dinner will be on me." Jessica paused again briefly, hoping to maintain the charade.

"I'm on my way, hang on."

"Great Mr. March that will be fine. I'll see you soon." With that, Jessica hung up the phone and slipped it back into her purse. She thanked God Peter March recognized that "not okay" meant she was in trouble. That had been the signal she used, previously, but she'd never imagined she'd need it again.

The little parade marched toward Jessica, single file, until they were all in the waiting room where she stood. The diminutive Mr. P. stepped out from behind Max Samman and Amy Klein. He had a hand on Kim Reed's arm, his grip distorting that image of Saraswati. "You paid me a visit, Ms. Huntington. I thought it only fitting to reciprocate." Jessica tried not to react as the two men glowered at her.

Max Samman steered Amy Klein back behind the reception desk and seated her in a chair, roughly. In a flash, the large, gangly man administered something from a hypodermic he must have had in one of his enormous hands. Amy Klein looked surprised and confused. Then she slumped forward over her desk, before sliding sideways from her chair onto the floor, with a thud. The doc bent down to check on her. When he stood up again, he spoke.

"I hear you've been asking around about me. What did you have in mind, Ms. Huntington? Your interest in me is likely to make Mr. P. here jealous, or maybe you were hoping to arrange a threesome?" He smiled,

A Dead Sister

revealing a wretched set of jagged teeth, more disturbing even than the grillwork worn by her assailant in Riverside. His voice had a harsh, deep sound, slightly raspy.

"What have you done to Amy, Dr. Samman?" She stared directly at him as she spoke. Jessica refused to yield to his efforts to intimidate.

"Put her out. Only temporarily, I assure you. She'll take a nap. When she wakes up, she won't remember much of what's happened here. It should help you relax knowing your friend here is out of harm's way." He leered at Jessica and she could almost hear his unspoken words: "... unlike you, Ms. Huntington."

"What is it you want?" She tried to sound calm. Her heart beat wildly as her mind raced through possible answers to that question. None of them were good. The doc had taken up a post next to Kim Reed, as Mr. P. stepped toward Jessica. Kim struggled to maintain her deadpan expression, but winced when the doc grabbed her arm.

"You've created quite a stink, Jessica. May I call you Jessica? I feel like I already know you so well. Our lives have become so intertwined." Mr. P. took another step toward her and reached out as though he might touch her. She shrank back away from him. It took all the restraint she could muster to take that step back rather than strike out at him.

"Now, that's not nice, almost as rude to me as you were to that client you just had on the phone. If you spoke to me like that, I wouldn't have dinner with you later. Even though there is something alluring about you. Not like that delectable friend of yours, Kelly Fontana, of course. She was so young, so wild, and innocent at the same time. You're feisty enough, but not the least bit innocent, are you, Jessica? You've had plenty of experience in all sorts of endeavors, like rocking the boat. One too many times, I should add. Thanks to you, I'm going to have to take a long vacation abroad while this all gets straightened out."

She balled up her fist, clenched and unclenched it, fighting the urge to punch the man. She could get in a couple quick jabs before he or the doc could stop her. That would accomplish little, however, and might accelerate their end game. Even if the doc was telling the truth and Amy was no longer in trouble, Kim Reed still was. Her only goal now was to buy time. Give Peter the chance to get to her and figure out how to help. Instead of punching the man, she spoke, calmly but defiantly.

"You still haven't answered my question, Mr. Pogswich. What is it that

301

you want? Would you care to sit down and discuss it?"

The Pogswich thing got to him. He fought to regain composure. The face that won out was that of a man used to getting his way. For an instant, though, she had broken through, and glimpsed the scared husk of a human behind the mask.

"Please, call me Chris, now that we're on a first name basis. What I want is to make you pay for the great inconvenience you have caused me. You should have walked away from that defective human being, Chester Davis. Running his mouth, talking to Arnold Dunne and his other cellmates, yapping to whoever would listen to him. Like that drab man in the cheap suit assigned as his lawyer. If you had stayed out of it, minded your own business, all of this would have blown over."

He looked her up and down, running his tongue back and forth over his bottom lip. That veil of composure seemed to slip a bit as he continued to stare at her. An angry curl formed at the edge of his mouth.

"You've been quite busy, haven't you? Talking to the Sheriff's Department, and bothering those poor people at the casino, and that other two-bit junkie, Bobbie Simmons. That disgusting punk had the effrontery to demand money to buy his silence. Can you believe that? After all I did for that no-good bum over the years, he threatens me. He's nice and quiet now."

He spat out those last words about Bobby Simmons' betrayal. Growing angrier, he rose up on the balls of his feet for a moment, then came back down. "Then, you walk into my office and do the same. Even after the favor, I did for you. Warning you off by leaving that little note on your car. How dare you!"

The volume and pitch of his voice had risen. He was working himself up into a snit like that day at his office. "Who do you think you are?" He bounced a little, transferring his weight from one foot to another and gesticulated with both hands. Jessica tried to think of something to say to stall him, keep him talking, without pushing him over the edge. The doc spoke instead.

"We should get going, Chris." He spoke to him quietly, delicately, wanting to reach him through the agitation. "We can discuss all of this later. You'll have plenty of time to lay it all out for Ms. Huntington once we're in Cabo."

A Dead Sister

That got Jessica's attention. They were leaving the country and taking her with them. How? Surely, Frank had succeeded in getting Mr. P.'s plane grounded. Jessica gulped. One of Mr. P.'s areas of expertise involved moving women across the border. Who knew what arrangements the duo had made, given their connections and experience?

They could drive, crossing the border at Calexico in less than an hour. But once in Mexico, it would take hours and hours to drive to Cabo. She couldn't imagine Mr. P. allowing her to inconvenience him further by forcing him to travel so uncomfortably, since he was going along, too. The most likely mode of travel befitting the spiteful, bantamweight was his plane. Maybe his jet was stashed at some private airstrip nearby, or had been moved across the border before Frank had it grounded.

Jessica felt trapped in one of those movies where the clear path for the bad guys was to wrap it up, kill whomever they intended to kill, and make a run for it. A bullet in the head, like that doled out to Bobby Simmons, would do it. In true revenge-addled, psychopathic fashion, however, Mr. P. seemed bent on dragging this out. Clearly, he knew he was in trouble. Still, he seemed convinced he could leave the country *and* take Jessica with him. The doc apparently intended to indulge him, which meant no bullet in her brain for the moment.

"You're absolutely right, Max. Time to go." With that, he stepped out of the way and the doc moved forward, dragging Kim with him. She didn't put up a struggle.

"I know you have taken a liking to our fetching companion. We found your phone number on her cell. Perhaps we should make it a foursome, Max, my friend. Would you like that?" A lascivious grin spread across the doc's face.

"Whatever you say, as long as we get going. What Chris means to say, Ms. Huntington, is that if you don't want your new gal pal here to get hurt, do exactly as you are told. I am most adept at adjusting the dose from one that offers temporary respite to one that's permanent. Kim can be paying your old friend, Kelly, a visit in no time at all." A hypodermic was cupped in his hand. Mr. P. picked up where the doc left off.

"We have a car parked out back. Not that lovely S class sedan with the midnight blue paint, but a sleek, new model. If we had more time, I'd be happy to show you what makes it such a great car. I might even convince you to abandon your penchant for those BMWs that have been giving you a bit of trouble lately. The four of us are going to walk downstairs and around the back, like two companionable couples heading out for an evening of entertainment. A double-date," he said, giggling, before going on.

"Give no trouble, get no trouble, and neither does the lovely Kim." He ran his hand over the young woman's face. She did nothing, even though her eyes blazed for a moment. "Kim knows full well what kind of trouble I can give you, and please don't push the doc too far. He really has been on his best behavior."

Jessica tried to think of something to do. She hadn't replaced the used-up pepper spray can yet. A quick survey of the room revealed nothing she could use to defend herself. Not that she had much of a chance against the two of them. Even though she had seen no other weapon than the glint of that hypodermic needle, she imagined they were armed. Perhaps both carried guns under the suit jackets they wore in the triple-digit, mid-July heat. In the end, she did as she was told. The doc had moved so swiftly when administering the substance in that needle to Amy, it would take him no time at all to carry out his threat against the young woman at his side.

Leaving the last vestiges of comfort behind, Jessica exited her office and stepped out into the sweltering late afternoon heat. She didn't bother to lock the door behind her. She hoped, in fact, someone would walk in and find Amy Klein.

Where are you, Peter? She wondered. If he'd called from his office, he couldn't have been more than fifteen minutes away. She and her party passed through the small courtyard along the walkway that led behind the building. Mr. P. sauntered to his sedan in the parking lot and climbed in behind the wheel.

"Please, be a gentleman and open the door for our charming companions while I get the air conditioning going. We want them to be comfortable."

The doc opened the door and held it, motioning Jessica to get in. She took one last look around. The sun shone abundantly in a cloudless blue sky. The palms swayed. Jessica spied no brawny security consultant, no swat team, disgruntled detectives, or handsome police officers on bicycles.

As she bent to avoid bumping her head on the door jamb, she felt a sudden stinging sensation on the back of her arm. *Bee sting?* She wondered as she reached to brush it off. The last thing she remembered, before blacking out, was the snaggle-toothed doctor bending close. His fetid breath was on her cheek as he shoved her into that back seat. Kim had

A Dead Sister

already climbed in next to her without making a sound.

CHAPTER 35

Jessica dreamed of fire. Flames danced around her as she tried to rouse herself to escape. At one point, she almost succeeded in waking up. She even sat up for a moment, and took in the room around her. Sweat was pouring from her, but she saw no flames, no smoke, no heat, just the cool comfort of sheets. She was in bed. *Dreaming*, she thought, as she slid back beneath the sheets and drifted off to sleep again.

"Jessica! Jessica Huntington, wake up! You have got to wake up, now." A gentle shaking became more insistent as the voice pierced Jessica's stupor. Jessica tried to do as she was told, but her head was pounding. She wanted to close her eyes and go back to sleep so the pain would stop. That voice roused her again. She opened her eyes and lifted her head to take a few sips of water from a glass offered to her. The water moistened her parched mouth and throat, but her stomach revolted. She threw up the sips she'd swallowed. With that, the young woman standing over her simply hurled the remaining water from the glass into her face.

"What? What's going on? Who are..." Jessica finally recognized the young woman standing in front of her. It was zombie girl, less zombie-like now, even though she was dressed entirely in black. In a simple black knit top worn over black leggings, she almost appeared to be a normal girl her age. She was more disheveled than when Jessica had last seen her. Her hair was in disarray, her makeup all but gone.

Jessica tried to make sense of her situation. She was in what looked like a hotel room, but where? How did she get there? A funny taste lingered in her mouth and a funny smell hung in the air. Then she remembered those psychos in her office. After that, the walk to the sedan, a pinprick, and

A Dead Sister

nothing. Almost nothing.

The tumult in her stomach began again as she remembered the way *he* had smelled. It wasn't just that moment in the car. In the night, he had come into her room and sat on the bed beside her. He had leaned over and said something to her before lifting her head and giving her a spoonful of orange-flavored syrup. The flavor did not entirely mask the odor or hide a bitter taste. That's where she had heard it—from him: "chloral hydrate. She'll sleep through the night." Standing behind him was zombie girl, expressionless as usual. She'd asked him what was on that spoon.

Jessica's eyes widened as she spoke to the girl, struggling to recall her real name. "You, you were with him. Why did you let him do that?" Jessica's eyes darted around the room.

"Yes, I was with him. Where would I go? I told you they'd come after me, and you too. They threatened to kill you if I tried to leave. You could have made a run for it a couple times as we were leaving your office. Playing the hero, that's why. You didn't run because he had that needle pointed at me."

As she spoke, she walked a short distance and refilled the glass with water. "I didn't *let* him do anything, Ms. Huntington. He's been giving you chloral hydrate, after that first round of fentanyl Sunday afternoon. I won't swear that he hasn't slipped us both a little something else. Max has kept me dopey, too."

"Sunday afternoon? What's today?"

"It's Tuesday. We're at a motel in Indio. We've been here since Sunday. Chris and the Doc had plans, but they hit a few snags along the way."

"Cabo," was the only word Jessica could manage to make her voice utter as the impact of her situation hit her.

"That's right. They had Chris's plane waiting at the municipal airport, Jackie Cochran. We were all on our way to catch that plane when a crew member called. He tipped them off that the plane was grounded and the authorities were waiting. You and your friends *have* been busy. That crew member said they were watching the border, too, and looking for the Mercedes we were in."

As she spoke, she did what she could to continue to bring Jessica around. She sat her up on the side of the bed, then handed her another glass of water. "Sip it slowly," she ordered. While Jessica sipped the water,

Anna Celeste Burke

Kim continued her story, at the same time digging around beneath the bed to find Jessica's shoes. "The doc took our cell phones and yanked the batteries and then we checked in here. He called somebody to come and get Mr. P.'s car. Paid some jackass to drive it off a cliff or torch it out in the desert somewhere, I guess. Maybe he had it taken to a chop shop, and it's in about a thousand pieces by now. Who knows?"

She looked up into Jessica's face, as she wiggled shoes onto her feet. "I don't suppose you remember any of this. You were really out of it. The doc had to haul you up the back stairs to get you in here. I thought that maybe you had overdosed. Chris said that was fine with him. He was furious, blamed you for all of this, and wanted to kill you right then and there. Max talked him out of it, suggesting you might make a good hostage if it came to that. He didn't say what 'that' was, but Chris bought it, and it's kept you alive." Kim stood up, went back into the bathroom, and returned with a damp cloth and a dry towel.

"Clean yourself up, Ms. Huntington," she demanded, handing both to Jessica as she picked up where she left off.

"No," Jessica said, shaking her head.

"What?" Kim asked.

"No more Ms. Huntington. I just threw up on you. You can call me Jessica."

"Whatever," she shrugged, then, went on with her story as Jessica used the cool cloth to clean up. The cobwebs hanging out in the corners of her mind refused to go away. She concentrated on Kim's voice, hoping it would help focus her mind.

"Chris had a major meltdown Sunday when he realized his grand plan was falling apart. The world-renowned Mr. P. was sure the desk clerk would recognize him so Max went in instead. Can you believe that? The doc isn't exactly a 'low profile' kind of guy; you know what I mean? Anyway, after we checked in, the doc left us alone while he got rid of the Mercedes. The longer Max was gone, the crazier Chis became. He started drinking scotch he pulled from his suitcase. He was guzzling, straight out of the bottle, ranting more, the drunker he got. The jerk called you and me, and even the doc, every name in the book. At one point, he was waving this stupid little gold gun around. I thought he might kill himself or us. Then he just laid the gun down and went in the bathroom to take a leak. I grabbed the gun, but the frigging thing wasn't even loaded!"

A Dead Sister

She took the towel and washcloth from Jessica and tossed them both onto the floor in the bathroom, then stood there a second recalling that first day at the motel. "When he came back out of the bathroom, he'd gone from raging monster to scared, sniveling rabbit. He was running around the room, raving that 'they're on to us,' and that 'we have to get out of here, Kim, Max or no Max.' The doc had been gone a couple hours so he was sure they got him and we were next. I played along, saying maybe he was right and we should get away while we could. Chris was about to use the phone here in the room to call a cab when Max turned up, with food. Whoever took the car off his hands must have stopped at a drive through, then, dropped Max back here at the motel before he left. Can you believe that? Like two guys out on an ordinary weekend outing, running errands." She looked at Jessica and shook her head.

"Chris went off the deep end again. This time he cussed out the doc to his face. I never saw him do that before. I wasn't sure what Max would do, but he stayed calm. He explained that they had to wait until the next morning, when someone was bringing them another car, an old beater of some kind. That horrified Chris. Not only that they had to wait, but that he was going to have to ride around in a 'piece of crap car,' as he called it. Max spent another ten minutes explaining why they were better off with a more nondescript car, and that they needed more than just that car. The doc had to get new 'paper' for them before they could go anywhere. You know, fake passports and drivers' licenses, social security cards, stuff like that? The madness continued for at least a couple more hours. Rants of rage followed by demanding, even pleading with the doc to leave, right then and there. The last time I saw the little schmuck Sunday night, Jessica, he was sucking his thumb and holding the corner of a sheet like it was a blankie. He was sitting in his bed, rocking back and forth like a lunatic. That's when Doctor Demento got out his bag of goodies and knocked us all out. I think he gave Chris a hit of whatever he had cooked up earlier for you and that woman you work with. It was a round of chloral hydrate for the girls, you first, then me."

Leaning over Jessica, she grabbed her by the shoulders, "Stand up and try out your legs. We have to get out of here."

Jessica did as she was told. Her legs felt like spaghetti, and her head spun as she stood. "Where is he? Where are *they*?"

"Let's just say Chris is indisposed, out of it, for the time being. The doc's out running errands. Whoever took the Mercedes gave Max a burner phone, and he's been on it nonstop. He was working angles all day yesterday, trying to score a couple passports, and find a way out of the country. That hasn't put him in a great mood, so I've tried to stay invisible. Turns out their old contacts are less than trustworthy now, so he's been scouting new ones, and that's taken time. Walk, Jessica, do it. We have to move." She gave Jessica a little push that nearly toppled her. Regaining her balance, Jessica paced around the bed and back.

"When the cops busted Arnold Dunne, they picked up most of their associates in the general vicinity. The ones that haven't been rounded up, have scattered, gone over the border, or underground like we are. Last night they were talking about giving up on Mexico altogether and heading north. Their latest scheme is to cross the border into Canada and head to Cuba from there. I didn't hear all of it. He knocked us out again." Kim shrugged her shoulders.

"Here's the thing. When I said Max is out trying to pick up a couple of passports, I *mean* a couple, as in *two*. So, maybe they plan to ditch us like the sedan. There are a lot of other options those sickos might have in mind for us. Please, keep moving." She was back in command mode. Jessica did her best to take more steps. Her head was pounding and she felt like she might heave again at any moment, but she was already steadier on her feet.

"I've put one more glitch into their plans, for the moment. The doc left me with Chris this morning without giving me one of his magic knock-out potions. The Mr. P. was feeling sorry for himself and wanted to whine. Yuck! That scrawny lowlife will be back in alpha dog mode soon. He'll start to feel invulnerable, maybe invulnerable enough to end our troublesome lives. In his mind, I'm an ungrateful wretch and you have done him a great injustice. We both deserve to be punished for our sins against the man forever at the center of his own universe." She went to the window near the door to the room, pulled back the edge of the curtain, and scanned the area around the motel. "You ready?"

"Can I go to the bathroom first?"

"Oh, good grief! Yes, but hurry up please?"

"Okay," Jessica replied on her way to the bathroom.

"I shot Chris full of enough stuff pilfered from the doc's supply to knock him out all day. He's barely breathing, so maybe it's going to kill him. Serves him right for all he's done. Your friend Kelly had a come-to-Jesus moment at the wrong time. They had to pack her off quick before she could squeal about what went on alongside Mr. P.'s legendary legit work. It was just a matter of time for her anyway. She was a favorite. Still, at nineteen, she was old and used up like me. I'm no longer awed by the man or the three-ring-circus he runs, freak show and all. You ready?"

"Yes, I'm so cold," Jessica said, wishing she had more time to steady her still wobbly mind and body. She was chilled to the bone, and her teeth chattered. A consequence of her physical condition combined with the twisted tale Kim told. Something didn't smell right.

"Let's hustle. Chris is out of it, but Max won't leave us alone much longer." Kim dug around in the bedclothes and came up with the blazer Jessica had worn when she left for her office on Sunday. She tossed the jacket to Jessica, who put it on hoping to ward off the chill.

"That monster doesn't trust me one bit. He doesn't think much of Chris right now, either. He's going to want to get back here soon to save his own neck. A neck your friend Kelly took a jab at with a steak knife before she died. That's how she got away. Well, that's how she got away as far as the parking lot. Chris told me all about it—as though the doc was the victim. The doc almost killed himself when he tried to follow Kelly and fell down a flight of stairs. He was really messed up when Mr. P.'s hired help found him."

"Do I smell smoke?"

"Yeah, there's a fire on the ridges above Palm Springs. The roads in and around the valley are crawling with fire fighters and highway patrol. Some roads that lead over the mountains to San Diego are closed, roadblocks set up too. More trouble for our outlaw pals." Kim was standing behind the curtain, looking out the window again. Jessica caught a peek. The skies over Indio were laden with dark clouds that had drifted east from the South Palm Canyon area where Kim said locals could see the ridges burning. A disconcerting sight, apparently. Not as disconcerting as the sight she glimpsed before they fled their motel room.

Kim had gone into Mr. P.'s bedroom and turned on the television with Jessica on her heels. It was in disarray, most notably, the hotel phone ripped out of the wall. Mr. P. was out cold. Drool pooled on the pillow near his lips. Kim worked quickly to lock the door to Mr. P.'s bedroom from the inside, while standing in the outer sitting area. The doc would have to pick the lock or break it down, once he figured out that Mr. P. was in there alone.

Outside, they edged their way along the open corridor on the second floor and around a corner to a set of stairs at the back of the motel. Jessica held onto the stair rail as they made their way to the ground level. The heat and smoke outdoors undid much of the progress she had made fighting off the drug-induced torpor. She stood at the foot of the stairs, trying to clear her head and figure out where they were.

When she had ventured there to interview Bobbie Simmons, Jessica realized how little she knew about Indio. Indio had hosted the Riverside County Fair and the National Date Festival for sixty years. She'd gone to the Date Festival numerous times while growing up in the desert, watching with delight as animals paraded across the stage at the finale of the annual Arabian Nights pageant. They had since added the hugely successful Coachella and Stagecoach music festivals to their credits as the "City of Festivals," but those were held at the Polo Grounds near La Quinta. She struggled to find a recognizable landmark or a street sign that might reveal where they were. From the second floor, she could see that the roadway in front of the motel ran along train tracks to an overpass some distance away, but there was not much in between. They needed to get to a phone.

"Why don't we go to the registration desk and ask the clerk on duty to call 911?" Jessica whispered the question to her companion.

"I tried to call the cops from our room, but couldn't get it to let me call out. Some creep at the front desk finally picked up and asked me what he could do for me. I made up some story about wanting to call out so I could get food delivered. He just laughed and said 'that big handsome doctor of yours told me *he* was going out to get food. I understand a couple members of your group are under the weather. The doc gave strict orders for you to rest, with no visitors or phone calls. Do I need to call him?' I told him that wouldn't be necessary, and yanked the frigging phone out of the wall. I was so ticked. That was about twenty minutes ago, right before I woke you. Any idea where we are? We need a gas station or a fast food restaurant, any place like that with a phone." Kim scanned the area around them.

"I think the main road out there is Indio Boulevard. There aren't a lot of shops along the roadway. That overpass west of us is Monroe, and that takes us back to town if we head south. Not close on foot. I'm not sure what's to the east. In front, we'll be more exposed, but maybe we can spot a place to run. I don't know what other options we have." Jessica leaned against the wall for support, wishing she could at least get a breath of fresh air to clear her mind.

"Yeah, I don't see a way out of here from the back or the side either. The motel and parking lot are completely enclosed by the fence. Let's stay close to the building in case the doc has someone else babysitting us besides

A Dead Sister

the creep at the front desk."

As soon as they came around the corner, Jessica spotted a gas station one street over. Unfortunately, Kim was right. There was only one way around the fence, and that was through a front entrance leading out of the parking lot to the street. The parking lot was nearly empty. A plain, unmarked white van sat off to one side, and two cars sat opposite the front entrance. Most of the distance they had to traverse was wide open. There was nothing to shield them from view if that guy at check-in was watching the parking lot.

"I think it's now or never. Are you ready to run for it?"

"I hope so. What other choice do we have?" With that, they dashed diagonally across the parking lot from the corner of the building where they were hiding in the shadows. As they neared the opening to the fence at the motel entrance, a car—two cars actually—approached at high speed. Sirens wailed in the distance. Jessica spotted the angular face of the doc at the wheel of the first car that turned into the lot. He didn't see them right away, because he was peering in his rearview mirror at the car behind him. When he returned his gaze forward, he spotted them, hit the accelerator, and raced right for them.

"Car," Jessica shouted, yanking Kim toward her as she lunged for the fence, hoping their forward momentum would get them out of the path of the car and closer to that exit.

"Gun," Kim shouted back, as she tackled Jessica and slammed them both onto the ground. Jessica heard the screeching of tires and a metallic crunch, as the doc's car must have come to a halt nearby. They also heard quick "pop, pop" sounds. A bullet whizzed past and pinged off the pavement in front of them. She heard Kim utter a cry of surprise. Jessica, the wind knocked out of her and with Kim's dead weight on top of her, froze as someone returned the gunfire. The sirens grew louder. More tires screeched, doors slammed, and a gun battle blazed around them.

A trickle of blood poured from Jessica's nose. A torrent gushed from Kim. Jessica managed to wriggle out from under Kim's body and found the bullet hole in Kim's shoulder. Taking off her jacket, Jessica used it staunch the blood flow, applying pressure as best she could, while staying low to the ground. As suddenly as the chaos had begun, it ended.

"Yo, Jessica, you okay?"

"We've got to stop meeting like this, Peter," she managed to say, smiling wanly, as she did her best to keep the pressure on Kim's wound.

EPILOGUE

"Where have I been all my life, Father Martin? It's as if I've been asleep, unaware of what was going on around me. Now, I'm awake, but I'm living a nightmare. First, I catch my husband in bed with Hollywood Barbie. Then, my best friend's husband is murdered. Now, I find out my poor, sick, childhood friend was part of underground porn that trafficked in drugs and people. Just kids really, most of them young girls. I must have slipped into one of those parallel universes my surfer dude buddy talks about. What's next, a zombie apocalypse?"

Jessica had sought out the priest, hoping to make sense of the latest bout of carnage that had left the doc dead, Kim Reed wounded, and Mr. P. in police handcuffs. Jessica and Amy Klein had gotten off easier. On Sunday, Peter March had sent the police to Jessica's law office on El Paseo as soon as he recognized Jessica's "not okay" code. The police had found Amy alone, out cold, but physically unharmed. When she regained consciousness at the hospital later, she recalled little of what had occurred that day. Jessica was hungry, dehydrated, and hung over from the mix of drugs used to keep her under control. She had some scrapes and bruises from evading the speeding car and bullets aimed at her by the doc before the police engaged him in a gun battle. The doc lost that battle, cut down by police officers in a matter of minutes.

When he called Jessica on Sunday, Peter had been in his SUV heading to pick up Kim Reed. He knew, immediately, that Jessica was in trouble. Even before she hung up the phone, Peter took off toward El Paseo. When the signal from Kim's phone began to move again, he followed. When they headed down Monterey to I-10, Peter was only a few miles behind. By the time they exited the highway at Monroe Street, and were driving into Indio,

315

he was closing the distance between them. But then, the signal ceased, and Peter was unable to locate them.

The reason the signal ceased was that a member of the flight crew at Jackie Cochran airport called the doc and tipped him off that Mr. P.'s plane was grounded. Border Patrol was watching for Mr. P.'s Mercedes at entry points into Mexico, and he suspected they were also being tracked. That's when the doc pulled the batteries from their cell phones. Minutes later, they checked into the closest motel, hoping to get out of sight before they were spotted. Using the phone in the motel room, the doc arranged to meet someone to pick up a burner phone and unload the Mercedes.

Meanwhile, the search was on in earnest, for Jessica, Kim, and the two wanted men. It didn't take long for the police to figure out that their plan to capture the men at the airport had been leaked, and by whom. Given how quickly they fell off the radar, Peter and the police figured they couldn't have gone far. They stepped up patrols in Indio near Peter's last point of contact.

On Monday, police had broadcast pictures of the two men, along with a brief news story that they were wanted for questioning in the disappearance of Jessica Huntington and Kim Reed. That should have been enough to get the creepy desk clerk to call the police, but the doc had paid him off. He continued keeping an eye on them using motel surveillance cameras and monitoring their phone calls. The investigators caught a break on Monday when someone spotted the doc at a drive thru in Indio and called it in. He was gone by the time the police reached the restaurant, but they were reassured that he was still in the area. They also had a line on the car he was seen driving: an older model, gray Ford.

The real break in the case, though, came from a call made by a member of the motel housekeeping staff. She caught a glimpse of "el doctor maligno" leaving one of the rooms at the motel, Tuesday morning. Instead of calling the police, she called a friend who had told her about a woman at Agua Caliente who won a big jackpot and was asking about el doctor, "más feo que Picio"—uglier than sin. That friend called another friend, and less than six degrees of separation later, they reached Bernadette. Bernadette called everyone: Peter March, Detective Hernandez, Frank Fontana, the Palm Desert police, and the Indio police. It took a few more minutes for Bernadette to get the original informant on the phone, directly. With Bernadette's help, they confirmed the location of the motel and pinpointed the room the doc had exited. Police converged on the motel.

Peter, armed with the same information, was on the move even before

A Dead Sister

the police were. He spotted the doc first and followed him for a few blocks, keeping his distance. The doc suddenly realized he was being followed and sped up, with Peter picking up the pace to stay with him. When the doc took that turn into the parking lot, Peter was nearly on his bumper.

In what must have been a fit of rage, the doc had tried to run over Jessica and Kim. Then, abandoning the car, he began shooting at them. One of the bullets hit Kim in the shoulder. Peter returned fire, and the doc took cover, as police poured into the parking lot. For the next few minutes, a flurry of gunfire was exchanged between the doc and the police. Two bullets felled the man, ending the firefight and his life.

The doped-up Mr. P. slept through the entire confrontation. Still barely conscious, he was hauled out on a stretcher, taken to a hospital where he remained until he was well enough for police to place him under arrest, and haul him away in handcuffs. He lawyered up right away and tried to get out on bond. There was no way the court would give Mr. P. another chance to flee. Word traveled like wildfire about the charges piling up against the infuriated little man. Given that one of his "sidelines" involved abusing children, the police had already put him in protective custody. When he wasn't ranting, he was sobbing, feeling sorry for himself and the way he was being misunderstood and mistreated.

Kim recovered quickly and turned out to be a credible informant about Mr. P. and the doc's furtive illicit enterprises. She led police to a cache of secret documents and private mementoes kept by Mr. P. behind a false wall in the "panic room" of his Hollywood Hills home. That included photos and video, all neatly stored. His office, Hollywood Hills house, and Malibu beach home were all wired, filming almost every move he made. He described the film archive to Kim as part of his legacy, a documentary of his singular genius. He sometimes added voice overs later or spoke to the cameras while alone, so not even a private thought might be missed. The voyeuristic narcissist enjoyed watching those films for hours, endlessly fascinated by his own life and an insatiable appetite for corruption.

In addition to even the most mundane aspects of the bizarre man's twisted life, the video recordings documented hours and hours of interaction with young girls and boys. In some cases, he "groomed" them, wooing them with gifts and the promise of stardom. In other situations, Mr. P. had the doc drug them or resorted to force to get them to take part in the illicit material he distributed.

The music-industry despot ruled his kingdom without objection or opposition. He was a pint-sized King Henry the 8th doling out royal favors and then issuing decrees to dispense with his subjects. That included smuggling young women over the border into Mexico, via a perverse take on the "underground railroad"—this one led into slavery, not out of it.

Never directly on camera, but lurking in the shadows, was the doc. Dr. Max Samman was useful to Mr. P. in so many ways. More than merely the doctor of record, he ran the porn studio. That included overseeing the networks required to distribute the materials they produced, legit or otherwise. Working behind the scenes, he also ran the drug smuggling and human trafficking "sidelines," as he and Mr. P. referred to them.

Sometimes the doc could also be heard in the background strategizing with Mr. P. about the best way to solve a problem with an unruly subject, like Kelly Fontana. "What to do about Kelly" had become an issue, in the fall of '98 when Kelly Fontana had a tantrum. On film, Mr. P. was hurt and angry that she had threatened him, and wondered if the doc could give her something to calm her down. The doc agreed to give her something, but argued that she had to go one way or another. He proposed they "export" her. She was still young enough to fetch a decent price in the marketplace; her red hair made her "an exotic," as he had referred to her.

Initially, Mr. P. balked, apparently having something akin to affection for Kelly. But then he must have yielded to pressure from the doc, or to fear, since Kelly disappeared shortly after that discussion. Some plan was afoot that night when fear suddenly morphed into savagery, and despite whatever misgivings he had, Mr. P. killed Kelly. He could be seen, on film, sniffling about it years later as he spoke to Kim Reed.

"What could I do? I had to stop Kelly, when she turned on me like a rabid dog. I couldn't let her bring my work to an end when I have so much more to offer." It was all melodramatic—King Richard the 3rd, a role better suited to the twisted little man even than King Henry the 8th. By the time Jessica visited Mr. P. at his office, he was alarmed, trying to stay ahead of events.

Kim said that, when Arnold Dunne informed them about Chester Davis, Mr. P. had a good laugh about it. That is, until Dunne mentioned that Chet had put together his very own dream team, with a lawyer from a big-time law firm to represent him alongside Dick Tatum. Mr. P. might have let that slide, too, but a day or so later, Bobby Simmons, tracked him down with a similar story about a nosy lawyer asking a lot of questions about Kelly. Bobby demanded help to get out of town, in exchange for his continued silence about what had happened to Kelly Fontana and other misdeeds to which he was privy.

A Dead Sister

Still in Bobby's possession were items taken from Kelly the night she was killed. Bobby had cleaned out her apartment, taking items Mr. P. had given her, some of them autographed. Bobby also had Kelly's cell phone. The doc had her cell phone on him the night Kelly had stabbed him. Once they made her disappear, permanently, the doc had intended to give her phone to a hired hand going on a cross-country trip, making it look as though Kelly had run off. In all the confusion that night, Bobby Simmons had been asked to go with the doc to the ER, and ended up with Kelly's phone. When Jessica had asked him specifically about that phone, Bobby Simmons must have figured the jig was up, and decided to "get out of Dodge."

Once Mr. P. decided to act, he had put Arnold Dunne, as well as Justin Baker and several other street kids, to work. The police had picked up Justin Baker, too. He wasn't talking, but the young man was another of Mr. P.'s "prodigies." When they searched the hovel where the young man lived in LA, they found a copy of a demo made by the aspiring rapper with the Mr. P.'s studio logo on it. They figured he'd eventually spill his guts when he realized Mr. P. was no longer able to bail him out—or seek retribution.

Arnold Dunne confessed to his part in the murder and mayhem. His price had been money and drugs, and a get-out-of-the-country-for-life gift package of drugs and smut that he could sell to finance his retirement in Mexico. He got Chester Davis released by putting up the bail money. After picking him up, it was easy to coax him into partying. He didn't have to kill him, exactly. He just kept feeding the addict drugs: heroin laced with fentanyl, in addition to pills and meth. When Chet Davis overdosed, Arnold Dunne was high too. It had never occurred to him to worry about leaving his fingerprints at the scene or on the man's body when he checked to make sure he was dead.

Bobby Simmons was another matter. Arnold Dunne set up a meeting where the not-too-bright Simmons showed up to make a trade—the items he held linking Mr. P. to Kelly in exchange for fifty thousand dollars. Bobby Simmons demanded to see the cash before he forked over the small box of items he'd taken from Kelly's apartment that linked her to Mr. P. A more public meeting place might have made it difficult for Arnold Dunne to complete the transaction in the way Mr. P. ordered it. He handed the money to Bobby, took the box from him, and then, put a bullet into Bobby's brain.

He then took Bobby's wallet, and placed drugs in Bobby's lap, aiming to make it look like a dispute about drugs had cost Bobby Simmons his life. Arnold Dunne ended up with the money, fifty thousand dollars, plus the couple hundred bucks Bobby had on him. The money was only part of Arnold's severance package. As he had learned later, that package included several hypos full of drugs like the deadly mix in the syringe found near Kelly's body. If he'd used one of them that would have indeed severed ties to Mr. P. and the doc, forever.

"We'll probably never know for sure what happened to Kelly. Maybe Mr. P. will tell us the rest of the story, but who knows? My guess is that they held her for days, drugging her like they did me," Jessica said. "I presume they were making arrangements to get her out of the country, dead or alive, when she attempted to escape. If the doc had administered the drugs in that hypodermic needle they found near her, she would have been dead. Poor Kelly. She almost made it..." Jessica's voice trailed off as she paused for a moment.

Jessica resumed pacing, as she had been doing while spilling her guts to Father Martin. She tried not to bump into anything in the cramped space. If she had been at home, she would have found something to kick or throw. Under the circumstances, pacing and ranting would have to do.

"Where's your God in all of this? Sleeping more soundly even than me, apparently. I'm sorry, but I just don't get it. What possible logic could there be in allowing the likes of Christopher Pogswich and Maxwell Samman to roam the earth long enough to become old men, while leaving a trail of dead and broken young women behind them? I know Kelly wasn't naïve, but she was young and stupid, and possibly dealing with an untreated mental illness. Why did she have to suffer and die so horribly?"

Jessica stopped pacing and hovered over Father Martin like a hawk about to pounce upon its prey. Before Father Martin could say a thing, she continued. "And if you say anything remotely like, 'God works in mysterious ways,' I will walk out of here right now."

"Jessica, I wish I could answer your question. I don't know any better than you do why such a bad thing happened to your friend. On the face of it, evil does appear to get the upper hand, at times."

"You think? A tidal wave of crud has swamped me. I'm not complaining about the ordinary, run of the mill, muck and mire that laps at your ankles day in and day out. That's old news. All the grease and grime that goes along with building a career and running a household, while trying to have a meaningful relationship with the corrupt man I married. Did I scream at God about that? No! Or how about blowing up like a balloon just looking at a piece of cake, while on fertility drugs trying to have a baby with that

A Dead Sister

unfaithful louse? That's not a problem for the soon-to-be second Mrs. James Harper, by the way. How is that fair?" Finally exhausted by her rant, Jessica slumped down in a chair opposite the priest.

"What I want is an explanation for the surge of depravity and horror that has engulfed me. My marriage was over, but was it necessary for me to witness my husband betraying me, in my own bed, with another woman? How is it fair that my friend, Laura, barely into her thirties, is widowed by a maniac who murdered her husband?" She looked up wearily, making eye contact with Father Martin.

"Kelly didn't even make it into her thirties. I've told you what a mess she was, how much she hurt me at times, but I loved her. She had just started to figure things out, Father Martin. Not only was she killed, but she was tormented for days before being mangled by Mr. Pervert and his sidekick, Dr. Doom. I don't get it, not fair, not fair."

"It's *not* fair, Jessica. Welcome to the human race. I'm sorry that you've suffered so much loss and witnessed such villainy. It's despicable. Your penchant for justice is a good thing, in the context of the profession you've chosen. Always putting everything on a scale and getting it all to balance out neatly is a risky proposition. There are a lot of people who would object to the privilege and prosperity you have, like your friend, Kelly, did at times. And the fact that some people have more even than you and Jim, may well have driven your husband to ruthless disregard for anything other than getting more. From what I've seen, he may have already gotten more than he bargained for in his pursuit of a new trophy wife."

"Et tu, bruté. Don't you priests have anything better to do than watch entertainment TV? Won't this humiliation ever end?"

"*My* God, as you have called him, has done a lot to try to steer us away from evil. You must have learned about the Ten Commandments in catechism. Do you believe Moses set down those laws for his people on a whim, or picked them out of thin air like a late-night TV 'Top Ten' list? Does it surprise you that human beings murder and steal, commit adultery, and covet what others possess?"

"No, I'm not surprised, in the abstract sense. I'm a lawyer. I get it that people do bad things. Just not to me, I guess, and not to Laura or her poor husband, Roger. Why Kelly?"

"Evil is more shocking when it strikes so close to home, I get that. I've said this to you before. You've been making the best of some very bad

321

situations. You and your friends have helped put a stop to some sick and vile people. You couldn't help Kelly, but you are able to help Kim. How many others might have fallen prey to Mr. P. and the doc if they hadn't been stopped? You've helped them too. You'll help more people, too, by practicing law again if you don't sit around feeling sorry for yourself because things aren't fair."

"I hear you. I'm trying to be strong, but I do feel sorry for myself. My privilege and prosperity haven't protected me one iota from betrayal, danger, and loss. The boost I get from buying beautiful new things doesn't last long, but it's better than nothing. I want to believe that good is stronger than evil but lately, it seems like a toss-up, at best."

"Toss-up isn't too far off, in the short run. We have our work cut out for us as humans. I ask myself the same things, and the best I can come up with is that it has something to do with God's desire that humans avoid hurting others, and pursue goodness, as a conscious and deliberate choice. It's that whole annoying free will thing, you know? If it's a matter of choice, lots of us will get it wrong much of the time. But I'm betting on goodness, over the longer term. Like that notion borrowed from the transcendentalists by Reverend King: the arc of the moral universe is long, but bends toward justice." Jessica's face must have reflected the doubt she felt.

"Oh, come on. On some level, you believe that, too. Otherwise, why would you put yourself in harm's way to find out the truth? That's not to say I agree with all the decisions you've made, in that regard. You scare me talking about some of the impulsive things you've done. God has sent you, not one, but three detectives to warn you about that side of your nature. You might want to listen." Jessica folded her arms across her chest, and began tapping her toe in protest. The lecturing tone angered her. Worse was the anxiety triggered by knowing he was right.

"Okay, okay, I'll stop preaching. There's one more thing. Truth-seeking requires work. It does mean 'waking up' to your own life. You've been given a wake-up call and a great opportunity if you heed that call. Where *have* you been all your life, Jessica, and where are you going?"

Jessica contemplated all that she and Father Martin had discussed as she drove back to Mission Hills. Was justice the antidote to envy, virtue the counterpart to vice? Could good prevail against even the vilest acts of desperate mortals? He had given her absolution for her "sins." Things she had long regarded more as psychological problems than religious transgressions. Anger, despair, impulsiveness bordering on recklessness,

A Dead Sister

compulsive spending, self-absorption, the line she walked between envy and outrage about injustice were all, no doubt, in the case notes made by her shrink.

He had challenged her to change her life. Could she read the books he'd given her, take time to pray and meditate, daily? Or keep a journal to write and reflect on the darkness that haunted her?

"Look deeper into the mystery, until you find the light past all that darkness," he had said. Could she do that?

Jessica's thoughts turned to her friends, who were struggling each in their own way. Laura was as lost as Jessica about all of this, preferring to keep her fight with demons in the realm of psychotherapy. "I'll add all of the new traumas to the list of crap I have to process in my grief group."

Tommy, reeling from the new revelations about Kelly, was furious. He was furious with Mr. P. and the doc, and with Kelly, too. He had asked Jessica, "How could she have been so stupid? Why didn't she ask for help? What on earth made her keep so many secrets?"

"Maybe she was ashamed or scared, Tommy? Or, trying to protect you..." He cut her off.

"Ashamed? Scared? How do you think I felt when I told her I was gay? I was terrified, but I still trusted her enough to tell her the truth. Why couldn't she?"

"I'll ask Father Martin for you. I'm going to go see him. Maybe he'll have some insights into how this has happened, and why."

"Are you kidding me? You still believe that hocus pocus they fed us at St. Theresa's? Kelly was a good little Catholic schoolgirl when she started hanging out with Bobby Simmons and his perv friends. All that holiness did her a lot of good, didn't it? Hell, the Church had guys like them wearing the collar, Jessica." His face had taken on that splotchy look that went with anger or other extreme emotions. Sparks flew from his eyes. No elfish twinkle, but a blaze of rage.

"Do you think Father Martin would sit down and talk about this with me, a gay man? Would he offer comfort and solace, absolve me of my many sins, or invite me back into the Church for Holy Communion? Why would I do that, anyway? Why would I want to go where I'm not welcome? There is no God. The sooner you face that, the better." Jessica had been speechless. Taken aback, she couldn't find words, even when he collapsed in her arms and sobbed. When he had exhausted himself a few minutes later, Jessica had tried to comfort him.

"To be honest, Tommy, I'm not sure what I believe. I'm still searching for answers, too. Despite the disaster my marriage has turned out to be, I am sure there's love. I loved Jim. Love is never wrong. I love you, too, with all my heart." That set off another round of tears for them both, but good ones. The kind that washes away the grime and leaves you feeling clean and refreshed.

Jessica was still deep in thought about that encounter with Tommy when she entered the kitchen. She hoped that Bernadette would be there and they could talk about the things Father Martin had said. Bernadette would support her. Share her own efforts to take up the challenge and live a more conscious life focused on the good in it.

"Hello, Jessica, how are you doing, darling? Bernadette has been telling me about Kelly and all you've been through. I had no idea, my sweet girl. I am so sorry."

"Mom, what are you doing here?" She asked as she tumbled into an open chasm; alarmed by nothing more than the sight of her own mother.

"Didn't you get my postcard? I came home to celebrate with you and your father. They're going to honor Hank next week and I didn't want to miss that. Let's go have lunch on El Paseo and see if we can find something to wear." Before Jessica could answer, Alexis rushed forward and embraced her, holding her so tightly that she nearly crushed her.

"I have something I need to tell you. I couldn't tell you on the phone, and I should wait, but..." Suddenly, her mother seemed to shrink in her arms.

"Mom, what is it? What's wrong?"

~~~~~~

THANKS FOR READING *A DEAD SISTER*! I would love to get your feedback. Please, pleases, please leave me a review on AMAZON and GOODREADS!

Stop by my website http://www.desertcitiesmystery.com Sign up to keep up with what's going on. Leave a comment or ask a question! Check out excerpts, blog posts, book reviews, news, and more.

A Dead Sister

What's up next for Jessica? Mom's back, why? In A Dead Daughter http://smarturl.it/deaddau, murder and mayhem take Jessica Huntington to new heights when Libby Van Der Woert wants to meet at the top of the Palm Springs Aerial Tramway. The disturbed daughter of Jessica's wealthy clients, Libby says she has information about her friend, Shannon Donnelly. Another mixed-up daughter of the rich and famous, no one has heard from Shannon Donnelly in over a week. Trouble begins the moment Jessica greets Libby in the Mt. San Jacinto Wilderness. Wild, manic, and sure she's being followed, Libby's got a gun. All hell breaks loose when Libby's Beverly Hills shrink shows up with a gun of his own.

What's up with the missing and misguided daughters of wealth and privilege in Dr. Carr's care? Jessica and her friends go toe-to-toe with more well-heeled heels in A DEAD DAUGHTER. Getting to the bottom of things Jessica-Huntington-style, sets off a whirlwind tour of fashionable enclaves, upscale rehab clinics, shops, restaurants and other haute hangouts. Behind all the glitz and glam: secrets, lies, corporate wheeling and dealing. How can Jessica and her friends outwit and outlive 'la crème de la crud' wreaking havoc from Palm Springs to Beverly Hills?

Here's an excerpt for you from book three: the prologue to *A DEAD DAUGHTER*, Jessica Huntington Desert Cities Mystery #3 http://smarturl.it/deaddau

Anna Celeste Burke

THE PROLOGUE TO *A DEAD DAUGHTER*

Jessica used her bound hands to tug at the jacket she was wearing. Keeping it closed retained more of her body heat. With her hands under the edge of the jacket, she worked to loosen the rope wrapped around her wrists. Seated, with her back was pressed against an outcropping of boulders near one of the scenic overlooks on the Desert View Trail, she could see much of the Coachella Valley. The spectacle below was breathtaking, a view she had always loved, but not now. Overlaid by a grid-work of roadways and buildings, colorful patches stood out in contrast to swaths of white desert sand. The lights in the desert resort cities below sparkled as the day languished and evening approached. It got dark so early this time of year.

The air was crisp and fragrant with the smell of the pine trees that flourished in the Mt. San Jacinto wilderness at the top of the Palm Springs tramway. Jessica had come here, many times, while growing up in the valley below. She loved the short tram ride that carried you from palms to pines in minutes. This trip was her first visit since returning to the Palm Springs area after retreating to her childhood home in the wake of unfortunate events that had wreaked havoc on her well-planned life.

Despite her best efforts to take refuge behind the gates of the tony Mission Hills Country Club in Rancho Mirage, calamity prevailed. Jessica had soon fought, like a junkyard dog, to survive a series of shocking attacks. Not even an earthly paradise could keep murder and mayhem at bay. Now, here she was again. This time, in the company of another wealthy, pampered, thirty-something woman whose life was in tatters. Libby Van Der Woert had a gun and was in the midst of a full-blown manic episode.

"Please listen to me. It's getting dark. Let's go inside where it's warm and talk this over. We'll get coffee and talk as long as you want."

The ties give as Jessica picked at the knots and then stretched, clenched and unclenched her bound wrists repeatedly. She had been working on them since she sat on the flat-topped boulder. Wiggle

A Dead Sister

room meant Jessica was making progress. An icy blast made her work harder. They had followed the trail, away from the visitor center at the top of the tramway, after Libby stuck a gun in Jessica's ribs. When they arrived at the overlook, Libby had bound Jessica's hands and forced her to sit on the ground.

"No, you're trying to trick me. If I go back, the police will arrest me. My screwed-up life will get even worse. Do you think I want to spend what's left of it in prison?"

"I'll help you. Nobody wants you to spend the rest of your life locked up."

"Oh yeah? They think I killed Shannon. Why not, since I've lied to everyone, over and over? Now, thanks to you, they can add kidnapping to my rap sheet. I've had plenty of help from you, Jessica Huntington. If you had followed me when I asked you to, I wouldn't have had to use the gun."

Libby hopped from one huge boulder to another closer to where Jessica sat. A wave of vertigo swept over Jessica. It looked as though Libby hovered above a sheer drop into the valley. That image was deceptive. The land fell away at a slope not visible from where Jessica sat. That didn't mean that falling, from where the hyped-up young woman now stood, wouldn't hurt. It might even kill her.

"Untie my hands. Let's go back to the tram station while we still can without breaking our necks. It's going to get icy when the sun sets. If anyone asks, I'll explain that this was a big misunderstanding. There won't be any charges filed against you for kidnapping, I promise. We'll find someone else to help you if you don't want me to be involved."

"I've already got help. I've had help since I was twelve. Dr. Dick is just the latest in a long line of shrinks. He used me, but I let him do it. He believed me, Jessica. Anything I said, and the grimier, the better. It was such a rush, you know, making up all this sick stuff about people? I had it all worked out. I'd pay back the smug jerks for everything they had ever done to me."

As she spoke, Libby paced along the top of a row of boulders. She pretended to be walking a tightrope, wobbling like she might lose her balance. That started another wave of vertigo, forcing Jessica to shut her eyes as she worked harder at the rope around her wrists.

"You should have seen how he worked me. He nodded with such concern in his eyes and spoke with so much admiration for all I had suffered. In fact, he was so sorry that I almost believed it myself. I even cried real tears! It was nothing but lies and more lies about my family. That's slander or libel or some crap like that, right?" She stopped pacing, abruptly, and almost lost her balance.

"Oh my God, Libby, no!" Jessica gasped. Libby steadied herself and picked up where she had left off. A wistful note entered her voice, for a moment.

"I thought he loved me. I figured that if I forced my parents to give me my inheritance early, I could run off with the love-of-my-life. Why not? If I waited until they died to get the money, I'd be too old to enjoy it anyway. That part was his idea—getting the money, I mean. I'm the one who tried to get it for him, though, so add extortion to slander and libel and kidnapping. Whatever." She shrugged and went back to her pretend high-wire act. That she had help from Dr. Richard Carr when hatching her scheme to harass her parents, was news to Jessica. Who knew how much of what Libby was saying bore any resemblance to truth rather than more lies or delusions?

"I'm not the first, but I will be the last psycho-tramp who falls for Dr. Dick. I pulled a 'Monica Lewinsky' on him, with enough of his DNA to make sure he never practices psychotherapy again. That's one thing I wanted to tell you when I asked you to meet me up here. It's all in a little blue bag, Jessica. Get it and use what's in it so I won't be a dead daughter for nothing!" She threw her head back and laughed, made a sudden turn like she was a gymnast reaching the end of a balance beam, and walked back. That dead daughter's statement and the routine that followed sent a chill down Jessica's spine that had nothing to do with the temperature up there at eight thousand feet.

"Libby, I'm sorry Dr. Carr took advantage of you. Why wait? Let's go get him, now." DNA evidence was one way to sort fact from

A Dead Sister

fiction. If he was taking advantage of his clients, perhaps the renowned psychiatrist had planted the seeds of false allegations in the confused woman's head, too.

"What's wrong with you? I broke my family! Don't you get it, or doesn't that mean anything to you?" With that, she stopped, hopped down closer to Jessica, with a menacing gleam in her eye.

"I care about my family," Jessica said. "I also understand how much trouble you can get into when you're angry and confused. Lots of us get in over our heads and hurt people, even the ones we love most." Jessica felt the ropes on her wrist give again, as she spoke those words to Libby in a calm voice. Only a little more and she could slip free. What to do after that wasn't clear. The gun Libby held wasn't more than a few inches away.

"Shut up! You don't know what you're talking about, except the part about being in over your head. It's over for me like it was for my so-called friend, Shannon Donnelly. I'm the one who told them what she was up to, so it's my fault she's gone. I'm going to pay for that one way or another. Here's an idea! Why don't I take you with me? I'll make you disappear too. Poof!" Libby waved the gun back and forth over Jessica as if it were a magic wand. Her face was pale, her dark eyes were wild, and her hair flowed in the cold mountain air. She was like a character from Harry Potter, a mad, wizard-in-training. "You should have left me alone."

"You called me, remember? I'm here because you reached out for help. Please, no more dead daughters, okay? Get rid of that gun. Toss it down below, and nobody will know you ever even had a gun. You don't want to hurt me, yourself or anyone else. I can help you. Paul can help you too."

Libby squatted down, fixing Jessica with a grimace on her lips. "Are you kidding me? Like he did when I had that car accident that killed Lela, you mean? Please don't tell me you believe that was an accident. I should have died, too, you moron. You aren't half as smart as you think you are." Libby stood up again and turned her back on Jessica.

"Paul Worthington was helpful, all right. All he did was let me get up to more mischief. That's what I've done, you know, caused a lot of mischief for Lela and Shannon and my oh so respectable family." Libby tossed her head back and cackled. The action caused her to wobble again. "My parents' lives are blown to bits. Such accomplished people with their rags to riches story, and all that overcoming hardship garbage. No matter what else they ever do, they're losers as parents. If I haven't already made that clear, I will soon, won't I?"

"Come on, Libby. I can't believe you want that for them, or for you. There's always a chance to make things right. You just have to give it another try."

"Oh no, not that old 'try and try again' line. At a time like this? Is that all you've got? Woohoo, it is a long way down. Come, look." With that, Libby climbed back to the boulder she had been using as a balance beam and took a couple of steps back without even looking.

"Stop! Don't back up anymore. You're so close to the edge already. You've got to believe me. Those rocks get slippery."

"Come here now or I'll shoot you!" Libby pointed the gun at Jessica.

"Then what? Who will help you make sure Carr pays for what he's done to you? Go ahead and shoot me because I'm not coming any closer."

"Do as she says or I'll do it."

Jessica's head snapped around, startled by the sound. There he was, on another of the boulders nearby, as if conjured up out of thin air by Libby's words. The doctor's white hair gleamed in the afternoon sunlight. Dr. Richard Carr was waving a gun of his own.

She was about to warn him off when Carr, belying his age, moved toward her, in a flash. He hopped from the boulder he was on to another, and then down onto a flat rocky area near where Jessica sat. Grabbing her by the ropes, he jerked Jessica to her feet.

"Libby has the right idea about you. You haven't been helpful to her at all. In fact, you've been a pain in the neck from day one. She'd

A Dead Sister

be fine right now if you'd kept your mouth shut tight around that silver spoon in it. It is a pity you two couldn't help each other though, since, under other circumstances, you might have been close friends. Two self-absorbed, poor little rich girls, with no real worries in your pointless little lives, you could have found plenty to whine about over manis and pedis. You and all the rest of the entitled children in my practice make me sick. What a bunch of naive, sheltered, self-centered monsters! Easy to manipulate, I will say that much for you, especially with the help of my liberal drug policy. Libby was doing fine until you stepped in. Now get up there, or I'll shoot her and then you." He motioned with the gun toward Libby.

"It won't work, Carr. They'll figure out you did it."

"How? Nobody even knows I'm up here. It'll be easy enough to believe you two psychos fought over the gun or something. Or maybe you decided you were Rodeo Drive's answer to Thelma and Louise and forged a murder-suicide pact. Who knows? There's ample evidence you're no more stable than Libby. You've been in treatment for years, with one therapist after another. Then a nasty divorce and all the other traumas you've been through in the last few months. It's enough to push anyone over the edge. Over the edge, get it?" Carr laughed at that last witty bit. His laugh was as unnerving as those that had issued from Libby earlier. Libby wasn't laughing now.

"How do you know I've been in treatment, or why?" Too wound up to answer, he continued to rant.

"I can't believe you had the gall to get Libby to turn on me. And you, Libby, are sicker and dumber than I ever dreamed. Why don't you do as Ms. Huntington suggested and toss the gun down below? Trust me, if you make even the slightest move, I'll shoot your meddlesome friend. I know you don't want another dead daughter on your conscience now that you seem to have found one."

Jessica stood, letting the new psychopath take his turn raging against the fates. His yank on the ropes had brought her to her feet but had also loosened them enough that she wriggled free as the madman spoke. In an instant, she reached over and shoved him. Caught by surprise, he went flailing backward. He slipped off the boulder and fell flat on his back with an audible thud and a grunt of pain. The gun flew out of his hands and wedged into a crevice nearby. Jessica scrambled up onto the boulder where Libby stood, grabbed her by the hand, and yanked her toward the jumble of rocks they needed to cross to get to safety.

"Let's go. This ends now! We're going to tell the authorities all about your esteemed psychiatrist. He'll never hurt you, or anyone else, again."

As they moved past the spot where the doctor had fallen, he climbed on the rocks behind them. He reached for Libby, who teetered as she tried to evade his grasp. Libby shoved Jessica and then turned as the man lunged for her. Dr. Carr grabbed hold of the arm in which Libby still held a gun and pulled himself forward onto the boulder with her. Jessica heard two sounds as she fell—a gunshot and a blood-curdling scream. The scream was her own as she fell back and plunged into nothingness. Maybe it was a sheer drop to the valley below.

Want to read more? Find the entire series on Amazon at: http://amzn.to/1WMdJrS

Before you go...

Bernadette and Jessica want to share a few of the recipes for food featured in this book. You'll find them below. Enjoy!

RECIPES

Chilled Avocado Soup

Serves 2

Ingredients

1/2 seedless cucumber
1 medium avocado
1 shallot
2 tablespoons plain Greek yogurt
2 tablespoons fresh mint
1 sprig fresh mint
4 teaspoons fresh lime juice
1 1/2 teaspoon salt
1/4 teaspoon ground black pepper
1/4teaspoon ground cumin

Preparation

Place the cucumber, avocado, shallot, yogurt, 2 tablespoons mint, lime juice, salt, pepper, cumin, and 1 cup cold water in a blender, and process until smooth.

Chill for at least 1 hour. Pour into chilled soup bowls and garnish with a sprig of mint leaves or sprinkle with a dash of smoky paprika or cayenne.

Bruschetta with Figs, Honey, and Feta Cheese

Serves 4-6

Ingredients

1 loaf crusty bread, cut into 1/2"-3/4" thick slices
2/3 cup feta cheese, crumbled
1/4 cup pine nuts
4 fresh figs, thinly sliced
1/4 cup honey

Preparation

Place bread slices on baking sheet and lightly toast both sides of the bread under the broiler (1-2 minutes per side) Remove bread from oven

Sprinkle feta cheese evenly over the toasted bread
Put 2-3 fig slices on each piece of toast
Divide pine nuts between the bread slices and lightly press into topping

Place under broiler for 1-2 minutes; figs will begin to sizzle and pine nuts will begin to toast

Remove from oven, drizzle with honey, and serve immediately

A Dead Sister

Red Potato and Green Bean Salad with Bacon and Dijon Vinaigrette

Serves 6

Ingredients

8 ounces green beans, trimmed, cut into 1 1/2-inch pieces
3 pounds small red-skinned potatoes, unpeeled, halved
4 slices bacon, cooked crisp and chopped
2 tablespoons dry vermouth
2 tablespoons white wine vinegar
1 large shallot, chopped
1 tablespoon coarse-grained Dijon mustard
2/3 cup extra-virgin olive oil
2 tablespoons chopped fresh parsley

Preparation

Cook bacon until crisp, drain on paper towels, and crumble when cool.

Cook beans in large saucepan of boiling salted water until crisp-tender, 4 minutes. Drain. Transfer to bowl of ice water. Drain; pat dry with paper towels.

Cook potatoes in large pot of boiling salted water until just tender, about 12 minutes. Drain; transfer to large bowl. Sprinkle vermouth over hot potatoes; toss gently and let stand 5 minutes. Whisk vinegar, shallot, and mustard in small bowl. Gradually whisk in oil. Pour over potatoes and toss to coat. Cool completely. Mix in green beans, bacon, and parsley. Season to taste with salt and pepper. (Can be made 1 day ahead. Cover and refrigerate.) Serve cold or at room temperature.

Anna Celeste Burke

Lemon Pilaf with Peas and Pistachios
Serves 8

Ingredients

4 teaspoons extra-virgin olive oil
2 large shallots, minced
1 1/2 cups long-grain white rice
8 tablespoons chopped pistachios
3/4 cups fresh or frozen peas [defrosted]
1 14-ounce can (or more) chicken broth
1/2 cup fresh lemon juice
1/2 teaspoon salt
2 1/2 tablespoons lemon zest [no white rind]

Preparation

Heat oil in heavy large saucepan over medium heat. Add shallots and sauté 3 minutes.
Add rice and 2 tablespoons pistachios; stir 2 minutes.
Stir in 1 can broth, lemon juice and salt; bring to boil.
Reduce heat to low; cover and cook until liquid is absorbed and rice is tender, about 20 minutes.
While still hot, mix in peas, remaining pistachios, and 2 tablespoons lemon zest. Season with salt and pepper.

A Dead Sister

Chipotle Roast Chicken
Serves 4-6

Ingredients

1 5-6 pound whole roasting chicken
1 bunch fresh cilantro, chopped [about 1 cup]
4 garlic cloves, chopped
2 limes, juiced, about 1/4 cup
1 7-ounce can chipotle peppers in adobo sauce
Salt and pepper

Preparation

Preheat oven to 425 <u>OR</u> prepare outdoor grill to cook over indirect heat.

Put cilantro, garlic, lime juice, peppers plus salt in blender or cuisine art, blend 1-2 minutes. Mixture should be almost like pesto in consistency—a little thinner in consistency is okay, too.

Remove giblets from chicken and rinse inside and out, pat dry. Rub cavity of chicken with salt and pepper.

Place chicken breast side up. Then, loosen skin starting at the neck, gently to disconnect but not tear it. Loosen around chick thighs and legs, too. Once loose coat chicken, *under* the skin, with the mixture you have prepared.

Place chicken on a rack inside a roasting pan. Place the roasting pan on oven shelf in the lower third of the oven. Roast 20 minutes per pound—about 1 1/2 hours or until internal temperature reaches 165 degrees. Remove from oven and let chicken 'rest' for 15-20 minutes before cutting into it.

OR

Prepare on the grill using a mesquite hardened charcoal [or mesquite wood chips with regular charcoal. Soak wood chips for 1 hour prior to use and drain well.]

Charcoal should be spread off to the sides with *the middle of grill left open,* so heat is *indirect.* Once the charcoal is ready [white edges to the briquettes and a temperature gauge registers about 400 degrees, spread wood chips over the charcoal, if you're using them], place the whole chicken in the space left open for it, *breast side up.*

Close the lid. About half an hour into the cooking process, check temp and make sure chicken's not getting charred or cooking unevenly, then let it continue roasting another 30 minutes.

At that point, add corn or veggies to the grill too, if desired and there's room on the grill. Cook another 20-30 minutes for chicken and veggies. [About 1 1/2 hours total for the chicken, 20-30 minutes for the veggies—depending on what you're grilling.]

Chicken is done when internal temperature using a meat thermometer reaches 165 degrees.

Hint: Hold back one or two chipotle peppers and a bit of sauce to rub shucked and cleaned corn on the cob before placing the corn on the grill.

A Dead Sister

If you have any of this chicken left over chop it, and use it to make roasted chipotle chicken salad.

Ingredients

2 cups chicken without bones, chopped or shredded
1/2 cup celery, chopped [about 2 stalks]
1/2 small red onion, diced
1 garlic clove, minced
1 medium avocado, peeled and chopped
1/2 cup mayonnaise
1/4 cup Greek yogurt
2 teaspoons fresh cilantro, chopped.
Salt and pepper to taste

Preparation

Mix all ingredients, season to taste, and chill. Serve on a bed of salad, a toasted bun, or fresh bread.

Bernadette's Spicy Triple-Layer Chocolate Cake with Fudge Icing

Serves 8-12

The Cake

Ingredients

2 cups boiling water
1 cup dark cocoa powder, natural unsweetened, [not Dutch processed]
1 tablespoon cinnamon [canela molida]
2 teaspoons cayenne pepper
1 cup butter, softened
2 1/4 cups sugar
4 large eggs
1 1/2 teaspoons vanilla
2 3/4 cups all-purpose flour
2 teaspoons baking soda
1/2 teaspoon baking powder
1 teaspoon kosher salt

Preparation

In a medium bowl, combine the boiling water with the cocoa powder and the red cayenne pepper. Whisk until smooth and set aside to cool.
Preheat the oven to 350 degrees. Prepare 3 8" cake pans by spraying with baking spray and by placing parchment paper rounds on the bottom.

In the bowl of a standing mixer, cream together the butter

A Dead Sister

and sugar until fluffy. Then add the eggs, one at a time until they are well mixed in.

In a separate bowl, combine all the dry ingredients.

Add the cooled chocolate mixture to the batter.

Then add the dry ingredients to the batter and mix well until it is smooth.

Divide the batter between the three pans evenly. Bake at 350 degrees for 25 minutes. Remove from the oven and let cool completely.

Run a knife or thin spatula around the edge of the pan, then invert the cake onto wire rack. It should come out easily and cleanly. Remove parchment paper from the bottom.

The Fudge Frosting

Ingredients

1 1/2 cups (3 sticks) unsalted butter, room temperature
1 cup cocoa powder, natural unsweetened [not Dutch processed]
4 1/2 cups powdered sugar
1/2 to 3/4 cup heavy cream, more or less as needed
1 1/2 teaspoons vanilla extract

Preparation

In a large mixing bowl, beat butter on medium-high speed until smooth and fluffy, 2 to 3 minutes.

Add cocoa powder and beat until incorporated.

Add powdered sugar, 1/2 cup at a time, mixing well after each addition.

As frosting thickens, add a few tablespoons of cream as needed. Depending on the temperature and consistency of your frosting, continue alternating adding cream and powdered sugar, then continue beating until frosting is light and fluffy. Beat in vanilla.

Assembly

To assemble the cake, first level each cake layer, if necessary, by cutting off the domed top with a long, serrated knife. [Tapping the cake pan lightly <u>after</u> filling and <u>before</u> baking can help reduce doming. Be sure to use the parchment paper, too.]

Place one layer, flat side down, on a cake stand or serving platter. Spread on about 1/2 cup of frosting onto cake using an offset spatula.

Position second layer on top and press to adhere. Repeat with another 1/2 cup of frosting, and then position final cake layer, flat side up.

Cover the entire cake with a thin layer of frosting. This "crumb coat" will keep the stray crumbs in place and make frosting the cake easier. Refrigerate for about 15 minutes to allow this crumb coat to set.

Remove cake from refrigerator and cover with remaining frosting.

ABOUT THE AUTHOR

Anna Celeste Burke is an award-winning, USA Today bestselling author who enjoys *snooping into life's mysteries with fun, fiction, and food— California style!*

A few words for you from Anna…

Life is an extravaganza! Figuring out how to hang tough and make the most of the wild ride is the challenge. On my way to Oahu, to join the rock musician and high school drop-out, I had married in Tijuana, I was nabbed as a runaway. Eventually, the police let me go, but the rock band broke up.

Our next stop: Disney World, where we "worked for the Mouse" as chefs, courtesy of Walt Disney World University Chef's School. More education landed us in academia at The Ohio State University. For decades, I researched, wrote, and taught about many gloriously nerdy topics.

Retired now, I'm still married to the same, sweet, guy and live with him near Palm Springs, California. I write mysteries set in sunny California! The Jessica Huntington Desert Cities Mystery series set here in the Coachella Valley and the Corsario Cove Cozy Mystery Series set in California's Central Coast, The Georgie Shaw Mystery series set in the OC, and coming soon, The Misadventures of Betsy Stark also set here in the desert. Won't you join me? Sign up at: http://www.desertcitiesmystery.com.

Made in United States
Orlando, FL
27 December 2021

12448231R00192